Simon Benjamin is a graduate of the University of Southern California and the University of San Diego. The writing of *Beyond Billionaire* is the fascinating sequel to Benjamin's *Scam Seduction*, his intriguing previous novel based on true events. A former real estate consultant, Simon is an avid baseball fan who enjoys spending time with his family. He is a native of a small town in California, where he currently lives with his charming wife.

As always, for my wife, Caren, and our children.

Simon Benjamin

BEYOND BILLIONAIRE

AUSTIN MACAULEY PUBLISHERS™

LONDON • CAMBRIDGE • NEW YORK • SHARJAH

Ordering Information
Quantity sales: Special discounts are available on quantity purchases by corporations, associations, and others. For details, contact the publisher at the address below.

Publisher's Cataloging-in-Publication data
Benjamin, Simon
Beyond Billionaire

ISBN 9781649790880 (Paperback)
ISBN 9781649790897 (ePub e-book)
ISBN 9781638295457 (Audiobook)

Library of Congress Control Number: 2021921685

www.austinmacauley.com/us

First Published 2021
Austin Macauley Publishers LLC
40 Wall Street, 33rd Floor, Suite 3302
New York, NY 10005
USA

mail-usa@austinmacauley.com
+1 (646) 5125767

My heartfelt thanks to my wife, Caren, who patiently listened as I developed the plot of *Beyond Billionaire*. Her support, sharp mind and attention to detail always seemed to help me find a way to improve my vision. I am eternally grateful to the remarkable team at Austin Macauley Publishers for their persistent hard work of examining, improving and making this all presentable. And finally, to those who originally inspired the story.

Chapter 1

Nearly a month had elapsed since Elliot Sterling had received an astonishing 100-million dollar wire transfer from the Central Bank of Nigeria. This unconventional business transaction had instantly made him a very wealthy man. Sterling, an experienced Los Angeles-based real estate developer, would have under normal circumstances automatically deposited the wired funds directly into his Beverly Hills Bank. Instead, he ordered all the funds transferred to an Israeli Bank managed by his trusted friend and previous Stanford University roommate, Benjamin Yaalon.

It was sunny in Los Angeles on this December day in 1993. Elliot and his charming wife, Felicia, formerly a high-fashion model, had been chauffeured the thirty-minute drive from their sprawling residential estate in Bel-Air to the Los Angeles International Airport. They meticulously made their way through rigorous security at the Israeli El Al airline counter. Before too long, they finally found themselves seated in the first-class cabin of the Israeli aircraft patiently awaiting departure of the nonstop flight from LA to Tel Aviv, Israel. Discreetly seated in the row just behind Mr. and Mrs. Sterling was Yonatan, an Israeli military special forces Mossad-trained bodyguard, privately hired to protect them from their imminent fear of retaliation by the government of Nigeria.

Before too long, they were in the air drinking Israeli Chardonnay wine and engaged in hours of conversation regarding the future of their two daughters enrolled at Stanford University. After drinking a little too much wine, Elliot instantly dozed off, leaving Felicia to start reminiscing about the painful decision to leave their stunning home and well-established life in Bel-Air for an uncertain life in Israel. Regrettably, her husband's somewhat naïve business dealings with dangerous high-ranking corrupt Nigerian government officials had forced them to a decision to leave the comforts of Bel-Air for the possibility of finding peace of mind and physical safety in Caesarea on Israel's Mediterranean coast.

As the aircraft kept racing toward Tel Aviv, Felicia could not refrain from sorting out in her mind the desperate chronological events that had led to this day. It was no secret that her husband's prestigious Sterling Development Company had been on the brink of collapse, and that Elliot had signed Personal Guarantees that included a major lien on his own home. Not even the brilliant mind of Elliot Sterling could have found a solution to the virtual depression in the Southern California housing market. Elliot's firm could not sell a single home during that time, pushing his lenders toward foreclosure on his real estate empire and his personal residence. Then one day, out of nowhere, came a faithful letter on stationary entitled Nigerian National Petroleum Corporation, Tinubu Square, Lagos, Nigeria, signed by Chief Abba Balla.

Felicia clearly remembered that she had insisted that her husband "throw that letter away!" Not only did Elliot keep the letter, but under severe protest by Felicia, her husband elected to travel to Lagos, Nigeria, in pursuit of a "fantastically over invoiced governmental contract". She understood all along that Elliot was intelligent enough to know that if it sounds too good to be true, in all likelihood it is. But, under significant financial and personal pressure, her beloved husband naively succumbed to the seduction of pursuing a 100-million dollar contract.

Felicia was infuriated that her honest and proud husband had become prey to a nefarious Nigerian network. Blinded by his economic turmoil, her remarkable husband did not realize he had been seduced into a scam by preeminent Nigerians organized to mask the true identity of a corrupt powerful syndicate. It took meetings in Nigeria with high-ranking government officials including the Minister of Finance and the Governor of the Central Bank of Nigeria, along with the assassination of a greedy American Congressman, and the apparent loss of a significant amount of personal money invested before Elliot ultimately discovered the truth about the scam artists.

Although Felicia remembered feeling scared during the Nigerian ordeal, she always had faith in Elliot.

This was especially true when Elliot decided to take matters into his own hands. Felicia instinctively understood that somehow, someway, her husband would figure out a method to win. That moment came when Elliot decided he'd had enough and it was time to fight back. He turned to his loyal childhood friend and street-smart business associate, Mark Goldman, along with his young brilliant attorney, Paul Norman. Together, they became the architects of a clever legitimate reverse scam on the Nigerians, and as they say, the rest is history.

Elliot's life had significantly changed on 2 November 1993. That was the euphoric day that Elliot had finally won the financial war against his Nigerian schemers. He received his wire fund totaling one hundred million dollars, making the Sterling family very wealthy. But little did Elliot know that his hard-fought business war against the Nigerians had actually just begun with the stakes having gotten graver by virtue of placing his family's future and physical safety in jeopardy.

Felicia couldn't get out of her mind what a dangerous position they were sitting in. Elliot's original Nigerian principal partner, Chief Abba Balla, was dead. Balla had been a victim of an assassination by the ruling military dictatorship. The story was that Chief Balla was the man who was going to politically lead Nigeria into a transition from a brutal military dictatorship to democracy. Any money made from the Nigerian contract was to have been shared equally between the Chief and Elliot.

Balla in theory had represented that the proceeds earned from the venture would go to finance his campaign for the Nigerian presidency. The truth turned out to be that although Chief Abba Balla was actually running to become President, he was nothing more than a crook whose true intentions were to steal as much of Elliot's money as he could.

An American Congressman was also killed in Nigeria during this awful ordeal. The rumor was that he too had been assassinated by Yemi Muhammadu, the Nigerian Head of State. Elliot had asked the Congressman while visiting Nigeria to check on the status of his contract. The next thing he knew, Congressman Jared Baron was dead. These acts were not coincidences. They were all premeditated murder in some way associated with the now infamous 100-million dollar wire transfer with consequences yet to come.

What worried Felicia wasn't that the Nigerian government was corrupt, or that the leadership was a military dictatorship. It wasn't even the horrific assassinations that kept her up at night. It was the circumstances surrounding how the wire transfer made it out of Nigeria.

A Central Bank of Nigeria official by the name of Stanley Roberts had met Elliot during his trip to Lagos. Once it was clear to Elliot that Chief Balla was up to no good, it became evident to Elliot that he needed to make a deal with someone in the Central Bank to assure that his contract payment was made. That deal was cut with Stanley Roberts.

Elliot would lawfully receive his one hundred million dollars and Stanley would be paid a fee of five million dollars to assure the funds were wired. Not exactly ethical by U.S.A. standards, but a pretty normal way of doing business in Nigeria. Since Roberts was a Stanford-educated attorney with a strong desire to move his family to America, he seemed like the perfect guy to trust.

It turns out that he was. He clandestinely programmed the Central Bank's computers to automatically wire Elliot the money, which had occurred a month ago on November 2nd. This was accomplished without anyone in the Central Bank or the government knowing. Although technically, he was acting legally within the bank's working rules and regulations, in reality, the military dictatorship would never have allowed for such a transfer.

This would be considered as an act of treason, especially given that the country was in the midst of a bloody Civil War. The nation desperately needed to preserve its cash reserves and the last payment they would have approved was an offshore contract depleting the country of one hundred million dollars during a time of serious civil unrest.

Elliot got his money, but Stanley ended up in jail. No one could verify whether he was dead or alive. The only certainty was that the ruthless Nigerian government demanded its money back forthwith.

Therein lay the panic and endangerment for the Sterling family. The tyrannical Nigerians played by their own rules. They had unilaterally claimed that the funds had been stolen by Elliot. This, of course, was not true, yet it would be impossible to prove Elliot's innocence in a court of law in Nigeria. Paul Norman, Elliot's exceptionally clever personal attorney, had responded to a harshly worded Nigerian letter demanding the return the money. The Nigerians had unconditionally rejected Norman's perfectly drafted response, showing evidence that the funds legally belonged to Sterling.

Felicia couldn't help but remember how she had pleaded with her husband to just forget about the wire and simply live within their means. The irony was that even if Elliot would have had second thoughts and listened to his wife's sound advice, he didn't have a choice. Stanley had set up the wire transfer to automatically fund, and no one, including Stanley, could have done anything to stop it without severe ramifications. Stanley had retired from the Central Bank without further security access. If Elliot would have informed the Nigerian government that Stanley had programmed the payment,

Elliot would have become an accomplice to treason, and Stanley would have been tried, then killed.

The way Elliot and Felicia had figured, they had no option but to keep the one hundred million dollars. It was lawfully their money. They had earned it by virtue of a contract. Effectively, they had outsmarted the Nigerians at their own game. If they gave the funds back, they would be admitting they had committed some form of fraud, which would certainly guarantee the death of Stanley Roberts, if he wasn't already dead. Either way, they understood that they would be spending the rest of their lives looking over their shoulders, fearful that the Nigerians would be seeking further revenge.

So, it was mutually decided that the Sterling family would be far better off keeping the money as opposed to forfeiting a hundred million dollars. At least they could try and defend themselves by contracting the finest security money could buy, which was exactly why Yonatan was seated behind them. It also allowed them to live anywhere in the world for security purposes. So, they had decided on Israel and bought a magnificent gated, guarded home in Caesarea on the Israeli Mediterranean coast.

Felicia was excited to visit their new home. This was one of the primary reasons she and Elliot decided to travel at this time. The residence had been discovered by Elliot's college friend and now banker, Benjamin Yaalon. The home had belonged to a wealthy customer at Yaalon's bank who had passed away. Elliot bought the house all cash, sight unseen, for four million dollars. Felicia was anxious to physically inspect the premises. She genuinely looked forward to converting it into a comfortable residence for her husband, their two daughters and herself. Felicia had come to terms with the fact that this was going to be the Sterling family home, at least until the initial expected danger had subsided.

The other reason they were heading to Israel related specifically to the new business venture Elliot was preparing to embark upon. Her husband and Benjamin had been planning this idea for a considerable period of time. All the legal paperwork for the Sterling Hedge Fund had been prepared and was ready for signature. The Sterling family had committed to make a 90-million-dollar investment into the newly formed Fund. Felicia was nervous about the size of their commitment, yet she knew deep in her soul that Elliot was about to build this Fund into one of the world's greatest and most profitable companies.

It seemed as if hours had passed while Felicia had been daydreaming and Elliot had been sleeping. So, with a loving nudge to Elliot's right ribcage, she got him to wake up saying, "You've had enough beauty sleep, it's time for me to beat you at gin rummy. Come on, wake up."

Elliot slowly responds, "I had a dream that we became billionaires through the success of the Sterling Hedge Fund. It all felt so real, especially the second part of the dream which had me seated at a table with a huge grin on my face as I destroyed you in game after game at gin!"

Felicia, with a gorgeous smile and a quick wit, answers, "I completely believe the billionaire part. As for the gin stuff, that's totally never going to happen!"

Elliot, who grew up poor, had earned a full scholarship to play tennis at Stanford, and was an extraordinarily competitive person. He lived his entire life with a philosophy that he must win to survive. It got him into the best schools, it pushed him to build a great company, and it put a hundred million dollars in his bank account. His wife's gin rummy challenge…well, that he considered a worthy provocation. Elliot stares into Felicia's beautiful blue eyes, gently caresses her hand, and with a confident charismatic expression says, "Oh, so you think you're better than me at gin. Okay, shuffle and deal the cards. The pleasure is going to be all mine."

They laugh, drink wine, talk, and play for hours. Toward the end of the game, Felicia stopped keeping score and simply declared herself the winner. Elliot did not protest her decree, but he didn't acknowledge it either. All he says is, "We'll keep playing at the new home in Caesarea. This is just the first round. A good warm-up. Consider it an early spring training baseball exhibition."

Felicia grins at her husband and says, "The pleasure will be all mine."

As the over fifteen-hour flight was coming closer to its destination, Elliot turns to his wife and says, "I'm sincerely sorry I put us in this situation. It was a bone-headed mistake for me to have placed you and our daughters in such a precarious position. There is no doubt that we'll live in danger until one day perhaps the thugs running Nigeria are either run out of office, or they steal so much money that they decide to give up power and go live some place outside of the country. In the meantime, we're going to need to live under tight surveillance. I feel terrible that I did this to us. I hope you'll forgive me."

Felicia, who has been Elliot's loving and supportive wife, even when he had no money, looks at her husband and responds with grace, "You made the best decisions you could have made under complicated circumstances. You have always come through for our kids and me. We'll make a great life for ourselves in our new home. We'll find new friends, and we will make the best of our new life. I don't blame you. You're my husband and I trust you. Elliot, all I ask is that you do everything that you can to keep our family safe!"

Grateful to hear Felicia's words, Elliot holds his wife's hand and thoughtfully says, "You and our daughters, that's all I got. No one is going to lay a hand on any of us. Yonatan, the guy sitting behind you, he's as good as it gets in personal security. Yonatan and his firm are getting paid a lot of money to make certain we're all safe. We must always be mindful of a potential threat, but I am very confident these men will allow us to go about our lives safely without incident."

Felicia looks straight into Elliot's eyes and says, "Alright, that's about enough on this subject. Is Benjamin going to pick us up at the airport?"

"Yes. Benjamin will be at the airport. The Israeli Bank is sending him in one of the bank's cars. Ben has arranged for that car and its driver to be assigned to us for our exclusive use during the entire duration of our stay. They're going to take us to the Hilton Hotel in Tel Aviv where we'll stay for the next seven days. The bank has also arranged for a hotel penthouse suite with magnificent views of the Mediterranean Sea at the bank's special discounted rate. By the way, the hotel is literally located on the Mediterranean, so I hope you packed one of your sexy bathing suits!"

Felicia says, "I didn't bring it, but I can't wait for you to buy me a new one. When do we see our home in Caesarea?"

"We visit the residence tomorrow morning. The driver is already scheduled to pick us up at 9 AM.

"It's about thirty-five miles from Tel Aviv. It'll take us around forty-five minutes to get to Caesarea. Ben will accompany us to the house. He also scheduled an interior decorator to meet with you at 11 AM.

"If you like the decorator, work hard over the next five days to brief her as to our lifestyle. Describe to her how we live and what we're looking for. If you're comfortable, go ahead and order window-covers, floor finishes, countertops, paint, and furniture. Choose art and all the interior decorating finishes we need. Design the house to end up as comfortable as our home in Bel-Air."

Felicia, now starting to feel really excited, asks with an innocent grin, "What's my budget?"

Elliot replies with a smile, "No budget. Just use your impeccable good taste and do it right. Obviously, spend our money wisely, but let's make this a warm and charming home. We need the Caesarea property ready for moving in within four weeks. We and our girls need to be living in that house by December 31st. You got a big-league project in front of you!"

"So, what are you going to be up to as I do all this residential heavy lifting?"

Elliot responds, "I am going to be working with Benjamin to finalize the new Sterling Hedge Fund. Ben has arranged for the attorneys and the accounting firm representatives to meet at the Caesarea residence to go over the final details regarding the legal and financial structure of the company. Additionally, Ben has prepared agreements for my signature for our first business deal.

"Naturally, I'm going to have a whole bunch of questions for Ben before I can get comfortable to sign any such agreement."

Felicia says, "Sounds like you're going to be busier than me. Tell me about the first deal?"

With a twinkle in his eye, Elliot says, "Because of Ben's longstanding Israeli government and banking contacts, the Sterling Hedge Fund has been awarded the right to purchase and resell the Savor assault rifle to the African governments of Algeria and the Sudan. The Savor is manufactured by the Israeli Weapons Industries and has replaced the American-made M-16 and M-4 as its first-line rifle in Israel.

"Sterling Hedge Fund will net over ten million dollars on our initial deal! We plan to sell this rifle in South America, Central America, African and Asian nations, including Colombia, Mexico, Guatemala, Senegal, and Nepal. By the time we're finished marketing the Savor, it's going to be in Vietnam, India, and all the way into the United States police departments. This rifle, along with everything else we're working on is going to earn us a lot of financial security."

Felicia responds with her clever sense of humor, "So, I guess that makes us international arms dealers!"

Elliot, who is laughing out loud and ready for rebuttal to his wife's comment, is interrupted by the El Al pilot announcing both in Hebrew and English, "Please fasten your seatbelts and bring your seats to the upright position in order to prepare for landing into Ben Gurion Airport."

Felicia and Elliot instantly drop the business subject while simultaneously looking out the window, spotting the coast of Israel off the Mediterranean Sea. That magnificent sight brings chills down their spines as they squeeze each other's hand. Neither say a word. They just keep admiring this historical land as they come closer and closer to shore. Before they know it, the aircraft has touched down and they have arrived safely to the beginning of what promises to become the adventure of their lifetimes.

Chapter 2

As Elliot and Felicia stand to leave their seats, they graciously begin thanking the crew members as they slowly make their way through the exit of the first-class section of the El Al aircraft. It feels good to be on their feet and getting some exercise while walking toward the International Customs area.

Although expectedly tired from the long trip, they both feel spirited to have arrived at their new homeland.

The Customs section is a very busy place with uniformed personnel and many armed guards carrying the Savor rifle. Elliot quickly enters a short line where travelers wait to be cleared into Israel by a Passport Control agent. Once they reach the actual booth, they are immediately asked by a young Israeli agent whether their travel is for business or pleasure. Without any hesitation, Elliot answers for himself and his wife saying, "Both business and pleasure."

With no further questions, the agent glances at Felicia, looks into Elliot's eyes, and simultaneously stamps the two entry visas. The young man then says in a distinct Israeli accent, "Shalom Mr. and Mrs. Sterling. We hope you enjoy your stay. Welcome to Israel."

Baggage claim is the final step before exiting Customs. Those travelers with something to declare were obligated to follow the "red" line. Conversely, with nothing unusual to declare, you were to pass through the "green" line. Elliot and Felicia, now starting to feel a bit worn out, decide to step into the "green" line and conspicuously walk right past several observing Customs agents without any incident. As they approach the exit leading to the public greeting area, Yonatan is quietly standing at the opaque glass doors waiting to escort his clients into the open public airport.

Elliot stares at Yonatan and says, "You're like a damn chameleon. For a moment there, I actually forgot you were travelling with us all this way!"

Yonatan, a ruggedly handsome Israeli military man of very few words, responds, "But I didn't forget."

Curious, Sterling asks Yonatan, "How did you get past Customs so fast? I didn't see you in front of me, and I was one of the first to make it through."

Somewhat uncomfortable with the question and reluctant to answer, Yonatan hesitantly provides his new client with a courteous explanation, "I was a high-level commander in the Israeli Defense Forces, known in America as the IDF. The man in charge of Customs at this airport served as my first assistant. Let's just say the government authorizes my expedited clearance, including my firearm.

"But enough on that subject. It's time to escort you and Mrs. Sterling into the public."

Elliot responds, "Very impressive, Yonatan. Well, I guess this is where you start earning your money. Should we follow you?"

"No sir. I will follow you and your wife. Please act naturally, and I'll take care of the rest."

As Elliot and Felicia move through the opaque doors, Benjamin makes eye contact immediately with his college buddy. With a great big smile and an equally colossal hug, the long-time friends greet each other warmly. Ben then kisses Felicia and says, "Shalom, Shalom. I'm delighted to see you! You are going to love your new home. It's simply amazing!"

Felicia responds, "Thank you so much for coming to the airport. How is your lovely wife, Shira, and those beautiful children of yours?"

Benjamin responds with, "They are very excited to see you both. You're invited to my home Friday for Shabbat dinner. We'll all get a chance to catch up with each other. Shira can't wait to see you!"

Elliot then turns to Yonatan and says to Ben, "This man is the head of security for the Sterling Hedge Fund. Yonatan, meet Benjamin Yaalon, my friend, banker and business partner."

Without further clarification, Ben fully understood that while in the public domain, Elliot was using code to introduce his personal bodyguard. Instantaneously, Yonatan and Ben begin speaking Hebrew to each other as if they are old acquaintances. Elliot then turns to Ben and says, "You know each other? I step into the country, and you Israeli bastards already have me at a disadvantage."

Ben, who can't stop laughing at Elliot's comment, says, "Sorry Elliot. Just a natural reflex to speak in Hebrew to an Israeli. I wanted Yonatan to know that if he needed anything during your stay to contact me immediately. I offered him my private cell number. I also told him I would be providing you and Felicia with cell phones to be used while you're here. Yonatan politely thanked me, then informed me he would not need any of my assistance, and told me to go to hell on providing you with the cell phones. I guess he didn't like the security risks. Oh, and finally, he said that I should concentrate on making you money, but to stay far away from the business of keeping you safe. So, I don't think you missed too much."

Now it was Elliot's turn to laugh saying, "You guys actually said all that in two minutes? I hope you understand each other. We all good here?"

With nothing further said, Yonatan nods in approval, and Ben winks at his college roommate as they grab their bags and proceed to a waiting black Mercedes Benz. Felicia, Elliot, and Ben step into the backseat, while Yonatan makes his way into the front seat with the driver. As they start driving away from the Ben Gurion Airport toward the exclusive Hilton Tel Aviv Hotel, the driver informs his passengers that the hotel is located approximately thirty minutes from the airport, and that they are welcome to the bottled water located in the side pockets of the doors.

The comfortable drive goes by smoothly as the driver pulls into the hotel's elegant entrance. Yonatan instantly gets out of the car, surveys the situation, then calmly opens the back door, advising Mr. and Mrs. Sterling to proceed into the hotel. They are followed by Yonatan and Ben into the spacious and grand lobby. To the right of the lobby entrance is the private concierge check-in reception desk.

Seated behind the desk is a special hotel assistant manager dressed in a dark blue suit. He warmly greets Elliot and courteously arranges for a high-floor Mediterranean water view suite at a specially discounted bank rate. The entire registration is skillfully settled within minutes.

As soon as Elliot turns to walk toward Felicia, a slender black man appears to be approaching Elliot.

Yonatan sees this man out of the corner of his eye and instinctively uses his fingers to locate the actual positioning of his concealed automatic weapon. He then walks right up to the man and says, "Excuse me. Can I help you?"

Somewhat intoxicated, the black man replies, "Who the hell are you?"

Yonatan does not act confrontational but says, "I'm part of the hotel's security team, and we've had an anonymous credible tip that someone who fits your description is prepared to carry out a possible terrorist act. You're obviously not that guy! Pardon me. Have a good evening."

Felicia, who is observing this scene, can't help but think to herself that she's only been in Israel for less than a few hours and she's already feeling an anxiety knot in her stomach. Was this how it was going to be every time they encountered a person with black skin? Felicia quickly composes herself and lightens the tension by advising Yonatan, "If I were you, I'd be asking my husband for a raise!"

Yonatan briskly responds, "He'd probably sue me for breach of contract."

It just took a few choice words from two clever people and all worries vanished. Ben turns to Elliot and Felicia, saying, "We'll pick you up at 9 AM tomorrow and head straight to Caesarea.

"We'll arrive in less than an hour. From the moment we get there, we'll be busy the entire day. First, I'll take you for a tour of the residence and the neighborhood. I know how much you appreciate your home in Bel-Air, but I promise you both that from the moment you step into your new home in Caesarea, you will fall in love. This place is architecturally designed with charm and warmth like I've never seen before. I know Felicia will customize it to your family's needs and wants, but I guarantee you, it's high quality all the way, and it is incredibly secure.

"By the way, since we'll be meeting with interior decorators, accountants and lawyers, I took the liberty to rent for the week a conference table, three sofas and a large dining table with ten chairs. Just wanted to make sure we could work comfortably!"

Elliot, who is inspired by the efficiency of his trusted confidante, grabs hold of Ben and gives him a huge hug of appreciation, saying, "We're going to do big things together, and I'm thrilled that after all these years of talking about jointly creating a business, we're finally going to do it! I can't wait to get started!"

"Thank you, Elliot. The feeling is mutual. By the way, did you know that I'm a very important executive at my bank? You want to know why? My customer is the largest individual depositor in the bank's history. We handle larger business depositors, but no individuals bigger than you and Felicia."

Elliot smiles and responds, "Just like our college days, I get the final word, and here it is. By the time you and I are finished, the Sterling Hedge Fund will be the largest business depositor in the bank's history by far, and I will remain the largest individual depositor! See you at 9 AM."

As Felicia and Elliot make their way to the elevator to go to their suite, they are trailed by Yonatan.

Felicia says to her husband, "I'm starting to understand how government heads of state live their lives. They have power but give up privacy in exchange for security. I guess I need to get used to it, even though I hate it." Then she raises her voice a little bit, looks back, and says, "No offense, Yonatan!"

Once inside their posh multi-room accommodations, which include a grand living room area with expansive views of the Mediterranean, Felicia looks at her husband and says, "This is heaven! I mean it, Elliot. Just magnificent!"

Sitting down on a lavish sofa, Elliot replies, "Well, it's all yours for the next seven days. After everything you've had to endure over the last year, I'd say you've earned a little rest and recreation."

Felicia starts unbuttoning her blouse and makes her way directly into the room's deluxe master bathroom where she spots, to her delight, an oversized tub and says to her husband, "You really did think of everything. I'm going to take a sumptuous bath!"

Elliot, knowing that his wife loves her baths, simply says, "Enjoy."

By the time Felicia completes her bath and both have unpacked their bags, room service arrives with dinner. Elliot has ordered them both the fresh fish catch of the day, vegetables, roasted potatoes and a salad with balsamic vinaigrette dressing. He asks room service to send up their best bottle of Chardonnay. The server beautifully organizes everything on a dining table in the suite so that they are seated to take advantage of the sweeping views of the sunset and the gorgeous sea.

Elliot thanks the waiter, adds a generous tip, and signs the check. Once the server has left, Elliot passionately kisses his wife, serves them both a glass of wine, and makes a toast, "To my lovely wife who has always stood by me, no matter what. I love you! I pray that we are blessed with a happy and fulfilled life while in Israel. I promise to do everything I can to accomplish that."

Felicia simply says, "I adore you, Elliot. All I ask for is that our family be safe. If I'm with you and our daughters, I will feel secure and content. We'll make this our home for as long as it is needed. We'll do so with great character and a smile on our faces. But I want you to know that the moment you tell me we can return permanently to Bel-Air, I will be anxious to return."

Elliot stares into his wife's eyes and says, "So will I. Now, tell me about Rose and Erica's Stanford University leave-of-absence. Are they going to get credit for foreign study abroad while living here in Israel?"

Felicia, who has spent countless hours working with her daughters and the university, enthusiastically answers, "Yes! The Hebrew University of Jerusalem has accepted our girls' expedited applications. Of course, I will admit, it didn't hurt having their father be a well-respected Stanford alumnus. And, it didn't harm us having an advocate like Ben leaking to the university that Mr. Sterling is the largest individual depositor in his bank.

"All kidding aside, Rose and Erica were accepted solely on their academic merits. They are both recognized as exemplary students and rising stars. But to be fair, their dad's name might have tipped the scales a bit with the expedited part of the acceptance."

Elliot was, of course, pleased that his daughters had been accepted into such a prestigious university, allowing them to continue seamlessly with their education. But Felicia, who understood her husband's range of emotions very well, instinctively knew Elliot was not sharing the same exuberant vibe she was feeling regarding the timely university acceptance. "Okay Mr. Sterling, what's going on in that head of yours?"

Elliot responds with one word, "Location."

Felicia pauses for a moment, then gets it right away, saying, "You mean the girls will experience more security risks living in Jerusalem as opposed to Tel Aviv University, which is closer to our home in Caesarea. I thought about that too. Although the girls will live in dormitories at the Jerusalem University as opposed to commuting from Tel Aviv University to our home every day, they will not only be safer but receive a better education."

"Alright Mrs. Sterling, tell me how you figured that all out."

"Well, that's easy. First, the Hebrew University of Jerusalem is the number one ranked university in all of Israel. But even more importantly, the university offers twenty courses taught in the English language, such as International Law and Human Rights. Stanford University will grant full credit toward the girls' transcripts in any one of those twenty classes! This even gets better.

"The exchange students are allocated to Israeli students throughout their stay at Hebrew University. All students are highly encouraged to join in on social activities in the Student Village, which will allow Rose and Erica the opportunity to make life-long friends. Finally, the university offers pre-semester language courses allowing exchange students a chance to study some Hebrew before beginning the academic semester. Need I say anything more on the academic university choice?"

Elliot just says, "Go on."

Felicia collects her thoughts and continues, "I spent a lot of time discussing the best university security alternatives with Yonatan. Together, we dissected the security risks from every angle. His unconditional recommendation was the Hebrew University of Jerusalem. He will assign one security guard to Rose and one to Erica. They will be under their watchful eye while living in Jerusalem.

"Yonatan felt the kids will be safer by not commuting every day from Caesarea to Tel Aviv. The routine of that would make it easier for the Nigerians to figure out. He felt that splitting up the family was also smart so that we are not one big target, but that it would be fine to have the girls come home to Caesarea for the weekends so long as there was no set pattern of travel.

"Yonatan was convinced that going to school in Tel Aviv and moving around that big city would pose a greater risk than living in less hectic Jerusalem. He gave me some other reasons he opted for this decision, but that's the highlights.

"Feel free to speak further with him, but I am confident this is the correct way to proceed. Satisfied?"

"Wow! Very impressive. You got this. I really should have known better. You've looked after our kids perfectly for their entire lives. Why should living in Israel be any different? From the first day we faced the Nigerian challenge, your number one concern has been the safety of our family. Not only do you have the safety issue for Rose and Erica read correctly, but you're spot on with choosing the right Israeli university. Very savvy of you to have consulted with Yonatan. And you were very wise spending the time coordinating between Stanford and the Jerusalem University. Did I ever tell you I have a very smart wife?"

Felicia, wearing a pink silk robe and very sexy negligee, stands after finishing her dinner and says with a gorgeous grin, "Stick with me, I'll never steer you wrong."

Elliot looks at his beautiful wife, then gets up, passionately embracing and kissing her, saying, "I know. The best decision I ever made was to marry you. So, Mrs. Perfect, let's go to bed. We've got a long day in front of us tomorrow."

Exhausted from their long trip, they instantly fell asleep until the next morning. They awoke well rested, got comfortably dressed, and went downstairs to eat the hotel's famous Mediterranean "Sabra" breakfast.

The buffet featured home-made hummus, pita bread, bagels, lox, green olives, an assortment of cheeses, and a tasty lemon marinated diced tomato with cucumber salad. You could order any style egg omelet imaginable while enjoying freshly squeezed orange or grapefruit juice. After completing the delicious breakfast, they relaxed in the hotel's elegant lobby waiting for Benjamin to arrive.

At precisely 9 AM, Ben makes his way through the revolving front doors of the facility and walks directly toward Elliot and Felicia, greeting them with the now familiar, "Shalom."

Elliot and Felicia respond with their own "Shalom". When they finish greeting Ben, they hear virtually out of nowhere a "good morning". Turning to look, it's none other than the clandestine Yonatan.

Elliot addresses Yonatan slightly irritated, yet mixed with some humor by saying, "You really got to stop creeping up on us like that."

The no-nonsense and unapologetic Yonatan answers his boss with, "You'll get used to it."

Feeling some tension, Elliot glances at Felicia, who unexpectedly reacts by bursting out laughing at Yonatan's comment, instantly relieving any anxiety. Elliot then breaks out in a smile and says to Ben, "Alright, let's get my wife to Caesarea so she can visit her new home!"

The drive to Caesarea from Tel Aviv takes approximately forty-five minutes following Road 2, which is the main coastal highway. The ancient city is located about the midway point between Haifa and Tel Aviv. Engaged in deep conversation, the car travel goes by quickly as they approach the picturesque Caesarea on Israel's Mediterranean Coast.

This is the city that Herod the Great had dedicated to Caesar Augustus more than 2,000 years ago. The area is composed of a magnificent township featuring a National Park with a Roman amphitheater and a historic port. The driver, born in nearby Netanya, encourages Mr. and Mrs. Sterling to take the time to visit the archaeological park with pillars and sculptures, and the remains of a hippodrome, with frescoes and stone seating. These ruins include the seafront Promontory Palace with fascinating remains of a mosaic floor. As the Mercedes Benz begins to approach the beautiful beaches and impressive elite modern residences, the car slows down as it makes it way toward a prominent security guard house with an impressive electronic gate.

The entire planned community is surrounded by a soaring wall. The wall is made from "Jerusalem Stone", which consists of a white, meleke, coarse limestone used famously in structures like the Western Wall. The security to enter the intimate private community is over the top. Not just because a Prime Minister of Israel maintains a residence there, but because some of the most prestigious people from across the globe have established their address in this extraordinarily secure complex.

Dressed in a dark suit, one security guard comes out of the bulletproof glass and stone structure, while a second guard remains inside. He politely says in Hebrew, "Welcome. How can I assist you?"

Ben rolls down his window and states in Hebrew, "Mr. and Mrs. Elliot Sterling are the new owners of the residence located at 18 Balfour Street. They are visiting their home for the first time. Previous arrangements were made by my bank with your security management to provide us with clearance to enter the complex by providing you with their passports."

The highly trained guard immediately says, "May I have a passport and drivers licenses for everyone in the car?" After gathering the identification documents, he walks into the secured guardhouse, hands the items to his superior, and waits for the clearance. Within a few minutes, the guard returns to the car, handing everyone back their credentials and now speaking in English, says, "We welcome you to your home, Mr. and Mrs. Sterling. Please be aware that we are available twenty-four hours around the clock.

"Shortly, one of our guard personnel will schedule an appointment to better brief you about how security is conducted here. In the meantime, we have been informed by your bank that you have various visitors arriving today. Upon clearance, we will direct them to your residence. In the future, you will be required to authorize anyone visiting this complex. Finally, as a routine reconnaissance practice, someone from the Prime Minister's security detail will visit with you later today. Thank you, and we wish you a long and pleasant stay."

As the heavy-set gates open slowly, the driver makes his way toward the Balfour estate and takes the opportunity to pridefully explain, "Balfour was the signatory to the famous Balfour Declaration, which was a historical document confirming support from the British government for establishment in Palestine of a homeland for the Jewish people. Balfour will forever be remembered in Israel."

It didn't take long to arrive at the property, which was located right on the coast of the Mediterranean.

Felicia initially focuses on the serious entry gate, security cameras, and a "Jerusalem Stone" wall, which literally surrounds the entire magnificent estate. Behind the gate, she begins to stare at a gorgeous two-level traditional French architecturally designed home. The serenity of the residence with perfectly manicured mature landscaping is a dream to observe. The custom cobblestone pavers leading to a wide circular driveway and entry fountain went beyond Felicia's expectations.

Elliot, who is sincerely impressed, asks his wife, "Well, what's on your mind?"

Felicia answers with what she's thinking, "The exterior is flawless! I just hope the interior is as spectacular as the exterior."

Elliot responds saying, "Let's go find out."

Benjamin, who has the gate transmitter, alarm codes, and keys to the home in his briefcase, opens the private gate granting access to the driver to enter the estate. Once at the entrance, Ben is the first to get out of the car, grab the keys and open the front door while simultaneously deactivating the alarm. He leaves the door wide open as he nervously awaits his friend's reaction.

Elliot affectionately holds his wife's hand as they make their way toward the home they have bought sight unseen. Before they enter the residence, Felicia looks at her husband, takes a deep breath, and walks by herself into the six-bedroom, seven-bath masterpiece home. The expansive entry foyer to the residence has a remarkable high ceiling with a Baccarat crystal chandelier and a custom designed marble floor. Each of the rooms features a high ceiling with crown molding. The large gourmet kitchen is organized with handcrafted custom cabinets and the finest appliances money can buy.

The detailed mosaic tile design of the calm Mediterranean shoreline above the cooktop, along with the seamless marble countertops, designer flooring, and natural light is unsurpassed first-class quality.

As Benjamin continues the tour of the home, it is evident the original architect had designed a floorplan that flowed to perfection. Each room is spacious with an abundant amount of natural lighting. Felicia just loves the serenity of the breakfast nook. She is very impressed by the formality of the dining room with its custom French doors and grand Swarovski crystal chandelier.

Elliot cannot hold back from smiling as he walks into the quaint movie theatre, the charming living room with a wood burning fireplace, and his library/study. The family room is especially impressive with expansive windows and a glorious unobstructed view of the Mediterranean Sea.

But it is the master bedroom that just blows Felicia away. From the double door foyer leading into the magnificent suite with a romantic fireplace, to the breathtaking views of the sea and the sizeable balcony off to one side. This room is simply stunning! The master bathroom, with two huge cedar-lined walk-in closets, could have been taken right out of a page from an architectural magazine.

Felicia, who literally is speechless, walks over to her husband, hugs him, and with a joyful tear rolling down her cheek says, "This place is phenomenal. Thank you."

Elliot quickly responds, "Don't thank me. Thank Ben. He got it for us."

Felicia turns to Ben and with her smart quick wit says, "You're off the hook, Ben. You don't have to worry any more. I just told my husband that we're keeping the place. Seriously, thank you very much for finding this amazing residence for my family. This home is superb! Consider this your home too."

Ben says, "I will admit I felt a little nervous thinking that perhaps you wouldn't find it to your liking, especially since it cost you and Elliot many millions of dollars to buy the residence without ever seeing it. The good news is that you like it, but I can assure you that if you did not, you could have re-sold it for a substantial profit within a week! So, let's go see the backyard."

The outside is as terrific as the inside. The swimming pool is oversized with a vanishing edge. It gave the impression that the pool melts into the horizon. The entire backyard has a soothing view of the Mediterranean Sea with direct private access to a beautiful beach. The concrete deck area features an outdoor fireplace and an enormous spa. The mature palm trees, expansive green lawns, and colorful bougainvillea plants give the gardens a resort vacation feel.

As the tour came to an end, Felicia looks at her husband's banker and close friend and says to Ben, "If you continue advising my husband on his hedge fund business as well as you have guided us regarding the purchase of this estate, you're going help make my husband a seriously wealthy man. We're sincerely grateful. I love this home!"

Ben humbly responds, "Your husband doesn't need my help to be successful. He's already very successful and wealthy. When it came to this home, Elliot described in meticulous detail the type of residence you expected. I just found him what he demanded. It has always been his leadership that brings the best out of everyone he meets.

"Much to the contrary, Elliot Sterling is the one who is going to make us all succeed with the hedge fund. I'll just be right there at his side opening every door I can, while informing him about everything I know. Believe me, he'll take care of the rest."

Felicia makes eye contact with her husband and asks him, "What do you think of those words?"

Elliot responds directly to his wife as if Ben isn't even standing there, "From the first day I met him at school, this guy has always had a gift to gab. Back then, I wasn't always sure that I could believe everything he had to say. Over time I began to understand that Ben was a man who said what he meant, and sincerely meant what he said. I am touched by his words, but I can assure you, without his considerable financial skills and amazing contacts all over the world, the Sterling Hedge Fund would be very challenged to succeed. With Ben, we will become a powerhouse all over the globe!"

Felicia smiles and says, "Okay. Sounds like a love fest. Shall we go greet our guests?"

Ben, who is now laughing at Felicia's statement, looks at his watch, which indicates 11 AM, and says, "Yes, the interior decorator should arrive any minute now. The attorney and accountant will also be here shortly."

Chapter 3

Feeling very comfortable with her new home, Felicia leads Elliot, Ben, and the ever-present Yonatan back into the residence. She navigates the floorplan as if she has lived there for years. Felicia feels a deep sense of security knowing that her husband has made an intelligent decision concerning the home, and that the people Elliot chose to surround their family with are exceptional. She has not experienced this magnificent sense of financial and personal security for years, and decides right then and there that she will never relinquish this sentiment again.

Waiting at the front door is the security guard they had met earlier, accompanied by an attractive young woman who wore absolutely no make-up. Felicia isn't quite sure whether this woman is the interior decorator or someone from the security detail. So rather than guess, she extends her hand and says, "I'm Felicia Sterling."

The charming young woman responds with her Israeli accent and says, "Shalom, Mrs. Sterling. A pleasure to meet you. I am Avigail Livnat, your interior decorator. Many people who meet me professionally for the first time have a hard time believing that I am an accomplished designer. So, I thought I'd just save you that awkward moment and tell you a little bit about myself. I have served as the interior decorator for many of the homes in this complex, including the Prime Minister's residence.

"I have been commissioned to do the interior decorating for the homes of many high-level Israeli Cabinet Ministers. I am often retained by high-net worth Americans who have bought second homes in Israel. As you can see, I'm very straightforward, and very confident you're going to appreciate my work.

"So, should we get started by showing me your splendid home? Please tell me every detail that comes to your mind. And, most importantly, talk to me about your family. Explain your lifestyle. Help me understand what makes you feel relaxed, and the color palettes that express your unique personality. By the way, you are the most beautiful American woman I have ever met!"

Mesmerized by this most interesting and energetic woman, Felicia responds, "Thank you for the compliment. I'm sure you say that to every new female client you meet."

Avigail interrupts, "No, I don't. I really mean it. You're gorgeous!"

"Well, thank you again. Besides your flattery, something tells me that you and I are going to get along famously. Let's take a tour through the home and we'll talk as we go. Did you bring your fee proposal?"

Avigail quickly responds, "No, I didn't. But as soon as we finish our walk-through and I listen to your thoughts, you'll have it by the time I leave here today."

With a grin on her face, Felicia starts walking as she says, "Fair enough."

Just as Felicia disappears into the home with Avigail, the doorbell chimes begin to ring. Ben, seated in the living room on one of the three temporary sofas he had prepared for the various scheduled meetings, gets up to open the front door and says to Elliot, "That must be the attorneys and the two accountants."

Elliot looks up at Ben and sarcastically says, "Do we really need two of each?"

Benjamin responds, "No, but you know how it works, the main partner has his name on the door, and the assistant does all the work. We learned that trick from you Americans."

Within just a few minutes, Ben returns to the room with the four professionals dressed in elegant dark suits with handkerchiefs and ties. Each were wearing short Israeli military style haircuts. All of them carrying sleek briefcases.

Just by looking at these guys, Elliot instantly sizes them up as a bunch of high-priced arrogant pricks. They remind him of the pompous academic bankers and other professionals he found despicable back in Beverly Hills. Although he has not even so much as said "hello" to these people, his instincts sound off alarms of distrust in his head.

Elliot stands to greet his guests as Benjamin says to the group, "I'd like you all to meet your client, Mr. Elliot Sterling."

One by one, they each extend their hand, starting with the senior attorney who says, "My name is Yair Katz and my associate is Naftali Lapid. It's a privilege to represent you."

Then the main accountant introduces himself as Moshe Ariel, who in turns introduces his assistant as Gilad Cohen.

After the obligatory hand shaking with each of them, Elliot requests that they all follow him to the dining room where a temporary conference table has been installed so they can conduct the meeting. Once they arrive, Elliot sits at the head of the table flanked by Ben. The two attorneys take a seat on the right side, and the accountants sit on the left.

A no-nonsense Elliot immediately takes control of the meeting by first requesting their retainer agreements. "My understanding is that you have been asked by Benjamin to represent us in the formation of my new firm, the Sterling Hedge Fund. Additionally, I am informed that you have drafted our first business agreement regarding the lawful sale of the Savor rifle. Let me get something really clear here. Whenever you work for my company, or myself individually, we must first sign a retainer or you will not be paid. Second, you will always provide an estimated fee agreement in writing before any work commences. So, who has your retainers and the associated estimate?"

A more serious Ben steps in and says, "I have the retainers, but frankly, I don't have any fee estimates."

Sterling then looks at Katz and says, "What's the cost for your services?"

Katz responds, "Depends on the scope of the work."

Sterling, disliking this guy more and more by the second, says, "The only services you've been retained for is to legally organize the Sterling Hedge Fund and do some transactional work regarding our agreement to sell the Savor to our customers in Africa. That's it. Now what the hell is your fee estimate to complete these assignments?"

Katz, starting to get his ego ruffled and not wanting to get pinned down to a fee estimate, says, "I don't have that answer for you, Mr. Sterling. We don't work this way in Israel. Our firm has hourly rates identified in our retainer agreement. We simply charge you by the hour until we complete the work you request. I can assure you we are quite efficient and very effective for our clients. We won't cheat you, if that's what you are insinuating."

Elliot, glancing at Ben, then looking back at Yair, says, "Pursuant to your retainer agreement, how many hours do you have into our account and what do we owe you as of this hour?"

Yair answers with a slight smirk, "I have no idea."

Sterling says, "That's what I thought. So, Yair, I want you to go back to your office. Figure out what I owe for your work. Produce a final statement. Deliver it to Benjamin's office. We'll pay you, then you're fired! That's the way we work in America. I'm sure you can find your way to the front door."

Stunned, Katz asks, "I apologize if I've offended you, Mr. Sterling. I'll be happy to make an exception and estimate our fees. Can we try to start fresh? Is there anything else I can do to assist you?"

Elliot quickly answers his question, "My American attorney, Mr. Paul Norman, along with my associate, Mr. Mark Goldman, will be in your offices within forty-eight hours. Please cooperate fully in transferring all your files and associated agreements to them. Of course, you can charge me for the time you or your staff spend in answering their questions during the transition. Thank you, Mr. Katz, and thank you, Mr. Lapid."

As they walk out of the dining room, everyone has a startled look on their faces. Ben, who is embarrassed, tries to break the ice by saying, "Well, I'm glad that went well. Anyway, Moshe, are you prepared to provide Mr. Sterling with your fee estimate?"

The wise and seasoned accountant answers briskly, "Yes Ben, I am."

Ben makes eye contact with Elliot and smiles. "Okay, at least I picked one smart professional."

Moshe goes on to say, "Mr. Sterling, we'll charge you ten thousand U.S. dollars per month for the next six months. We will adjust the fee up or down depending on the real workload accessed at that time.

"Either party can cancel the arrangement at the end of the six months. If you're satisfied, keep us. If we're comfortable, we'll stay. Agreed?"

Sterling takes a glance at Ben and remarks, "That's a deal, Mr. Ariel. You're my accountant!"

Ariel then says, "Very good. Now I have one more suggestion, if I may."

Ben says, "Go ahead, Moshe."

"As Ben will advise you, it is a mistake to try and use an American attorney to navigate the Israeli legal system. You can rely on the good consul of your personal attorney and associate, but it will be business and legal suicide if you don't retain an Israeli attorney."

Sterling, already one step ahead of Moshe's comment, says, "Got someone in mind?"

Moshe answers, "Yes I do. He's one of the very best transactional lawyers in the country. His family was originally from the United States and immigrated to Israel decades ago. He has a degree from Harvard Law School, but is humble and down to earth. His name is Yitzhak Bennett. Please trust me when I tell you that this guy is amongst the best in Israel."

Sterling likes what he hears and has only one question, "Can you get him to Caesarea this afternoon?"

Moshe says, "I will call him now and ask. Most likely, we're talking about sometime tomorrow. I'll contact Yitzhak and see how quickly he's available. If not, perhaps you can visit with him in Tel Aviv tomorrow morning before you travel here to Caesarea."

"Fine. Give him a call."

As Moshe was contacting the lawyer, Sterling says to Ben, "Excuse me. I'm going to step out for a moment. I got to make a call too. Let's get Paul Norman and Mark Goldman to Israel right away. I want them engaged with our consultants right from the beginning. You alright with that Ben?"

"Perfect. Get them over here. Paul can start working with Yitzhak immediately, and I can get Mark briefed on the Savor deal. He's the man you're sending to Algeria and the Sudan, right?"

Elliot says, "Yeah, that's right. Let me go call them."

Sterling makes his way to the private office, closes the door, and calls his people. Mark answers and says, "Hey, Boss. How's the holy land?"

Elliot responds, "You're about to find out! Get on the next plane out of Los Angeles to Tel Aviv.

"I just fired our fucking Israeli lawyer and I need you and Paul over here for some backup. Call Norman and tell him to carefully read the copy of the Sterling Hedge Fund organizing legal documents I left him prior to my departure. Additionally, tell Paul to review the Savor Agreement regarding Algeria and the Sudan. He needs to fully brief you on that deal because you're going to be on your way to Algeria very soon to close our first hedge fund contract. So, get your butts over here as fast as you can. Plan to be away for several weeks, maybe even a month. Any questions?"

Knowing that Elliot would not ask them both to come if he did not instantly need them, the fiercely loyal Mark responds simply, "We'll be there within twenty-four to thirty-six hours. I'll call you with our airline information. Just let me know whether we meet you at the hotel in Tel Aviv or at your home in Caesarea. See you soon."

Elliot responds to his childhood friend by saying, "You're a good man, Mark. Tell Paul that I apologize for the short notice. Safe travels to the both of you."

As Sterling is slowly strolling back to the meeting, it is becoming more and more evident that the only way the new hedge fund will succeed is to get Mark and Paul completely immersed in the daily operations of the Fund. He understood at that moment that there would be no substitutes for his brilliant young American lawyer and the street-smart Goldman. The big challenge is how to get them both to move to Israel for the next year to jointly build the business together.

Sterling enters the dining room and asks Ariel, "So, what did your legal prodigy have to say? Is he on his way to Caesarea?"

"Yitzhak can see you tomorrow in Tel Aviv at his office at 10 AM or he can visit with you here in Caesarea at 3 PM. Your choice."

Thinking that it would be smart to see the Israeli attorney's office firsthand, Sterling pauses for a moment, then answers, "Tell Mr. Bennett I'll see him in Tel Aviv at 10 AM tomorrow."

Moshe says, "Yes, Mr. Sterling. I'll call him right now."

Elliot goes on to instruct Moshe, "Advise Mr. Bennett that you will be dropping off copies of the Sterling Hedge Fund organizing documents, and the Savor Agreements. Tell him that he should base his retainer agreement and fee proposal around the review of these documents in consultation with my American attorney who will be collaborating with him closely. I want him to establish a retainer agreement like yours for the next six months. Do you understand me, Moshe?"

"Much better than you think, Mr. Sterling."

Now starting to feel in control of his business, Elliot says, "Very good, Moshe. Very good. Alright, so go call Yitzhak, then let's get started discussing the financial structure of my Fund. Also, Ben, please make immediate arrangements to get this gentleman his ten-thousand-dollar retainer."

Benjamin smiles, saying, "So long as Moshe can figure out how to properly document the expense on the Sterling accounting books, he'll have his money tomorrow morning. Seriously, how are we paying vendors from now on? United States dollars or Israeli Shekels?"

Moshe answers, "That's easy. We'll establish two operating bank accounts. One in US dollars, the other in Israeli Shekels. Whenever we pay anyone in Israel, it will be in Shekels. Whenever anyone outside of Israel will accept payment in Shekels, we'll pay in Shekels. Everyone else gets paid in dollars. We'll need you, Ben, to constantly have your hand on the pulse of the daily exchange rates regarding conversion of dollars to Shekels, and vice versa."

Sterling tests Ben by asking, "What's today's exchange rate for an American dollar?"

Without any hesitation, Ben answers, "Each US dollar is equal to 3.51302 Shekels."

Sterling winks at Moshe and says, "Wow! I'm impressed."

Now, it was time to get down to the financial structure of the Sterling Hedge Fund. Seated around the dining room table was Moshe and his assistant Gilad, Benjamin, and Elliot. Gilad had previously placed a white binder at each chair, outlining in detail the proposed capital structure for the new Hedge Fund.

Sterling looks at Moshe and just says, "The floor is yours, Mr. Ariel."

Moshe responds, being brutally honest, "You have in front of you a notebook full of a bunch of theoretical financial models. When I refer to financial structure, I mean the balance between all the company's liabilities and its equities. We accountants describe this as the entire 'Liabilities + Equities' side of the balance sheet.

"The capital structure, by contrast, includes equities and only the long-term liabilities. In Hebrew, I call this a bunch of chara. A bunch of shit. Since we're new, we don't have any liabilities, just equity. And since we haven't even signed any agreements with any customers, all you have in those binders is the model for how to financially organize the Fund's accounting in the future. Typically, the optimal capital structure is the best debt-to-equity ratio that maximizes its value.

"Often, the optimal capital structure for a company is one that offers a balance between the ideal debt-to-equity range and minimizes the firm's cost of capital. Any questions about this boring stuff so far?"

Ben jumps in and sarcastically states, "I believe what you're saying is that the company is worth shit!"

Elliot, Moshe, and the assistant burst out laughing. It takes Moshe a moment to compose himself into a more serious mood as he says, "This week, Mr. and Mrs. Sterling will be transferring a sum of ninety million dollars as the start-up capital for the Sterling Hedge Fund. Mr. Sterling has granted options to Mark Goldman, Paul Norman, and Benjamin Yaalon to acquire shares in the Fund up to one million dollars each. The option to contribute into equity will expire one year from the official start of the firm. And of course, the first transaction regarding the Savor rifle is anticipated to net over ten million dollars. So, no, this company is not worth shit. It has the potential to grow into one of the most important financial firms in all of Israel. That binder in front of you will be our financial blueprint!"

Listening carefully, a thoughtful Sterling asks, "What about debt finance. Do you recommend it?"

Moshe turns to his assistant, Gilad Cohen, who is considered an expert in debt structuring. Gilad answers, "The trade-off theory of capital structure is the idea that a company chooses how much debt-finance and how much equity-finance to use by balancing the costs and the benefits. An important purpose of the theory, illustrated in the binder, is to explain the fact that corporations usually are financed partly with debt and partly with equity. Our recommendation is to owe no one anything. Self-finance is the riskiest option in that you will be taking the entire risk, but you also receive the entire reward plus full autonomy."

Having lost his previous real estate development company to an over-zealous financial institution foreclosing on him due to disproportionate debt, this is precisely the answer Sterling wants to hear. "It will be the policy of this Fund to always self-finance. My goal for the Sterling Hedge Fund is to owe no money to anyone. Ben, am I perfectly clear?"

Ben answers with only one word, "Yes."

"Mr. Ariel, I am very comfortable with your preliminary thoughts. Ben will take over from here. He will review the binder page by page with the two of you. By the way, I'm changing the name of the binder to the 'Bible' because we're going to follow it like a Bible from now on. Ben has my authority to make amendments as he sees fit. He knows exactly what I'm looking for. Please follow his directions.

"If there is a grey area that requires my involvement, just let me know. I'm now going to excuse myself. Please make yourself at home and stay for as long as you'd like. We'll see you all back here tomorrow afternoon at 2 PM to continue with the review and comments. Let's build this Fund into an international sensation. Work hard every day toward advancing the Sterling Hedge Fund. Every detail must be analyzed until it's right. Communicate clearly with each other, and with our clients.

"Take pride in your work. As we grow, your extraordinary efforts will eventually result in significant financial rewards for each of you."

Ben, very fired-up by Sterling's pep-talk, enthusiastically asks his old friend, "So Elliot, what's your goal?"

The charming CEO of the company answers with a charismatic smile, "One day, I expect my net worth to be documented by Moshe as beyond a billionaire!"

Elliot then quickly gets up out of his seat, shakes everyone's hand, and makes his way to the second level of the residence to catch up with Felicia and Avigail. He is curious to see what type of progress they are making. He is equally eager to get a handle on the costs and fees Avigail has in mind for the interior decorating. As he's walking up the steps, he can't help but overhear the astute questions that his trusted college roommate was asking the accountants. But he is even more impressed with Moshe's answers. Sterling's instincts are telling him that this team, combined with Mark, Norman, and Yitzhak has the foundation of a world class organization.

Elliot locates Felicia and Avigail in the master bedroom. The two appear to be engaged in a spirited conversation as if they have known each other their entire lives. The eye contact, the hand gestures, and the laughter is a pleasant site to observe. It is almost as if Elliot doesn't want to interrupt them.

Felicia notices her husband and waves him into the room.

Avigail, who is holding a yellow legal pad filled with handwritten notes and sketches, says, "You are a very lucky man, Mr. Sterling."

"And why's that, Avigail?"

"Because your wife is smart, drop-dead gorgeous, very kind and extremely practical."

Elliot thanks Avigail for the lovely compliments and extemporaneously asks, "Give me an example of smart."

Avigail, without any hesitation, answers, "She insists on saving you money!"

Elliot thinks, then says, "Go on."

"Not one shekel will be spent on the exterior of the estate, even though I made some suggestions. Felicia informed me she loves it as-is and instructed me to save her husband any expenses on the exterior."

Elliot says, "I agree. Very smart! So, how many shekels am I going to need to set aside for the interior? And what are you going to charge us?"

Avigail, a talented street-smart Sabra (a Jew born on Israeli territory), responds with, "Ten percent."

Elliot, who understands exactly what she means by ten percent, tests her character by asking, "Ten percent of what?"

Avigail, who knows that Sterling is in the real estate development business and who knows he's just testing her, says, "Ten percent of the price you paid for the house."

Elliot is not initially sure whether she is serious or not, but then figures out that she's just having fun with him and says, "If you're going to charge a percentage of the entire estate, you'll need to drop the zero from the ten percent and you've got a deal. What I think you're saying is this, you're going to charge ten percent of whatever the actual new interior home improvements costs. So, if you spend five hundred thousand dollars, your fee will be fifty thousand. Did I hear you right?"

"Mazel Tov, Mr. Sterling. You really do understand the housing industry."

"Much better than you think, Ms. Avigail. So anyway, how much is this project going to run to?"

Avigail answers directly, "Fortunately for you, the home needs very little in terms of physical improvements. It's glorious as it stands. As for the estimate, plus or minus five hundred thousand US dollars. That will get the job done. This will include all furniture, flooring, window treatment, fixtures, everything required to customize the home to your family's lifestyle. My fee is in addition to the estimate.

"I'm confident that I clearly understand Mrs. Sterling's expectations. While you're here in Israel, she and I will be going through catalogues and samples. We will visit with many of my interior decorator vendors, and we'll make as many selections as possible. Anything we miss on this trip will be handled by phone or computer. I have assured Felicia that the job will be completed by your permanent move-in date of December 31st."

Elliot faces Felicia and asks, "Anything you want to add to this conversation?"

"Thank you for locating such a competent professional. We will work very well together. I am certain Avigail recognizes what our family needs. She appreciates that we're looking for quality, yet she knows we insist on value. She gets it, and she gets me, so let's get her on board."

Elliot responds with a grin and a wink, "Sounds like you don't like this woman! And just for the record, I did not find Avigail. You can thank Ben for that too." Now focused on Avigail, he continues, "It looks like my wife just hired you. Congratulations! Bring us your retainer agreement.

"Make sure the budget does not exceed five hundred thousand dollars plus your ten percent."

"Todah Rabah. Thank you, Mr. and Mrs. Sterling. I do have one final request."

"Sure, what's that?"

"All payments to the vendors will be in Shekels, but my professional fees are to be paid in dollars."

Elliot, without any hesitation, says, "We'll accommodate your request. Just put it in writing. That's why we have a retainer."

"Thank you, Mr. Sterling. I'll bring the agreement with me tomorrow. Your confidence in me is sincerely appreciated."

Elliot faces his contented wife and says, "So, Felicia. This has been a very productive day. You hired an interior decorator and made a good friend all in one afternoon. I retained an impressive accountant who's going to assist us in establishing the financial structure for the Sterling Hedge Fund, one of Israel's most important emerging companies. What do you say we get back to our hotel, grab some dinner, and watch the sunset disappear into the Mediterranean? Sound like a good plan? We'll be back here tomorrow by 2 PM immediately following the meeting with my proposed new Israeli attorney in Tel Aviv."

Felicia responds, "That's fine by me. Why don't you go tell Ben to start informing all of our guests that we plan to head back to Tel Aviv in about fifteen minutes."

"Will do."

Avigail grabs the hand of Felicia and says, "It's been a delight meeting you. Your husband is a charming gentleman. Please be assured I will give you my best efforts to meet, or surpass the goals you've set for your lovely home. Tomorrow afternoon I'll bring some upholstery swatches along with furniture, window treatment, and flooring samples for your review. We'll need to start making some decisions in order to meet the move-in timeline. I promise you this will be fun!"

Felicia says, "I have no doubt. I'll just feel much more at ease when we move in on December 31st."

Avigail responds, "Completely understandable. We'll get started tomorrow at 2 PM."

Chapter 4

Elliot and Felicia spent a pleasant evening in their hotel suite after returning from Caesarea. Again, they decide to order room service and enjoy the splendid Mediterranean sundown from the balcony of their room. They spend the night in deep conversation envisioning their new life in Israel and discussing the inevitable challenges they know they are about to face. The more they spoke, the more they understood that as long as they have each other, everything will be alright.

The sunrise the next morning is glorious. Elliot got up early to prepare for his important meeting with Yitzhak Bennett. He makes his way to the hotel's buffet to eat a hardy breakfast, enjoy his coffee, and make copious notes for the attorney meeting. Before he knew it, Ben is standing at his table and saying, "Good morning, Elliot. We must go now because many of the streets have been closed due to a stabbing of a police officer by a terrorist. This animal set off a bomb strapped to his waist, killing ten innocent people waiting at a busy bus stop. A baby was killed along with her mother. Just horrible, but regrettably, this is a part of our life here in Israel.

"We never get used to this type of news, but life must go on despite these despicable acts, or the terrorists will feel a sense of victory. I can assure you that these bastards will never accomplish their goal to terrorize our citizens. They have accomplished a moment of horrific pain from grieving families and the nation, but these acts of cruelty will never defeat our soul as a nation."

Elliot, stunned by the loss of life and inhumanity, asks, "Where did this happen?"

Ben answers, "Right outside of Tel Aviv in Ramat Gan where Yitzhak's office is located."

Elliot responds, "Was it near the Diamond Exchange in Ramat Gan?"

Ben answers, "Right across the street."

It did not take long before Ben's car was in heavy traffic to enter the Ramat Gan financial district. The Magen David Adom, Israel's national emergency medical disaster ambulance, along with blood bank service personnel were everywhere the eye could see. The

41

police were doing the best they could to keep traffic flowing, but the scene was just plain chaotic. After some time, they finally arrive at their destination and make their way into the underground parking facility.

Elliot and Ben rush to the elevator and travel to the eleventh floor. Bennett's office is at the end of the corridor. As they enter the suite, they are courteously greeted by a young receptionist who smiles and says in perfect English, "Welcome, Mr. Sterling and Mr. Yaalon. We've been expecting you. Mr. Bennett will be with you shortly. Is there anything I can get you?"

Ben answers, "No, thank you."

Before they even sit down, Yitzhak walks into the reception area wearing an unpretentious white short-sleeved shirt, khaki pants, and a black religious skull cap (yarmulke). He calmly introduces himself, "My name is Yitzhak Bennett. Thank you for coming to my office. I realize how complicated that must have been after the attack. Please follow me into the conference room."

Already positively impressed with Bennett's demeanor and the way he's dressed, Elliot sticks his hand out and says, "I'm Elliot Sterling, and this is my associate Benjamin Yaalon. Moshe Ariel tells me that not only can I trust you, but you're the best lawyer in all of Israel. Pleasure to meet you."

With a charming smile, the Harvard-educated Bennett quickly responds, "He's correct on both counts. Come, follow me to the conference table."

Sterling, now quite comfortable, tests Bennett's character by asking, "Do you always dress this way?"

Yitzhak instantly answers, "Only when I'm about to meet an important new client!"

Seated around the table, Bennett gets right to business. "I have been briefed by Mr. Ariel as to why you are here. With certain conditions, I would be pleased to legally assist you."

Sterling automatically asks, "And what are those conditions?"

"I'll review your former Israeli attorney's work product only as a general overview, but when I complete my review, his paperwork will be thrown in the trash. I will only rely on the original legal documents and my thoughts regarding the legal formation of the Sterling Hedge Fund. All organizing documents will be my new work product customized to your needs and requirements. I will work closely with Mr. Ariel and I will report to your American personal attorney. I have no problem collaborating with your attorney, except that Israeli law will prevail. I will not spend any time arguing with your counsel when it comes to Israeli law. He must be instructed by you to trust my judgement when it comes to this country's laws, as I will adhere to his concerns regarding the Sterling business plan. We agree so far?"

Sterling says, "What else?"

"I am very expensive. I work at a professional rate of eight hundred dollars an hour. The good news is that I am exceptionally efficient and get things right the first time. For example, as we speak, I know exactly how to proceed with your matters. We'll be done here in less than an hour. Perhaps other Israeli lawyers may drag you into a three-hour conference identical to this, and still not understand you. I'm certain you comprehend my example and the mathematics regarding my fees. In the long run, you're far better off hiring me. High quality advice at what will surely end up being comparable legal fees."

Sterling asks, "What else, Mr. Bennett?"

"I only work under a retainer agreement. Your retainer will be fifty thousand US dollars. Should my legal fees exceed the fifty thousand, you'll be required to replenish the retainer with a fresh fifty thousand. You may terminate your relationship with me at any moment you please so long as you pay me what you owe me through termination. Any further questions?"

Sterling thinks for moment, then says, "My attorney from America, Paul Norman, along with my associate, Mark Goldman, left a message earlier at my hotel informing me that they will be arriving in Israel later this afternoon. They were instructed to meet me at my Caesarea home at 2 PM this afternoon. Are you available to attend this meeting?"

Bennett responds without hesitation, "Do you agree with my terms and conditions?"

Sterling smiles and says, "Almost."

Amused, Bennett says, "Almost what."

"My previous attorney charged me half of your proposed retainer amount. I can live with all that you request except for the dollar amount of the retainer. I'm sure you're very good at what you do, but are you twice as good as Yair Katz?"

"That's what I hear. Look, Mr. Sterling, I don't pretend to understand all the sophisticated economics behind what constitutes an excellent hedge fund trade. But the one thing I do know is legal work. My fee structure, it stands as quoted. Take me or leave me. If you don't think the legal services merit continuing, you have the perfect right to fire me at any time you wish. Yes or no, Mr. Sterling?"

Sterling, who quickly realizes that Bennett means business, says, "Your initial work will be to legally organize the Sterling Hedge Fund and provide the original agreements regarding the sale of the Savor in Africa. Is that your understanding?"

"Yes Sir, Mr. Sterling."

"Alright, Yitzhak. You're my lawyer. Benjamin will arrange for your fifty thousand dollars later today. Just so you know, we only pay Israeli firms in equivalent shekels. Is that understood?"

"That is acceptable, Mr. Sterling. I'll draw up the retainer agreement and bring it with me to the 2 PM conference at your home in Caesarea. I look forward to meeting and working closely with Mr. Norman and Mr. Goldman."

Satisfied with his arrangement, Sterling instructs Yaalon to organize the retainer funds. "As long as we're here, go ahead and jot down Yitzhak's bank routing number so that you can wire him the money today. We'll sign the retainer as the first order of business this afternoon, then release the funds."

Benjamin, starting to recognize the decisive manner by which Sterling operates, simply responds with, "Consider it done."

Sterling then looks straight at Bennett and asks, "Okay. Anything more you need from me?"

Bennett looks right back at Elliot and says, "Just one more thing."

Thinking to himself what else could this guy possibly ask for, Sterling responds, "Alright Yitzhak, what's the thing?"

"I need your opinion on an investment I'm about to make. I trust I'm not indulging, but I thought since your firm is a specialist in finance, well, perhaps you might be good enough to express a quick word.

"I am the attorney that just recently won a ruling for my client that may open the door to an international flood into what's being called 'Israeli Cryptocurrency Trading'. Our Supreme Court ruled last week that one of the country's largest banks could not stop digital currency broker bank accounts until a public regulatory review can be completed. The court's temporary injunction forbids the bank from indefinitely closing the bank account of my client. My client hosts the trading and currency exchange in bitcoin and in other cryptocurrencies, all powered by what's called 'blockchain technology'. My client is a blockchain start-up entrepreneur. Am I boring you?"

Elliot, now hanging on every word Yitzhak is saying, glances at Ben then remarks, "Please, carry on."

"Well, anyway, if the court decision will be upheld, then it would be much easier to convert regular money to cryptocurrencies. Effectively, more people will hold cryptocurrency accounts, and it will in all probability increase the amount of trading. Digital currency is here to stay, and Israel is at the forefront. If my client has this read right, the reason this type of currency is going to go worldwide is because the cryptocurrency is going to be backed by diamonds, not gold, but diamonds.

"We have a serious diamond industry in Israel with diamond relationships all over the globe. I think this thing is going to be groundbreaking, along the lines of the cell phone or internet technology. What do you think, Mr. Sterling?"

"What else can you tell me?"

"Well, just for the record, everything I'm discussing here is public knowledge, so we are free to discuss this openly. And, since you have agreed to retain me, this will, of course, be considered an attorney-client conversation. The only thing else I wanted to share with you is that the banks are concerned about money laundering and adhering to bank regulations.

"The Central Bank of Israel has yet to formulate clear-cut cryptocurrency rules, therefore, they are afraid that the whole concept is going to undermine traditional banking as we know it! Transactions will be able to be completed immediately, and reliably without the need for a brick-and-mortar bank to complete the transmission of funds. What a concept!"

Very intrigued, Elliot says, "On the tip of the iceberg, this sounds like a winner. I need to study this more with my team. I love the fact that this is in its infancy, basically unregulated, and will be backed by the full faith and credit of diamonds. A lot of people have made enormous fortunes in black markets.

"Since the Sterling Hedge Fund will be selling the Savor in emerging African markets, this type of currency might even work for us. I'll get back to you within a few days on a more thoughtful opinion. Any comments, Ben?"

"I've of course heard of this for years. The banks hate the idea. As far as our Hedge Fund, I think we should put this under the microscope and study it hard. My gut feeling is it will work. The initial exchange rates will be far less than a hundred dollars per bitcoin. Once the world discovers they can use the cryptocurrency, it could be worth over a thousand dollars per coin. Who knows, they could have a value of well over ten thousand per coin one day!"

Elliot turns to Yitzhak and says, "Do you mind me asking how much money you plan to invest in this start-up?"

"I have an option to earn my legal fees in US dollars or the 'funny money' we're discussing. I have a further option to buy, during the initial private placement, up to one hundred thousand dollars. My legal fees will exceed that amount."

Sterling, fascinated with the conversation, says, "My first thought is to take your fees in dollars, then exercise your option for as much as you'd be prepared to risk. Figure you're going to potentially lose the entire investment. That way you can sleep at night. Who knows, you might even strike it rich.

"Give me a few days and you'll have a much better answer. By the way, if we like this deal, can we get in on it?"

The shrewd Bennett smiles and says, "I'll see what I can do."

Sterling, grinning right back at him, says, "While you're seeing 'what you can do', keep in mind that if I get involved in a deal like this, I'm talking about investing upwards of five million dollars in the initial placement. I'm pretty sure your client will be asking you what it takes to get me involved."

Bennett says, "I'm sure you're right, Mr. Sterling. I'll speak with them after you study the merits and you confirm to me that you do in fact want to make that kind of a sizeable commitment. I can't guarantee that the company will accept you as a preferred initial investor into the private placement, but I'm reasonably sure they'll find a benefit and embrace a high-powered investor."

Sterling then says, "Look at us, Yitzhak. We meet each other for twenty minutes, and I'm sending you fifty thousand bucks, and we're already talking about a 5-million-dollar investment. Yeah, I'm sure we're going to make a great team! See you at 2 PM in Caesarea."

As Elliot and Ben leave Bennett's conference room and make their way toward their car, Yonatan appears in the parking lot literally out of nowhere and says, "I'm not comfortable with the current risks on the public streets after the bombing. The police suspect that there may be a second terrorist ready to strike near this building. There is still much commotion on the streets, and I recommend that we stay in this building until I say so. I have arranged with one of my close friends for you to use his conference room and computers right here in the building. Plan to stay for about one hour. So, please follow me to the twentieth floor."

Sterling thinks for a moment, then holds back his resistance to the precautionary step, saying to Yonatan, "I trust your friend has coffee in his office?" With that said, Elliot gathers some paperwork, then facetiously states, "I hope this is worth our valuable time!"

Yonatan very calmly responds, "How much do you value your life?"

It didn't take much time for Yonatan to escort Elliot and Ben to the twentieth floor and straight into the reserved conference suite. The views of Tel Aviv are spectacular from this floor, and the room is especially well decorated. Yonatan tells his boss to take a seat and informs him he'll be back when it is safe. Ben, who is seated across the table from Elliot, waits for Yonatan to close the door and says, "This cryptocurrency thing is real! Our bank has fought for years to block its legitimacy in the courts.

"We know for sure that one day cryptocurrency is going to be the currency of choice for the business and investment communities. I didn't want to say too much in front of Bennett, but his client is the real deal, and this form of currency is going to make it on the world market."

Elliot pauses, then says, "So you recommend that the Sterling Hedge Fund invest? Don't you think it would be smart to study this some more?"

Ben just says, "No. I'll tell you why we don't need to go deeper. Our bank already did. We have studied this inside and out. I have all the financial models. In fact, the bank has spent countless hours trying to figure out how we could profit from the currency once the government approves its use. Let me give you an example.

"My bank projects that the initial private placement will come out at ten dollars per coin. Very quickly that same coin will resell at more than one thousand dollars per unit. The profits are staggering. Even the politicians are salivating at the thought of investing. Once Bennett wins his case, there are hundreds of millions of dollars to be made with this endeavor. If there is a graceful method to buy out Bennett's client, I'd highly recommend it!"

Sterling, staring into Ben's eyes, says, "Do you realize that if your bank's mathematical equations are correct, a 5-million-dollar investment, at ten dollars a coin, has a potential to grow to approximately 500 million dollars! This is beyond belief! Explain to me once again how this stuff works."

Benjamin says, "Sure. These coins are a digital currency that are not tied to a bank or government. It allows users to spend money anonymously. The coins are created by users who 'mine' them by lending computing power to verify other users' transactions. They receive the coins in exchange. The value of these coins can swing sharply. The legal tender represents lines of computer code that are digitally signed each time they travel from one owner to the next. That's it in a nutshell.

"Now, the reason that Bennett's client has come up with a world-class intellectual property is that he will be the first to tie the cryptocurrency to the spot value of diamonds. So, for instance, if a one carat diamond is worth one thousand four hundred dollars, the cryptocurrency will initially be tied to that spot market value. This will instantly give the digital currency extraordinary worth, especially for the initial investor who will buy the coins at ten dollars per coin.

"When the rest of the world figures out it is tied to one carat diamonds valued at one thousand four hundred dollars, the coins will instantly trade at over a thousand dollars per coin. This is precisely why we need to buy as many of these coins as we can get hold of."

Sterling, who is slightly dazed by the enormity of the wealth that could be realized by this type of transaction, says, "You're serious, aren't you?"

Ben answers, "Never been more serious in all my life! Either buy out the start-up company, or buy every single crypto coin from this son-of-a-bitch you can. This is a once in a lifetime fortune to be made on this deal. Well, in your case, a second in a lifetime fortune to be made. Don't let this go."

Elliot asks, "Who else do you think is going to try and get in on this with Bennett's client?"

Ben says, "That's easy. We hear that the prime minister himself, along with the finance minister. If the banks can't stop the regulatory restrictions, they will also be amongst the first to try and swallow up the coins. I wouldn't be surprised if a silent partner in the initial offering isn't already a politician."

Sterling is silent for about a minute and then says, "What's the downside?"

Ben answers, "New markets tend to enjoy a boom when professional investors start entering the market. Generally, that follows by euphoria as other players rush in to capitalize on the gains. I am certain that this virtual currency is going to rise much further than the spot price of a one carat diamond. When it comes to the bubble bursting, the question is when, not if! This kind of thing never ever lasts. The trade value might go up as much as to ten thousand per coin, but it won't sustain that price because its true value is a whole lot less. We will need to calculate precisely when to sell these holdings."

Sterling pauses saying nothing, just thinking. He gets out of his chair and walks to the end of the room and says, "What else could go wrong?"

Ben responds quickly, "Government could go wrong. They can decide that the virtual currency is impossible to regulate, and declare this type of virtual currency not in the national security interest of the country. In the United States, your currency is governed by the Bank Secrecy Act. The guidelines require people in the business of exchanging money to register with the government and follow other anti-money laundering measures as banks do, including knowing the identity of the customer and reporting any transactions over ten thousand dollars.

"Many states also require money transmittal businesses to be licensed. We must always be worried that politicians could pass laws heavily regulating the coins or decide to outlaw the currency in its entirety. In the meantime, a company such as the Sterling Hedge Fund could have made an agreement to accept payment in the form of cryptocurrency from a country with an unstable national currency. If that country's national currency should seriously be devalued, and governments decide to simultaneously overregulate, or for that matter outright ban the use of the coins, then we're all fucked!"

Sterling does not pause and says, "We'll buy the coins, sit on them, then time their sale to perfection."

Ben reacts, "Does that mean you don't want to buy the Bennett client start-up company, just the coins?"

"That's exactly what I mean. We're going to buy as much of this currency as they will allow during the initial private placement. I'm willing to go as high as a 10-million-dollar investment using that old reliable formula of buy low and sell high. The risk should be manageable because the virtual currency we will be buying is not only based on those complicated software codes, but will be backed by the one carat diamond value.

"In the short term, I expect the coins to go from ten bucks, to near the value of a one carat diamond. I agree with you that the coins will soon be priced at over a thousand dollars per unit. As soon as it hits that benchmark, we'll decide what to do. Perhaps we'll sell off the entire portfolio, or maybe we stick with all of it, or a portion. Who knows, we might even accept the virtual currency when it comes to those countries with unstable national currencies paying us for the Savor. Let's see what happens."

Just as Elliot and Ben are finishing up their discussion, Yonatan walks into the room and says, "My sources have informed me that it is safe to leave. The law enforcement officials tracked down some other terrorists that were all part of a conspiracy to kill other innocent Israeli citizens here in Ramat Gan. They have them all in custody. This is a very good time for us to leave now. We'll pick up Mrs. Sterling at the hotel and still make it to Caesarea by 2 PM."

The traffic from the office building to the hotel is mild. They pick up Felicia and make it to Caesarea well before their anticipated meeting time. As they make their way toward the entry security gate, Sterling notices a car parked at the entry gate with a tall rugged-looking guy having a discussion with the now familiar security guard. It doesn't take long for Sterling to recognize that man as his life-long friend and confidant, Mark Goldman. Seated in the car is his trusted young attorney, Paul Norman. This is a great moment for Elliot to be reuniting with his "business family" on Israeli soil.

Elliot gets out of his car and walks straight toward Mark, and without his knowledge that he's standing just a few feet away from him, says, "Hey Goldman, you can't even convince our innocent young security guard to let you into my house. How the hell are you going to persuade some General to buy Savors!"

Mark, a former United States Marine, turns his attention from the guard to his boss and close friend. "The reason you'll assign me to sell the rifles is because you don't have the balls to face a General!" As they now move toward each other, the two men are smiling and then laughing as they affectionately hug.

Goldman says, "How the hell you doing, Boss? Did we get here fast enough for you?"

Elliot responds, "I'm doing a lot better now that you guys are here. I'm impressed how quickly you made it to Caesarea. Thanks for coming on such short notice. You guys are my rock!"

Slow to get out of the car, but listening to the conversation, the Harvard educated Norman makes his way toward his boss and business hero, extending his hand while saying, "Very good to see you, Mr. Sterling. I sure miss working with you daily. I trust all is well with Mrs. Sterling and you."

Sterling, who can't even hide his excitement about being surrounded by his two top lieutenants, remarks, "It's very good to see you too, Paul. I sincerely apologize for dragging you all the way over here without any planning. but we got a ton of important work to do here. I got to have the guys I trust standing right next to me as those decisions are rendered. By the way, how's that beautiful young girl from the bank in Beverly Hills?"

"She called me while I was in the airport in LA and told me she hopes to marry me, Sir."

"Well, let's take care of our pressing business here, then get you back into her lovely arms. Alright, gentlemen, follow me." Sterling gestures toward the security guard, who in turn opens the gate for the two cars to proceed into the complex.

As they enter the front door and to the residence, Sterling says to his entourage, "Follow me to the dining room area. We've set up a make-shift conference table."

Mark is delighted to see Felicia as he gives her a hug and says, "Great to see you. You look relaxed and beautiful as ever. Wow, what a spectacular home! This beats the Bel-Air place."

Felicia, very comfortable in her relationship with Mark, says, "Thank you. Elliot and I are delighted that you're here. We want you to know you will always be warmly welcome in this home." And then she quips, "I'd really like to return your nice compliment to me, but frankly, you look like hell!"

Mark bursts out laughing. "You try flying fifteen hours straight, cram in nine non-stop hours of sleepless preparation desperately trying to figure out how these Israelis conduct business, then drive to Caesarea to have this meeting, all in a day's work for your husband!"

Felicia, using her wit, says, "Paul doesn't look half as bad as you. I'm just messing with you, Mark. Elliot really needs you guys right now. Thanks very much for coming. You're a deeply loyal friend and we love you for that. Elliot set up super rooms for you and Paul at the hotel. The moment you're finished with this afternoon's business, we'll get you some well-deserved sleep!"

"Very kind of you, Felicia. I appreciate the words. You know that whenever Elliot asks me to 'jump', my only response is 'how high?'. He's a special guy and I love him to death!" Then, with his trademark charismatic grin, Mark says, "By the way, I slept the whole damn way from LA to Ben Gurion. It's the nightlife with my girlfriend that exhausted me."

The last man into the dining room is Mark. As he takes a seat, the doorbell rings at exactly 2 PM.

Felicia opens the front door and finds Avigail Livnat, Moshe Ariel, and his assistant, Gilad Cohen. As she's about to close the door, she hears a man's voice saying, "Excuse me, please wait!"

51

Felicia, who does not recognize the voice nor the person, responds, "Who are you and how did you get past security?"

The man responds, "I actually arrived at the same time as the group of people that just entered the house. Mr. Sterling authorized the security guard at the main gate to grant me permission to enter the complex. Just as I was entering the residential private security gate leading to the house, I received a phone call while in my car. That's why I didn't simultaneously arrive with the rest of the group. To be honest with you, I'm pretty much uncomfortable being part of any group. Not quite sure why I disclosed that, but anyway, I'm Mr. Sterling's Israeli attorney, Yitzhak Bennett."

Felicia recognizes his name, then reaches out her hand to introduce herself. Yitzhak does not reciprocate with an outstretched hand. Instead, adding a little bit to the awkward moment, he explains, "By tradition, I do not touch, let alone shake another woman's hand, unless it is my wife. There are some exceptions, but I'm not going to get into them right now. I do hope you'll give me a second chance to show you that I'm clearly not as complicated as it appears!"

Now smiling, Felicia says, "I'm very familiar with that beautiful tradition. Please say no more. By the way, I'm Felicia Sterling, and Elliot is my husband."

Feeling slightly chagrined, Yitzhak responds, "I wouldn't blame you if you just instructed me to go back to my car and return to wherever I came from. Please excuse my clumsy behavior. My good friends keep telling me that I may have some form of an avoidant personality disorder. But I guarantee you, if you were to witness me in a courtroom or in my law office, you'd see a completely different personality. Sorry about that."

Using her adorable wit to break the ice, Felicia says, "For whatever it's worth, Mr. Bennett, I don't find you awkward. Weird, yes, but not awkward. Welcome to our home. Please follow me to the dining room." As Felicia drops off Yitzhak, she picks up Avigail and proceeds to her decorating meeting.

The Sterling Hedge Fund management team is assembled for the first time around that dining table.

Each member stood and introduced themselves by providing a brief narrative of their background along with how they met Elliot Sterling. It was quite evident that these men have achieved extraordinary accomplishments. These were serious people with character and vision. Even Yitzhak, the brilliant lawyer with a self-proclaimed personality disorder, seemed to fit in with this group. The common thread was a goal to achieve at superior levels.

Every member, in their own unique manner, expressed their willingness to collaborate and trust one another. Mark Goldman sums it all up when he stands and says, "Trust each other, share a strong sense of group identity, and have confidence in our collective effectiveness as a team. Look, I've known Elliot Sterling since we were kids, and I'm positive he won't have it any other way!"

Elliot is the last man to speak. He stands slowly and contemporaneously begins to speak.

"I did not come to Israel to start this company by choice. I came due to circumstances that were not planned, or even that well thought out. I'm here because I fear for the life of my family and myself.

"I am not proud of the last business venture I participated in before coming here. In fact, if I had it to do all over again, I wouldn't do it. I put my wife and two daughters at risk. For that I am ashamed. Not even for the hundred million dollars I made, was it worth it taking that kind of risk.

"Mark Goldman and Paul Norman, they know the story because they were the courageous men that stood next to me, even when they may have thought I was wrong. We won because we were smart and we stuck together. We had trust! We fought in the trenches protecting each other no matter what the outcome. I know first-hand that these are men of character, and they will be your colleagues."

Mark stands and says, "Before you finish, Elliot, I've got one more thing to say."

Elliot looks at Mark and says, "Go ahead, say it."

Mark continues, "In case you were wondering who the quiet guy sitting toward the back of the room might be, well, he goes by the name of Yonatan. He is an Israeli Mossad trained expert on security. He will consult with us as needed regarding safety and security matters in general. He also has been assigned to Mr. Sterling and his family as a personal guard. Yonatan is considered one of the best and brightest security experts in the world, and he is an important part of our team. Thanks for keeping the boss safe. Round of applause for Yonatan. How about a few words, Yonatan?"

Yonatan, in his thick Israeli accent, responds with three words, "No, thank you."

Mark smiling, says, "I guess I did insinuate to keep it to a few words. Well, since he's too big of a pro to speak about himself, I'll tell you. He's a loyal man who knows his stuff. He's a guy who will never let you down. As they say in Hollywood, this guy will take a bullet for you. Rely on Yonatan as you need him. He'll be your go-to guy on security."

Sterling stands back up and takes control of the meeting, commenting, "I also have one last thing to say. The Sterling Hedge Fund will be built with a strong foundation from the bottom up. I will insist that every move we make be double and triple verified.

"Gentlemen, my role will be to make our company the most respected hedge fund in the world. I want this company to be long remembered after all of us are no longer around. The Sterling Hedge Fund is destined for beyond greatness. With your tireless best efforts, and that of mine, our name, along with the brilliant work we are about to accomplish together, will live on forever!"

The people sitting at the table spontaneously break out clapping, then standing for their new chairman.

Sterling looks out at the faces of the men gathered in the room, then chuckles and says, "I haven't accomplished a damn thing for this company and yet, I receive a standing ovation. I can't wait to see how you guys will respond when I finally do something. Okay, so let's get down to business. The way we'll work this afternoon is to subdivide all of us into smaller groups in order to maximize progress.

"Paul and Yitzhak, you'll start off together and settle the approach toward organizing the Sterling Hedge Fund legal operating documents. Additionally, I want you on the Algeria and Sudan agreements regarding the Savor rifle. Make sure our business practices start off kosher.

"Mark, I need you to get with Benjamin, Moshe, and Gilad. You guys make sure the financial plan and the accounting foundation is in order. Try to get it as close to our old Sterling Development company ideas, but of course, operating as an international Hedge Fund based in Israel.

"Hey Mark, for your working knowledge, Moshe refers to our business plan as the 'Bible'. Didn't want you lost with any of the lingo! I'll be moving around to each of your meetings. Engage me where you need me. Alright, let's get to work!"

Chapter 5

Sterling starts off with the 'Bible' meeting being led by Moshe Ariel. The first thing that Moshe does is have his assistant, Gilad, hand out a ten-page summary highlighting the critical accounting and financial points that make up the essence of the 'Bible'. Ariel is aware that traditional American business meetings started with the guy leading the meeting painstakingly following an outline word by word, presuming everyone was attentively listening and clearly understanding the concepts. Knowing that this approach was universally flawed, Ariel begins by asking, "How many of you read the memo I handed out yesterday, and understand the bullet-points?"

Everyone raises their hand except Mark. Even Sterling raises his hand. Then Moshe says, "That's total bullshit. I wrote the fucking thing, and it's even difficult for me to comprehend it! Usually, people just plain lie about having read these things. They figure they're about to receive a thorough explanation from the author of the work, so they just play it lazy and rely on their listening skills to get up to speed. Am I right, or am I right? I know that, I'm the same way if I'm not presenting. So, here's what we're going to do first. I'm going to give you about thirty minutes to read the memo. Try your best to understand it, then formulate questions. Go ahead. Take your time. Read it. See you in thirty minutes."

Sterling, who winks at Moshe as his sign of approval, lowers his head and begins reading the 'CliffsNotes' version of the 'Bible'. He, along with all the others in the room, takes the full allotted time to jot down their notes and questions. What a brilliant way to demand everyone's attention on the subject matter. More importantly, each person could now be engaged in a quality conversation allowing for the participants to even add value or ideas to the 'Bible' instead of only listening to the concepts for the first time. Sterling knew Moshe was a man he could trust, and grateful he is his accountant.

Upon his return, Moshe looks at Mark and asks, "Tell me in a few words how you'd summarize what you just read. Did you understand it?"

Mark, taken back by the 'did you understand it' comment, looks at Elliot, and says, "Nah, it's Greek to me, or should I say Hebrew, since I don't speak Hebrew. I don't get it, Moshe."

Ariel, expecting a different response, says, "Hmm, probably because you weren't present at yesterday's initial briefings."

As Ariel starts an explanation, Mark interrupts him and says, "Of course, I understand it! Just playing with you. It is clear you have sensibly set up our accounting practices almost to mirror that of our previous real estate company. We converted two outdated accounting methods to finally get to the program you have selected. So, how do you say it here? Mazel Tov? You just hit a home run with that one! The principles, the objectives, and the goals you sight, you're spot on. You know what the fuck you're talking about. I am positive that between Benjamin, you, and Gilad, we got this wired. You're just missing one bullet point to the financial plan."

Now staring at Elliot, Moshe asks, "And what's that, Mr. Goldman?"

Mark glances at Moshe and says, "Take care of the customer. Make sure we understand our products perfectly, then service the customer. Without our customers, we don't have a business. Add that to your plan, and now you have my endorsement."

Sensing at minimum a verbal altercation, and in the worst case, a fist fight, Sterling steps in and says, "By adding the 'customer amendment', sounds like you ratify Moshe's work. Right, Mark? I'm not that positive Moshe caught all your good-intentioned humor. I don't speak for him, but I'm pretty certain Moshe has just been insulted by you. If so, I'm positive, Mark, you'd like to make a few additional comments."

Mark looks at Moshe, then glances at Elliot, and says, "No Sir, I got nothing further."

Sterling looks at Mark and responds with a tint of anger, "You just finished addressing the team passionately explaining how trust was so important, blah, blah, blah. Why the disrespect for your distinguished colleague?"

Mark answers, "Oh, I trust him. His theories and his financial framework are right on. My problem is that he thinks of us as a bunch of students learning from the master. Back home, we call it arrogance. I call Moshe's approach bullshit. Don't behave as if you're better or smarter just because you spent hours preparing the material, which took us only thirty minutes to understand. Talk to us like men, not kids.

"You're smart, Mr. Ariel. You know your stuff, but your teaching style belongs in some prep school versus men ready to launch a world-class Hedge Fund."

Moshe steps in and says, "You're right, Mark. I forgot who I was presenting to. You don't need to say another word," as he extends his hand to shake Mark's hand.

Sterling, who is just sitting back and observing the events unfold by the second, says absolutely nothing. Out of the corner of his eye, the next thing he sees is Mark getting out of his chair and shaking Moshe's hand. Then he gives him a hug. Elliot thinks to himself, what could have been a disaster turned out to be a pretty good moment for the Sterling Hedge Fund.

As Mark releases Moshe, he addresses the small group and laughs out loud, "In retrospect, I think Moshe's style is gifted," which is received by a roar of laughter led by Sterling.

The Sterling Hedge Fund avoided its first upper management personality conflict. Elliot walks over to the Mark and whispers, "You almost cost us our accountant! Yeah, you made a good rebound, but you got to learn to control yourself. We operate in a foreign country. Dammit Mark, this isn't LA."

Sterling looks into Mark's eyes and goes on to say, "Remember, this is about winning. You need to be much more emotionally intelligent. Not everyone is going to understand your humor here. You dodged a bullet with Moshe, but trust me, the next time could be fatal."

Mark, who knows Sterling since childhood, realizes that his boss is very annoyed and says, "I had to rough him up a little bit. I get we're in Israel and that we need to adapt. I understand. But we're the investors! It's our company, and it is our fucking risk, not theirs. So, I felt that we needed to take charge and show that the Hedge Fund's senior management is from America, and it is our culture that will internally prevail here. The alternative will be that the tail is going to wag the dog. Trust me, Moshe is going to think twice about how he presents anything further to you or me in the future.

"I want Moshe, Gilad, and Ben thinking more like us, as opposed to the alternative. I know there will be times that we'll need to do it their way. I fully get that, but we need to run the company our way from day one."

Sterling glances at Mark and says, "I knew I brought you over here for a reason. Yep, you have this read right. I guess I just wanted to accumulate the finest Israeli team I could, but you're one hundred percent correct. We're not going to manage our company from fear.

We'll manage it from a total position of strength. You and I have watched each other's back for a long time, and we sure as hell aren't going to stop now. Thanks for the sound advice!

"Hey, let's leave this group for now. Moshe will provide all the details to Ben. I've briefed Ben for countless hours on what we're looking for. Ben will get this accounting and financial crap right for us. Let's go over and see how Paul is doing with Yitzhak. You don't know this yet, but we need to get Yitzhak to allow us to buy up to ten million dollars' worth of a virtual currency from a company he legally represents."

Mark responds saying, "Virtual what?"

"You heard me. Virtual currency."

"There you go again, Elliot. The last time you talked to me about this kind of crazy financial shit, we ended up on a wild goose chase in Nigeria. Do we really need to take this type of high risk again?

"I thought the Sterling Hedge Fund was about investing in sure-bet solid transactions. Jesus, I'm wasting my breath, aren't I? Uh-oh, you've already made up your mind, haven't you?" Understanding that once the boss has made a business decision, it will be next to impossible to convince him differently, Mark succumbs to reality and asks, "Alright, let's hear it!"

Sterling says, "You might recall that the last time we ventured into a high-risk complicated deal, which I insisted on doing, we made hundred million dollars. I'm sure you didn't forget that! But anyway, this deal isn't even close to the gamble we took with Nigeria. I promise you, once you understand the mechanics, you're going to be the biggest advocate for this agreement. So, listen me out."

Mark sarcastically responds, "I'm all ears."

"Yitzhak represents a client that has just won a landmark legal case here in Israel regarding digital currency broker bank accounts. The court issued a temporary injunction forbidding a particular bank from indefinitely closing the bank account of Yitzhak's client, thus paving the way for legal trading of cryptocurrencies in Israel. This client hosts a digital currency backed by diamonds all powered by what they call 'blockchain' technology.

"Yitzhak's guy is a blockchain start-up entrepreneur coming out with an initial private placement at far below a hundred dollars per digital coin. It might even be ten dollars per digital coin! Once the world markets discover that each coin is pegged to the spot market of one carat diamonds valued at near one thousand four hundred dollars per diamond...well, Mark, you do the math! Ben thinks the cryptos have a real chance to actually trade at up to ten thousand dollars per coin. Can you imagine that?"

Mark, quickly warming to the idea, asks, "How much do you plan to invest?"

"As much as Yitzhak can arrange for us to purchase. I'm hoping up to ten million dollars."

"Elliot, we're talking about profits well into hundreds of millions of dollars here! How do you know this is real?"

"Because the bank that Ben works for has been closely following the results of the court case for years. They too want to invest in this currency. They see this as the way of the future. Even the finance minister wants in on this. Trust me, this is a winner."

Mark, mimicking how women curtsy to royalty, lowers his head, extends his right foot behind the left, then bends his knees, and gracefully brings himself back to his original position saying, "I shall never doubt you again, your majesty. Now let's go get this son of a bitch to sell us as many of these fucking cryptos as we can get our hands on!"

Smiling, Elliot says, "Sounds as if you like me now! Let's go convince Bennett to let us into the early placement."

As they step into the meeting between Norman and Bennett, it is very apparent that these two Harvard-educated lawyers clearly have synergism. They could be heard discussing complex legal issues while at the same time laughing. This is music to Sterling's ears. These are the type of colleagues he envisioned working for the new company.

Norman looks up and says, "Glad you're here. Let me quickly clean up a few items. First, Yitzhak's retainer is in order and if you agree with the fee, you can execute it. Here. Take a look."

Elliot reviews, then responds, "The number is correct."

"Very good. Go ahead, sign and initial the two copies where indicated... Alright, the deed is done. We just hired ourselves an excellent Israeli attorney that will integrate seamlessly into the organization."

"Second, per your instructions, Mr. Sterling, my title will be General Counsel. Mark's is Senior Vice President/Operations, and Ben is Senior Vice President/Finance. Each of us, Mark, Ben, and I, will be entitled to stock options in the amount of up to one million dollars. Mr. Sterling, you will hold the dual titles of Chief Executive Officer and President."

"That's right, Paul. Everything is correct. Now, let's take a break from all the legalese and spend a moment on digital currency. The Sterling Hedge Fund is prepared to write a check for a lump sum amount of ten million dollars to buy the crypto coins currency during the initial private placement. Can you deliver that, Yitzhak?"

Bennett glances at Norman, then addresses Elliot, "As I told you earlier, Mr. Sterling, I do not control who gets to buy what. In fact, I really cannot be talking about this any further. Whatever information is public, well, everybody has access to that. I'm sure you understand, I will not discuss private or privileged information. No more discussion please."

Mark jumps into the conversation and says, "Howdy. I'm Mark Goldman. I just met you a little earlier. Would you be uncomfortable if I asked you where I could buy the equivalent of ten million dollars of the new digital currency that was recently featured in the local newspaper?"

Bennett, playing right along with where Mark is heading with the question, answers, "I have no problem with that question."

"Would you have a problem if I asked you to introduce me to the man in charge of making a decision regarding our possible interest? Of course, that's only if you knew such a person."

Bennett answers, "I could do that."

Starring at Elliot, Goldman says, "That a boy! So, how about you get on the phone and request a meeting today, or as soon as possible since the investor must return to America very soon. I'm pretty certain your source will accommodate a short notice meeting, especially when he hears that someone wants to hand him a massive check within the next couple of days. Can you make that call?"

"Sure. Give me a few minutes."

"Take as much time as you need, my good friend Yitzhak."

As Bennett leaves the room to make his phone call, Elliot walks over to Mark and says, "You realize that Yitzhak wasn't going to budge for me, yet it took you just a moment to get him to do exactly what we needed him to do. Glad to see you're as street smart as ever. In retrospect, you're the one that should be named CEO. Very impressive, Mark. I mean it, very impressive. The timing of your words, and the simplicity of your questions could potentially result in our Hedge Fund profiting hundreds of millions of dollars. Dazzling work, Mark, amazing how quick you are on your feet."

Grateful for the comments, Mark says, "Thanks boss, but as you have consistently taught me since the early days, results are the only thing that counts. Yitzhak could come back and tell us his client said go to hell."

Sterling responds, "Yeah, you're right, but at least you got us to the point where we even have a shot at the conversation."

It doesn't take long before Yitzhak re-enters the room. He shows no expression on his face until he says, "As Mark accurately predicted, my friend and client, Yair Erdan, is willing to meet today. He will be here in two to three hours. Before he hung up the phone, Mr. Erdan reminded me to be certain that Mr. Sterling brings a big checkbook to the meeting. Of course, I'm kidding about the checkbook! But seriously, it sounds as if he's prepared to make a deal. We're about to find out."

Mark is the first to respond, "Now, that's what I'm talking about, Yitzhak! Good job, dude! You're the man!"

Elliot then chimes in, "Well done, Yitzhak! Thank you!"

Yitzhak responds, "Well, first of all, as you both know, I was just responding to Mr. Goldman's question. Second, I have a serious conflict of interest. I cannot in any manner whatsoever represent you regarding the possible transaction you may potentially have with Mr. Erdan. In fact, I cannot even be in the same room. I must disclose in writing to both Mr. Sterling and Mr. Erdan of the existence of a conflict of interest due to my separate legal representation of each of you. Am I clear on this?"

Mark responds, "Of course, you're clear, but can I ask a question?"

Yitzhak says, "Something tells me I'm about to be convinced to do something I'm sure I going to regret. Let me hear your clever question, Mr. Goldman."

"Could you please stop calling me, Mr. Goldman? By the way, that doesn't count as my question, okay?"

Yitzhak broadly smiles as Goldman continues, "Please call me Mark, alright? That doesn't count as a question either. Here's my real question. If Mr. Erdan and Mr. Sterling waive any conflict of interest solely related to this particular crypto currency agreement, could you legally represent both parties on a one-time only basis?"

Yitzhak does not say a word. He then openly starts laughing, but doesn't answer the question until Goldman says, "What's so funny? Can you let us in on the joke?"

Yitzhak puts on a more serious face and says, "You know, Mark, it makes me laugh how simple your questions are and how easy the answers should be. I think the legal community, and society as a whole, have made lawyers like me overthink and complicate things. The simple answer is, 'Yes, I could'."

Mark can't help but smile as he glances at Elliot, who is also grinning. He then blurts out, "Yitzhak, my man, I'm liking you more and more by the minute. I'll bet you ten to one that Erdan will agree to the waiver. No, I'm sorry, make that twenty to one. You might as well go ahead and prepare the waiver agreement right now. As sure as I'm standing here, this guy is going to sign!"

Elliot adds, "Once again, Yitzhak, thanks very much for thinking outside the box on this matter. I'm grateful for your good intentions and your willingness to cooperate. I'm reasonably certain that once Mr. Erdan listens to our offer, he will not only agree to our proposal, but he will wholeheartedly appreciate our serious confidence in his start-up company. He knows, and we know, that there's a hell of a lot of risk in investing in his digital currency even though the fundamentals appear in order.

"The truth is that the Sterling Hedge Fund could lose its entire investment, or make a shitload of money. Nobody knows for sure. We're willing to put our money where our mouth is. My impression is that Mr. Erdan will welcome our investment. So, I think Mark is right, go ahead and draw up the waiver and start working on the draft of the agreement granting the Sterling Hedge Fund the unconditional right to buy the new cryptocurrency at the initial private placement amount anticipated to be less than one hundred dollars per unit.

"Of course, the digital coins that we will be offered will only be those backed by one carat diamonds. We are prepared to purchase the first ten million dollars. So just to be clear, if the initial price per digital coin is one hundred dollars, we will be buying one hundred thousand crypto coins. Benjamin will set up Letter of Credit in the amount of ten million dollars, which will serve as our performance guarantee to Mr. Erdan. If I'm wrong and Erdan doesn't agree to do the deal with us, be assured that I'll cover your legal fees related to your extra work. We good?"

Yitzhak responds, "Yes. We're good. So, if you'll excuse me, I'm going to get to work on the waiver and the purchase agreement."

The following hours are spent discussing the pros and cons of investing into the unconventional and potentially risky digital currency. Sterling had requested that Benjamin join them to gain his insight on the subject and better educate Mark and Norman as to the in-depth analysis that Ben's bank had conducted into the cryptocurrency. It didn't take long before Ben had convinced Norman as to the great potential of the digital coins.

Norman seemed to be the sole skeptic of the group because he was very conservative by nature, and strongly believed that the government should be the only entity that should be responsible for issuing currency. He felt that without government regulation, the legitimacy of this type of currency would collapse. The one component that was slowly making him a believer was the fact that the coins would be backed by diamonds. He could live with that.

Two hours passed and no one had heard or seen Yitzhak until he walks into the residence through the front door holding the waiver and the purchase agreement. Yitzhak completed his work in a quiet corner of the home, then convinced the security officers at the entry guard house to accommodate him by shooting five full copies of each. Armed with the agreements, he was ready to meet with both of his clients.

Almost as if planned, Yair Erdan shows up at the front door and introduces himself to everyone near the doorway. The first to greet him is Yitzhak who says, "Shalom. Thank you for coming. We're very appreciative that you made the trip all the way here to Caesarea. I would like to introduce you to Mr. Elliot Sterling, the president of the Sterling Hedge Fund; his close associate, Mr. Mark Goldman; his attorney from America, Paul Norman; and his Israeli Senior Vice President for Finance, Benjamin Yaalon."

Erdan apathetically shakes hands with all of them, then indifferently addresses the group with a no-nonsense Israeli accent, "My privilege to meet all of you, especially you, Mr. Sterling, since I hear you sign the checks. As Americans are famous for saying, time is money, so, let's get to work!"

Sterling, not feeling the best of vibes from this guy, sarcastically answers, "Nice to meet you too, Mr. Erdan. Just for the record, I don't technically sign the checks, that is done by Mr. Yaalon. Also, for your working knowledge, if the rest of the gentlemen you just met don't like a deal, we don't do the deal.

"Oh, and one final clarification, while it is true that the phrase is usually credited to Benjamin Franklin who used it in an essay in 1748, the idea that 'time is money' has an even longer history dating back to Antiphon of ancient Greece in 430 BC when he stated that 'the most costly outlay is time'. Funny we're talking about ancient Greeks while here in Caesarea."

"I'm sorry if you are offended, Mr. Sterling. I hope you don't feel insulted by my desire to get right to the point. I'm not really into small talk. All I really want to know is whether there is a deal here. If there is, let's make it; if there isn't, I've got plenty of things to do, as I'm certain you do too."

Sterling looks at Mark and quickly glances at Yitzhak, understands that the reason for meeting Erdan was the opportunity to make an incredible windfall profit. It was in Sterling's interest to stop slapping this arrogant prick around and concentrate on getting a deal done. So, Elliot answers, "I'm not insulted. I agree with you. Time is money. Welcome to my home. Let's go make a deal."

Sterling walks Erdan to the dining room table and takes a seat at the head of the table. The egomaniac Erdan takes a seat at the head of the opposite side of the table. Yitzhak sits right next to Erdan and immediately says, "Before we start this meeting, I have prepared a waiver that expressly releases any conflict of interest either one of you might claim against me as it specifically relates to the possible purchase by the Sterling Hedge Fund of Mr. Erdan's subject digital currency. Read the waiver and if you agree, sign and date where indicated. Once you both sign, I will participate in the deliberations."

Without even reading the waiver, Erdan signs it and says, "I trust Yitzhak blindly. If it's good enough for him, it's good enough for me."

Sterling does not sign the waiver. Instead, he hands it to Norman for his review as he addresses Yitzhak, "Just an old habit. Nothing personal."

Norman takes a moment to scan over the waiver and swiftly hands it back to Sterling advising that he can sign the conflict of interest waiver, paving the way to get down to business.

With both parties having signed the waiver, Yitzhak then distributes copies of the purchase agreement and states, "I have done the best I could to be fair and balanced with this agreement. It's my understanding of what you both intend to accomplish. Neither of you should feel as if I favored one over the other. That did not happen. Please read the purchase agreement, then let's discuss openly what questions you may have, or any changes we need to make."

After a good fifteen minutes later, Erdan, with an exaggerated sense of his own importance, says, "Look, let's cut to the bottom line. I'm here because I want your money. You're here for my money. I assume Yitzhak has fairly written the agreement to cover both of our butts. From my point of view, the purchase agreement is fine.

I'm prepared to sign it with a simple change. My alteration is final without any room for discussion.

"The Sterling Hedge Fund will not be granted the right to purchase the first ten million dollars. Again, cards on the table. During what we call the Initial Coin Offering, or ICO, the first buyers are scheduled to be me, followed by high level members of the Israeli government, members of my family, government and business associates of mine, then you, Mr. Sterling. After that priority list, you can purchase your ten million dollars of crypto coins."

Sterling responds with a simple question, "What's your estimated ICO price per digital coin?"

Erdan illusively responds, "If I knew the answer to that question, I wouldn't be here talking to you. My guess is that it will come out at around fifty dollars per coin. That will buy you two hundred thousand coins! I expect the value to ratchet up to one thousand per coin within a month!"

Mark, who can't hold himself back, says, "Hey, my name is Mark Goldman. I sort of met you a few minutes ago. Anyway, where the hell are you getting your assumptions? And why do you keep using all those weasel words like 'expect' and 'guess'? Why don't you just talk straight to an investor ready to pay ten million dollars in cash for a currency that very well may be worth shit? What the hell is up with you?"

Erdan does not back down and responds, "You asked for this meeting. I accommodated your request. I'm not in court and I don't have to answer all your questions. In fact, I don't even need to talk to you.

"Now, having said that, I'll voluntarily answer your bullshit questions. I say 'guess' because I'm guessing. I said 'expect' because that's what I expect to happen. Mr. Goldman, you are going to buy my coins based on your expectation that the digital currency has a true value greater than one thousand dollars per coin. Why am I positive you will buy my stuff? Because the value of a one carat diamond is worth more than a thousand dollars.

"My cryptocurrency is backed by one carat diamonds. If I decide to grant you the right to buy at the preferential ICO price of fifty dollars a coin and, within a month, those same coins are worth more than a thousand dollars, can you even image how much profit you can make if you own two hundred thousand coins? So please, don't bullshit a bullshitter.

"You and your group should be grateful that you know the best lawyer in all of Israel—Yitzhak Bennett. I have two final investors ready to buy coins up to five million dollars each. No one investor has agreed to invest ten million dollars in one lump sum, other than you. I prefer to place the ICO sale of the final ten million dollars with one buyer, as opposed to two. Yitzhak has known for some time that I was searching for an investor of your size. He validated you. That's why I'm here. Are you in or out?"

Sterling steps in and asks, "When is the ICO scheduled to launch?"

Erdan glances at Yitzhak and says, "Subject to any unforeseen circumstances, the initial sale will be within three to four weeks. What's your answer, Mr. Sterling?"

Mark consults with Elliot, Benjamin, and Norman for a brief side bar, then says to Erdan, "We're in, with one minor adjustment to our purchase agreement."

Erdan, annoyed, impatiently asks, "What?"

"We reserve the right to withdraw our ten million dollars in the event the ICO offers the coins above one hundred dollars per digital coin. Other than that, we have a deal."

"Sorry Mark, and the rest of you greedy bastards, no deal! You're going to take the risk, just like the rest of us. I'm not given you some custom deal! I've just wasted a whole bunch of time. Thank you, Yitzhak, we'll talk later."

Sterling, sensing the deal is rapidly falling apart at the seams, immediately says, "Don't you think it's fair and logical to set a reasonable ceiling on the original ICO pricing? You know better than me, the ICO could set a value equivalent to the one carat diamond that is closer to one thousand four hundred dollars as opposed to opening at fifty dollars. There goes all that profit! So, we got to set a minimum framework on the ICO."

"No Sir, Mr. Sterling, we don't have to do anything I don't feel like. Now here's my final offer. There will be no minimum ICO price! Now, let me hear your final decision!"

Sterling focuses on the eyes of Yitzhak and his body language, remains dead silent for more than sixty seconds, then says, "I guess I'll sign the agreement. Yitzhak will serve as our holder of our ten-million-dollar Letter of Credit guarantee. Yitzhak will solely be responsible for the release of funds as will be documented in the Credit Letter. Very well, Mr. Erdan, you win today, but I trust we will all win soon. I assure you I'll be watching carefully. Thank you for coming to Caesarea."

"Good decision, Mr. Sterling. Why don't you sign the agreement so I can head back to Tel Aviv?"

Sterling asks Norman whether he had reviewed the Erdan purchase agreement. Norman instantly responds by saying, "No sir."

Elliot stares at Norman and Yitzhak, saying, "Since I'm committing ten million dollars to this deal, I'm pretty sure I have a right to take a peek at what the hell the agreement says. In fact, that's exactly what I'm going to do. Alright, so give us a moment while Paul reviews the document."

Erdan, looking more and more impatient, says, "That's fine Mr. Sterling, but I've been here far longer than I expected and I'd like to get the hell out of here!"

Yitzhak hands the purchase agreement over to Norman, who takes it to one side of the room and instantly begins his examination. Upon his completion, Norman sits back down at the dining table, looks at Sterling with a serious face, and says, "I recommend we do not sign this agreement. It is way too open-ended regarding the ICO opening price. I'm not willing to recommend taking this risk. That will be your business decision, but the way I see it, this is business malpractice. We can live with the Sterling Hedge Fund having the obligation to perform, at let's say, a hundred dollars and below as a benchmark, but open-ended, that's suicide."

Erdan comes out swinging, saying, "You weren't asked to conduct a business analysis. You're a lawyer, not an MBA. Your boss already told you that he agrees to no minimum. Obviously, there's no legal issues. So, sign the fucking thing or I'm leaving. What's it going to be, Mr. Sterling?"

Elliot looks toward Paul and asks, "Is it a legal matter or is it a business issue?"

Norman responds, "Both. The business decision is up to you and Mr. Erdan to decide, but here's my concern with the legal side, which effects the business side. Not that they would do it but this is what we're facing. The ICO could create two classes with two separate minimum prices. One class could be for the founder and one class could be for the initial investors. There is nothing in the agreement prohibiting such a legal maneuver.

"So, in order to protect ourselves, we need a minimum, or we are wide-open to way overpaying for the digital coins. Yes, we trust Yitzhak, but Mr. Erdan could terminate him or change his mind as to what is in the best interest of his company, and we'd be legally obligated to purchase the crypto coins under the Letter of Credit at whatever price Mr. Erdan established under the hypothetical second class."

Sterling slowly gets up out of his seat, walks over to Norman, and shakes his hand while saying, "Bravo Paul, you're one hundred percent correct! No offense, Yitzhak, but he's right. We'll insist on either a minimum initial coin value or an unconditional statement in the purchase agreement clarifying that there will only be one class of initial buyers. Not only will we be in the initial single class, but we will be entitled to purchase the digital coins at the identical price as Mr. Erdan. This is a break point with us."

Visibly upset, Erdan blurts out, "Yitzhak, you don't have to make any further amendments because I'm leaving. What a waste of my valuable time to have come here. You guys are amateurs. Have a nice life, Mr. Sterling."

Without any hesitation, and much to the surprise of Erdan, Sterling calls his bluff, "Mr. Goldman will walk you to the front door. As you travel back to Tel Aviv, I hope you reflect on what an idiot you are from having walked away from a 10-million-dollar crucial investment into your company. I'd say that the only amateur here is you. Good day, Mr. Erdan."

Astonished by how quickly Elliot dismissed him, Erdan hesitates, then gradually pushes back his chair, stands up, then sits back down, and says, "Well, perhaps you have a legitimate concern. How about I set an initial minimum amount of not to exceed one hundred dollars per digital coin?"

Sterling reacts, "Good, very good. We will accept your minimum with the condition that there will only be one class of investor. The Sterling Hedge Fund will be in that initial class with you. Agreed?"

Erdan responds, "Almost. I agree to the minimum one-hundred-dollar ceiling, and I agree that your Hedge Fund will exclusively enter into the class that includes myself or any of my affiliated entities, but I reserve the right to establish a second class at my discretion. Do we have a deal?"

Elliot glances at Mark, Paul then Ben and says, "Yeah, we got a deal. Let's have Yitzhak write up the amendment and we'll sign it together. Shouldn't take him more than fifteen minutes. You okay with that?"

Erdan responds, "Sure. Go ahead, Yitzhak. I'll wait."

Within thirty minutes, Yitzhak makes the changes to the purchase agreement and makes the copies at the security guardhouse. He returns to the dining room and hands four copies to Norman, then delivers one to Erdan. Norman speed-reads it and is the first to say, "It's in order, we're prepared to sign."

Erdan says, "Yitzhak wrote it, I don't need to read it, so let's sign it!"

And just like that, the Sterling Hedge Funds has made its first investment with the real potential of making a staggering profit or, perhaps, losing its money. Time would tell. But in the meantime, the old reliable Sterling team of Mark, Paul, and Elliot demonstrated once again how to outsmart its opponent while arranging for the best terms and conditions available for them.

Erdan executed the purchase agreement and was long gone back to Tel Aviv. A three-week waiting period officially started and the suspense surrounding these coins has just begun.

Chapter 6

The next day, the primary business emphasis shifts to Mark Goldman and the sale of the Savor rifle to the Hedge Fund's customers in the Sudan and Algeria. Yitzhak and Paul had worked late into the previous night making certain that they had the finishing touches incorporated into the Savor purchase contract that Mark would use while visiting his customers in their countries. They made certain that in the event there was ever a disagreement between the parties, the jurisdiction for conflict resolution would be Tel Aviv, Israel.

The balance of the contract were fundamental boilerplate provisions. All payments to the Sterling Hedge Fund were to be made in United States dollars and routed to the Hedge Fund's bank account in Ben's bank. The contract was organized with the simple philosophy of 'we give you guns, you give us money', and everyone goes home happy.

The meeting in Caesarea consisted of Sterling, Goldman, Norman, Bennett, and Yaalon. It was very important that Mark thoroughly understand the contract he would present to the high-level government officials he was scheduled to meet with. He also needed to be briefed on the economics of the deal, along with the logistics and timeline for delivery of the Savor. The afternoon would be spent immersing Mark with the knowledge required to close two deals valued at one hundred million dollars each.

Elliot begins the discussions by providing a general overview surrounding the first contract with Algeria, officially known as the People's Democratic Republic of Algeria. He starts by telling Mark that Algeria is a North African country with a Mediterranean coastline and a Saharan desert interior. Its capital is Algiers where Mark is to meet with what is considered the equivalent of the Secretary of Defense in America. Although the native language is Berber alongside Arabic, French is widely used in government, culture, media, and education due to Algeria's colonial history. Goldman is told that he would have no problem speaking English with the government officials.

Sterling continues by laying out the general economics of the Savor deal. He tells Mark that the Savor rifle trades on the street for around 1,500 US dollars. The Sterling Hedge Fund, due to Ben Yaalon's extraordinary contacts, was set to buy the Savor at a wholesale price of 750 dollars per rifle. The Hedge Fund would turn around and sell the Savor to the Algerians for one thousand dollars per unit plus shipping costs. The Algerians had placed an order through one of Ben's military connections for one hundred thousand rifles.

The math was simple. The Hedge Fund would pay seventy-five million dollars for the rifles, and the Algerians' contract would obligate them to buy one hundred thousand Savor rifles for a grand total of one hundred million dollars. The anticipated net profit to the Sterling Fund was forecast to be slightly less than twenty-five million after some money was paid to a few of Ben's connections and brokers.

Sterling faces Goldman and says, "Welcome to the arms business. Twenty-five million in one transaction! Hard to believe, but true. So, we'd all really appreciate it if you don't fuck this deal up."

Mark responds, "For twenty-five million, I'll learn how to speak Arabic! The deal will get done, but are you sure I'll make it out of Algeria alive? Remember the last time I was in Africa, you sent me to Nigeria.

"To this day, I have nightmares dreaming about rotting in some Nigerian jail for the rest of my life. To tell you the truth, I didn't even know where Algeria was until today. When are you sending me there?"

Sterling jokes, "I wasn't expecting you to return. I thought you'd just take one for the team."

Everyone breaks out laughing, then Mark responds, "Ha-ha. Very funny. So, when do I go?"

A much more serious Elliot says, "We're going to send you with one of Yonatan's Mossad-trained associates who has experience with Algeria. Every place you go, he'll go. You leave in two days. We need the contract signed and the rifles delivered within two weeks, or a portion of our Savors will be allocated to a different dealer. Get in, sign the contract, and get the hell out."

Mark then asks, "What about the Sudan?"

This time Ben jumps in, "You're not going to Sudan until we receive payment in full, or should I say, cleared funds in our bank account from the Algerians. We're extending seventy-five percent of our credit line toward the Algerian deal. We'll get paid, and then we proceed with Sudan.

"Virtually, it's the same financial structure as with the Algerians. They buy a hundred thousand rifles, we get a hundred million, we pay off seventy-five million for the guns, and make twenty-five million. Same contract, just some name changes."

Sterling continues, "The Sudan is located in Northeast Africa. Its capital and largest city is Khartoum, where your meeting will take place. Sudan's armed forces are slightly over one hundred thousand. They urgently need the Savor rifle. We've arranged for you to meet directly with the Minister of Defense who is a Major General. We'll confirm your timeline regarding Sudan once we determine the closeout date with the Algerians."

Mark asks, "So, does that mean I do the deal in Algeria, then come back to Los Angeles and wait?"

Sterling answers, "Sign the contract. Tell them to wire their money. Confirm the proceeds are wired, then, I repeat myself, get out! Now, once Algeria pays, you'll have two options. The first, return to Israel and wait for further instructions as to when to depart for the Sudan. Or second, fly directly to Los Angeles where I physically will be until the end of the month."

Goldman asks, "What do you suggest I do, boss?"

Sterling answers, "Finish your business in the Sudan, I'll see you in LA."

Mark simply says, "Done."

Talking to everyone around the table, Elliot says, "Please brief Mark carefully on the remaining details.

"Paul, Yitzhak, make sure Mark understands the contract well. If a defense minister or some prick assistant military guy asks a question, Mark needs to fluidly respond without hesitation. Ben, make certain you go over delivery and shipping details. Mark must be able to answer questions about logistics, or call you on the spot to get answers for the military personnel he'll be dealing with. The bank wire instructions must be clear and Mark has got to understand the banking mechanics in detail.

"We're asking for a hundred million bucks to go through the banking wires. There is absolutely no room for error! Alright, I'll leave you gentlemen for the time being. You can find me on the second level talking with my wife and her interior decorator. I've got to get this house in order within weeks. By the way, Ben, go ahead and lease that initial small office space in Ramat Gan. For the time being, we'll use that office as our official address and corporate office. Yitzhak, place the address in the contract."

As Sterling is about to walk up to see his wife, Ben asks, "Do you want me to also give Mark an overall briefing regarding our big picture goals for the Savor rifle beyond Algeria and the Sudan?"

"Yeah. In fact, start right there so he sees where we're going with this. Smart thinking, Ben."

Although the Savor long-term vision briefing was intended for Goldman, Ben knew that Sterling wanted everyone on the team to know the astonishing potential associated with marketing the Savor. "So, let me start by explaining that Elliot sees Algeria and the Sudan as simply a pilot. The objective is to distribute the Savor to every nation in Africa who will buy it from us. We will soon be selling the rifle in Latin America. In fact, our target is to sell these units to every United States police department, SWAT division, and each law enforcement agency in America who has a use for it. This will be a huge undertaking that will eventually require a sizeable sales force. Elliot feels like this business will have no growth limits. By the way, this will all be headed by you, Mark."

Goldman smiles and says, "Funny, Elliot told me that after the Nigerian deal, we should take it easy!"

Laughing, Ben responds, "He lied."

Ben goes on by explaining that the biggest hurdle to the sales was not the efficiency of the Savor product itself or, for that matter, the money that would be required to keep purchasing the high quantity of rifles needed to supply the market. It would be the Israeli manufacturers' inability to produce enough rifles to keep up with the demand. Elliot believes that since the Savor's demand will be way greater than the supply, an epic opportunity will become available for the Sterling Hedge Fund. "Can anyone guess what that is?"

Mark, who knows his old friend and boss very well, instantly answers, "We'll either be the lender to the Savor manufacturer so they can seriously expand their facilities to produce more rifles, or we're going to buy these bastards out with an offer they can't refuse. Wow! Elliot is really starting to think big. Like beyond billions!" Mark, chuckling to himself, says out loud, "I can't believe I played little league baseball with this guy!"

Everyone in the home was working hard well into the late evening. Progress was made on every front as the Sterling Hedge Fund was putting the finishing touches on what was shaping up to be an important Israeli business. Even the final interior decorating preparations for the residence had made great strides. The dedicated work continues for the next few days leading to the eve of Elliot and

Felicia preparing for their flight back to Los Angeles to pick up their children and personal possessions.

The last night before their journey back to the United States, Elliot summons Mark to the gardens of the Caesarea home to take a walk together. Elliot opens the conversation by saying, "How do you feel about traveling to Algeria?"

Mark stops walking, looks at Elliot, and says, "I'm scared shitless to go down there. The more I read about that place, the more uncomfortable I get. To be honest with you, Elliot, you're the only guy on the face of this earth I would do this for. We have a 25-million-dollar profit to reel in. We're starting a brand-new business with stunning possibilities. The success of this first deal will serve as a domino effect for the rest of our ambitious Savor plans. The players are in place and this deal requires me to step up and get it done, which is exactly what I'm going to do. Let's face it, after we deliver the rifles and get paid on the first contract, there's no stopping us. So, I got to go. Nothing more to talk about on this subject."

Elliot, concerned for his friend's safety, asks, "Do you think we can do the deal without you physically travelling to Algeria?"

"No chance in hell! I don't show up, they'll pull out. I got this, but I'll tell you what, let's ask Yonatan to add one more security guy to the trip. Sound good?"

Elliot stares at his loyal friend and simply says, "Done."

As they continue their walk, Mark asks, "How do you feel about moving to Israel? Are you, Felicia, and the kids going to be alright?"

Elliot sincerely answers, "I have no choice. Do I prefer to live here, no. But I am terribly frightened for my family living in America. The Nigerians can come after us at any moment, and our best odds favor us living in Israel. We'll make the best of it for as long as we need to. I'm even worried travelling back to the US just to pick up my girls and the rest of my stuff."

As these two old friends continue with their heart to heart, Mark lightens the moment and says, "Well, when were you going to pop the question?"

A baffled Sterling responds, "What the hell are you talking about?"

The fun-loving Mark says, "You know, it goes something like this. I need you more than ever! I can't live without you! Will you please come live with me in Israel?"

Elliot, who dissolves into laughter, responds, "Oh yeah, that question. I was working on the timing to ask. But since you brought it up, well, here goes. I've asked you to do a lot of things for me in our lifetime. You've taken a hell of a lot of risks for me. You know that I love you like the brother I never had. You're the man I can always rely on for the truth, and for straightforward great advice. So, yes, I'm going to ask you to join me here in Israel for as long as I need to be here. I can't do this without you! Will you join me?"

Mark says, "Sounds like I'm the mistress here! Can you at least buy me a condo and place a nice car in the garage? I thought you were never going to ask! Of course, I'll join you. Besides, I've noticed a lot of pretty women in Israel. Hell, I'd be bored in LA without you."

"Thanks very much, Mark. Ben has a real estate agent looking for a condo on the Mediterranean coast for you in Caesarea. And, yes, there will be a car waiting for you in the garage. We're going to have the time of our lives together. We've spent an entire lifetime watching out for each other's back. We'll just have to keep doing that until the end of time."

As they complete their walk and just before entering the residence, Elliot stops and gives his friend a heartfelt hug of appreciation. "You know this isn't going to be easy. Everyone is going to try and defeat us. But knowing that we will fight this fight together gives me a sense of strength that I can't really put into words. I just know that we're going to be the ones standing at the end."

As he enters the residence, Benjamin sees Elliot and tells him, "All the preparations are in order. The Sterling Hedge Fund is organized and ready for business. The office in Ramat Gan has been secured.

"Mark is ready to close our first contract in Algeria. The accounting books are set and prepared."

Sterling responds, "Terrific! Everything good with the bank wire instructions? What about the Savor shipment? Do the Israelis have a hundred thousand units ready to go?"

Ben says with conviction, "The Savor manufacturers have set aside the rifles for us and the bank is one hundred percent prepared to receive the Algerians' money. All we must do is ship those guns by the end of next week and we're home free. If Mark misses the deadline, all bets are off. As we have discussed earlier, those rifles are ours so long as we pay for them by the end of next week. If we don't, the supplier reserves the right to ship them to the dealer of their choice. By the way, if we miss the first deadline, you can kiss the Savor relationship goodbye. The Israelis won't respect us anymore."

A challenged Mark looks at Elliot, then says to Ben, "Piece of cake. Get the fucking guns ready to ship, and tell the bank they'll have a fresh one hundred million bucks sitting in our account by Friday of next week."

Very impressed with Mark's confidence, Ben responds, "You sound like a man I want to go to war with. If there's anything, I mean anything, you need from me, be assured I'll get it done for you."

As all three men make their way toward the living room to sit and wrap up a productive week, Sterling spots Yonatan quietly standing toward the back of the room and says, "Can I have a word with you?"

Yonatan responds, "Since I'm on your payroll, you can have as many words as you'd like with me, Mr. Sterling. How can I help you?"

Sterling gets right into it. "I've got a knot in my stomach thinking about two things. The first is related to Mark's travels to Algeria. I'm afraid for his life. Any suggestions?"

A man who prefers not to talk too much says, "My sources say this is an excellent time to travel to Algeria. The government appears to be stable for the moment. We can add a second man for security."

Sterling responds, "So, what are you saying? Mark will be safe?"

"I wouldn't worry about Mr. Goldman's safety. We'll add the second security guy as a precaution."

"You probably don't need a second man, but let's err on the side of caution. The world is a nasty place. There's no such thing as pretending danger is not imminent, but from my read of this, Mr. Goldman will be fine. We'll take good care of him. Now what's your second concern?"

Sterling bluntly says, "My instinct is that the Nigerians are going to want to kill me the moment we arrive in Los Angeles. I worry for my wife and children's safety. I figure these bastards have a price on my head. They know by now that they're not getting a dime back from me so they're going to act.

"Yonatan, I think they're going to strike or use Felicia and my kids as bait. My guess is that it will happen before we permanently return to Israel. I have followed my instincts my entire life, and I'm pretty sure this premonition is correct. What should I do?"

Yonatan pauses briefly, then with his very distinct Israeli accent calmly says, "Nothing. You do nothing."

"My job is to keep you and your family safe. None of us can prevent an assassin from trying. But we can, and we will do everything in our power to protect you and your family. Each of you must take the least amount of risk possible and always listen to our advice. I'll be honest with you, our biggest vulnerability will be at the Los Angeles airport when we arrive. I have already spoken to our people in California to bolster security at the LA airport. That place is just too public, and we must be very cautious while moving through the public area to the car pick-up. In addition to myself, I've arranged for three of my best people to assist in escorting you from the international arrival area to your waiting limo. You and your wife's job will be to stay alert and follow our lead. Let us do the worrying."

With a serious look on his face, Sterling responds, "Jesus! That's even a lot sooner than I thought it could happen! Do you really think we're going to get attacked at the Los Angeles airport?"

Yonatan answers, "Maybe. Maybe not. We'll be prepared for it and hope there's no incident. The enemy is a foreign sovereign nation. They have access to information and clandestine resources that are very powerful. We will assume that they are around the corner and motivated to strike. We are a much bigger target in the United States because of the open society. The sooner we can return to Israel, the better.

"You and your family will be much safer here than in America. Do yourself a favor. Let my team and I do what we're trained to do. There will always be risks, but we are here to mitigate those risks."

Sterling stares into Yonatan's eyes and says, "Promise me you will never let anything happen to my wife or my children."

"What I promise you, Mr. Sterling, is that we will do everything in our power to keep you and your family from undergoing any distress. Will Mr. Norman be travelling with you back to Los Angeles?"

"Yes, he will."

"Anyone else?"

Sterling says, "No, except you."

"Very good, Mr. Sterling. Please trust that we will always be right at your side, and well prepared."

"That doesn't concern me. I know you'll do your job. It's the assholes that want me dead that are keeping me up at night. But, as you have counselled, I'm just going to allow you guys to do the heavy lifting and the worrying. We'll be extraordinarily careful, and I promise we'll listen closely to your advice. Alright, I've had enough on this gloomy subject. Let's go back into the residence and close out this exceedingly successful week."

As Sterling makes his way into the living room, he feels a sense of pride for what he and his team have accomplished in such a short period of time. The Sterling Hedge Fund is now organized and functioning as an entity. The Savor operations are set and ready to be implemented. And ironically, the cryptocurrency coins could end up being the greatest business move of his lifetime. He is happy that he has found brilliant consultants to work with, and very pleased that he has authorized the signing of an office lease in Ramat Gan for his Hedge Fund. All as his home is being designed into a masterpiece of warm comfort and design.

Chapter 7

As their aircraft is about to touch down at the Los Angeles International Airport after a long flight from Tel Aviv, Elliot is reflecting on what a remarkably successful trip it was. All of Felicia and his goals had been accomplished both personally and professionally. Elliot was also deep in thought with concern for his good friend Mark regarding the risks he was about to undertake in Algeria within the next 48 hours. His mind could not stop thinking about the fact that he had authorized eighty-five million dollars for business transactions. Ten for the digital currency and seventy-five million for rifles.

Questions kept popping in his mind. Would Mark get the Savor deal with Algeria on time? What would the ICO opening price be regarding Yair Erdan's cryptocurrency? And even more importantly, would there be an attempt on his life at the airport?

As the El Al aircraft taxies its way from the runway to the gate, Elliot glances at his watch and sees that the digital timepiece has adjusted to California time, which is precisely 1:30 PM. There is no doubt that Elliot is nervous about the prospects of a Nigerian operative coming out of nowhere and gunning him and his wife to death.

Elliot stares at his beloved wife, gives her a warm kiss, then grabs her hand, and simply says, "I love you with all my heart and soul."

Felicia, sensing a concerned disposition in her husband's face, says, "I adore you, Elliot. Now tell me, what's bothering you?"

Elliot, snapping out of his moody demeanor, yet being very sensitive to his wife's safety concerns, says, "Nothing is going on, just a little anxious."

Felicia and her husband, then Yonatan and Paul grab their carry-on bags from the overhead bins and find themselves departing the plane. They look like a herd of sheep as they continue their way toward the international customs area.

They are all greeted back into the United States by courteous customs agents who process them into the country in an efficient manner. Once the Sterlings retrieve their bags, Yonatan addresses

Elliot, Felicia, and Norman, "We have three of our men waiting for us at the top of the exit ramp leading to the public area in the airport. They will spot us immediately. Stay together as they, along with myself, will escort you out of the building. We are trained to create a protective shield in order to keep you safe. Just follow our lead. In the event of an incident, one of my people will guide you through it. Please do as you are told. Your life may depend on our split-second instructions. Any questions?"

Somewhat startled, Felicia looks Elliot in the eyes, then asks Yonatan, "Are you anticipating a problem? All of a sudden, I'm very concerned."

Yonatan calmly says, "Mrs. Sterling, it is our job to always anticipate a problem. We will escort you through the public area directly to your waiting limousine. Okay, let's go."

Elliot grabs his wife's hand and Norman positions himself adjacent to Elliot. Yonatan stands in front of all of them as he leads them up the ramp together. Midway up the exit, Yonatan makes eye contact with his personnel and begins to speed up his pace. As they approach the public area, the additional three security agents seamlessly join the group in what appeared to simulate protection by the Secret Service guarding an American President.

Without any incident whatsoever, the door to the limo is opened and Mr. and Mrs. Sterling, along with Norman, enter the car securely. Within seconds, they are on their way to Elliot's Bel-Air estate.

Yonatan is seated in the front of the limo, while the three other guards are trailing them in a black SUV.

About thirty minutes later, the limo turns slowly onto Eagle Way, moving toward the Sterling estate's private gate located at the street level of the fenced-in residence. The limo driver asks Elliot for the security code to the gate. As Elliot states the digital code, the driver punches in the numbers.

For some odd reason, the four-number code cannot open the gate and the housekeeper will not return until the next day. The SUV carrying the three Israeli security personnel drive past the limo to the end of the cul-de-sac, intending to quickly turn around and position themselves in front of the home.

Elliot, sitting in the middle backseat with his wife to the right and Norman to the left, says, "Hey Paul, do me a favor and try to manually punch in the security code so we can get up into the house?"

Paul answers, "Sure."

On a pleasant Los Angeles afternoon where all you can hear are the birds chirping, Norman steps out of the limo and instantly, there is a 'pop, pop, pop' sound heard by everyone in the limo.

Norman has been hit with three bullets to the head, chest, and abdomen. As chaos erupts, the sniper instantly disappears. A composed Yonatan yells, "Keep your heads down! Keep your heads down!"

The black SUV carrying the three security guards cautiously exit their vehicle with their guns drawn, but it is too late. Norman was on the concrete driveway, lying in a pool of blood. With no visible assassin in sight, the concentration is focused on Norman, but it is too late. The brilliant Harvard educated attorney and a trusted advisor to Elliot is dead even after Yonatan desperately tries to resuscitate his lifeless body.

Elliot and Felicia are horrified and in a state of shock. Felicia is crying as she views Yonatan handing Norman's body over to his associate. Then Yonatan abruptly stands up, walks over to the security gate control box, and follows Elliot's instructions permitting for the gate's manual opening.

Once the gate is open, the driver swiftly moves the limousine to the porte-cochere at the residence's entry. Yonatan gets out of the limo and says to Elliot and Felicia, "I apologize, but you will need to stay in the automobile. I must go into the house to determine if any further threats exist. I've got one of my men assigned to the entry gate and another will stay here with you. The third is assigned to inspect the perimeter of the house's exterior.

"Mr. Norman's body has been placed, with dignity, at the back of the SUV. We have contacted the police and expect them to arrive shortly. The moment I find that it is safe, you will be permitted into your home forthwith. On a personal level, I am very sorry for the loss of your attorney. I realize he meant a lot to you. Please bear with me, I promise to get this search done quickly."

Elliot, who is emotionally shaken, quietly says, "You need to immediately secure my two daughters at Stanford. Act on this without delay! Beef up your security personnel assigned to them this instant.

"Please get me the telephone number to Mr. Norman's parents. They deserve to know what has happened. Additionally, we need the telephone number for his girlfriend. She works at a bank in Beverly Hills. Mark can assist you with this. As painful as it is, they must be advised at once."

While the search takes place, Felicia holds on to her husband for nearly 30 minutes. She is scared and Elliot is struck concerning the brutal murder of his attorney. The thought that he had placed his own family into this type of future makes him nauseated. What words can he find to comfort Norman's parents in explaining the catastrophic loss of their son? How will he be able to face shattering the life of such a beautiful young woman? Then it occurs to Elliot that the most important single action he needs to do is communicate with his two children instantaneously, as he starts speed-dialing his oldest daughter from his cell phone.

To the great relief of hearing her voice, Elliot says, "Hello Rose, this is dad. Are you alright?"

"Of course, I'm alright. Have you returned from Israel? You don't sound so well, dad. Is mom okay? You've got me frightened. What's going on?"

"Where is your sister?"

"She's across the hall in her dorm room! Enough! What wrong?"

Elliot takes a deep breath and says, "My attorney, Paul Norman, was shot to death in front of our home in Bel-Air just as we arrived from the airport. I'm sure the sniper was aiming for me. So, calmly go get your sister and stay close together. Yonatan's security people will take good care of you. Listen carefully to every word they say. Everything is going to be fine."

As Rose is about to respond, her bodyguard enters the room with her sister Erica. Rose then says, "Erica just walked in with her security guard. In fact, my security guy just came into my room too. Where's mom? Is she okay?"

"She's a bit unsettled, and very sad for Paul, but she's fine. Mom's right here with me. I'm so grateful you're both safe! I'll fill you in with more details later. I'll put mom on in just a second. Just let me speak to your sister for a moment. Love you."

Erica, who has been informed of events by the bodyguard, is crying as she says, "Daddy, is mom safe?"

"Perfectly safe. You don't need to worry about her, she's worried sick about you. Thank God you're both fine. Okay, I've got to talk to the police. Listen to Yonatan's people. I love you; here's mom."

Elliot hands the phone over to his wife, then looks up to see police officers in every direction. He gets up out of the limo and is immediately greeted by Yonatan and a law enforcement officer. Yonatan speaks first, "The residence and the grounds are secure. Mr. Norman has been transported to a local morgue facility. We can now go into the home. Officer Johnson and I will escort you and Mrs. Sterling into the house."

Once comfortably inside, Officer Johnson says, "I'm sorry to be bothering you during this awful moment, but I need to do my job and ask you some questions. I'll start with you, Mr. Sterling, and we'll see if we require Mrs. Sterling's statement later. So, where can we sit and talk?"

Understanding that it is the officer's job, Elliot says, "Follow me into the breakfast nook. We'll get you some coffee and I'll answer any questions you have."

Elliot softly holds his wife's hand as they all walk into the home. Felicia excuses herself and goes on to the bedroom to take a bath and compose herself. Elliot leads the officer and Yonatan into the nook. He makes a fresh brew of coffee, then says, "Alright, how can I help?"

Officer Johnson, a seasoned veteran of the Los Angeles Police Department, starts by stating, "Apparently, somebody wanted you, or a member of your entourage, dead. I'm pretty sure you know exactly who that might be. So, let's start there. Who is it?"

Without hesitation, Elliot answers, "The Nigerian government."

Astonished with the response, the officer says, "A country wants to kill you? What in Sam Hill did you do to them?"

Elliot says, "I sued them in the United States District Federal Court for breach of contract and a whole bunch of other causes of action. The man that they just killed was my lawyer who brought the legal proceedings against them. I eventually got paid a lot of money, which they decided they wanted back.

"We said 'no' and they obviously didn't like our answer. There's plenty more to my story, but that's it in a nutshell."

Officer Johnson continues, "Must have been quite a bit of money! Have you or Mr. Norman ever been threatened by the Nigerians before?"

"Well, they wrote us a letter demanding the funds be reimbursed. If you do a little research on them, you'll discover that they are a brutal military dictatorship. People get killed over there all the time. In fact, not too many months ago, the US Congressman from this district was found dead in a mysterious automobile accident while riding in a Nigerian government official's car. They led Mr. Norman to believe that there might be a price to pay if we didn't return the money."

"Did you feel that the threat was real?"

"Very real. You met Yonatan. He's one of this country's top security people. He and his staff are hired full time to guard my family and myself 24-hours around the clock. That's how real I took the threat."

"Okay, Mr. Sterling. I think I get the picture for now. No need to talk about motive any further. We'll work under the preliminary theory that the Nigerians are the suspects. Anyone else you can think of that would want to see you or Mr. Norman dead?"

"No sir. Paul Norman was one of the finest people I've ever met. The Nigerians did this. Please find this butcher! I wouldn't be surprised if he isn't on his way to the LA airport as we speak."

The officer turns to his assistant and instructs him to warn the LA airport to be on the lookout for any suspicious travelers destined for Nigeria, especially those with limited or no luggage. Then he turns to Yonatan and says, "Okay, explain to me what happened."

Yonatan says, "The driver of the limo, Mr. and Mrs. Sterling, Mr. Norman, and I arrived at the entrance driveway. We were returning from the airport. The driver could not seem to get the digital code to open the security gate. I was sitting in the front seat at the passenger side and Mr. Norman was sitting on the left backseat, window position. Since he was the closest person, other than the driver, to the digital security code box, he got out of the car to firmly push the buttons to get the gate to open. We heard three shots. One hit him in the head. The other two hit his chest and abdomen. He died instantly. In my opinion, this was a professional job."

"Were any other shots fired? Did you get a look at the assassin?"

"No other shots were fired. The sniper vanished without a trace."

The officer thinks for a minute, then asks, "Who hired the limo driver? Could he be in on it?"

Yonatan says, "The limo service was hired by Mr. Sterling who has used this reliable company for many years. Were they in on it? Anything is possible."

Officer Johnson continues asking Yonatan, "Give me your theory on what happened."

Yonatan says, "This is just a theory, but probably true. I've walked the crime scene and here's my take.

"The house across the street is where the shots came from. That home is for sale and no one apparently lives there. The sniper had either been waiting for days, or got a tip that Mr. Sterling would be arriving today. He took his shots from behind a large tree with a clear vision to the driveway. His target was most likely Mr. Sterling, but he accidentally killed Mr. Norman. Although it is possible that the target could have been either one, I'm very confident they wanted Mr. Sterling. Once this son of a bitch hit his mark, he departed out a back gate, into the alley, and into a waiting car. Perfectly executed plan with an exception of killing the wrong person."

Officer Johnson follows up, "Did the Nigerians have a picture of Mr. Sterling or Mr. Norman?"

Elliot answers that question, "Both Mr. Norman and I travelled and met with Nigerian government officials in Nigeria. They had a good profile on both of us."

Officer Johnson says, "The working theory sounds just about right. We'll need to speak to the limo company and the driver. One of my officers authorized him to leave. We do have his statement, but we'll interview him and his company in much greater detail. Also, it is possible that Mr. Norman may have been targeted. The assassin may have been told to shoot to kill either one of you. If they got Mr. Norman, it would serve as a serious warning shot to Mr. Sterling to hand over the money or you're next.

"Keep us informed if you hear formally or informally from the Nigerians. These guys mean business. Be very careful. They could strike again at any moment. Now, Mr. Sterling, we have a detective assigned to this case. He's out at the driveway and across the street inspecting where the sniper allegedly set up. I'm going to brief him, then he'll need to speak with you some more. Yonatan, we'd appreciate it if you could stick around for that talk too."

Elliot glances at Yonatan, then says, "Sure. I need to make a call to my associate, then we'll meet."

The moment the officer leaves, Elliot gets on the phone and calls Mark. It is near 2:30 AM in Israel, but the call needs to be made. After many rings, Mark answers the call a little nervously. "Hey boss, I got some company with me. Thanks for letting me know you're back. Okay if we talk tomorrow?"

Realizing that Mark is with a female acquaintance, Elliot is torn between withholding the truth or just blurting out the details of the horrible tragedy. He opts to speak the truth and says, "Paul Norman is dead. He died in my driveway in Bel-Air upon our return from the airport. The fucking Nigerians probably mistook him for me. He was assassinated by a coward sniper. Mark, I'm devastated, but I'm trying to stay strong for Felicia and my kids. Sorry to be the bearer of such bad news, but you needed to know."

Mark says, "I'm speechless. I can't imagine what kind of pain you feel. Shit, what a devasting loss! I loved the guy. Paul was my friend and colleague. Oh man, his parents! Jesus, the girlfriend. What a disaster these bastards have caused! Elliot, how can I help? Should I cancel the Savor business trip?"

Elliot responds in a choked-up voice, "Paul is dead. There is absolutely nothing you can do except be especially cautious. I won't be able to stand another loss like this. If you're up to it, we need you to do the Algeria deal. Way too much riding on the success of that agreement. Finish the deal, then get your butt back to LA in one piece. When you get a chance, call Yonatan and get him the telephone number and address for Paul's parents. It would help if you had the girlfriend's number too.

"I'll need to go tell these people in person. If the parents will permit, we'll wait to bury Paul until you get back here. Sorry for the bad news and sorry for ruining your night. Apologies to your guest."

Mark says, "No apology needed. This is a gut-wrenching blow to all of us. Give my best to Felicia. I'll leave for Algeria tomorrow. I'll get the deal signed, then head to you. It would mean a lot to me if I could be present at the funeral, but I'll understand whatever the parents decide. Elliot, please get your wife and kids out of Los Angeles as fast as possible. I guarantee you, these guys are coming back faster than you think. Pull together your personal affairs and once we bury Paul, get the fuck out of LA! In fact, tell Yonatan that the funeral could be the site of the next attempt on your life!"

Elliot listens carefully, then says, "I really appreciate you making the Algeria trip happen. Make sure you stay in constant communication with me throughout the trip. In light of the disaster here, Yonatan will be in touch tomorrow morning, Israeli time, regarding his plan to tighten up security measures for your travels. Best of luck. Godspeed."

Just as he hangs up the phone with Mark, he dials Benjamin in Israel to break the troubling news. Half asleep, Ben answers, "Shalom Elliot. You and Felicia make it back okay?"

"No Ben. I have some bad news. Sorry to bother you, but I felt as if I was compelled to inform you.

"Paul Norman was shot to death on the driveway of my home in Bel-Air. He was professionally killed by a sniper. I'm certain it was the Nigerians probably looking to hit me. I'm feeling a ton of grief over this. Paul was a good man. He's survived by his parents and a steady girlfriend. That's it for now. I got to go talk to some law enforcement people here."

Ben sadly responds, "My condolences for such a senseless loss. Such a bright future, and what a delightful man he was. Is there anything I can do for you, Elliot?"

"No. Just make sure that Yitzhak Bennett is informed. Tell Yitzhak that he'll be in charge of my legal affairs from now on regarding Israel. He'll need to be retained as my personal and business attorney for my Israel matters. I'll call him soon to discuss the new role. Please watch yourself. Be cautious.

"Mark is aware of the murder and will be travelling to Algeria tomorrow. He's beat up over Paul's death, but understands the significance of the Algerian deal. Please be certain that both Yitzhak and you are readily available should Mark contact either one of you from Algeria for your advice. Listen, Yitzhak, I've got to go talk to the detective who's waiting to speak to me. Sorry to wake you with such distasteful news. I'll fill you in much better later. Stay safe."

Elliot makes his way back to the breakfast nook where he finds Yonatan and a man dressed in a wrinkled grey suit, white shirt, and a blue tie opened at the collar. He has grey hair combed straight back, somewhat overweight, and appears as if he has not slept in days. Yonatan looks at Elliot with a concerned face and says, "This is Detective Rick Gore. He is assigned to this case and has a few questions for you."

Elliot extends his hand and says, "I'm Elliot Sterling. What can I do for you?"

Speaking with a Southern accent, Gore gets right to the point, "Did you have anything to do with the murder of the victim?"

Elliot glances at Yonatan, then says, "What did you just ask?"

"You heard me, Mr. Sterling. Did you conspire to have Paul Norman killed? Pretty easy question. Yes or no?"

Elliot, now thinking to himself that he's got an asshole to deal with, answers, "What kind of a stupid question is that?"

"Just answer the question."

Elliot says, "No."

The detective then asks, "Did you owe the deceased any money?"

Elliot thinks for a moment, then says, "Mr. Norman had earned money with my company and was entitled to receive his funds either in cash or in the form of stock equity. You'll need to speak to my attorney about the mechanics of all this as opposed to me."

"What is the name of your attorney?"

Elliot has heard enough and says, "You seem to be approaching this interview as if I am a suspect. If that's the case, then this discussion is over without my attorney present. Do you clearly understand, Mr. Gore?"

Gore shoots right back, "Look. We got a dead guy on your driveway who you owe money to. I don't know you from the man on the moon. Given that you were out of the country for over a week, how many people on the planet could have possibly known that you and Mr. Norman were going to be on your driveway, at that precise time? And how much of a coincidence is it that your entry gate would not function at that very moment?

"Or that Mr. Norman just happened to be seated next to the security gate pad and is the only one in the limo to get out of the car, which results in three bullets instantly ending his life? On top of all of that, the body gets moved to an SUV right in the middle of a homicide investigation without the authority of law enforcement officials.

"Do you have any idea how much evidence was affected by that stupid decision? You guys contaminated gunshot residue, hair, soil, pollen, and fibers! I can't swear to a judge that you were simply naïve and had no nefarious intent. So yeah, you are a suspect until I rule you out. Now, do you understand me, Mr. Sterling?"

Elliot then stands up and says, "By the way, Mr. Norman was my friend and my lawyer. He was lying in my driveway soaked in blood, open to the public for anyone to take a picture of him with the risk of the news media announcing his name before his parents were informed. We did the humanitarian thing. We were driven by dignity and compassion given the circumstances. Now, for your information, it was the Nigerian government who killed Mr. Norman, not me. So, if you're not going to arrest me, this meeting is over. I'm not going to answer another one of your fucking questions without my attorney present. So, go finish your investigation, then get the hell out of here!"

Gore looks at Elliot and says, "Have it your way, Mr. Sterling. Here's my card. Have your attorney call me, but don't stay quiet too long! I'll be waiting by the phone."

The remainder of the afternoon is full of sorrow. Elliot experienced the deep heartache of breaking the painful news to Paul's elderly parents face to face. The description of the tragedy that unfolded is by far the most difficult conversation Elliot has ever encountered. He cannot stop thinking of the grief he witnessed on Mr. and Mrs. Norman's faces when learning of their son's death.

Elliot will never be able to forget the image of Paul's father falling to his knees with tears running down his face, despondently asking, "Why did this happen to my son? My beautiful son? My only son!"

Although Paul's mother remained composed under the circumstances, the mournfulness of her face said it all, as the depth of her sadness could not be measured. Elliot would for the remainder of his life remember the words of Mrs. Norman when she graciously said, "Thank you for having the courage and the decency to inform my husband and I in person of this horrifying news. We know that you are under no obligation, nor are you required to come here yourself. My husband and I are very grateful for your making the effort to come to our home."

Elliot was struck by the fact that neither of the parents asked him any questions regarding their son's assassination until he was about to leave, when Mrs. Norman whispers to Elliot and said, "We'll let you know when the funeral will be. At some point, my husband and I will insist on hearing more of the particulars as to precisely what happened."

The next step that dreadful afternoon was the delivery of more bad news directly to Paul Norman's fiancé at her employer's Beverley Hills bank office. This too was a moment that Elliot dreaded, yet clearly had no choice but to do.

Elliot had prearranged with the bank for Paul's girlfriend, Emma Adams, to meet in a private conference room. He felt an obligation to inform Emma that afternoon because he was afraid the news media would pick up on the story and disclose Paul Norman's name. So, Elliot took a calculated risk and decided to inform Emma of this horrific disclosure at her place of work. He got to the conference room ten minutes prior to the meeting, just so he could build up enough nerve to rehearse the words that might be comforting to a young woman whose life was about to be turned upside down.

The problem is that there are no words, just the agony of the truth.

As Emma enters the room, she has already realized something is terribly wrong. She knows exactly who Elliot Sterling is. This strong-willed woman instinctively understood that there is only one reason a person of this stature would ever be meeting her, and it isn't going to be good. As she stares into Elliot's eyes, Emma anxiously blurts out, "What's wrong? Where is Paul?"

Elliot desperately tries to maintain his emotions, but simply can't as he sheds a tear from his left eye while telling the lovely young woman that Paul has been killed.

Emma first glances at Elliot with pain etched across her face, then covers her eyes with her hands, and simultaneously lowers her head. Nothing is said for what feels like an eternity, until Emma composes herself and asks a simple question, "How?"

Elliot answers, "Paul was shot by a sniper in front of my home this afternoon as we returned from the airport. I believe the bullets were intended for me. I am certain that the assassin was a hired by the Nigerian government. I know Paul loved you very much, and I cannot express to you how genuinely disturbed I feel for your loss."

With teardrops rolling down Emma's face, she says, "It's worse than that, Mr. Sterling, I'm pregnant."

For a brief moment, Elliot is speechless. He literally couldn't utter a word until he says, "Congratulations! Through your child, Paul's legacy will continue to live on. I promise to assist you in whatever manner I can to assure that your child will grow up having a great future. I want you to contact my associate, Mark Goldman, whenever you're ready to discuss this further. We're going to help you.

"We'll make it our business to be certain that Paul Norman and Emma Adams' child will be raised with a good education and a good life. I've jotted down Mark's private cell phone on this paper, as well as mine. Make sure you keep in touch with us, and absolutely make sure I'm advised when the baby is born! If you personally need anything, please don't hesitate to let us know."

Emma responds, "My life will never be the same without Paul. I will miss him beyond comprehension. I am a person of faith, so I have no choice but believe that God has a plan for all of us.

"I will do my best to accept this fate. You are exactly the kind of man that Paul described to me. I'm grateful for your effort to come and visit with me in person. I can imagine how difficult it must be for you to deliver this terrible news. I also am aware of how much pain you must be feeling regarding your loss of Paul. Thank you for coming and thank you for caring about the well-being of my child. Paul would have been very proud of his 'boss' today."

Elliot gets up from his chair and gives Emma a hug, just like a father would have done for a suffering daughter. He then looks at her and says, "Emma Adams, you are exactly the kind of woman Paul described to me, and believe me when I tell you, Paul would have been very proud of how you have handled this moment today. Can my driver take you anywhere?"

"Thank you, Mr. Sterling. I live close by. Walking and some fresh air sounds pretty good to me."

As Elliot makes his way out of the room with Emma, he simply says, "Take good care of yourself."

Chapter 8

Yonatan has become Elliot's shadow. Effectively, he had moved into the Sterling residence, taking over Mark's guest suite and office. No one entered or left the home without Yonatan's careful surveillance. Although this was the day Paul Norman is to be laid to rest, Yonatan insisted that Elliot not attend. The risk was just too high that the Nigerians would make another attempt on his life. Elliot made a futile argument expressing that he should at least be present at the indoor chapel ceremony, but his wife and Yonatan would hear nothing of the sort. So, he sent one handwritten note to Paul's parents and a second one to Emma. He explained why he would be unable to attend the funeral and expressed his warmest condolences.

It was not like Mark to have failed to check in with Elliot regarding his travels to Algeria. It was even more unusual that Mark had not even attempted to ask about Paul's funeral date. Elliot was worried, but he wasn't sure whether Mark was just letting him get some rest from all the drama going on, or whether something had terribly gone wrong. He checked his fax machine and asked Yonatan if had heard from Mark. With no new information, Elliot went right to his phone and placed a call to Mark. The phone did not even ring. The operator's message was, "All circuits are busy, please call back."

Elliot then asked Yonatan to step into his office and said, "There's got to be something going wrong in Algeria. I can't reach Mark and I'm positive Mark can't reach me. I need you to figure out what's going on. See if you can get through to your guys guarding Mark, and if you can't, I want you to get to the root of what's happening over there! Please do this right away."

Within minutes, Yonatan returned. "All phone and internet services are down in Algeria. Rumor is that the government shut all the services down due to the threat of a coup d'état. No commercial aircrafts are entering or departing the country. We have our contacts in the Israeli government checking into the facts. I should hear back from them within the next hour."

"Listen carefully to me, Yonatan. I don't care what you need to do, get Mark and your personnel out of Algeria immediately! I don't want to hear anything other than they are safe and on their way back to the United States. We clear?"

"Yes, Mr. Sterling, very clear, except without any form of communication, we're paralyzed, short of sending our people clandestinely into Algeria. That will require serious planning and a lot of money."

"Yonatan. Do what you need to do. Just get Mark out of there alive!"

"I understand your instructions, Mr. Sterling. I'll get you a plan of action promptly. Please excuse me."

Anxious and very uneasy, Elliot begins calling his congressional contacts, trying desperately to gather information. Each response sounds like a broken record, "We have no information to share with you at this time, but we'll get back to you shortly."

Elliot understood that the United States and Algeria did not have a good diplomatic relationship. In fact, US-Algerian relations had ranged from outright hostility to limited diplomatic engagement. This complicated the challenge of locating Mark. If Mark was not found within the next hour, it was apparent to Elliot that he would need to work through Yonatan's unorthodox method of sending Israeli mercenaries, "professional soldiers of fortune", to get the job done. The haunting thought of losing Mark immediately after the death of Paul was just too much to bear.

Within an hour, Yonatan returns to Elliot's office and without any emotion says, "We've located Mr. Goldman and my security detail. They are safe."

Elliot responds, "Thank God! Where are they?"

"They are all in the hotel under a benevolent house arrest. They are not allowed to leave, but they are not being mistreated. The Algerians do not give their permission for any form of communication to the outside world. We located our people because the Israeli Mossad have one of their operatives staying in the same hotel. The Mossad is the national intelligence agency of Israel, and they just happen to be conducting a secretive mission in Algeria. The Mossad agent recognized one of my guys from when they served in the Israeli military together. At the request of my security guard, the Mossad guy sent off an encrypted message to my office with this information."

A very impressed Elliot looks at Yonatan and said, "So how do we get them out of there?"

Yonatan answers, "We wait. My people are extremely well trained for this very situation. They will follow the lead of the Mossad agent. Trust me, Mr. Sterling, Mark will get out of Algeria without a scratch on him."

Elliot asks, "How long will it take before I can speak to Mark?"

"I wouldn't be a bit shocked if we didn't talk to him by this evening."

Elliot responds, "You sound pretty confident. You must know something I don't."

Yonatan stares over at Elliot and simply says, "I know the Mossad. That's all I need to know. You'll speak to Mark very soon. You can trust me on this."

It was not until late into the night that Yonatan finally had an update to share with Elliot, who was patiently working at his desk. Again, without any emotion, Yonatan says, "Mark and my personnel have safely been escorted out of Algeria to neighboring Morocco. They are in the capital city of Rabat en route toward the Rabat-Sale International Airport. Within two hours, they will board an Air France aircraft with the destination of Los Angeles. Mark will call you upon his arrival at the Rabat airport."

Elliot, relieved and all smiles, addresses Yonatan, "Don't you ever flash a grin? This is great news! How the hell did you get them out of Algeria?"

Yonatan says, "This was all Mossad, but it doesn't hurt to be friendly with the right people. The operation was impressive because the Israelis do not have diplomatic relations with Morocco, even though the United States does maintain bilateral economic ties with them. Behind the scenes, Mossad cleverly figured out a way to use American diplomacy, as opposed to Israeli muscle, to get them out.

"I'm sure Mark will fill us in with more details later. As I said earlier, all I needed to know was that Mossad was involved."

Just about two hours later, the phone rings with the telephone screen reading 'Mark Goldman'. Elliot quickly answers the phone, "Mark, are you okay?"

In that great booming voice of his, Mark says, "Never better, boss. Never better. Listen, I'll be brief because I need to board some French plane, so I can get the hell out of here. Here's the punch line. The Savor deal is done. Our contacts clearly understood in advance that Algeria was about to go through some turbulent civil unrest. Since they urgently required possession of the rifles, they quietly prearranged for their payment to be made through a bank in

Morocco versus Algeria. Tell Ben to be on the lookout for a 100-million-dollar wire. When he's got it, ship the fucking Savors!"

Elliot says, "Mark, you are unbelievable! You're really the man! I'll call Ben as soon as we hang up. By the way, I thought you were scheduled to meet with their top military people, what happened?"

"It was weird, Elliot. There was not one military guy at our meeting. Just a bunch of low-life thuggish-looking guys. My take is that the wackos I met with were middlemen for the military or perhaps even the head of state. I'm not even sure the Savors are going to stay in the country. Well, maybe some, but not all. I wouldn't be surprised if these bastards aren't going to resell the rifles and make some huge profit for the president and his crony generals."

Elliot responds, "Sounds like you may be right. I guess we shouldn't care what the hell they do with the Savors so long as we get paid, although they could effectively become our competitors. I'll tell Yitzhak to be certain to place a non-resale provision in the upcoming agreement we have with Sudan."

Mark interrupts Elliot, "Am I going to make Paul's funeral?"

Elliot says, "You'll see him again in heaven one day. Take care of yourself. Safe travels."

Understanding he would miss the funeral, Mark then says, "Hey Elliot. Make sure you thank Yonatan for saving my ass. That guy is worth every penny you're paying him. See you in LA."

Knowing that Mark was safe and the Algerian deal was made, Elliot was feeling much less stress.

He was deeply grateful that his childhood friend was on his way home. Although anxious to determine whether Ben had received the bank wire, it just didn't seem as critical anymore. The fact that Paul was dead, Mark had been held hostage, and the Nigerians had a price on Elliot's head seemed to have put everything into perspective. Life was short, and he was more determined than ever to enjoy making the most of it with his wife, children, and business.

Before Elliot gets a chance to call Benjamin, his cell phone rings, indicating that it is Ben. Elliot answers immediately, "Hello Ben, I was just going to ring you."

Ben enthusiastically cuts in, "Good news! We have received the Algerian wire for the hundred million! Actually, it came from some low-level bank in Morocco, but we'll take it. I've got the money off the wires and placed the funds into the Sterling Hedge Fund account. I'll clear the funds within two to three business days. As soon as the funds are confirmed to be good, I'll pay the Savor manufacturer and we'll ship the rifles. Elliot, you're spoiling me. First the Nigerian hundred million, now the Algerian hundred million, and soon the Sudan transfer. I can really get used to this!"

"Awesome, Ben! Welcome to the big leagues. Now the trick is to figure out how to stay in the major leagues. Any team can win a game once in a while, but can they do it consistently? We've got a scrappy group of guys on our team, now let's find out if we're the real thing. When you get a chance, make sure you call Mark and tell him what a spectacular job he did making sure the money was wired on time. He went through hell to get this done. He's boarding a plane right about now. So, you might catch him."

Ben says, "I'll call him. Is Mark okay? How are you holding up? I still can't get over the shock of Paul's untimely death. I know you've got a lot on your mind, but here's my advice, Elliot, get the hell out of LA as fast as you can. Get Felicia, and your daughters, and yourself to Israel now!"

Elliot says, "I agree. I'm going to speak to Yonatan and start making the arrangements. Yeah, Mark's fine considering he was effectively held hostage in Algeria. He'll give you the details. As far as myself, I'm very sad for Paul's parents and his close girlfriend. No doubt, this is a big loss for me. It just shows you, Ben, life can turn in the blink of an eye. Remember, we're at war with the Nigerians. So, all of us need to be extra cautious. Don't play Israeli commando, just be extra careful."

Feeling that his good friend was emotionally hurting, Ben says, "Please know that whatever you need from me, consider it done. Although we've had a serious setback with the murder of Paul, we will come back stronger than ever. The team you have assembled will faithfully go to war for you, and none of us will be satisfied until the people responsible for Paul's death are brought to justice. And I assure you that the Sterling Hedge Fund will be stronger each day of its existence. Together, we're going to make this company the most powerful of its kind in the world. That, I promise you, my friend. Just do us all a big favor. Get out of LA and come home to Caesarea."

Touched by Ben's words, Elliot says, "I'll get out of here very soon, I give you my word on that. Hey, listen, just a few last things. First, please tell Yitzhak to insert a boilerplate clause in our purchase agreement indicating that the buyer is prohibited from reselling the Savor to a third party. We need that done before Mark leaves for the Sudan to sell the Savor.

"Make sure Yitzhak understands that we must protect ourselves from our own buyers becoming chief competitors. Second, tell Yitzhak to prepare a new retainer whereby Yitzhak will represent me personally. Again, I want this separate from his representation of the Sterling Hedge Fund. I'll sign it as soon as I get back to Israel. Last, I want Yitzhak to get a reading from Yair Erdan as to when the ICO is planning to go public with the crypto coins and at what price? Alright, that's it. Call me when the Algerian funds clear. Shalom, Ben."

"Shalom, Elliot."

Elliot wasted no time organizing his expedited plan to move to Israel. He calls in Yonatan to his office and gets right into it, "Yonatan, I'm very fearful for the lives of my family, and for that of my own. For that reason, we must leave Los Angeles for Israel within the next ten days. I want my children transferred here the moment they complete their final exams at Stanford. They'll both be done within the next three days. We won't be flying commercial anymore, I'll be buying a private jet shortly."

Yonatan glances at Elliot and says, "The private jet idea will resolve many security issues. Primarily walking through public airport areas. Just the thought of going back to the airport with a killer on the loose was concerning. Many of my clients have private jets. May I make a suggestion?"

Elliot says, "Sure. Go right ahead."

"First of all, Mr. Sterling, you need two pilots with extensive international experience. The jet should have a long range of between 7,500 to 8,500 miles at minimum. The seating should accommodate eight passengers. You can go as high as eighteen. I highly recommend buying a Gulfstream aircraft or its equivalent. A new Gulfstream will run you around fifty million dollars. The problem is that you'll need to wait approximately two years to fulfill the order of obtaining a new Gulfstream. So, we need to purchase a pre-owned jet with a first-class maintenance record. A previously owned Gulfstream jet will run you approximately twenty-five million dollars."

Elliot looks at Yonatan and asks, "Did you say it will take two years in order to buy a new jet?"

"That's exactly what I said!"

Elliot responds, "I don't have two years!"

Yonatan responds, "I have a source that has been trying to sell their Gulfstream jet for the last year and a half. I heard that the jet is sitting in Australia ready to be picked up. The sale is being conducted by a previous client of mine. Do you want me to make some calls and determine if the plane is available?"

"Absolutely. Call today. And get me a couple pilots while you're at it."

"Very well, Mr. Sterling, I'll secure you a plane and two pilots. Just get ready to pull out a big wallet!"

The next seven days seemed as if they had passed by quickly. Elliot and Felicia were sincerely grateful that their two daughters had safely returned home. Yonatan had successfully made the deal to purchase the private jet from his former client. He also arranged for the two pilots who previously flew the plane to stay on with Mr. Sterling. And, it was quite a special moment when Felicia, Rose, and Erica got their first glimpse at the Gulfstream aircraft and its beautifully decorated cabin.

During that week, Paul Norman had been buried with dignity and Mark had triumphantly returned from Algeria with much to discuss. With just a few days left before the Sterling family is prepared to move to Caesarea, Elliot summons Mark to his office to discuss some important matters. As Mark arrives at the office, he sees Elliot pouring himself a shot of tequila. Mark responds, "It's kind of early in the day to be drinking tequila, don't you think?"

"No, it's not. Here, have one. In fact, have two."

A little startled, Mark asks, "What's up, Elliot?"

Elliot seriously says, "I'm terrified that I'm going to get all of you killed! Paul had his whole life in front of him. Now he's lying six feet under because of me. He didn't even get a chance to get married or meet his new kid. And those poor parents of his. They're not supposed to be burying a child, it's the other way around, goddammit! What have I done?"

Perhaps for the first time in his life, Mark is observing his close friend experience a psychological meltdown. It is apparent that Elliot felt responsible for Paul's death and is deeply concerned for the well-being of his wife and children. The murder of Paul before his very eyes has brought the severity of the Nigerian threat to the forefront of his mind. Elliot is grieving hard for his late attorney and he is just plain scared about the real possibility of a new brutal act lying around the corner.

Mark is not quite certain what to say under the circumstances. He is sympathetic to the realities Elliot is expressing, yet he feels a need to snap his boss and friend out of his funk. After a moment of reflection, Mark aggressively responds, "Get over it, Elliot! Whatever has happened, happened. The Nigerians killed Paul and they are the ones responsible, not you. Nothing is going to change that.

"Paul is dead, but life must go on. You're our leader. If you're weak, we're all weak! For the sake of Felicia, your kids, myself, and our beautiful new company, wake the fuck up. Strength and brains will keep us all living prosperous lives. Your choice, my friend, show us the way, or tear this fucking empire apart!"

There is dead silence after Mark's risky comments. In fact, there is no movement by either one of them. This goes on for several minutes until Elliot clears his throat and says, "We fight, Mark. We fight on, just as we've done together all of our lives. First, we must get out of Los Angeles and on to Caesarea. It's just too dangerous here. Let's get the Hedge Fund humming like a fine-tuned Ferrari.

"Hey, who knows, maybe the current Nigerian regime gets overthrown, and the new government will let us off the hook. If all else fails, we'll just rely on ourselves and make billions to buy our safety. I know we'll be the last guys standing. Thanks for the talk. I needed to be reminded of what is at stake."

Reassured, Mark changes the subject and asks, "When you were referring to Paul's kid, I'm pretty certain you meant the hypothetical child he could have had with his future wife, right?"

"No. Emma is pregnant."

Mark reacts, "Holy shit. You're kidding me?"

Elliot looks right at Mark and says, "No, I'm not. So, I want you to go see her in person. We're going to give her Paul's one-million dollar share in the Hedge Fund. We'll set up a trust for her and the kid."

Mark says, "You want me to go see her in person? I've never met her. I didn't even go to Paul's funeral. No, boss, I'm the wrong guy to go talk to her. You'd be better at this than me. I don't want to go see her. You see her."

Elliot, now laughing out loud, says, "You show such courage, Mark. Wow, what leadership you reveal.

"Here's her number. Get on the phone and call her. Jesus, how difficult can that conversation be? You're offering her a million bucks plus security for her kid. You just came back from being kidnapped in Algeria, and you tell me you can't visit with a lovely woman like Emma? Give me a break. Call her!"

"It's not that, Elliot. I don't like to talk to grieving women. They make me nervous, especially a pregnant woman."

Elliot, looking at Mark, says, "Get on the goddamn phone and call her. Help Emma get on the right path. She's been through a lot."

Without responding, Mark steps out of the office, calls her, and returns saying, "She's very nice. I'm going over to meet her for some coffee right now."

"Now that's the spirit! Just one more thing to discuss. You're not going to the Sudan. Way too dangerous. Algeria was enough drama. No more suspense. We'll need to handle the deal by phone."

Mark stares at Elliot and says, "The sale will never get done by phone. These people need to see us in person. If I don't go, you can kiss the deal goodbye. We don't have their trust yet. Maybe a future contract might work, but not the initial one. If we're going to do business with the Sudan, I must go. Period! Fly me in there on the new Gulfstream. I'll take a couple of Yonatan's guys. I'll be fine, and we're all going to get a little bit richer. We're building a new business, Elliot, we don't have an option."

Elliot reflects upon Mark's comments and says, "Alright. Alright. You win, but here's how we're going to do this. Your meetings with the Sudan military personnel will be shifted to an indoor airport hangar that Yonatan will arrange. Do your dealings aboard the jet. Everything gets done inside the jet. Do you hear me?"

Mark, who appreciates his best friend's concerns, says, "I can live with that, but will the Sudan people agree?"

A confident Elliot responds, "Leave that to me. Just fly in there. Do what's necessary, and fly out. Ben tells me these guys are very anxious to get their hands on the Savor. They want to sign the purchase agreement even more than us. So, here's the plan. You'll fly with Felicia, my kids, and I back to Israel. You'll get briefed by Ben and Yitzhak the next day, then you'll be off to the Sudan with Yonatan's security guys. We good?"

"Yeah, we're good."

Elliot then directs his attention to Emma and says, "Look, that's Paul's kid she's carrying. Give her a sense of security. Let her know that she's not in this alone. Tell me how it goes."

Right as Mark makes his way to meet Emma, Elliot receives a call from Ben. "Elliot, the funds from Algeria are good funds! The money has been cleared and is sitting in our bank account ready to move on your instructions."

"Thanks for the good news! Mark will see you and Yitzhak in four days. After you guys brief him, he'll take off for the Sudan. Make sure he's ready. Anything new on the ICO opening value?"

"Nothing official, but my guess is the opening value will be less than one hundred dollars. Personally, I think the cryptocurrency will shoot to over a thousand dollars per coin. Brace yourself, you're about to make an unimaginable amount of money! Give this about a week before it rolls out. Also, start giving some thought as to whether we hold or sell our position in the coins. Big decision! Give me your thoughts as soon as you're ready."

Elliot responds, "Sounds promising, but I really don't like counting my chickens before they are hatched. So, I'll pass on giving you any direction until we see the real values. Cool, Ben?"

"Sure, I'm cool. But you got to listen to me, Elliot. Minutes in this kind of work can cost you tens of millions of dollars. Do what I'm advising. Give it some thought and let me know whether we sell or keep the currency. You'll thank me later."

Chapter 9

Mark parks his car in a public metered parking spot along Beverly Drive in Beverly Hills. The popular coffee shop he is to meet Emma at is located about a block away. All along this swanky street are restaurants with outdoor seating, gorgeous jewelry stores, and a collection of high-priced boutique clothing stores featuring the latest fashions. As he makes his way into the coffee shop, Mark looks for a young woman that Elliot had previously described. Within seconds, he spots her seated at an upholstered oversized red chair intently reading a book and sipping her coffee. Mark approaches her and says, "Excuse me. Are you Emma? I'm Mark Goldman."

Emma puts down her book, stares at Mark, and says, "Pleased to meet you. I saved you a seat. I tried really hard to get one equally comfortable as mine, but it is so crowded in here you'll just need to settle for whatever I got you. Take a seat, or better yet, go get yourself some coffee."

Mark immediately senses a bond with Emma. He isn't quite sure what it is about her, but he is positive he likes her. Perhaps it is her kind soul. Maybe it is her innocence combined with her natural beauty. Whatever it is, the connection is real. As Mark returns to the empty chair next to Emma, he places his piping hot coffee on a table in front of Emma, then takes a seat.

Mark asks, "What are you reading?"

Emma responds, "A fiction novel about a great young lawyer and the cases he tried in the South. I find this author's books fascinating and very entertaining. You like to read?"

Mark, who has a chance to paint himself to be much more intellectual than he is, decides to just tell it the way it is, "No, I don't."

Emma responds with a beautiful smile, "I won't hold that against you. Well, at least for now."

As Mark drinks a little of his coffee, he asks, "So, how you holding up? Feeling alright?"

Emma glances at Mark and says, "These days have been the worst of my life. I feel sad, yet I must look to the future with optimism, or what kind of a life will I give my baby. The thought of raising a child without a father worries me sick. The fact that my child will grow up without a father frightens me. Let's face it, what kind of a man is going to want to marry me with a kid? And to top it all off, the guy I was about to marry and spend the rest of my life with is gone. So other than that, all's good."

Mark notices a tear running down Emma's cheek, hands her a napkin, and says, "By the way, your eyes turn very blue when you cry. First of all, any man would be very lucky to have you as his wife, with or without a kid. Trust me, that is not going to be your problem. Your challenge will be to find a man like Paul Norman. A man who will protect you and will help you raise your child in the best of traditions. Hey, I've known you for a few minutes and I'll guarantee you that your child, and you, are going to live full and honorable lives."

Emma, much more relaxed after the kind words Mark expresses, says, "Now, how do you know that, Mr. Mark Goldman?"

"Anyone who has the brains and character to win the heart of Paul Norman tells me everything I need to know. Paul was my trusted friend. We worked very well together for many years. Your man was a first-class individual. A Harvard educated lawyer with a heart of pure gold. Although he was a bit of a nerd, he knew precisely how to interact with common and simple people from all walks of life. Even though we were almost exact opposites, we understood each other perfectly because we always seemed to be seeking practical solutions while living life from a good place. I too will sorely miss him."

Emma and Mark went on to talk for hours. They spoke comfortably about everything from baseball to banking to babies. There was no doubt that the chemistry between the two of them was real. Neither one wanted the conversation to end until Mark finally says, "You got any plans for dinner?"

Emma smiles at him and says, "To be honest with you, I don't really have any immediate plans for anything. Are you asking me out to dinner? So, if you are, my answer is yes."

"Great! Let's go. What do you like to eat?"

Emma says, "How does Chinese sound?"

"Great. I know the perfect place right on Wilshire Blvd. We can walk there from here, and since it after 6 PM, I don't even need to move my car from the public parking spot. So, let's go. Besides, I've got something important I wanted to talk to you about. We can do that over dinner."

Emma, a little concerned and with a serious look on her face, asks, "What do you mean? What do you need to speak to me about?"

Mark, trying to lighten up the moment, says, "Oh, it's just a boring message from Mr. Sterling. I'll fill you in over Chow Mein and Kung Pao chicken. I just love their hot and sour soup. The sweet and sour sauces are out of this world!"

Much more relaxed, Emma gets out of her chair and says, "Come on, let's get out of here. You're making my mouth water. This place better be as good as you say it is!"

It is a short walk to the restaurant. The place is packed, but Mark knows the owner, who gets them seated right away. Emma opens the conversation by curiously asking, "Are you married? Any girlfriend?"

Feeling more and more at ease, Mark decides to give Emma a straight answer and says, "Married and divorced to the wrong women. Then, I could have been married about ten years ago, but I was just too stupid and selfish to go through with it. She warned me she wouldn't wait forever. Of course, I didn't believe her until one day she moved out of my house and went back home to Texas. I wanted her to reconsider in the worst way. It's that classic story of you don't know how good you have it until one day you lose it.

"I chased her hard, but she was convinced that our marriage would never work, so she quit on me. It took me a long time to recover from that relationship. She just decided to never give me another chance. Personally, I thought she showed no character. I didn't cheat on her. I was making great money and there wasn't anything I wouldn't do for her, except marry her at that time. It all eventually worked out. She stayed in Texas, got married, and has a couple of kids. I concentrated on building a dynamic company with Mr. Sterling. I guess I'm a little scared to go through that kind of pain again."

Emma appreciates the sincere explanation and says, "I hope retelling the story didn't get you upset."

"No. Not at all. That's all water under the bridge. As far as a girlfriend, well, to be honest with you, I've had my share. None of which I ever considered marrying. Recently, I broke off a pretty serious relationship. She just didn't know how to be happy. Besides, she wouldn't even consider coming with me to live in Israel for the next year while we got our new business off the ground. I kept telling her it would be a great adventure. She wouldn't have any part of that proposal, so here I am, single and hoping for love again. I really do want to find a wife and have a family. I'm ready for that."

Emma, staring into Mark's eyes, says, "Thanks very much for the explanation. By the way, I would never have allowed the man I loved and trusted to go to Israel without me. Anyway, let's order all that delicious food you promised, then I'd like to hear Mr. Sterling's mysterious message. Do you always speak on his behalf like this?"

Mark responds, "No. I don't. But I always speak for him whenever he asks me to. Let's order. I'm starving!"

Emma is enjoying the evening and the good food. The meal is even better than advertised by Mark.

Even though she is grieving and hurting on the inside, she seems to find some relief from the constant pain she is enduring by simply talking to Mark. They sincerely enjoy having a conversation, and perhaps more importantly, they enjoy laughing with each other. Although Emma and Mark only met hours earlier, they interact as if they have known each other for much longer.

Feeling sad yet comfortable, Emma asks, "Am I ever going to see you again, or is this a one-night stand?"

Laughing, Mark says, "Well, I guess that depends on you."

Feeling a bit of guilt, Emma thinks for a minute, then hesitantly responds, "I'd like that."

Looking at a beautiful, intelligent, yet fragile young woman, Marks says, "So would I."

"Well, Mark Goldman, are you going to tell me what the boss wants me to hear?"

"Yeah. Sure. Mr. Sterling has instructed me to set up a trust in the amount of one million dollars in you and your baby's name. It will be organized to assure that your child and you will have the security to live without the fear of financial worries. The money will be invested so that it will generate additional income and equity growth. We will set aside funds for your kid's education, and you will receive monthly funds to assist in the growth and development of both your child and you.

"Paul had been promised these funds by Mr. Sterling as a part of a previous venture. Although Mr. Sterling could easily retain Paul's funds due to his death, he decided to reach out to you and the baby. Our attorneys and accountants will organize the trust within thirty days. I'll then fill you in on the mechanics."

Speechless and shedding a grateful tear, Emma finally says, "Wow! I don't know what to say. I'm overwhelmed with emotion and joy, yet sadness that Paul will never meet our baby. Wow! You guys are too much. Please extend my heartfelt thank you to Mr. Sterling for this gracious gesture. I will forever be appreciative for this act of kindness. I would like to thank him in person. Can you arrange that?"

"Believe me when I tell you that Mr. Sterling feels that this is the least he can do for you. Besides, Paul earned that money, and I'm sure Paul would have wanted you and his kid to be well taken care of with those funds. Unfortunately, you're not going to be able to see Mr. Sterling. He is very busy getting ready to move to Israel within the next few days, but he did extend you an invitation to visit him in Israel whenever you're up to it."

Emma glares at Mark and asks, "Are you for sure moving to Israel too?"

"Yes, I am. Well, at least for the next year. I'll be flying back with Elliot and the family."

Thinking for a moment, Emma then says with a smile, "Well, perhaps one day, I'll take Mr. Sterling up on his invitation and visit with him in Israel."

Mark, staring at this bright young woman, says, "I hope you do. In the meantime, you have my personal cell number that Elliot gave you. So, should you need anything, well, give me a call. Just remember Israel is about ten hours ahead of Los Angeles."

Mark, who had previously paid the bill, looks at his watch and stands up saying, "I know this has been a very distressing time in your life, but I promise, time will help you heal. Let me walk you back."

After dropping Emma off, Mark drives to Elliot's Bel-Air estate and goes directly to the private office where he finds Elliot on the phone speaking with the mayor of Los Angeles, his close acquaintance.

Elliot completes the conversation by thanking the mayor and expressing his appreciation for getting involved in Paul's death investigation. It seems as if Elliot says the words "thank you" more than a half-dozen times. As Elliot hangs up the phone, he looks up at Mark and says, "The goddamn limo driver was in on the plot with the Nigerians to kill me or Paul!"

Mark says, "What!"

"The limousine company apparently is discreetly owned by a guy that was born in Nigeria. An anonymous source, very likely an agent of the Nigerian government, paid off the limo people to provide them with my flight number and pick-up date. This morning, the driver was arrested on conspiracy to commit murder, but it looks like the owner made it out of the country back to Nigeria.

"The mayor says the Nigerians conducted a major undercover investigation in order to figure out which car service I was using. Then, they turned around and paid a huge bribe to the limo guys to obtain my time of arrival on that fateful day. Those bastards tipped off the fucking assassins!"

Mark, who can't believe his ears, asks, "Did they find the killer?"

"No. They think the sniper who pulled the trigger is long gone. But they're confident the limo driver is going to sing like a canary. Eventually, the mayor believes that the LAPD are going to bring all these criminals to justice. The mayor also advised that Detective Gore has eliminated me as a suspect of the investigation. In fact, Gore told his Chief that he apologizes for having even suspected me in the first place. Officially, I'm no longer a target of this investigation. To tell you the truth, it worries me that a moron like Gore would have the authority to handle Paul's case. Anyway, please update Yonatan."

Mark says, "I just can't believe that piece of garbage limo driver was in on it. It's amazing what people will do for money. Well, I just hope the judge locks him up and throws the key away. I'll go brief Yonatan right now."

As Mark is making his way out the door, Elliot says, "Could I have an additional word with you before you go?"

"Sure Elliot, what do you need?"

"Remember Stanley Roberts, the guy who released our 100-million-dollar contract payment from the Central Bank of Nigeria? He's one of the many Central Bank officials that the government summarily rounded up and placed in a Nigerian prison. As you will recall, I promised him a 5-million-dollar consulting fee payable as soon as he released our contract funds.

"A few weeks ago, I had Benjamin pay off the fee to his family at the designated bank account he requested. That part of our obligation is settled. My problem is that I may have foolishly over-reached in promising his daughter, Adeleye, that I would do all that I could to get Stanley released from prison. Yesterday, Adeleye called, begging me to save her father's life before the Nigerian government executes him for treason. She claims they're going to legally try him in some 'kangaroo court' in Nigeria, then the government is going to kill him."

Mark says, "Of course, I know who he is! When is this court going to convene?"

Elliot somberly answers, "Next month. I can't let that happen. This man stuck his neck out for us. I made a promise and I have an obligation to help save his life. Stanley is not going to die without us putting up a fight. Any thoughts?"

Mark stares at Elliot and says, "Yonatan will get him out. Leave this to him. He'll get Stanley out!"

Elliot stares back at Mark and asks, "What makes you so sure?"

"Yonatan was a member of the Sayeret Matkal special operations unit that performed a famous raid conducted by the Israelis back in 1976. It was a counter-terrorist hostage-rescue mission carried out by commandos of the Israel Defense Forces in some country in the middle of Africa. These guys flew over 2000 miles into the heart of Africa to bring home to Israel over 100 hostages whose French commercial aircraft flight had been hijacked into Africa by Palestinian and German terrorists abetted by the leader of that African country. This was one of the most heralded rescues in history, and our friend Yonatan was in the thick of all the action. Believe me, he'll get our boy out of that hell-hole."

Elliot says, "Can you find Yonatan and tell him to come in here? I'd like to hear what he can do to bust Stanley out. I wonder what it would cost?"

"He's outside near the pool talking to some guy about making arrangement for the private jet hangar in the Sudan for me. He should be finished by now. I'll brief him on your conversation with the mayor regarding the limo driver and the owner. I'll also let him know about Detective Gore's apology. I'm sure I'll get a rare smile on Yonatan's face after he hears about that one. I'll be right back."

About fifteen minutes later, Mark and Yonatan returned to Elliot's office. As they entered the office, Mark closed the door and says, "I've informed Yonatan about the Stanley Roberts situation. Additionally, I'd like to report to you that our head of security actually laughed out loud while sporting a big smile on his handsome face when he heard about the Gore apology."

Elliot looks straight at Yonatan and asks, "Can you save this guy's life?"

Yonatan quickly responds with a question, "Do you have two million dollars for the mission?"

Elliot says, "You guarantee me Stanley Roberts in Palo Alto, California, and I'll guarantee you two million bucks."

Yonatan says, "I won't guarantee anything but our best efforts. There is never a guarantee on these types of missions. Too many things can go wrong. I wouldn't bet against my team getting him out alive, but I'm not going to warrant some heroic ending. I'll recruit the finest former Sayeret Matkal soldiers with nerves of steel. I'll hire a man on the ground in Nigeria to gather all the reconnaissance we need. We'll require two pilots flying a state-of-the-art military style helicopter.

"I'll figure out how to obtain a diagram of the prison and its surroundings. We'll need gratification money to pay off a whole hell of a lot of officials and guards. We're going to need to organize a refueling airport for the return home to Israel after the operation is complete. I think we can succeed with the mission with eight commandos. The ultra-sophisticated helicopter, the best of the best soldiers and the gratification money is not going to come cheap! From the day you give me the green light to proceed, I'll be ready for the rescue operation within sixty days."

Realizing that Yonatan is dead serious, Elliot says, "Suppose I give you the green light. I get the sense you really think you can do this, don't you?"

"Yes sir, I can organize and execute this mission. I believe my men will succeed in getting Mr. Roberts out of the Nigerian prison. Best case scenario, he'll be sitting in Palo Alto within sixty-five days from your approval. Worst case, he and my men die in a failed mission. As for Roberts, well, let's face it, if we don't make this attempt, he's a dead man walking anyway. It's the high value of my men returning alive that should give you some comfort that I will do everything in my power to assure that everyone returns home safely! Do I make myself clear, Mr. Sterling?"

"Yeah, you do. Here's the problem. This guy may be dead in thirty days. We can't wait sixty days!"

Yonatan thinks for a moment, then angrily responds, "Without the proper planning, this mission will fail and each of my men will die! I will not send these brave soldiers into a death trap. Not under my command. You give me sixty days to prepare, I'll send my people. Not one day less. Now let me tell you something else. If the weather conditions are not right, our mission will be delayed. The only way I give the order for the commandos to proceed is that they have a fighting chance to succeed. There can be no further discussion on this. I'm in full control, or there is no deal."

Elliot, getting slightly annoyed with the long lecture, says, "Nobody is asking you to send your mercenaries to go die. How stupid would that be? I spend two million to get your guys and my guy killed. Now there's a winner. The only thing I'm telling you is that Stanley Roberts may be dead within thirty days. Can you plan and train for the rescue to go faster? That's it. Nothing else."

Yonatan simply answers, "No."

Elliot looks at Yonatan, then says, "Give me a moment."

Elliot then picks up the phone and calls Adeleye. He explains that a rescue mission is being planned for her father. Elliot goes on to explain the risks and the timing dilemma. He advises that the mission will cost her family two million dollars, and requests that if she wants this operation to proceed, she must wire-transfer to Yonatan's trust account one million dollars by tomorrow, and one million dollars thirty days later.

Adeleye, without any hesitation, responds, "You will have the first installment tomorrow. Just tell me where you want the money sent. I trust you with my father's life. I understand that there is no guarantee, but we must fight for his precious life. All I can ask is that you do everything that you can. I am confident you'll get him out alive. Thank you, Mr. Sterling. Please keep me informed. Goodbye."

Elliot hangs up the phone and says to Yonatan, "Alright. Go set Stanley free. You got sixty days and two million bucks. You get a million tomorrow and a million in thirty days. I'm not your client."

"Stanley's daughter, Adeleye Roberts, is the one who will hire you. She knows exactly who you are, and here's her private cell phone number. Adeleye is expecting your call so that you can provide her with your bank routing number. Thereafter, she will wire you the first fee installment. Please do everything in your power to save the life of Adeleye's father. His wife and family are counting on you, and so am I. Thank you, Yonatan. Now, go save our boy!"

"I will do my best, Mr. Sterling. The commando recruiting will start today. I know some guys in the Israeli Defense Forces (IDF) who owe me some big-time favors. I'll convince them to allow me to pay a very large fee to the government in order for them to grant us access to a state-of-the-art combat ready helicopter. They'll make us responsible for buying a very expensive insurance policy covering the IDF's helicopter potential loss. It's worth it to us to borrow the helicopter and pay the high insurance premium."

Elliot gets up out of his chair and says, "It's your show, Yonatan. Just get my guy out alive!"

Chapter 10

Felicia and Elliot had spent the last night in their Bel-Air home before leaving for Caesarea discussing their future. They both expressed uncertainty regarding their safety and anxiety about living more permanently in Israel. They were worried about Rose and Erica. The rest of their lives didn't feel so bright and comfortable anymore. Although they were blessed to have each other, they felt as if their lives had been reduced to looking over their shoulder every moment of every day. Even though Yonatan was amongst the best security men in the world, it was apparent by the tragic death of Paul Norman that anything was possible. This was a complicated way to live.

For the sake of their children and each other, they decided that they would leave their destiny to the man upstairs and just do the very best they could to live a full life without fear. It just felt right to stop worrying about things they couldn't control and concentrate on the things they could.

As they are lying in bed, Felicia, out of nowhere, says to Elliot, "You know what I've decided?"

Elliot asks, "What's that?"

"It's best to sell this home. Paul's murder in our driveway is an indelible memory. Every time we pass through that driveway, we will remember his awful death. I don't think either one of us wants to live with that memory. Sell the home, Elliot."

Elliot, not disagreeing with her thoughts, says, "You want to buy a different home in Los Angeles?"

"Yes, I do. Let's buy a home in the 'Flats' of Beverly Hills. It doesn't have to be an estate like this one. It just needs to be very comfortable. Our home is worth about fifteen million dollars. We can buy a wonderful residence for that or less in the 'Flats' on one of the upper 800 blocks. I'm sure we can locate a beautiful home on one of those famous tree-lined streets in the heart of the 'Flats'."

Elliot jumps in, "Sounds like you've given this quite a bit of thought. I'll tell you what, before we leave for the airport tomorrow morning I'll call one of my broker friends on Canon Drive there in Beverly Hills. I'll tell him to run an appraisal on our home, and be on the lookout for a property in the Beverly Hills 'Flats'. If he gets back to me with the right numbers, you and I can revisit what we want to do. Sound good?"

"No, Elliot. Sell the home. Tell your guy to send you a listing agreement, then sell the home. I'm not going to live in this house anymore. It's just too painful. Get top dollar but get rid of the house!"

Elliot, seeing that Felicia has made up her mind on this subject, says, "Okay, tiger. We'll sell it. Obviously, we're in no hurry to sell it tomorrow. I promise you we'll sell it, but I'm not giving it away. We'll get fair market value, then I'll find you a home in Beverly Hills. Now get some sleep. We've got a long trip in front of us tomorrow."

Felicia, very appreciative of her husband, looks Elliot in the eyes and says, "I'm sure we're making the right decision. I love you very much."

Elliot, recognizing the wisdom of Felicia's position along with the sincerity of his wife's anguish, holds his wife gently and says, "Why do I deserve such a smart wife? I'll sell this place as soon as we get the right price. Deal?"

Felicia, wearing a gorgeous powder blue nightgown, turns in the bed to face her husband and says, "Yes, Mr. Sterling, we've got a deal."

At 10 the next morning, a shining black Cadillac Escalade limo is parked in the porte-cochere at the front entry of the home. Yonatan had already conducted a thorough interrogation of the driver and had walked around the entry gate to the residence. His men had driven around the entire neighborhood looking for anyone suspicious. Everything appears in order. The luggage has already been loaded onto the Cadillac and it is time to depart to their private jet waiting for them at the airport. Mark, Felicia, Rose, and Erica are seated in the limo waiting for Elliot and Yonatan. Everyone seems very subdued. In fact, no one has said even one word until Elliot enters the limo and Yonatan gets into the front seat with the driver.

"So, why all the long faces? This trip marks the beginning of the rest of our lives. Think of this as an adventure. We all have our health. We don't need to ask anybody for anything. We have a terrific home waiting for us in Caesarea. We're all going to make new friends and learn a new language. I'd say this is a pretty interesting time in all of our lives.

"So, let me put it to you this way. I am not going to tolerate anything less than an optimistic way of life from each of you. These are the cards that have been dealt to us. I will expect nothing less than a good attitude and a great character from all of you. Be positive. It's contagious. Do you hear me?"

For a very brief moment, no one responds until Rose says, "Hey Dad, if I fall in love with an Israeli, promise me you'll get him immigrated so I can bring him back to live in the States?"

Elliot, reminded of the quick wit and humor of her mom, says smiling, "I promise."

From that point forward, the Sterling family is ready to leave the security of their home in Bel-Air to start a new life. Elliot carries on conversing with Rose, and Erica is deep in conversation with Felicia. The ride to the airport goes by quickly and without incident as the limo enters the private jet hangar.

The moment the Cadillac is parked next to the private jet, three attendants instantly begin unloading the baggage and escorting the passengers onto the aircraft. Mark takes a short stroll by himself to a quiet place toward the rear of the hangar and calls Emma. He confirms to her that they are at the airport and ready to depart to Israel. Mark wishes her well and tells Emma that if there was anything she needed, she should feel free to contact him. He also tells her that if she ever decides that she wants to visit them in Israel, of course, she would be welcome. Although the conversation is short, Mark feels an honest connection with Emma. He isn't sure if he just feels sorry for her or whether it is something else. Time would answer that question.

As Mark returns to the airplane, he sees that Elliot is in deep conversation on his phone. He can't tell whether there is something terribly wrong or something very good. As he stands waiting for Elliot to complete his call and board the jet, Mark realizes that the discussion is regarding the initial pricing of the cryptocurrency private placement. The heavy conversation is taking place with Benjamin.

Apparently, the coins came out at a remarkably low price of fifty dollars per coin. Within hours of trading, the digital currency unexpectedly had a meteoric market rise to the one carat diamond spot price of one thousand four hundred dollars per coin. Since the Sterling Hedge Fund had invested ten million dollars at the confirmed new initial virtual currency price of fifty dollars, they controlled two hundred thousand coins. The math was staggering. Those two hundred thousand coins bought at ten million dollars were now valued at two hundred eighty million dollars!

An astonished Elliot looks up at Mark and says, "Benjamin has just confirmed that the cryptocurrency we bought for ten million is currently worth two hundred eighty million dollars! We invested ten million dollars in coins at fifty bucks per coin. That equates to two hundred thousand coins. Since the price went from fifty bucks to one thousand four hundred dollars and we own two hundred thousand coins, we're sitting on two hundred eighty million dollars. Unbelievable!"

In somewhat of a state of shock, Mark stares back at Elliot and says, "Unbelievable is all you have to say! Elliot, this is fucking incredible! We invest ten million. In less than a month, that ten million grows to two hundred and eighty million! Oorah!"

Mark is so excited and loud with his comments that Felicia actually hears him while sitting in the cabin of the jet. Concerned, she steps out of the plane and asks Elliot, "Everything okay?"

Elliot responds, "Perfect. I'll be up in a moment to explain."

With all the commotion, Elliot forgot that Benjamin is still on the phone and says, "Ben. You still there?"

Benjamin, who has heard all of the verbal exchanges, answers, "Yes Elliot, I'm right here celebrating with you, Felicia, and Mark."

Elliot, feeling a release of dopamine in the brain causing a euphoric feeling, reacts to Ben, "Now what?"

"We're faced with a big decision, Elliot. Do we sell off the coins and take the windfall profit, or do we stay with our position? The street is estimating the currency is heading to ten thousand dollars per coin! That could be hype or it could actually happen. Who knows?"

Elliot thinks for a minute, then asks, "What are the politicians, Mr. Erdan, and Yitzhak Bennett doing?"

Ben says, "As of ten minutes ago, Yitzhak confidentially advised that no one is selling."

Without any further thought, Elliot gives his clear instructions, "Sell off fifteen thousand coins. At one thousand four hundred dollars per coin, we'll receive twenty-one million dollars back.

"That will get us back our investment of ten million, plus an 11-million-dollar profit. We'll continue to hold our speculative position at one hundred eighty-five thousand beautiful digital coins. This way, we recover our investment with over a one hundred percent return. From this point forward, we can't lose, we can only win big. Any questions?"

Ben, who is incredibly impressed with the quick decision, says, "I'll sell the fifteen thousand coins today, then deposit the twenty-one million in the Sterling Hedge Fund operating account. Very good decision, Elliot. I endorse this move, even though I think the currency is going to hit ten thousand per coin. It's still the right decision because we're now playing with other people's money. You realize that if the cryptocurrency ends up trading at ten thousand bucks per coin, our position will be worth well over a billion dollars!"

Elliot reacts, "From your mouth to God's ears. By the way, we all owe you a debt of gratitude.

"It was your vision that was correct from the first day we discussed digital currency. Everything you told me turned out to be accurate. Had you not introduced me to Yitzhak, there would be no profits.

"Not only are you a good friend, but you are an exceptional financial wizard. Thank you for your good advice. Hey, listen, I got to jump on this waiting jet. We'll see you tomorrow."

"Shalom, Elliot. Safe travels."

As the two men are walking quickly toward the jet, Mark says, "Besides me, did anybody ever tell you you're a master CEO? Your business instincts are second to none. By the way, I'm really starting to like this hedge fund stuff. Let's go kick some butt in Israel."

Felicia has been observing through the jet window what obviously is good news. She can't wait to hear. As Elliot settles into his seat for the long trip to Ben Gurion Airport, he starts to tell the story.

After take-off, Elliot continues explaining the mechanics of cryptocurrency and the fact that the coins are backed by one carat diamond pricing. The more Elliot describes the virtual currency, the more Felicia appears to be rolling her eyes with disbelief. He tries to make her understand that the coins are not tied to a government or a financial institution, and are designed to allow users to spend money anonymously.

Elliot continues by stating that the coins are created by users who "mine" them by lending computing power to effectively verify other users' transactions. He goes on to discuss that the users receive digital coins in exchange, and that the coins could be bought and sold on legitimate market exchanges with US dollars and other currencies.

Felicia, who is very irritated with the idea of a digital currency not backed by the traditional full faith and credit of a government, says, "This sounds worse than the Nigerian scam. Elliot, I don't like this kind of business. It sounds like it has been set up by criminals who need to launder their money. Do us all a favor and get out of the currency as soon as you can.

"I guarantee that, in the long run, this type of business will not end well for us. The traditional banks and national governments cannot possibly want this type of currency to succeed. They lose total regulatory control, and gives criminals and terrorists the autonomy they're looking for. Believe me, Elliot, eventually the governments will put an end to this nonsense, but not before a bunch of people end up in jail for long periods of time."

As Elliot tries to get a word in, Felicia interrupts him, "This sham will fail because it is a currency that derives its value exclusively to the extent that individuals at any given time choose privately to assign them value. When people stop giving the coins value, after the government starts prosecuting and banks commence lobbying hard to get rid of this voodoo currency, these coins will vanish into a value to zero."

Elliot, highly impressed with how astutely Felicia has captured the subject matter, says, "Now look at you. I think you may have this better analyzed than most high-powered economists. Wow! That is some serious commentary. I don't know where to start. So, I'll begin by disclosing the amount of our investment. We have, or should I say, we had two hundred thousand digital coins. We bought them for ten million dollars. They are currently worth two hundred eighty million dollars!

"I just instructed Ben to sell fifteen thousand coins, which will pay us twenty-one million dollars. We get our ten million back and make a profit of eleven million dollars. Not bad for one month's work. Now the good thing is that we still have a position of one hundred eighty-five thousand coins at our discretion with no financial risk whatsoever.

"During this hyper-enthusiastic market frenzy, Ben predicts that the currency is going to ten thousand per coin. If we stay in the position, we stand to make well over a billion dollars! Still want to sell immediately?"

Felicia, somewhat embarrassed with her aggressive lecture, turns to her quick wit to say, "Good thing I put you in charge of the finances." With both of them now smiling, Felicia looks at her husband and says, "We have no risk. So, wait until it gets to ten thousand dollars per coin during this unrealistic euphoric market time, then sell every last one of these poisonous coins. Please Elliot, do what I'm asking of you. I don't want us to have anything to do with these coins after our final sale."

Feeling confident, Elliot says, "Your wish is my command. That could be within the next month, or it could be over a year, but we'll sell at ten thousand. You've got my word."

Proud of the manner by which her husband has handled the virtual currency investment, Felicia says, "Sorry about my stupid lecture and the low blow regarding Nigeria. I guess the whole idea of reliving the traumatic Nigerian experience is completely unacceptable. My instincts still tell me that this currency will come under deep attack, which will result in coins eventually becoming worthless. Do what you have to do, but just don't wait too long to do it."

Elliot looks over his shoulder and notices that Rose is out of her seat and appears to be listening to her parents' conversation. Then Elliot looks over his other shoulder and sees Erica also standing and listening, which prompts Elliot to annoyingly ask, "So, did either of you eavesdroppers learn anything? Or should I ask did one of you wiretap my conversation with your mom?"

Rose responds, "Just curious, Dad. We accidentally overheard you talking about some weird currency that no one appears to recognize. Then, Mom seemed to get kind of passionate, so we just got really interested. Especially the part about Sterling Hedge Fund making near three hundred million dollars on trading some goofy money. We're sorry, we just got fascinated with the story. We should have never listened without your knowledge or permission."

Elliot, who deeply loves his daughters, says, "You're both forgiven. Now tell me what you're thinking."

Rose looks over at Erica and says, "I love this kind of stuff. When I finish school and get my degree, I want to work for our hedge fund. In fact, I'm in the process of changing my major at Stanford to finance. To be honest, my ultimate goal is to be admitted to the Wharton School at the University of Pennsylvania. By the way, I totally agree with Mom. You need to sell off those remaining digital coins the second you hit your goals. The fundamentals of these coins will lead to nothing more than a loss. On the other side, a billion dollars in coins controlled by you sure sounds pretty amazing!"

Elliot, who is baffled by his daughter's keen interest in the hard-nosed arena of finance and business, says, "Wow! Listen to you. Business instincts and a passion to make money. I like it!"

Rose's confidence is rising by the second as she says, "I'm sure I'm cut out for business. I'm going to make you very proud, Daddy. I just hope you're not mad at me for choosing Wharton."

Elliot, now standing and looking at his smart and beautiful daughters, says, "I'm already very proud of both of you. You guys make feel like I'm the luckiest man on earth. Just keep doing what you are doing. The sky is the limit. Reach as high as you choose. Just make sure you enjoy the ride. As for Wharton, well, if Stanford has to lose you to the University of Pennsylvania, I guess I could live with Wharton. It's the top-rank business school in the nation alongside Harvard. Did you know it was the first business school in the USA established in 1881? I'll remind you for the record though, only Stanford students scored higher on the GMAT."

Erica jumps into the conversation, "Pretty impressive, Dad. You seem to know as much about Wharton as you do your own alma mater."

Elliot slowly responds, "Well, I'll let you in on a secret. I applied to Wharton at the same time that my application was submitted to Stanford. To tell you the truth, I wanted to attend Wharton more than anything in the world. They wait-listed me while simultaneously Stanford offered a full scholarship to play tennis. I took the sure Stanford deal, and I've never really looked back on that decision. It's so ironic that you're considering the same options I did!"

Rose, who is holding back a tear, says, "Thank you for sharing that story." Now feeling at ease, Rose looks straight at her father and begins to smile while saying, "I would have done the same thing."

The balance of the long trip was spent talking and eating, then repeating the same. Felicia and Elliot battled at their famous gin rummy games. Felicia was delighted to proclaim herself champion, while loving every second as her husband asked for a rematch. The girls kept reading and sleeping the entire flight, while Mark and Yonatan were in deep conversation in what appeared to sound like old war stories, one a little more interesting than the next.

Although it had been a long journey, the travel had been very comfortable as the pilot suddenly announces, "Please place your seats in the upright position, and fasten your seatbelts for our final descent into Ben Gurion International Airport."

Upon hearing the pilot's voice, Elliot and Felicia look out the window and see that now familiar view of the Israeli coastline. The thought that this proud nation is about to become their homeland gives them a unique sense of joy. Elliot places his hand on Felicia's hand and said, "For as long as we decide to stay, I promise you we're going to have a successful and stimulating life here. Shalom, and welcome home."

"I'm ready for whatever comes our way, Elliot. As long as our family is safe, healthy, and together, I'll be happy wherever we choose to live. Israel is as good as anywhere, and Caesarea is as good as it gets in Israel. So, let's go make a good life for ourselves."

Throughout their beautiful marriage, these were the kind of words that had given Elliot the confidence to accomplish remarkable goals. He was more determined than ever to make this work for the benefit of his wife and children. As the wheels of the private jet touched down on the tarmac, there was no turning back. The moment of truth had arrived and it was the beginnings of a new chapter in the lives of the Sterling family.

Chapter 11

Nearly a month had passed by since the Sterling family had arrived in Israel. They had settled into their comfortable new home in Caesarea and were living a rather normal life. Felicia was busy filling her day keeping the residential estate running well and looking after her family. There was always plenty to do and think about. The kids had started classes at Hebrew University of Jerusalem and had acclimated incredibly well.

Mark had travelled to and return safely from the Sudan. He had successfully sold them one hundred million dollars of the Savor rifles and made a nifty twenty-five million profit for the Sterling Hedge Fund. Needless to say, the Savor rifle business was off to a spectacular start with an ambitious plan to sell this product all over the world.

Of course, Yonatan was kept very engaged running the security for the entire Sterling family. He did it as if he was in charge of an Israeli head of state. So far, everything was going pretty much as planned, and life seemed good.

Mark, with the assistance of the Hedge Fund, had purchased a nearby condominium. His daily routine was to meet with Elliot at 10 AM to discuss the various business matters they faced for the day and beyond. Often, Benjamin Yaalon would be invited as was the case this day. Elliot had been closely tracking the cryptocurrency through his investment contacts in the United States.

It appeared as if one of the mutual fund giants in the US was forming a new business to manage digital assets for hedge funds, family offices, and trading firms. This American mutual company was prepared to offer security and storage services, trade execution and customer service for digital assets. The business, dubbed Digital Resource, had taken a serious interest in the Israeli firm that belonged to Yair Erdan.

The information Elliot had obtained on deep background predicted that Erdan's Israeli digital coins, similar to those the Sterling Fund controlled, were about to surpass ten thousand dollars per coin!

Elliot's instincts were telling him that something big was about to happen with the cryptocurrency. He faces Ben and asks, "So, what do you hear on the streets regarding digital coins?"

Ben, feeling very excited to answer the question, says, "Elliot, this stuff is taking off! It's got wings. I wouldn't be surprised if the coins don't end up somewhere between ten and twenty thousand for each coin. The bank predicts nothing but upward value. Digital Resource is the real deal regarding assessing digital coin value, and they say Erdan's coins will surpass ten thousand dollars a coin! It seems like anybody who can get their hands on these coins are buying. This, of course, is driving the value through the roof."

While Mark kept mostly silent, Ben seemed inclined to sell at a price over ten thousand dollars. Elliot turns to Mark and asks, "Care to share an opinion on the digital coins?"

"Yeah sure. Get the fuck out the moment our fake currency value hits ten thousand. Sell this shit into the strength of the market. As fast as this stuff is rising, I'm positive it will plunge. Have you done the math on this yet? We control one hundred and eighty-five thousand coins. If the market hits ten thousand bucks per coin, we stand to make nearly two billion dollars. That's billion with a B. That doesn't even take into account that we just cashed in for twenty-one million about a month ago. Listen to me, Elliot, and you too, Ben. Sell this crap at ten thousand, and thank your lucky stars we improved our assets beyond a billion."

A smiling Elliot glances at Ben and says, "Sounds like he has an opinion on this."

Ben says, "I happen to agree with him. The bank, the investment community, and the politicians are betting that the price will rise to at least fifteen thousand. We should sell into the strength of the demand for the coins. We probably could hold out and sell closer to twelve to thirteen thousand, but why risk a sudden drop in the market. I say sell at ten thousand. We'll enter the billionaire club just about overnight."

Elliot then asks Ben, "When do you think this run will occur?"

"It may well have already started. Yesterday, the price per coin increased by fifteen hundred dollars. My guess is that we could get to our magic number by the end of the week. If the worldwide market smells a winner, all hell will break loose with the digital coin's value. We should make our preparations to place a sell-order the second the coins reach ten thousand per coin in value. The order will sell every last coin we own for one billion eight hundred fifty million dollars. If you give me the order to sell, I'll make the arrangements."

Eliot stands, places his two arms over his head, then stretches his neck and shoulders. Once completed, he stares at Mark and says, "What makes you so sure of yourself?"

"Look, boss. I got a ton of experience dealing with government. Our bureaucracy does not want to lose control of its national currency. The Feds love tracking the money supply. The Federal Reserve needs to regulate interest rates and provide the nation with a safer, more flexible, and more stable monetary system. The FBI aren't going to standby with their arms folded allowing for dirty money to enter and exit the country. Ben can attest to the fact that the banks want and need customer deposits. Remember my words, the American bureaucracy will never allow for digital coins to operate free from serious regulation within the United States. It's just a matter of time."

Elliot, now standing next to the window, says, "Well, my judgement remains steadfast. We sell at ten thousand a coin no matter what. That's it. That's my final answer. Ben, make the requisite preparations to sell. Question. If we make this big money, do we leave it here or move it to the US?"

Almost simultaneously responding to the question, Ben says, "It should stay here in Israel in order to send a message to the Israeli government that we are a serious and important company. The more capital we control in this country, the more power and prestige we gain. Keep the money here for a while. Let the politicians understand that we are a force to deal with. This will open more doors for us."

Elliot asks, "What do you say, Mark?"

"Well, I prefer the money in the good old US of A, but I guess Ben might have it right. Let's show some muscle here. We could always move the money around as the circumstances require. Yeah, just keep it here for now."

Elliot says, "Well, it's unanimous. We all agree. Any future earnings from the digital currency stays in Israel, at least for the short run. Alright, that's all I got for you today Ben. So, if you don't have anything further for me, you can head back to Tel Aviv. Please start arranging for the decisions we just made here today. Keep a close eye on the market trading value of the coins. Get the hell out at ten thousand. We'll talk later."

Once Ben leaves the office, Elliot says to Mark, "I need you to go to LA on your way to Columbia. By the way, Columbia was an awesome choice to start off the Savor sales in Latin America. Bravo on that decision. The Colombian military is the second largest in the Western Hemisphere in terms of active military personnel, behind only the United States Armed Forces. They have a Columbian Army, Navy, Air Force, and Naval Infantry. I predict we are going to do exceptionally well in that country. In fact, once you introduce the Savor into Latin America through Columbia, that region may end up being the best market we have opened for the rifle in any part of the planet."

Mark says, "I can't take all the credit, Ben did the research, I just said yes. What's up in LA?"

Elliot answers, "I already have a buyer for my Bel-Air home and my agent has identified a new residence in Beverly Hills. The buyer is a big-time movie producer. He's going to pay fifteen million bucks in cash. He says he'll close escrow in thirty days. My agent tells me to grab the deal. He claims it's the highest price per square foot he's ever heard of in the Bel-Air community. Given that I paid a total of four million for the place, looks like Felicia and I will come out alright on that deal.

"We're probably going to accept the offer, but I want you to inspect a home I may make an offer on to buy in Beverly Hills. The home is brand new on gorgeous tree-lined Maple Street. It's on the eight hundredth block of the prestigious 'Flats' not very far away from the Beverly Hills Hotel. The builder wants eighteen million for the property. I want you to physically visit the house, and determine if the market supports the value. Then, I want you to offer fifteen million cash, subject to appraisal, physical inspections, and all the standard contingency bullshit you can throw into the purchase agreement."

Mark looks at Elliot with a little bit of cynicism and says, "You want me to go to Beverly Hills, make a fifteen-million dollar offer on a property you've only seen in pictures, and you want me to offer three million below the asking price. While we're at it, why don't you have me arrange that the movie producer buying Bel-Air cast you for a lead role in his upcoming movie? For Christ's sake, be reasonable, Elliot!"

Elliot strikes back at Mark, "I am reasonable. Their house has not sold in well over a year. The only reason I'd pay fifteen is because I must reinvest the money from the Bel-Air sale. I face a huge capital gains tax in event I sell the Bel-Air home. If I sell Bel-Air at fifteen, I've got to roll over the capital gains into the Beverly

Hills property, or else I'll be paying a shitload of taxes. I bet you the developer takes our offer.

"He's been sitting on the property for over a year. The taxes, insurance, maintenance, and interest carry must be killing this poor bastard. We know that feeling. Go there, make the offer; we can always drop out of the deal if we exercise any of our contingencies. I say the guy sells us the home!"

Mark responds, "I'll make him the offer. It's possible the guy could be desperate so I'll give you a fifty/fifty chance of buying the house. I'll leave Israel for LA late Saturday night. I'll finish up with Emma's paperwork, settle the Bel Air and Beverly Hills homes, then get my ass to Latin America where the big money is waiting to be made selling the Savor. I understand my marching orders."

Elliot just looks at Mark, then says, "Yes, you do, Mark. Indeed, you do."

Mark randomly asks, "Do you believe in destiny? Do you think our lives are preplanned, or in some cases, just plain sheer luck?"

Appreciating the sincerity of the question, Elliot says, "About a year and a half ago, I was on the brink of financial collapse. I was facing the real possibility of the bank foreclosing on my home in Bel Air, and losing my long-standing business. Then, completely out of the blue, I get some stupid sealed envelope from Nigeria signed by Chief Balla offering me fifty percent of a one hundred million contract. Of course, I end up with all one hundred million.

"Then, we move to Israel, buy a lovely home, and by chance I hire an attorney who stumbles onto an interesting concept of buying and selling cryptocurrency, putting me in a position to become a billionaire. This is all happening during the time when my best buddy from college and I decide to start a new Hedge Fund featuring the selling of the famous Savor rifle in Africa and Latin America.

"So, if anyone asks me whether there is a God, I immediately answer, 'Yes there is.' Just look at me. An exceptional wife. Two beautiful kids, and money to spare. So, my answer to your question is all of the above, destiny, planning, and sheer luck. I think I'd add hard work to the list because it places you in a position to capitalize on the moment."

Mark responds, "So how do you explain Paul Norman's destiny? Was that just bad luck?"

Elliot, detecting that Mark was silently worrying about something serious on his mind, says, "It was God's will. I have no further explanation. You can call it destiny. You might even call it bad luck, but when your time is up on this earth, it's just up."

With a concerned expression on his face, Mark softly says, "What would you think of me if I told you I have feelings for Emma?"

Somewhat exasperated, Elliot says, "You don't mean Paul's Emma? You can't possibly be talking about that Emma, right?"

"I'm ashamed to say that I am."

"Mark! Are you fucking out of your mind? Please tell me you weren't having an affair with her!"

"No Elliot, I wasn't having anything with her. I didn't even think I knew her name."

"Not knowing the girl's name hasn't stopped you in the past!" Realizing that he has crossed the line, Elliot recants, "Hey, I'm sorry for the low blow. What the hell is going on here?"

With an optimistic twinkle in his eyes that Elliot recognized since their childhood days, Mark says, "I had dinner with Emma to explain your generous proposal, and I haven't stopped thinking about her since. You've got to trust me when I tell you it's all innocent."

"I trust you, but the optics of this are just plain ugly. My dead attorney has a baby due very soon with his devasted pregnant girlfriend, and you have a romantic interest in your closest colleague's fiancée that I've recently pledged a million bucks to. Man, your timing sucks!"

Mark answers, "Well, had you not sent me to talk to her, things would be different. I didn't want to go. You insisted, so your sense of destiny and timing wasn't all that good either!"

Smiling, Elliot says, "Alright, so we're both idiots. What do you plan on doing about this?"

Mark now grinning says, "I plan to marry her before she spends your million bucks. Seriously, she's going to have a kid and that kid is going to need a father. Emma deserves a man in her life and I plan to be that guy if she'll have me. I've never really been able to settle down, but I think I'm ready to take on that responsibility. I know I can be a good dad and a good husband.

"Hey, who knows, she may send me to hell, but I'm willing to try and see what happens. I'm sure that Paul wouldn't want his child nor Emma feeling alone. I'm also certain that Paul would understand this all to be innocent and not disrespectful of him. I'm glad you know my feelings, and now you know my plans. I hope you can find it in your heart to accept that I'm trying to do the right thing."

Elliot, who has known his good friend his entire life, turns his attention to Mark and says, "You're my loyal friend and I will never turn my back on you. Follow your heart, but do not force things. If Emma naturally feels the same about you, as you feel about her, well, go for it!"

Very relieved, a grateful Mark says, "Thank you, Elliot. I guess I just needed to hear you give me your blessing. Do you still want me to have her sign the million-dollar trust documents?"

"Yeah, sure. Who knows, she may not like you as the marrying type. So, until further notice, don't deviate from our plans."

Mark feels as if the entire weight of the world has just been lifted. He understood that in the end, Elliot would make the right decision and find a way to help his friend win.

The week had gone by quickly. It was time for Mark to leave for Los Angeles and on to Latin America.

Mark had been called by Ben to urgently meet at Elliot's house about six hours before his flight departure. By the time Mark arrived, Ben, Yitzhak Bennett, and Moshe Ariel were already seated waiting for Elliot to make his presence. As Mark makes his way to his seat, Elliot enters the room saying, "The day has finally arrived. The Sterling Hedge Fund is about to become valued far in excess of a billion dollars. Any objections? I didn't think so. Without any further notice, I will order the sale of all our digital coins at the price of ten thousand dollars to one!"

Just as he was about to sign the order instructions drafted by Yitzhak, the accountant, Moishe Ariel, says, "I object, Mr. Sterling. I object."

A very surprised Elliot says, "This should be good. What's on your mind?"

Moishe stands and says, "We are prematurely selling. The price is going to settle within a short term at between fifteen and twenty thousand a coin. We are going to leave a small fortune on the table by selling way to early. There is not one politician or savvy investor selling at this point in the trading. In fact, every investment banker and financial expert advises to stay with the investment until the currency reaches at least fifteen thousand per coin. If the Israeli prime minister and the minister of finance aren't selling, I'd say that's a pretty good indicator that there's more equity in the coins than we're allowing credit for."

Elliot asks, "Which one of you think the same way?"

Yitzhak jumps in, "I don't get paid to give financial advice so, no charge for this consult, but Yair Erdan isn't selling either. If anyone understands the coin's value, it's going to be the founder of the company. I say wait a week. What do you have to lose?"

Elliot, looks around the room and points at Ben, saying, "So, what's your opinion?"

"My opinion is sell right into the strength of the market. I'd sell even if we're going to leave some money on the table."

"Is that your final answer?"

"Yes."

Elliot, seated next to Mark, looks at him, then says, "This is an equal opportunity group. What wisdom are you going to contribute to this fine group of gentlemen?"

Mark stares at Ariel and calmly states, "Get the fuck out of these shit coins as fast as possible. Instruct Ben to sell now."

Unable to hold back his laughter, Elliot says, "As usual, Mark has no opinion to share with us, but I do.

"My information, coming from the highest levels of the American government, seems to indicate that cryptocurrency is on a collision course with Western governments' need to control and regulate national currency. The Feds are worried about money laundering and banking rules. The powerful big banks will not stand by and allow there to be a change in the status quo norms of transacting finance.

"These institutions employ very well-paid lobbyist in Washington DC who assure their clients that business will be conducted as usual. My guess is that the Congress of the United States will be persuaded to seriously regulate, or should I say, over-regulate the digital coin markets. The President of the United States will join in on the effort to stop the growth of cryptocurrency. We have a window of opportunity to sell our investment into an incredibly strong market, and that is exactly what I intend to do. Ben, sell the coins today! All of them."

By the end of the day, Ben had sold the entire Sterling Hedge Fund portfolio of digital coins. All one hundred and eighty-five thousand. He sold at ten thousand dollars per coin, which was converted into a staggering one billion eight hundred fifty million dollars! Nearly two billion dollars in one day! Elliot Sterling went from being a multi-millionaire to becoming one of the wealthiest people on earth. With all the trades completed, Ben jumps on the phone and calls Elliot.

"Hello Elliot, this is Ben."

Elliot, anxious to get an official word on the sale, says, "I know it's you, Ben. Your name pops up on my telephone screen. Well, what's the verdict?"

"You control a great deal of money. Let's just say amongst friends, you're filthy rich! All of the trades are done, and you're sitting on nearly two billion dollars. Again, that is billion with a B. Every investor we know stayed in. Effectively, these guys bought our coins. I'm talking about our prime minister, the minister of finance, Yair Erdan, you name it, they either bought, or simply held onto what they controlled. Time will tell as to whether we were the fools or they were. I trust we got this figured out right."

Elliot, dead silent for a moment, says, "We will be proven to having read the future value of digital coins perfectly. We're a hedge fund, this is what we do. The rest of these poor souls are working on emotion and instinct. We have the financial and governmental fundamentals understood correctly, and sooner than you think, everyone from around the globe will be begging to do business with the Sterling Hedge Fund. Have you heard from Mark? Has he arrived in Los Angeles yet?"

Ben says, "Mark will touch down in LA shortly. I'll call him and give him the good news."

Again, there is a long pause before Elliot says, "What the hell are we going to do with all this cash? I know we decided to keep it here in Israel, but is it safer in America?"

Ben immediately answers, "Keep it here, at least in the short term. I'll tell you why. We may have just become the biggest private financial player in Israel. We are a huge fish in a small pond. This will buy us significant leverage in virtually everything we want to do here from now on. It will buy us political muscle, social significance, and international fame in the world of finance. This will open new doors for us regarding business opportunities.

"Israel is rapidly becoming a thriving mecca for start-up companies. It is advancing the world with technological inventions, ranging from drip irrigation and water creation technology to breakthrough medical advancements. We will have the pick of the litter. If we choose carefully, we will invest our capital in some of the fastest growing companies in the world. Pretty soon, we're going to make the two billion bucks look more like four!"

"Alright, I hear you. You still didn't answer my question. What are you going to do with our money tomorrow?"

"The funds will be deposited to our existing Israeli operating bank account. The moment that all of the funds have cleared, they will be placed in an interest-bearing savings account or a thirty-day time certificate of deposit. During the thirty days, Moshe Ariel and I will meet with the top investment banking people in Israel and come up with a plan to precisely indicate where we will place the funds to derive the highest yield. Moshe and I will present you with our recommended plan in about three weeks. You will either approve it, or, provide your thoughts on how we can do better. Once you give us the final green light, we'll implement your approved plan."

Elliot says, "Sounds reasonable, but you're making me feel like I'm bigger than what I really am."

Ben decides to paint a better picture for Elliot so that he could come to terms with his new reality by saying, "Ever heard of David Rockefeller of the famed Rockefeller family?"

Elliot answers with, "Of course I have."

"You've got more money than him!"

"Oh, is that so? Well then, I just came up with an idea."

"What is it?"

"If I'm so rich, I should be able to buy myself out of a problem, don't you think?"

Ben, not quite sure where Elliot is going with this, says, "Go on."

With a serious expression on his face, Elliot says, "I want to pay off the fucking Nigerians. They get money, and I get the target off my back. I'm pretty sure these bastards will take fifty million. Half of the hundred million they accuse me of stealing from them. Of course, I would prefer that they'd look at it more along the lines that I outsmarted them, as opposed to having stolen from them. Afterall, it was their contract they paid me on, not mine.

"As you know, the original intent of that contract was that they would receive fifty million, and I'd get the same. Well, whatever. I'd pay fifty million to get back my life without their threat looming over my family and me. What do you think?"

"I think yes, Elliot. Hell yes! Let's get this done. We've got to pay the head of state, Yemi Muhammadu.

"Don't mess around with paying anyone but this guy. He's a military dictator who has the last word on this type of matter. Offer him the fifty million anywhere in the world he wants it, and I'll discreetly get him the money. He'll take it and run. Exceptionally astute as always, Elliot. Just brilliant!"

Elliot responds asking, "How is it that you know so much about Muhammadu?"

"Confidentially, I've got a banking friend in London who's an acquaintance with a banker who allegedly has been handling a bank account for the General's wife. Apparently, it's not their main account, but it's one of the bank's more sizable individual accounts. He gives me some interesting generic insight once and awhile as to what some of these heads of state are up to. The Nigerian General has a healthy financial statement and loves money. Especially US dollars."

Elliot, taken aback, angrily says, "I am astonished that you never disclosed this information earlier to me! You should have told me about this relationship months ago. Any bit of information would have been helpful to me. I lost Paul Norman to these bastards! Your confidential insight could have helped save his life, goddammit! This relationship could have assisted me with my deal with them. I'm really pissed! What else aren't you telling me?"

Ben, sincerely dumbfounded by the response, says, "Hold on, Elliot! I don't even know who the acquaintance is. I couldn't even recognize him if I saw him. I was told about him in total confidence and between friends discreetly talking shop about interesting customers and their stories. I could never have asked another banker to break our unwritten rule to violate the sacred confidentiality of a banker with their client, or a banker to another banker.

"Besides, the moment I would seek some kind of favor or insight, my friend would immediately stop being my friend and become my enemy. Do you think for even a second that I would ever divulge any information to my friend if he were to ask me to provide any personal information on you so that the Nigerians could use it against you! Have you gone crazy, Elliot? You owe me an apology!"

"You're right. I apologize, Ben. Nigeria and the loss of Paul make me a little crazy. Stupid of me!

"Please forgive me. Paul meant a lot to me. And God only knows how much I've suffered with that Nigerian deal. I understand your explanation. I realize that if there was anything that you could have done for me or Paul, you would have been the first to contribute. I hope my bone-headed comments won't affect us."

Ben, who understood Elliot's character since their college days, simply says with a warm and gentle smile on his face, "You idiot, I accept your apology."

With that exchange of words, this subject between these two true friends was over and the attention shifted to the real challenge of how to quietly make a deal with Muhammadu.

Elliot opens up by saying, "Mark knows the Nigerian Ambassador to the United States in Washington DC. We can arrange a meeting with the Ambassador through the current chairman of the House Foreign Relations Committee, who is very friendly with Mark. Due to the ongoing threat these assholes pose, we won't send Mark into an actual meeting at the Embassy with the Ambassador, but we will send one of our pricey Washington attorneys to explain the proposition to them. It's going to cost us quite a bit of 'gratification' money to the Ambassador, plus some serious campaign contribution funds to the Congressman, but as they taught me oh so well in Nigeria, that's just the price of doing business."

Ben, who is listening carefully, asks, "What if the Ambassador won't take the meeting?"

Elliot instantly responds, "Trust me, he'll take the meeting. When these crooks smell money, they'll move heaven and earth. Unfortunately, I'm going to make our request just a little more complicated. I'm going to throw into the deal the unconditional release of Stanley Roberts from jail along with the dropping of all charges against him."

Looking somewhat dejected, Ben says, "Not a little more complicated. You may have just killed any opportunity we had to make this happen. You're pushing too far, Elliot. You have to look after you and your family first. Roberts is a good guy, but if the only way to make the deal is to save your family and you, there's no doubt what you must do. I think you're making a tragic mistake to add Roberts into the equation. I'm telling you, take him off the table."

"Look, Yonatan is very close to sending in a clandestine group of mercenaries to break Stanley loose from jail. They may succeed, they may not. Stanley might get killed and so may some of our guys. The operations is going to cost at least a couple of million dollars paid by his family. I promised his daughter that her father was going to dance at her wedding, and I intend to make good on that promise.

"So, I either make a goddamn deal with this piece of shit General, or I do my level best to fish him out through Yonatan. The most practical way to succeed, and potentially save a bunch of lives, is to make the deal I propose. If it's not possible, I'll re-evaluate my options. You on board with me?"

"Yeah. I'm on board. But listen to me! I don't care what you promised his daughter. You owe it to your own daughters and your wife to end the threat to their lives and yours. They come first, and Roberts and his family follow. Do you understand me, Elliot?"

"Very clearly, Ben. I appreciate your looking after my family and me. You're my good friend and I will take your words seriously. Alright, let's get to work on this right away before Yonatan gets us all killed."

Chapter 12

Upon his arrival into Los Angeles, Mark had been fully informed by Ben as to the sale of the digital coins. He was apprised of the significant wealth that had been accumulated due to the liquidation of the cryptocurrency, making Elliot the newest member of an elite world club of billionaires. Additionally, he was briefed regarding the new plan to "buy out" the price on Elliot's head established by the Nigerian government.

Although Mark was never really in it for the money, he couldn't help but think about the fact that his shares in the Sterling Hedge Fund had just made him a millionaire. He didn't feel rich. He just felt free. Mark recognized that for the first time in his life, he could—on his own dime—do anything he wanted or travel anywhere in the world he desired. But what kept on swirling through his mind was that he didn't have anyone to share this new beautiful freedom with. Emma was the answer to this void.

Mark knew that from a practical point of view, it wasn't such a bad idea for Emma to try and make a life with him. But that's not what he wanted. He was determined to win over her heart. His fear was that she would reject him. Maybe it was asking way too much to set aside her love for Paul and the emotions of the child they would have had together. Well, as his great friend and mentor Elliot had consistently said to him, "plan for success, not failure". So, with that in mind, he got on the phone and called Emma, requesting to visit with her that very evening. To his great delight, she had said, "Yes."

The days had gone by quickly for Mark while in Los Angeles. In between settling an approved purchase agreement for the sale of Elliot and Felicia's estate in Bel-Air, he also was able to negotiate and get approved a contract to buy the Maple Street residence in Beverly Hills for a price of fifteen million. This was precisely what Elliot had authorized him to buy it for. Mark had sold the Bel-Air property at an astonishingly high value and bought the Beverly Hills home at what a "high-powered" broker on Canon Street described as a "bargain".

Mark had found time to privately visit the gravesite of his friend and colleague, Paul Norman. While at the grave, he couldn't help himself but to talk to Paul. He asked him for forgiveness. He told Paul that he would raise his child as if it were his own. He whispered to his friend that he would always love Emma with all his heart. He promised to take as good of care of her as he knew Paul would have.

As he shed a tear, this rugged, former Marine asked that Paul give his blessings to Emma, and to him, for the lives they intended to share together. After a moment of silence, Mark stood at military attention, upright with his chin up, chest out, shoulders back, and stomach in. He saluted his colleague, then left.

Everything he had been responsible of taking care of in LA was complete. The housing deals were done, and Emma's Trust documents had been signed before a notary assuring Emma's child of a very good life. Mark and Emma had completely changed their relationship from business-like platonic to planning a future together with love.

Neither one of them had to work very hard at it. Each had a sense of humor, and they laughed together as if they had known one another for many years. They naturally felt very relaxed and felt a deep sense of security together. Emma was at peace knowing that her child and her would be taken care of by a good man. Mark took great solace in recognizing the wonderful stability of having a solid life companion at his side. He gratefully had found what he had been looking for all of his life.

This part of Mark's travels had been perfectly executed, but the itinerary for the balance of his trip was about to be dramatically altered. Sitting in his five-star Beverly Hills hotel room, Elliot was about to brief Mark by phone about a dangerously ambitious plan to pay off a brutal dictator fifty million bucks.

Elliot begins the call by asking, "Mark. Everything well?"

"Yeah, boss, things are well!"

A curious Elliot goes on to ask, "And Emma. You guys figuring things out?"

"As a matter of fact, I think we are."

Elliot decides to not ask any more personal questions and says, "Thanks very much for selling my place for top dollar, then turning around and buying the Beverly Hills property at a terrific price. As your last name implies, you, Mr. Goldman, are worth your weight in gold. You're a phenomenal friend and a sensational negotiator. I'm grateful you play for us! You're also, by my count, pretty damn wealthy after our digital coin sale! Handsome, charming, rich. I'd say Emma made a smart choice."

Mark, who knows all the flattery is about to turn serious, says, "Okay, okay, enough of the bullshit. How the hell are we going to pull off paying probably the biggest bribe, oh, I'm sorry, gratification, in the history of Nigeria? We're not a country trying to transact a government deal with another nation.

"We're a private individual effectively paying off a guy to stop trying to kill him. Elliot, I don't think this is going to turn out so well. Have you thought this through? I mean, maybe you're better off spending all the gratification money toward a lot more security personnel. I just don't think you can make a deal with the devil and live to tell about it."

Elliot responds, "You may be right, but I need to give this a good old-fashioned try. My gut tells me he takes the bait. Even to a Nigerian dictator, fifty million dollars in some Swiss bank account sounds awfully tempting. I don't care who you are! Hey, listen, as far as I'm concerned, I'm just lawfully returning the money to the government since I lost my Nigerian national partner to death."

Mark, who burst out laughing, says, "Your partner, Chief Abba Balla, the dead guy you're referring to, was assassinated by the very same guy you propose to return the money to."

"Like I said, I'm returning the money to the Nigerian government due to the death of one of their citizens, which of course, I'm obligated to do."

Mark, once again understanding that the decision by his boss to pay Muhammadu was already made, surrenders by simply saying, "Alright, put me out of my misery, let's hear the plan."

Elliot, no longer joking, earnestly begins outlining the plan by initially saying, "Ben will depart for Latin America to conduct the Savor sales deal. He knows exactly your itinerary, who to see, and what to do. He'll pinch hit for you for as long as you need to be away. You are heading immediately to Washington DC.

"There, you will organize a meeting with the Chairman of the Foreign Relations Committee in the United States Senate. You will also be retaining a very high-powered international law firm with close ties to the Republic of Nigeria. These two will assist you in arranging for a meeting with your old friend, Ambassador Mohammed, the current Ambassador to the United States from Nigeria. The proposition will be made by one of you. I just haven't made up my mind as to which one of you."

Mark, who is just listening, finally says, "You have really lost your fucking mind! You can't possibly be serious about having one of us offer a bribe to the sitting Ambassador to call off a hit on your life.

"Elliot, this isn't going to work. First, no serious American attorney is going to openly offer gratification. Second, no US Senator is going to set up a meeting with the intention of paying off a goddamn head of state. For Christ sake, this is not an oil company doing a private deal in Nigeria for oil leases! The Ambassador is going to tell us to go to hell and then shoot one of us right on the spot!"

Starting to get upset, Elliot says, "Obviously, you're not listening to one goddamn thing I'm saying, right?

"So, this time, open up your ears and listen carefully to my words. First, I have verified that we are permitted by law to do exactly what I propose to do. I was granted special permission by the university to retain advise from the Dean of the Stanford University Law School, Anna Mann. Anna is a scholar of constitutional and international law. I outlined to her what we are preparing to do along with an explanation of the original intent of the Nigerian contract to equally split the proceeds with Balla.

"Her advice and counsel was that not only did I have a legal obligation to return the money to an authorized agent of the Nigerian government, but I had an ethical duty to do the same. So, what better agent is there than the head of state? Now, as you can see, you are the fucking fool and I have got this exactly right. Agreed?"

Mark sarcastically responds, "Well, I guess all those huge endowment donations you've made over the years to the university have finally paid off a nice dividend. But did you tell the good scholar that our fine head of state friend will be requesting your highly ethical gesture be wired to his private foreign bank account? Or did you forget to inform our well-educated dean that this son-of-a-bitch has ordered his hit squad to shoot live bullets at you with the goal of blowing your head off?"

"Yeah. She knows all about that stuff, including my generous donations. Now, listen very closely to me. We're doing this deal, with you or without you. You either get on the same page with me, or step aside, go to Latin America, and I'll fly solo without you. Do I make myself clear?"

Mark, regretting he questioned his friend and boss, simply says, "When do I leave for Washington?"

"You leave tonight on the red eye. You have a meeting tomorrow afternoon with one of the partners of the international law firm that Anna arranged for us. They have been thoroughly briefed and prepared. The partner will outline the correct method by which to conduct the return of the money to the General.

"Once you understand the structure for lawful payment to Muhammadu, you will be ready to meet with Senator Lindsey White, Chairman of the Foreign Relations Committee. His chief of staff has already been informed by Dean Mann that you will be requesting a meeting regarding organizing a visit with the Nigerian Ambassador. So, as you can see, we have thought this plan through a lot more than you give me credit for!"

Mark's sheepish response, "Sorry about that. Just trying to be sure we weren't making a big mistake. Okay, I own it. I screwed up. I shouldn't have questioned you. Just thought I needed to speak my mind. I was looking after my friend and our company. I got no more words of apology. We good?"

Elliot, smiling from ear to ear, says, "I just love hearing you say sorry. It never gets old. It's got such a beautiful ring to it. I've been enjoying this kind of moment since we were kids. Of course, we're good!

"Just get your butt on the plane tonight and use all your charm and brains to make this deal a reality. My life may very well depend on your success. I'll send you all the contact information for the lawyer and Senator via fax to your hotel in a few minutes. You can pick it up at the front desk. Since you've been to the Embassy before, I won't send anything on them. Make sure and call me after you meet with the attorney. Hey Mark, you know I'm just messing with you. I trust you with my life. Safe travels."

Mark is sincerely happy that he patched up his little scuffle with Elliot. He knew better than to challenge Elliot the way he did, especially after he had already made up his mind. As he thinks about it some more, he feels like such a fool questioning a brilliant plan that could represent the best way out for Elliot and his family from the imminent danger they face day in and day out. Mark recognizes that Elliot has specifically chosen him for this role, but more importantly, he owes it to Elliot to win.

Mark and Emma had previously planned to spend the entire night together before Mark was to depart to Latin America. With the travel plans modified, sending Mark to Washington later that night, he would need to break the news gently to his new-found love. Rather than by phone, Mark decides to tell her in person. He was determined to maintain her trust, and genuinely wanted to spend as much time as he could with her before heading to the airport later that night. Since Emma had prearranged with Mark to meet at her apartment after work around 6 PM, he decided it would be best to stick with that plan.

When Mark arrives at the apartment, he is greeted with a heartfelt kiss hello, along with a very upbeat Emma. She excitedly tells Mark that she has received a job promotion that same afternoon.

Her new job is chief of staff to one of the highest-level executives in the bank. Her paycheck is going to double in size and she is moving to the highest floor in the building. The sincerely thrilled Emma says to Mark, "Ever since you came into my life, I have security for my child, a high-paying job, and a man that I can share my life with. You've brought me nothing but good luck. I love you, Mark Goldman!"

Feeling a bit overwhelmed, Mark takes off his coat and says, "I love you too, but I don't think I deserve very much credit. Elliot Sterling merits your thanks concerning the kid. You fought for that promotion.

"It sure as hell wasn't me or luck. It's simply good old-fashioned persistent hard work. Now, your comment about 'the man I can share my life with'. Okay, that my lovely, radiant, pregnant future wife is completely accurate. And just so you know, it is me who is the lucky one from the day I met you!"

Emma, hugging Mark, says, "You are by far are the sweetest guy on earth!"

Mark says, "Hey, you hungry? Just needed to tell you something before we go."

With slight concern, Emma responds, "Starving. What's on your mind?"

Reluctant to address the issue, Mark slowly says, "There's been a change of plans regarding my travels to Latin America. Mr. Sterling needs me to go to Washington DC tonight. I'm so sorry I can't spend the whole night with you the way we planned, but I'm all yours for the next four hours."

Emma, who is expecting something way worse, says, "That's it?"

A very relieved Mark says, "Yeah, that's it."

Suppressing her giggle, Emma remarks, "Business before pleasure, my gorgeous prince charming. So, I've got a change of plans for you. We order food in, and we spend the next four hours together right here. Deal?"

"Yes ma'am. You got yourself a deal!"

The next few hours felt as if they were made in heaven until it was time to leave. As they are lying in bed, Emma grabs ahold of Mark and with a serious voice says, "Promise me you'll never leave me. I love you and I want to spend the rest of my life with you."

Mark looks right into her beautiful blue eyes and says, "I'm not going anywhere. You'll have me for as long as you want me."

Smiling, Emma asks, "What about my job? Should I take the promotion? Are we going to live here in LA or we are moving to Israel?"

The light-hearted Mark, now laughing, responds, "Take the new job for now while we sort out all of our plans. I don't expect to be there for more than a year. Mr. Sterling just bought a house in Beverly Hills. I plan to live with you right here. I'll speak to Elliot and let him know that I have to be here with you.

"He's not going to have a problem with that. I'll share my time between Israel and Los Angeles. Just know I'll be here with you when the kid arrives. Trust me, everything is going to work itself out."

Emma looks into Mark's big sincere eyes and says, "I trust you, Mr. Goldman. I trust you."

As Mark gets up out of bed, Emma asks, "When will I see you again?"

Mark answers, "As soon I finish my work in Washington, I'm coming back. Besides, I promised you an overnight stay! I should be able to get back here within a week. I'll call you every day."

With a smile on Emma's face, Mark hugs her and says his goodbyes with both feeling the security of a stable life partner. Each knew that this was the real thing and that they wanted to be with one another. They had found love even though neither one of them had sought it from each other.

It didn't take long for Mark to get back to his hotel, gather his things, and make it over to Los Angeles International Airport. The company private jet had been dispatched back to Israel to pick up Ben and fly him to Latin America for security purposes. Mark had boarded a commercial flight to make his way to Washington. The flight left on time and before he knew it, the five hours and fifteen minutes flight had touched down at Washington Dulles International Airport.

Mark had gotten a good night's sleep and was on his way to the very important meeting with the high-powered international lawyer, Gabriel Andrews. The prestigious, intricately designed black glass and granite constructed high-rise office building was located on the top floor near the White House on Pennsylvania Avenue NW. Mark was first greeted by a courteous receptionist, then met by Mr. Andrew's assistant who escorted him into a fabulously decorated conference room. She offered, then brought Mark a cup of coffee. Moments later, the attorney entered accompanied by a young lawyer.

Gabriel Andrews was an impressive man, standing six-foot four inches tall and dressed in a navy-blue pinstriped suit. He had a distinguished look about him and sported greyish long wavy hair. His pronounced wrinkles at his forehead showed years of experience. He stood erect and focused his bright blue eyes right into Mark's eyes as he extended his hand and said in his deep courtroom voice, "Welcome to Washington DC, Mr. Goldman. We have been remarkably well briefed by Anna Mann.

"We are prepared to proceed right into the heart of this matter unless you believe we should address something else first. Allow me to introduce you to Carrie Baker, she will be assisting me with this matter. Don't hesitate to contact her as you please."

As they all take their seats in the impressive conference room, Mark says, "It's my pleasure to meet you, Mr. Andrews and Ms. Baker. Yes, I do have one curious question I'd like to get your thoughts on. Has it been determined who will meet directly with the Ambassador?"

Andrews calmly responds, "No, not yet, but your name is at the very top of my list. Why, would you like to volunteer?"

"Who else is on that list?"

Andrews looks over at Carrie, then says, "You're number one because you know the Ambassador and the Embassy from your previous dealings. I'm number two, and Senator White rounds out the 'A' List. Any other suggestions?"

Mark, looking straight at Andrews, responds, "The list sounds about right, but I'm the only guy who has a chance of pulling this off. So, if Mr. Sterling approves that I be the one, then I'm your guy. I think the Ambassador will respect me, and he will recognize that I am very close to Mr. Sterling and our business operations. The only concern I have is whether I'll ever be able to walk out alive. Let's talk about that, and then let's discuss how the hell a private citizen wires fifty million bucks to a military dictator!"

Andrews sits up in his chair and addresses Mark's concerns, "I get that this government wants Mr. Sterling and everyone around him dead. I also get that individuals do not make payments to heads of state. Now, I assume that you understand that the Nigerian government accuses you folks of being the bad guys. They say you ripped them off for one hundred million dollars.

"I'm not going to pass any judgement on this situation. You say it's a legitimate contract and you're entitled to all the money. I haven't seen your agreement but you're my client, and if you tell me the money was made fair and square, then that's good enough for me. But, as you are well-aware, the Nigerians feel quite differently and they're willing to kill you for it. So, do we need to take serious precautions?

"Damn straight we do. But one thing I won't guarantee, and that's your safety. You could get killed. That's going to be on you, Mr. Goldman. Don't go if you are not prepared to take that risk."

Mark, who is listening carefully, says, "I heard your speech, but you forgot to inform me what kind of plan you have up your sleeve to save my life. Obviously, you must have that part of the game plan figured out. There's just no way you would have considered me being 'the number one' guy on your list to go into the Embassy and become a sacrificial lamb. Right?"

With a confident grin on his face, Andrews answers, "That's right, Mr. Goldman. We do have a plan. We just don't want your heirs blaming us for sending you into harm's way where something might happen.

"Consider this our way of informing you of the risks, and effectively obtaining a waiver from you since Carrie now has all this documented. So, if you decide to go, you're now on notice that you'll be doing this at your own risk."

Annoyed with the legal jargon, Mark says, "Could you please skip all your legal bullshit and get to the fucking plan! Oh, by the way Carrie, make sure to add into your notes my 'sacrificial lamb' comments, and please accept my apologies for my bad language."

Having accomplished the protection for his law firm that he required, Andrews begins outlining the plan, "Let me address the strategy for keeping you alive. We're going to send you into the Nigerian Embassy accompanied by Senator Lindsey White. These guys, no matter how ruthless they are, won't dare lay a glove on you in the presence of a sitting United States Senator. Stick to the Senator like glue. Never leave his sight while inside the diplomatic compound. We understand each other so far?"

"Yeah. Go on."

Andrews proceeds, "Senator White will be in charge of explaining to the Nigerian Ambassador that Mr. Sterling, at the urging of the American government, has voluntarily decided to return fifty million dollars, half of the contract funds. The Senator will advise them that this gesture is an act of good faith, since Mr. Sterling's Nigerian partner was killed leaving no one to distribute fifty percent of the contract funds too. He will explain that the fifty million will be returned, as it should, to the Nigerian Central Bank upon full acceptance by General Yemi Muhammadu of this arrangement. Any questions?"

Mark expresses one word, "Proceed."

"Of course, prior to the meeting, we'll get the message clearly to the Ambassador and the General that the funds are for the direct control and possession of Muhammadu. The bank wire instructions will be routed into a two-step structure. The first arranged destination for the funds will be a designated bank account located in Cypress with instructions indicating the second and final stop being the Central Bank of Nigeria.

"Of course, the General, having the power and discretion to act as he pleases, will take the funds off the wire in Cypress. Those funds will never see the light of day in Nigeria. Muhammadu gets fifty million without a trace, and the Sterling family entourage is no longer at risk!"

Mark looks over at Carrie then addresses Andrews, "Let me get this straight. Senator White and I jointly go to the Embassy. The Senator explains to the Ambassador that the General can grab fifty million bucks for himself off the wires at the Cypress bank transition stop even though the funds are documented to wire transfer to the Central Bank of Nigeria. It seems as if our working theory is that no one will ever say anything or recognize that the fifty million never made it to the Central Bank for fear that they'll be killed. Do I have this right? Is this what you're telling me?"

Andrews quietly answers, "Yes. That is correct."

With a wink and a smile, Mark says, "You're much smarter than you look! Alright, what's next?"

Carrie, who at this point has broken out into laughter regarding Mark's comments concerning her boss, takes over the conversation, "We have been in communication with the Embassy and the Senator's office. The Senator will meet with you in his office tomorrow afternoon at 2 PM. He has been fully briefed on this matter by his staff. By the time you get to his office tomorrow, the Senator will have the Ambassador well versed on the subject matter.

"Senator White has assured me that he has a prearranged conference call scheduled with the Ambassador tomorrow at 10 AM, which should result in positively influencing the General to accept the proposition. The Senator should have a firm date for the upcoming meeting with the Ambassador by the time you visit with him tomorrow. Do you have any further questions, Mr. Goldman?"

"Go ahead and confirm with the Senator's office that I'll see him tomorrow at 2 PM. Kudos to both of you on a well-structured game plan. It could very well work. I'm impressed, but I do have one question. What is going to stop the General from collecting his fifty million, then deciding to kill us off one by one anyway?"

Andrews understands that the question is astute and answers, "The reason your lives will be spared is because Muhammadu is going to sign an agreement with us before he ever touches our money. As your lawyer, I can't guarantee you anything, but I will assure you that the General will sign an agreement acknowledging that the fifty million dollars is being paid in full settlement of any claims the Republic of Nigeria may have against Mr. Sterling and or any affiliated entity. The agreement will be witnessed by the Ambassador of Nigeria.

"On top of that, the General will be asked to sign a personal side letter, similar to that of a pardon, which will absolve Mr. Sterling and affiliated entities of any crimes that may have been committed. This letter will include a definitive statement that Mr. Sterling, along with any member of his family or business will be welcome to visit Nigeria and conduct business whenever they desire. Effectively, Mr. Sterling will be exonerated from all wrongdoing."

Mark looks over at Carrie, then addresses Andrews, "I like the way you're thinking. Good words. Good thoughts, but here's my problem. These agreements and pardons, they're not worth the paper they're written on. If this bastard decides to renege on his word, he'll end up with our fifty million bucks; yet, Mr. Sterling and his family will continue to be hunted and possibly killed!"

Andrews, starting to look agitated and getting tired of Mark's pessimism, responds abruptly, "That, Mr. Goldman, is the price you're going to have to pay, although I'm very confident you're going to have it our way. Besides, the rumor is that Muhammadu and his government are not too far away from transferring power to a democratically elected President with an election within a year. What we propose is the very best option open to Mr. Sterling and his family. I suggest he grab it!"

Mark locks eyes with Andrews and says, "May I call you Gabriel?"

Andrew responds, "Sure."

Mark then seriously says, "You better be right, Gabriel."

A very self-assured Andrews says, "At the rates I charge, I'm rarely wrong."

Without a pause, Mark says, "Very good, Gabriel. Very good. Go ahead and write up your agreements. Please have them hand-delivered to my hotel so that I have enough time to review them before I meet with Senator White at 2 PM tomorrow. Pleasure meeting both of you. We'll be in touch after my meeting with the Senator. Thanks very much for your good counsel."

Chapter 13

Mark had spent the entire evening catching up on calls to Elliot and Emma. Elliot had dedicated most of his conversation toward trying to convince his close friend not to go to the Nigerian Embassy, fearing for Mark's life. All of this concern fell on deaf ears. Mark was certain that if he did not show up to meet with the Ambassador, there would be no deal. Feeling as if there could be some legitimate truth to his argument, and understanding that there would be no capitulation by Mark, Elliot simply dropped the dialogue and shifted to advise on what to expect.

Mark had informed Elliot that he had stuck to their plan of not informing Gabriel Andrews, or anyone else, of the Stanley Roberts matter. They both had agreed it was best to keep the Roberts situation silent until it was raised in the meeting with the Ambassador. The thinking continued to be that if his lawyers or the Senator new in advance of the Ambassador's meeting that Mark was going to throw in the release of Roberts as a condition of the deal, it most likely would result in a failed pact.

Elliot reiterated the point that if the General and his advisors prematurely knew that Elliot wanted Stanley Roberts' release from jail as a requirement of paying the fifty million, the General would most likely raise the hardline concept of treason. Not only would Roberts continue to face the deeper threat of conspiracy to defraud the Nigerian government, but this could directly impact the results of precisely the covenant that Elliot needed done for his own peace of mind. Muhammadu would now possess a "smoking gun" potentially proving "bloody treason" and drag Elliot into a foreigner's conspiracy to defraud the Republic of Nigeria. An act of treason punishable by Elliot's death.

The tricky part was how to raise Roberts' release request without effecting the fifty-million dollar deal.

Mark explained to Elliot that the plan was to outline the overall proposal to the Ambassador, then at the very end of the presentation, he'd say that there was just one contingency that must be added for humanitarian purposes. He would explain how the Central Bank had previously approved the original Sterling 100-million-dollar contract much prior to the actual payment date. He would argue that Roberts was just doing his job when he released the Central Bank's wire transfer to Sterling.

Mark would go on to inform the Ambassador that before his brutal abduction, Roberts had honorably retired from government civil service. It was well understood by his colleagues that he was in the process of immigrating to the United States where he was to meet his wife and children that were already in America. Mark would insist on Roberts' release without jeopardizing the main goal of the meeting.

Elliot felt that the Roberts plan, and the overall game plan, made sense. He wanted to warn his good friend that he should expect the greedy Ambassador and the slippery Senator to ask for money.

Elliot went on to say that the Ambassador would most likely ask for a 'gratification' amount for his cooperation. He also warned Mark that it wouldn't surprise him if the Senator had his hand out for a big amount of money too. Elliot made it a point to tell Mark that there would be no way out of the gratification. The key was to make it as small as possible, or barter something. As for the Senator, Mark was told to "tell him to go to hell!"

Elliot felt that if the Senator insisted on money and Sterling paid it, the Senator would forever have leverage over him. Elliot had a terrible feeling about what Senator White would be asking for and what he would expect of him. So, Elliot instructed Mark not play ball with the Senator if the bribe money request was asked for. He told him to gracefully say "No" to Mr. White the moment the request was made, and "Yes" to the Ambassador.

Mark had understood the advice Elliot suggested, but asked whether he should walk away from the Senator's meeting in his office without securing any of the Senator's participation and assistance.

Without any hesitation, Elliot had answered "Yes", adding that Mark would have total discretion to replace the Senator and add attorney Andrews to accompany him to the Embassy. Elliot went on to explain that he would call the Stanford Law School dean, Anna Mann, and have her contacts arrange the Ambassador's meeting as opposed to the Senator. This move would assure Mark the flexibility to read the Senator's demeanor, then make the decision as to whether or not to remove the Senator from the team.

Elliot assured Mark that Anna would clearly inform the Senator's staff not to pursue making any further arrangements with the Ambassador. She would have this all under control by the time Mark walked into the Senator's office.

With everything now well coordinated with Elliot, it was time for Mark to get some rest and prepare himself for both the Senator and the Ambassador. After a lengthy telephone conversation with Emma, the night had gone by quickly. It was now the moment to make the short trip by cab from the Hotel to the Russell Senate Office Building near the Capital. It was precisely 2 PM as Mark checked in with an assistant seated at the front desk.

Mark was politely welcomed by the Senator's staff. He was asked to wait in the seating reception area because the Senator was on the floor of the Senate casting a vote and was running late. After a near thirty-minute delay, a young pretty woman with a smile asked Mark to "please follow me".

Mark was ushered into Senator White's private office where he was asked to take a seat on a plush pastel yellow sofa. The office was formally decorated with exceptional dark cherry furnishings. It was adorned with unique accessories from the nation's most important heirlooms including several original oil paintings with ornate gold frames from the Senate's decorative art collection. As soon as he stepped into the office, Mark instantly felt the power of the Chairman of the Senate Foreign Relations Committee.

Within a few moments, a short, grey-haired, balding elderly man wearing a dark navy suit with a pin of an American flag on his lapel entered the room, extending his hand toward Mark and saying, "Please don't get up. Good to meet you! My name is Senator Lindsey White. Sorry I'm late, but the President had insisted on a 'Continuing Resolution' to keep our government funded for the next few months while he figures out what the hell to do after that. I've been here almost thirty years, and I still can't understand why we can't balance the goddamn budget. We don't need to be on the brink of shutting the federal government down every six months. Anyway, I'm pretty sure that's not why you're here, so what can I do for you?"

"Not sure I introduced myself. I'm Mark Goldman, an associate of Elliot Sterling."

The Senator responds, "I know exactly who you are, and I know exactly why you're here. So why don't we just cut right to the fucking chase. Sounds good to you, Mr. Goldman?"

Not knowing precisely what the Senator knows since Anna Mann took over, Mark says, "Of course, why don't you tell me what you might be able to do for us."

The Senator says, "Every time I deal with the Nigerians, it always involves their bullshit gratification. I mean, they don't even go to the bathroom without gratification. What's with these guys? Looks like you gentlemen need to pay off some 'Guinness Book' of world record gratification totaling fifty million bucks. Lordy, that's a shitload of money.

"And I guess you want me to make sure these bastards don't end up killing you guys, or something like that. You'd think that for fifty million dollars, you could bribe someone on your own. Who needs me? Also, I hear you need some kind of meeting with Ambassador Mohammed, or was that taken care of by your Stanford people? Yeah, sure, I can help you. Of course, you'll need to take good care of me. Your Mr. Sterling knows what I'm talking about. Do you?"

Mark stares back at White and says, "Senator, Mr. Sterling informed me that you should consider an amount that is reasonable. Of course, we know that the so-called Super PACs accept unlimited contributions. So, tell me, what's reasonable?"

The Senator, now liking what he's hearing, says, "Mr. Goldman, sounds like you also know what I'm talking about. Let me make this quick and easy for you guys. I arrange the meeting with the Ambassador. I organize the gratification to him and I make sure that we get the message to General Muhammadu that we got fifty million bucks for him in exchange for the Nigerians permanently taking the target off Sterling's back.

"After everyone gets their money, we all go home and kiss our wife, girlfriend, mistress, whatever, and the deed is done. Alright, so here's what I need. You guys contribute half of one percent to my PAC. Fifty million dollars multiplied by half a point equals two hundred fifty thousand dollars. If you say yes, send me over one hundred twenty-five thousand today or tomorrow.

"The rest you pay at the close when you wire the funds to the General. Agreed?"

Mark stays silent for a moment then says, "We never pay for services rendered upfront. We only pay when we see results. I'm pretty sure I said 'reasonable' as opposed to highway robbery. No, Senator, there's no deal."

With the Senator's face turning more and more red by the second, he says, "That's the price you'll need to pay to have the Chairman of the Foreign Relations Committee taking care of your nasty business. Now get the fuck out of my office!"

Mark, who wanted to get rid of this guy and was hoping for this kind of reaction, turns while leaving and says, "I joined the military believing that people who served their country did so with the higher purpose of making this nation greater, not for windfall profit. So, no Senator, you get the fuck out of the people's office that elected you!"

As soon as Mark leaves White's personal office, the Senator summons his chief of staff, Mitch Price, to immediately join him. He goes on to tell him that he doesn't trust Mark or Sterling and calls them "the enemy". He informs Price, "I want this guy Sterling brought before a Senate committee and investigated for possible international financial crimes. I'm pretty sure they have 'dirty hands' and I need to teach them a lesson. Nobody, I mean nobody, walks into my office and insults me like Goldman just did! Mitch, get them up against the wall, then squeeze them hard for the truth. I think a lot of shit is going on here that's going to assure me some excellent media coverage. Just the kind I've been looking for."

Mitch acknowledges his boss with a simple, "Yes sir. I'm on it."

As Mark is walking out of the Senator's office building, he doesn't know who to call first, Elliot or Andrews. He opts for Elliot and calls him on his cell. "Hello Elliot, it didn't go so well with the Senator. Senator White is a crook. He just tried to shake us down for a quarter of a million dollars. But that's not the worst of it, he wants half upfront, then the rest when we pay the General. For all I know, White could be working for the Nigerians. Let's not forget what happened in our first deal with this government when Congressman Jared Baron flipped on us over to the Nigerians."

Sterling facetiously responds, "Sounds like we didn't make a deal."

Mark says, "You got that right! In fact, White told me to get the fuck out of his office!"

Elliot, finding this story intriguing, says: "And did you follow his request?"

"Yes sir, except as I was leaving, I told him to get the fuck out of the office the good people in his State elected to serve. Anyway, we need Andrews to take his place. I'm headed over right now."

Elliot replies with a combined sense of seriousness and humor, "Yeah. I think you handled all this right, with the exception that the Senator has an ego the size of the continent of Africa. He also has a vindictive reputation. Call Andrews, then get your butt over there as fast as you can. Advise the lawyer as to what went down in White's office, and while you're at it, bring him up to date regarding how we want Stanley Roberts to be part of the deal. Keep me informed. We'll speak soon."

Mark realized that his own ego may have caused him to make an error with a powerful Senator like White and instantly calls Carrie Baker. He informs her that the meeting with the Senator was a disaster and he must urgently talk to Gabriel Andrews. Carrie, understanding that the situation requires immediate attention, simply says, "Come right over. I'll brief Mr. Andrews."

The attorney's offices are a short distance away, and before Mark could even organize all his thoughts, he is sitting in their conference room waiting for Andrews and Carrie. Mark gets up and greets them both as they enter, then gets right into what happened. As Mark replays the White meeting, he realizes that he unnecessarily antagonized a vindictive crooked politician with a tremendous amount of power.

Andrews and Carrie understood the gravity of the predicament right away, yet Andrews calmly addresses the circumstances, "Well, not your best moment, Mr. Goldman. I've had a few of them myself. My reading of the situation is like this. Senator White will not let this go. Brace yourselves for some kind of retaliation. If and when it comes, we'll help you with that. In the interim, let's concentrate solely on taking care of what you came here to accomplish. With the brilliant cooperation of Anna Mann, we have already organized a meeting with the Nigerian Ambassador set for tomorrow morning at 9 AM. Obviously, I will substitute myself in for the Senator. Carrie will advise the Embassy that I'm in and White is out. We'll take care of your safety."

Feeling as if he has betrayed the team, Mark says, "Thank you. I'm sorry that I exercised such bad judgement with the Senator. I'm a former member of the United States Marine Corps, and I believe that I allowed my duty to defend this nation to cloud my better judgement as to how to have professionally behaved while dealing with this despicable so-called public servant."

Andrews looks at Mark and sympathetically says, "No apologies necessary. I can assure you, we feel the same way! But not everything is that gloomy. Allow me to share some important news with you.

"General Muhammadu has been diagnosed with life-threatening lung cancer. Our sources tell us he'll be leaving office within the next three months. Rumor has it he'll be dead within six. Also, we have it on good authority that Ambassador Mohammed is on his way out too! He will leave his post on or before the next six months or less. Our assessment clearly indicates that the General and the Ambassador should be very motivated to take our bait. The timing couldn't be better!"

Listening to Andrews' comments brings a sweet smile of revenge to Mark's face, and only one word comes to his mind to express his feelings at that moment—the Marines' saying, "Oorah!"

Both Andrews and Carrie cannot stop themselves from smiling until Mark says, "We need to add a little something to our Muhammadu Proposal. For humanitarian reasons, Mr. Sterling will demand release from a Nigerian prison of his good friend, Mr. Stanley Roberts. He was brutally kidnapped and tortured while unlawfully detained. Stanley has been inflicted excruciating pain while in prison as punishment or revenge for having assisted Mr. Sterling in lawfully releasing his one-hundred-million-dollar contract. I really apologize for introducing this at the last minute and adding one more layer of drama to this ordeal. We have desperately tried to keep this demand silent due to the risk it might pose to Stanley and others in custody."

Looking a bit concerned with a frown on his face, Andrews says while maintaining his now familiar calm demeanor, "In my opinion, I'm reasonably sure that adding Stanley Robert to the proposition may very well kill your deal with the General. Let me tell you why. Dictators like Muhammadu are often driven by the symbolism of strength as opposed to being sensible. The act of releasing a 'traitor' like Roberts could cause a revolt amongst the influential people in his ruling party, even though he's got a short-term hold on power. This is a very tricky demand.

"On the one hand, he could be tempted to just do it since he is ill and on his way out of office. On the other hand, he might simply stonewall our request. So, if you want to pull the trigger on this demand, understand the consequences of perhaps coming away with an even angrier madman looking to gun you all down.

"This is the choice you need to make. I would advise to remove Roberts' from the equation at this time. We can perhaps deal with the Roberts' matter after we get what we need from the General. The timing feels off to me, but it's your choice. I'm prepared to pursue either track."

Mark glances at the expansive window overlooking the beautiful Washington DC boulevard, then looks at Carrie and finally into the eyes of Andrews. "Regrettably, we don't have time to wait. We are told that Stanley Roberts will die in prison any day now, if he hasn't already been beaten to death. Mr. Sterling told his family many months ago that he would do everything in his power to get him out of prison alive. He informed his daughter Adeleye to her face that she should advise her mother that Stanley would dance at Adeleye's wedding. Since you have never had the privilege of meeting Mr. Sterling, I will cut this conversation short—we ask for the release of Stanley Roberts as a part of our request. End of discussion!"

Andrews responds, "You're the boss. Do you bring it up to the Ambassador or do I?"

Mark says, "I'll handle the Roberts' demand for release, but don't hesitate to help me out if you see me in a jam."

Andrews then goes on to explain that the time differential between Nigeria and Washington is six hours ahead. He explains that they will be meeting the Ambassador at 9 AM making it 3 PM in Nigeria. Andrews informs Mark that it would be smart to have Mr. Sterling on standby in the event his approval was required. He also suggests that it is entirely possible that the General could very well be consulted at any time by the Ambassador during the conversation. Andrews informs Mark that he would pick him up at the hotel precisely at 8:30 AM in a black SUV driven by armed security personnel which would escort them both to the Embassy.

Andrews closes the briefing by informing Mark that as a precaution, he has arranged for security to drive him back to his hotel. He is firmly warned to order room service then stay in his accommodations until an armed security agent picks him up at his room to accompany him to the SUV in the morning.

Mark acknowledges the instructions, shakes Andrews and Carrie's hand, and proceeds to the hotel. As he is seated in the back of the SUV traveling the short distance to his hotel, he senses by Andrews' serious tone that there is a real concern over the possibility of a security breach. It worries him that he may be in danger of meeting the same fate as Norman, but then quickly eliminates the thought.

As Mark is rushed into the hotel by Andrew's security personnel, he can't help but notice from the corner of his eye that Senator Lindsey White is at the check-in reception area accompanied by a young blonde woman half his age. There appears to be no luggage, just a tall attractive woman wearing a tight red skirt and a sexy white silk blouse. Mark immediately recognizes the girl as the Senator's aide.

He can't help but laugh out loud when he notices what appears to be a newspaper photographer shooting a photo of the Senator as he places an official Senate file over her embarrassed face.

Mark settles into his room for the night. While he is waiting for his food to arrive, he calls Elliot to bring him up to date. Elliot is happy to hear Mark's voice. "So, how's my best friend doing?"

Mark responds, "I think we got this under control."

Elliot, sensing trouble, says, "What do you mean think? Either you do or you don't. Which one is it?"

"Andrews believes asking for Roberts' release is going to ruin the deal. He thinks the General may walk if we insist. The only thing we got going for us is that Muhammadu is about ready to kick the bucket and maybe he won't give a damn because he'll be leaving his office and the world within six months or so. Other than that, Andrews is under the impression that it shows weakness to release a 'traitor' to us."

Elliot, now laughing, says, "The asshole who ordered my death but ended up killing Paul is dying. 'Ding dong, the witch is dead!' He must have cancer. Couldn't happen to a nicer guy. This is music to my ears.

"Now, listen carefully to me, Mark. Roberts stays in the deal! Do not under any circumstances cave into their pushback or demands. If the deal goes sideways, we'll just keep our fifty million and wait him out. Fifty million bucks will buy us a small army of security. And who knows, even if we give this bastard the money, there's no guarantee that he won't still try to shoot me!

"Besides, I'm not throwing Roberts under the bus. This guy risked his life for us and I gave my word to his family to do my best to spring him loose. If we need to get him out under Yonatan's prison invasion instead of under this plan, then so be it. By the way, is it cancer?"

"Yeah, lung. Also, Andrews requested that you be available tomorrow by phone at 9 AM Washington time in case we need you for something. Alright, I know what to do. I just hope they don't kill me and Andrews with all these hard-ass positions. Hey, just kidding. I'll call you with the verdict."

Concerned for his friend, Elliot asks, "Did Andrews prepare the proper security for you? If you're going into harm's way, I don't want you going. Just send Andrews. They won't have the balls to murder him. Mark, I want you to pull out of going. I'm not taking the risk. You're out! Goddammit, I should have just sent that piece of shit Senator White along with Andrews!"

This time it's Mark who is doing the laughing. "Elliot, the Senator's schedule would not have permitted him to make our meeting with the Ambassador. He had far more important work to do than screw us out of money. You'll never guess who I saw checking into the hotel with his girlfriend this evening. You're correct. None other than the powerful Chairman of the Foreign Relations Committee.

"And believe me, the only thing on his mind was the beautiful, tall, and curvy blonde at his side. In fact, you might be able to see it in tomorrow's newspaper because I'm pretty sure a press photographer got a picture of the two lovebirds checking in. I'm sure he can't wait for his wife and kids to see the lovely photo. So, anyway, I'm going to the Embassy tomorrow. Andrews has the security angle handled.

"Nothing is going to happen to either one of us. Andrews can't handle this on his own. Besides, I need to assess the situation first-hand. Trust me, if I thought I was going to take a bullet tomorrow, that's the last fucking place I'd be. We're good, Elliot. We're good."

"Alright. Okay. Just remember that it's not just you anymore. Take into consideration Emma and the new kid. Besides, I wouldn't be able to live with myself if anything should happen to you at the hands of these gangsters. You sure you got this?"

The charismatic Mark responds, "Piece of cake. I'll call you tomorrow with the results."

Chapter 14

At exactly 8:30 AM, a man dressed in a black suit, white shirt, and black-tie knocks at Mark's hotel room door. Mark, who has already eaten breakfast, looks through the peephole and elects to open the door. The security agent simply says, "Good morning, Mr. Goldman. Please follow me."

The guard escorts Mark into a freight elevator leading to the back of the hotel where the loading dock is found. As they walk pass the loading dock, they enter a black SUV Cadillac where Andrews is sitting in the rear seat and says, "Sorry for the elaborate tour to get you here, but your boss gave me a call last evening insisting on beefed-up security. Then he called me this morning to make certain I did it. So, please do me a favor and let him know I did what he asks. It's apparent that he cares a whole hell of a lot about you, that's for sure."

The Nigerian Embassy is less than fifteen minutes away from the hotel. Once they arrive at the compound's gated and heavily armed entrance, they are greeted by a young black soldier with an automatic weapon who immediately requests everyone's drivers' license as a form of identification.

The soldier returns in short order and asks that the driver move his SUV into a specially designated parking space. The soldier informs Andrews and Mark that they are cleared to enter the Embassy and they will be shown into the Ambassador's personal office where their discussions will take place.

The Embassy is magnificent with large open corridors and extraordinary high ceilings. The exquisite original oil paintings and gorgeous granite flooring are meant to make a visitor feel as if they are in the company of influential people. The fresh flower arrangement at the entry foyer gives the place a sense of warmth and elegance. Of course, the interior design is intended to lower your guard and deceive the visitor into softening any tough position they were there to present.

The guard walks Mark and Andrews directly into the Ambassador's elegant suite. Mark had previously met with Mohammed in this very same impressive office under contentious circumstances related to the initial 100-million-dollar agreement. He remembers the high ceilings, the spectacular Baccarat Crystal chandelier, and impeccable décor. But it is the grand solid wood carved executive desk, where Mark had exchanged verbal counter-punches with the Ambassador, that is etched in his mind forever.

The Nigerian Attaché enters the room. Mark instantly recognizes the tall, distinguished, gray-haired black man resembling a diplomat cast straight out of Hollywood. They all shake hands and the Attaché says in his familiar British-style accent, "Welcome again, Mr. Goldman, and welcome to you, Mr. Andrews. I will state quite candidly that I never expected to ever see you again, Mr. Goldman, but such is life. Please take a seat," as he points to a professionally decorated lush apricot-colored sofa.

Mark candidly says to the Attaché, "Last time I saw you, I thought you told me you were looking to retire. What the hell are you still hanging around here for?"

The Attaché chooses his words carefully, "Sometimes, assisting people through public service is a much higher calling than anything I can think of to do."

The Attaché then addresses the two men, "The Ambassador has set aside a few minutes for the both of you. He will be brief and to the point. Please organize any thoughts you have, but do not approach the Ambassador unless acknowledged."

Mark, who doesn't much care for diplomatic formalities, sarcastically asks, "Why, is he contagious?"

The Attaché, now getting a little annoyed by the comments, says, "You don't want to find out."

Once they are seated, it doesn't take long before Ambassador Mohammed enters the private office. Just as the first time they had met, the Ambassador immediately makes eye contact with Mark and says, "I remember you, Mr. Goldman. You verbally insulted me and you were very ungracious. I'm quite intrigued as to why you risked returning to this office given our past dealings. You must really need me, don't you?"

Paul Norman's image flashes before Mark's mind as he uninhibitedly responds, "You're not the first Nigerian I've insulted, and I'm pretty damn sure you won't be the last. As far as 'ungracious', if I recall, Mr. Ambassador, you were the one who changed your deal, then shoved it up our ass without giving us any option other than to accept your bullshit offer. Or did I get that wrong?"

Andrews, who is nervously worried that Mark is about to get them both killed, steps in, "Mr. Ambassador, we did not come here to exchange insults. Quite to the contrary. We're here to discuss the possibility of a truce between the Sterling organization and the Republic of Nigeria. Now, before we get started, let me inform you for the record, the American FBI, State Department, and Members of Congress have duly been advised that we are having this visit. Of course, we let them know solely as a precaution.

"Although they do not know the particulars of our meeting, they do recognize that one of Mr. Sterling's close associates was murdered in cold blood in front of his home and that one of the suspects may be linked to the Nigerian government. Again, we let them know that we were paying you this visit in the unlikely coincidence that no one ever saw us again. Alright, so with that having been said, why don't we get down to business. Shall we?"

All of a sudden, Mohammed starts laughing loudly. "You really think we we're going to kill you in our Embassy, then dispose of your bodies? You Americans really are crazy! Besides, what terrible publicity! No, we granted the meeting so that you may handsomely contribute to Nigeria's economy."

Andrews says, "Very good. Let us reiterate the deal. We are prepared to reimburse fifty million dollars to the Republic of Nigeria via 'Swift' bank wire routing instructions previously provided to your staff. As far as Mr. Sterling is concerned, the ultimate destination of the funds will be designated to the Central Bank of Nigeria. Now, if for some reason, those funds are lifted off the wire by one of your official government agents prior to hitting the Central Bank, that will be, of course, entirely up to your government.

"We're going to wire as instructed by the Central Bank. In exchange for the return of the fifty million dollars, you will provide us with a receipt for same, and you will sign an agreement acknowledging that Mr. Sterling has fulfilled all obligations expected of himself, and his company. Upon receipt of this payment, Mr. Sterling and his companies will be secure against any legal liability for their actions, and the original contract will have been deemed completed in its entirety. We will receive your personal assurances that Mr. Sterling and his family, along with his business associates, will no longer be targeted as your enemy. Do we understand each other so far?"

With a puzzled look on his face, the Ambassador answers, "What do you mean by 'so far'?"

Andrews turns to Mark and says, "The floor is yours."

Mark looks straight into the eyes of Mohammed and says, "We want you to release Stanley Roberts from your prison. He's an innocent man that has no business being in jail. Let him go!"

The Ambassador glances at Andrews, then looks straight back into Mark's eyes and says, "Who the hell is Stanley Roberts?"

"He's a political prisoner that you guys have associated with having nefariously assisted us in getting our 100-million-dollar contract paid. His crime is that he did his job. We're asking you for humanitarian reasons to release him. He's innocent, and I'm fucking certain you know who he is!"

The Ambassador glances at Mark for a moment, then says, "It sounds to me as if you owe this Mr. Roberts something, not just simple humanitarian gratitude. I can't help but to think to myself, why do you people care so much? If Roberts is in prison, it's certainly none of your business. There must be much more to this story! Why on earth would you even consider exchanging Mr. Sterling's peace of mind for that of a person you might have met perhaps once or twice in your life. Put yourself in my shoes, this makes no sense."

Mark says, "It's none of your business. You guys have no sense of decency, so why should I expect you to understand our reasons to ask for Mr. Roberts' release?"

The Ambassador calmly says, "Try me."

Mark, sensing a trap, just says, "Here's our deal, you get fifty million, you stop chasing us down, and we get Roberts. That's it, no more bullshit!"

The Ambassador quickly says, "I hear you, Mr. Goldman. That's fine, no more distractions. You'll need to pay a gratification of one percent of the fifty million, or shall I say five hundred thousand dollars. That payment will be made directly to me at the designated bank account of my choice. I can assure you that this money does not all come to me. Many governmental agencies and government officials will need an incentive to cooperate allowing for this plan to be seamlessly executed. Do not ask me to discuss this fee any further. It is not negotiable. Do we have an arrangement or would you like to hear my second option?"

Mark looks over to Andrews, then Andrews stares at Mohammed and says, "I didn't realize there was a different option. So, yes, by all means, let's hear the second option."

The Ambassador sits back in his chair, clears his throat, and says, "You are correct, Mr. Goldman. I am quite aware of who Mr. Roberts is and what prison he resides. Stanley Roberts was once considered a rising star in the Nigerian government. Well educated at Stanford University and a man with a photographic memory. We gave him the full power to release contract funds at the Central Bank of Nigeria.

"Unfortunately, his love for America became much greater than that of his native country. We think he made a deal with Mr. Sterling to release his contract even during our serious civil unrest when we needed every dollar we could get our hands on. Roberts was looking after his own self-interest instead of that of his country. He sold out Nigeria to you instead of looking out for the best interest of our nation. Stanley Roberts is a traitor, and he should be hung for treason, not released! Why don't you simply leave Roberts to us? Drop him from your request and we will complete our arrangement."

Mark jumps in, "I thought you had a second option. What is it?"

"Well, I really didn't want to get into it. I'll admit, it's somewhat hypocritical, but since you insist, I'll explain. My brother-in-law is in charge of the prison where Stanley is being held. I believe you call that position in the United States, 'warden'. Our leader, Yemi Muhammadu, is on his death bed. We don't think he has even a month to live.

"So, Mr. Goldman, this presents a very interesting opportunity for Mr. Sterling and me. Fate has created this moment and perhaps you can seize on the timing. Here is what I propose. Since our head of state is dying, I suggest that you save yourself forty-five million dollars. The General will never know what happened. He will be dead. I will make certain that his successor will never bother Mr. Sterling again. My brother-in law will officially make arrangements to have Stanley walk out of the prison a free man. He will be picked up by one of our people and driven one hundred miles to the nearest airport. Stanley will get on a plane provided by you and whisked off to freedom in America. All that service for just five million. You save forty-five million. Interested?"

Mark looks up at the ceiling, crosses his arms, glares at Andrews, and says, "Do you get paid after we get Roberts out of Nigeria?"

The Ambassador answers, "Partially. I receive a down payment of five hundred thousand immediately. This will cover some of my initial expenses. Upon my confirmation to you that we have a specific date for Roberts' release, you will transfer two million dollars to my bank account in London, England.

"The moment Mr. Roberts is confirmed to be identified by his family at the United States airport where his aircraft has landed, you personally, Mr. Goldman, will escort my designated agent to your car parked in the airport parking facility. There, in the trunk of your car, will be baggage containing two million five hundred thousand dollars in cash. That equates to twenty-five thousand one hundred-dollar bills. You will hand over those bags to my agent and the deal will be done. You get Stanley, Mr. Sterling and family are no longer our target, and I get my five million dollars."

Stunned at the detail by which this son-of-a-bitch had thought through 'option two', Mark says with a grin on his face, "Sounds like you didn't give this much thought. Tell me, what happens if the General lives? I'll answer that. You'll have five million bucks, Stanley will be walking around free in America, but Mr. Sterling will still have a big target on his back, worse than before because he's going to get accused in some way of colluding in Roberts' release. You can't assure me Muhammadu is going to die. In fact, you can't even assure me that Roberts will walk free on the date you'll give me. And you know what, you aren't even able to guarantee me that the new regime, after the General's alleged death, won't decide to kill Mr. Sterling anyway. Your deal sounds pretty one-sided, don't you think?"

Getting tired of Mark's insults, the Ambassador angrily responds, "Take it or leave it, Mr. Goldman. That's the risk you'll need to take. If things don't go as planned, I will die in prison for treason. This is the risk I will take. Now you have exactly ten seconds to give me your answer!"

Mark expresses absolutely no emotions. He had been taught by Elliot that your face is your sword, so he remained outwardly composed, but felt shaken by the time urgency placed upon him by the Ambassador. He understood the ramifications and consequences of the wrong decision. Not only were people's lives at stake, but he could very well get scammed for an enormous amount of money in this high-stakes poker game. He has ten seconds to process his decision and wastes no time using his brain.

He doesn't even glance at Andrews for fear of giving any impression that might be misinterpreted by the Ambassador.

The first thought that crosses his mind is that paying out five million in lieu of fifty million is a no-brainer if Mr. Sterling achieves the same results. Mark focuses on the simple fact that they could pay out fifty million and there really is no guarantee that Roberts would be released, or that Elliot would no longer continue to be on the Nigerian government's 'most wanted list'. Mark calculates that the payout structure would minimize their losses to two and a half million as opposed to five million.

If Roberts never made it out, the second two million five hundred thousand would never be paid. The worst-case scenario was that Elliot would lose two and half million, Roberts would be killed, and Elliot would still be hunted. The best-case scenario included Roberts would be freed, Elliot's target would be lifted, and the Sterling Hedge Fund would save forty-five million dollars. His decision was made.

Mark looks into the eyes of the Mohammed and says, "We'll give you what you ask with some minor adjustments. All five million dollars will be paid via bank wire to your designated bank. The payment structure will be the identical method we proposed to the General, except that the General's name will be replaced with yours and the amount will be five million dollars.

"Mr. Andrews will prepare an agreement that outlines our deal. As far as we're concerned, we will be legally returning to the government of Nigeria five million dollars as the negotiated settlement of our old contract. As soon as you sign Mr. Andrews' new agreement, we will transfer the first five hundred thousand. When you provide Mr. Andrews with the official release date for Mr. Roberts, we will wire you the next payment of two million dollars.

"The final payment consisting of two million five hundred thousand will not be in cash, it too will be a wire transfer to your designated bank. You are welcome to send your agent to Mr. Andrews' office to witness the final bank transfer upon Roberts' successful return to the United States. Any questions?"

The Ambassador says, "Yes. I do have a question. Are the wire transfers to the Central Bank of Nigeria or are they to me?"

Andrews, who understands that Mark wants to make the transaction legally clean for Mr. Sterling, answers for Mark, "Just as we had proposed for the General, we will do the same for you, Mr. Ambassador. Each bank wire will be organized with two designated stops. The first stop will be the bank of your choice, the second will be the Central Bank of Nigeria. You, as the named government power of attorney, will be granted the right to lift the funds from the bank wire at the first stop.

"You will collect all five million dollars at the first stops, and no money will ever make it to the Central Bank of Nigeria. No one in the Nigerian government will ever be privileged to know about these funds or the bank wire structure, except you. If you do what you say, you will receive all five million dollars. My office will assure you of that. Any other questions or comments? Do you accept?"

"Very well, Mr. Goldman and Mr. Andrews, I accept. I want your agreement by 5 PM today. I will contact my brother-in-law by secure communication this afternoon, and we will sign the agreement this evening. I will expect your first wire within forty-eight hours from the full execution of our agreement. Trust me when I tell you that General Muhammadu is on his death bed. We must act immediately. I will receive you back in my office at 5 PM."

Upon shaking everyone's hand, the Ambassador simply gets up and leaves the room without uttering another word. Likewise, Mark and Andrews stand and make their way toward the entry door to the Ambassador's private office. They are immediately met by two Nigerian Embassy armed security guards who escort them to the main entry of the Embassy. From there, they are taken to their vehicle and whisked off the compound toward Andrews' office.

As they are making their way back, Andrews says, "Well done, Mark. Very well done. You were under enormous pressure to make a split-second difficult decision, yet you stayed cool and made the right one! Not only did you save the Sterling businesses a ton of money, but you're going to get Roberts out alive without having to fire a bullet. I think all the threats regarding Mr. Sterling and his family will cease in their entirety. I'd say, Mark Goldman, you've done a magnificent job. Congratulations!"

"Well, thank you, counsellor. I appreciate the words, but only time will tell how good a decision it really was. We'll see whether events go our way. Alright, so I guess I just stay at your office while you put the agreement together, then we'll go back to the Embassy together for the 5 PM meeting to sign."

Andrews responds, "Sounds like a plan. Carrie will arrange an office for you to conduct any work you may have. You'll have the privacy to call Mr. Sterling and brief him on how we have modified the Nigerian deal. It would be very good if you would procure Mr. Sterling's approval.

"Additionally, I would like Mr. Sterling to forward to me a signed power of attorney granting you, Mark Goldman, the full rights to sign the final agreement I draft."

Mark tells Andrews, "Just give me the power of attorney form you want him to sign and I'll get Carrie to assist me in faxing the document over to Elliot. We'll have that for you within thirty minutes."

Once back at the law offices, Andrews goes right to work while Carrie walks Mark to a private office.

Mark instantly calls to brief Elliot in detail regarding how they are going to save forty-five million dollars, and that it would be smart to inform Yonatan that the planned raid to free Roberts is very likely not going to be necessary. He goes on to advise Elliot that he'll be sending him a power of attorney granting Mark the right to sign the Ambassador's agreement. Elliot listens carefully and does not ask one question. The only comment he makes is, "Good job. You've done a good job, Mark. Send me the power of attorney the moment you receive it, I'll sign it, then get it right back to you."

As Mark is waiting for Andrews to finish his work, he couldn't help but think to himself what a tremendous amount of confidence Elliot has in him regarding such a risky venture that includes his wife and children's well-being. Mark took this kind of responsibility personally and was determined to make certain that the Ambassador had the power to deliver on his promises. He is anxious to get back into the meeting with Mohammed to get a final gut feeling as to the truth.

In the meantime, Carrie efficiently forwarded the power of attorney to Mr. Sterling and received it back signed. She brought in the copy of the power of attorney and informed Mark that Mr. Andrews was in the process of his final review of the agreement. She advises Mark that Andrews would join them shortly, and that Mark would be permitted to read the final agreement prior to the Embassy meeting.

Within a few minutes from Carrie's comments, Andrews walks into Mark's makeshift office and hands him the final document, saying, "I apologize for the last-minute review, but I needed every moment I could get. This agreement is a heck of a lot more difficult than I thought it would be. I'm confident I got it right, but we're working with tight time constraints and I did the very best I could to keep the Sterling Hedge Fund clean from any future legal issues. Additionally, I was very careful to reserve our rights to legally pursue these guys in American courts if they don't do what they say."

Mark took the next twenty minutes to read the agreement. It seemed that Andrews had captured the essence of what was agreed to, but the truth was that it didn't much matter what was written on that piece of paper. What really mattered was that Elliot, his family, and the Sterling business personnel were potentially free from assassination.

Additionally, it was clear that Stanley Roberts would soon be liberated, but the question remained, would he? And was the Ambassador really in it just for the two and a half million? Only time would tell. So, with a heavy heart and a lot of doubt, Mark looks up at Andrews and says, "The agreement is very well drafted, but does the Ambassador have the will and the power to deliver on his word? If he is lying to us, he'll walk away with two and a half million dollars and a lot of people could find themselves dead! So, let's get on over there and try to read between the lines as we interact with this guy in person."

Carrie says, "The SUV is parked in front of the building ready for both of you to join them. Before you leave, let me remind Mr. Goldman that we were willing to give the Nigerians fifty million dollars for effectively the same deal. The only difference is we're paying five versus fifty, but of course, we've got to trust the Ambassador as opposed to the General. For whatever it's worth, if I had to lay a wager between the two, I'm placing my money on the Ambassador. Follow me to the SUV."

It doesn't take long to arrive back to the Embassy. After checking in with the guards at the entry to the compound, they park the SUV in the same location as before and are then escorted to the Ambassador's private office where they are asked to wait for him to arrive. It took an annoying thirty minutes before the Ambassador made his presence.

As soon as Mohammed joins the room, Mark hands him the signed power of attorney along with the new agreement and suggests that the Ambassador review the documents. Without saying anything further, Mohammed takes the documents in his hand and walks directly out of the room, leaving Andrews and Mark guessing.

It doesn't take long before a young Nigerian man dressed in a black pinstriped suit with a white shirt walks into the office and states in what sounds like a British accent, "The Ambassador is in the company of our attorney reviewing the documents you have presented him. He will return to visit with you upon his completion. Please feel free to make yourselves comfortable. Thank you."

It takes well over an hour before the young Nigerian official re-enters the office saying, "The Ambassador has sent me to inform you that the document review is in its final stage of analysis. He will be joining you shortly. Thank you for your continued patience."

Mark looks at Andrews and says, "This bastard is downright rude. Who does this kind of shit? I'm inches away from calling the goddamn agreement off. I'm really getting pissed. Who the hell does this joker think he is?"

A very composed Andrews responds, "He thinks he's the Nigerian Ambassador to the United States of America, and you're sitting in his Embassy knowing that you need something from him, so he's going to do whatever he pleases. That's who he thinks he is."

As Andrews completes his sentence, the Ambassador returns to the office without his attorney and says, "I apologize for the delay, but Mr. Andrews has a very well-respected reputation in Washington DC for protecting his clients well. So, we took our time to review the documents carefully and find them reasonably written. We will sign the agreements with one condition. You must be prepared to wire me the initial deposit of five hundred thousand dollars by tomorrow. If that is agreeable, I will sign your contracts this evening. Do you, agree Mr. Goldman?"

"Sure. Go ahead and sign. We'll get you the money by tomorrow, but I have a condition for you too."

Staring annoyingly at Mark, Mohammed says, "Very well, my good friend, Mr. Goldman, what is your condition?"

Mark asks, "How will you guarantee that the Sterling family and their associates will be safe from Nigerian attempts to harm them?"

The Ambassador says in a flippant manner, "I thought you had a condition as opposed to a question. We'll do the best we can to keep your Mr. Sterling and related people alive."

Mark, who is irate with what sounds like frivolous disregard for the sincere safety of Elliot and his family, says, "Listen to me carefully, Ambassador Mohammed. I guarantee you that you're going to receive every penny of the five million dollars you bargained for. Now here's my condition. If Mr. Sterling, or any member of his family, or any person in his company, should ever find themselves dead, or so much as a scratch laid on them by your people, we will hunt you down and we will kill you. This is not a threat, Mr. Ambassador, consider this a fact. Now, do you clearly understand my condition?"

Without agitation, Mohammed states, "I respect your fierce loyalty to your boss, but let me explain something to you about the Nigerian government culture. If someone within my government is still targeting the Sterling entourage after the General has passed, I guarantee you that I will have been exposed as a traitor to the country and will be long dead before you shall ever even get a chance to hunt me down. One thing you can rely on is that our goals are mutual.

"Now, let me address you, Mr. Goldman. I don't like you, but I am confident you will fulfill your promises to me out of your deep loyalty to Mr. Sterling. So, I will sign the agreement now, but then I do not want to see or speak to you again. All remaining communications will be conducted through Mr. Andrews. Good evening."

Mark retorts, "You don't need to like me, just make sure my people stay alive, then all's good."

Chapter 15

The deal with the Nigerian Ambassador was signed as agreed and settled for Elliot at a bargain price. Andrews was left in charge of the relationship with Mohammed and given the enormous responsibility of saving Roberts' life. The question that Mark kept spinning through his mind as he was flying back to Los Angeles to spend some time with Emma was whether the Ambassador would stay true to his word.

He certainly had enough incentive to get it right, but would he? It wasn't going to take too long before the moment of truth regarding Roberts' release would be revealed.

Mark had informed Elliot of the final deal points and his boss was one hundred percent behind all the decisions. Elliot had given Mark a heads up that a Canadian cryptocurrency exchange reported that it could not repay at least two hundred fifty million dollars to clients after its chief executive had mysteriously died suddenly while visiting India. Simultaneously, the United States Congress had enacted a law strictly regulating all digital coin transactions over ten thousand dollars to be reported by American citizens to the government.

Those two events caused an earthquake in the cryptocurrency market, causing a freefall in the value of digital coins back down to less than one hundred dollars per coin. All earnings were wiped out overnight and the investors had immediately begun filing lawsuits throughout the world. Some investors in Israel had publicly questioned how it was that just one brand new hedge fund operating in Israel had sold its entire portfolio for "well over a billion dollars" before the collapse.

Media rumors were surfacing claiming that the Sterling Hedge Fund had "insider trading privileges" and would be eventually charged with "criminal misconduct". Elliot was deeply concerned that this bad publicity would drag them into time-consuming government investigations both in Israel and the United States.

As he was flying to California, Mark understood that things were going to get rougher regarding government oversight of the Sterling Hedge Fund. The fact that they had made a huge profit, catapulting Elliot into the billionaire category, while his fellow investor colleagues broke even, put an instant target on Elliot's back. People from all over the world were dying to know exactly what Elliot knew when he decided to sell while everyone else decided to hold.

The scary truth was that the fundamentals dictated that the cryptocurrency was destined to fail due to eventual government intervention. The irony was that the politicians were the ones most eager to conduct the investigating, yet it was the anticipation of their future regulatory policies that prompted Elliot to sell his entire portfolio.

Politics and jealousy were about to rule the day as opposed to the merits and great vision of a stellar businessman like Elliot Sterling.

Mark was very grateful that Elliot had suggested he go back to Los Angeles to be with Emma even though the heat was building around the worldwide collapse of digital currency. He remembered that Elliot had told him to "bring her back to Israel if you think that would be best for the two of you, but get back here ASAP." Elliot never exaggerated the urgency of a matter unless it was actually urgent.

So, when he said to Mark "this crypto thing may blow up in our faces real soon due to many politicians having lost while we won", Mark instinctively understood the matter was serious.

The plan was for Mark to spend two days in LA with Emma while he waited for Benjamin Yaalon to arrive from Latin America. Benjamin had completed an incredibly successful business trip selling the hell out of the Savor, adding to the rapid growth and wealth of the Sterling Hedge Fund. The private jet would be serviced in Los Angeles for a day, then would be boarded by Mark and Ben for the flight back to Israel. Mark had thought through whether Emma should return with him, but decided that she would be better off staying in LA until Mark diagnosed the depth of the political challenge.

The time spent with Emma was precious. Mark and Emma had fallen deeper in love and Mark had decided that he was ready to marry her a lot sooner than he had expected. He told her that he wanted Emma to leave her job and come live with him in Israel for as long as Elliot needed him there.

He promised her a nice home and a good life for the baby. Mark told her that he would make whatever kind of wedding she wanted, big or small, in the US or in Israel. They both decided that the timing was right and that she should provide proper notice to her employer. Mark made it clear that he would return to Los Angeles for her within a few weeks and that she should prepare herself to come live with him in Israel.

The flight back to Israel in the corporate jet with Benjamin went by quickly due to all the business chatter between the two of them. Before they know it, they are sitting in Elliot's office in Caesarea drinking some coffee when Elliot walks in, greeting them both with a handshake and a hug while saying, "You guys look like you've been on vacation. You both look terrific! Your telephone briefings sounded to me as if your situations were in constant chaos. I expected to see two dead-tired old men.

"Instead, I see two fresh faces, both looking to conquer the next big challenge. All kidding aside, you guys both did phenomenal jobs that were beautifully executed!"

Mark butts in, "We're just doing our job, Elliot, but frankly, you're the one who actually looks a bit worn out. We're here to help, what the hell is going on?"

Elliot looks down at his desk and grabs a subpoena delivered to him by his attorney, Yitzhak Bennett.

The subpoena had been issued to Mr. Elliot Sterling, President of Sterling Hedge Fund. The document required Elliot to testify as a witness before the United States Senate Committee on Banking of which none other than Senator Lindsey White was the acting chairman. He also pointed to the front-page headline of a New York newspaper reading: PRESTO. A MILLION BECOMES A BILLION.

Although the headline was actually funny, Elliot was not laughing. He explained to Mark and Ben that the subpoena also came with a huge laundry list of documents requested to be reviewed by the Senate staff including "any and all documents related to Yair Erdan". Elliot was not worried about the legitimate purchase or sale of the cryptocurrency, but was sincerely concerned about the smear tactics, which were sure to question his integrity and that of the Sterling Hedge Fund. This type of high-profile, bad publicity would be terrible for his personal and professional standing in the business world.

As Elliot hands the subpoena to Mark and the newspaper article to Ben, he says out loud, "We're going to need to aggressively defend the integrity of our company, or else our enemies will paint an ugly picture of us. We can't allow people like Senator White to perceive us as weak or having anything to do with insider trading.

169

Our worldwide customers and business relationships dictate that our reputation for conducting ourselves be of the highest commercial standards. We can't afford to have our Latin American or African clients buying the Savor perceive us as shady. I need to go to Washington and set the fucking record straight in front of that group of morons that sit on the Senate Banking committee.

"I'm positive newspapers like *The Washington Post* and *The Wall Street Journal* will have a field day covering a story like this. I refuse to be the punching bag for all of these assholes!"

Mark, who always gets pumped up when the boss is ready for a big fight, says, "These bastards have no idea who they're messing with. You're one of the wealthiest men in the world and you got nothing to hide. Go kick their butts!"

The more conservative Benjamin remarks in his thick Israeli accent, "Perhaps we don't need to be quite so, how do you say, belligerent? Maybe we don't need to be so contentious. Sometimes just a quiet, but intelligent explanation might serve us best. Don't you think?"

Almost in unison, both Elliot and Mark answer, "No!"

After several weeks of intense preparation for the Senate Banking Committee hearing, Elliot, Mark, and Yonatan landed at the Dulles International Airport in Virginia near Washington DC. They came well organized for what promised to be a circus with the ringleader being Lindsey White. Their lawyer, Gabriel Andrews, had done a terrific job working with the Senate staff, and Elliot felt as if he was ready for the hardball questions he was about to be asked the next day at 10 AM in the largest hearing room located in the Dirksen Senate Office Building adjacent to the United States Capitol.

Although Elliot was very concerned that Andrews had not heard a single word from Ambassador Mohammed on the fate of Stanley Roberts, he chose to stay focused on the business at hand. Elliot understood that he had his hands full with the hearing and elected not to confuse things by mixing in the Roberts' matter. He would deal with Mohammed after the hearings were over.

Yonatan kept a very close eye on the security of Elliot and Mark as they entered a waiting black sedan Cadillac for their travel to Andrew's office for some final preparations before the all-important hearing the following day. Mark seemed uncharacteristically quiet and Elliot decides to call him out on the weird silence by asking, "So, why the long face?"

Mark says, "It's not the right time to talk about it. Let's talk later."

Elliot, who has known his buddy since childhood, responds, "Okay. Cut the bullshit, what's up?"

"I feel responsible for Stanley. I'm afraid he's dead and that son-of-a-bitch so-called ambassador scammed our money. The press would have reported by now whether General Muhammadu has kicked the bucket. He's obviously still alive, even though that asshole told me to my face that he was on his death bed. I just can't take the thought of telling his daughter and his wife that we failed, let alone knowing that I lost you a ton of money. Just having a hard time with this, but let's just concentrate on White."

Appreciative that Mark is taking the potential loss of company money and the well-being of a perfect stranger like Roberts to heart, Elliot responds quietly, "That's right. We concentrate on White, then we go after the Ambassador. I guarantee you that Yonatan will get to the bottom of all this.

"Don't worry about the money. I would have given it to him myself, just the way you recommended. While we're battling the Senators, remember what I have always told you, your face is your sword. We'll take care of business here, then we'll go fish out Stanley with or without Mohammed. We understand each other?"

Mark snaps back into himself and says, "We're not taking any prisoners at the Senate!"

Elliot, now smiling, says, "That a boy! By the way, did I ever tell you that your face looks like my ass?"

Mark, now laughing aloud, says, "Yeah, I've heard your comparison before."

The final preparation with Andrews and his team of attorney went smoothly. The lawyers threw grueling practice questions at Elliot and helped structure his responses over and over again until Elliot had the correct answers down perfectly. After helping edit Elliot's brief opening statement, there was nothing more to do but get a good night's rest and face the Senators' questions the next day.

It was a gorgeous morning in the nation's capital as Elliot and his entourage entered the famous Senate Hearing room. Elliot felt confident with his team that included Andrews, Carrie, Mark, and Yonatan.

The room was a blend between classical tradition and modern aesthetics. The walls featured rich walnut wood panels as guests entered through imposing heavy bronze doors featuring impressive dark bronze lighting features. The granite flooring and columns throughout had all the trappings on power.

The Senators' seating was elevated similar to a judge in a courtroom. They sat in dark red leather beefy executive chairs behind a beautifully designed over-extended walnut curved desk.

The committee was made up of twenty-five Senators, thirteen Republicans, and twelve Democrats. The Chairman was Senator Lindsey White, the right-wing ultra-conservative Republican. As he enters the room, the clicking and camera lights from the numerous photographers become evident as Elliot is seated at a small desk with a temporary nameplate facing the Senators that simply said, "Mr. Sterling".

The hearing is about to commence.

White pounds the gavel twice demanding silence and states, "The Senate Committee on Banking shall come to order." He goes on to explain for the record the reason for the hearing and then faces Elliot. "Please stand, Mr. Sterling. Raise your right hand and I will administer the following oath: Do you solemnly swear or affirm, under penalty of law, that the testimony that you are about to give is the truth, the whole truth, and nothing but the truth, so help you God?"

Elliot simply replies, "Yes."

The Chairman then says, "You may be seated. I understand you have a brief statement you'd like to make for the record. So, go ahead, the floor is yours."

Elliot then says, "Thank you, Mr. Chairman, members of the Committee, and your staff for the many courtesies extended to myself and my associates. I would like to begin by being unconditionally clear."

"At no time have I ever participated in any form of insider trading or any other illegal act or unethical act related to why you have requested me to come here. Yes, I made over a billion dollars trading in the cryptocurrency market. Every penny was earned lawfully and ethically. I sold the digital currency when our internal matrix model told me it was time, not because I knew something from someone that gave me an unfair advantage. In fact, I alone made that decision based on the fundamentals. I assure you, there was no insider trading, just good old fashion hard work and precise timing. It was actually a very conservative decision.

"Finally, I will leave you with a very important observation, or perhaps I should call it a prediction."

"Undoubtedly, there will be many cycles in the volatile world of cryptocurrency. I experienced a cycle whereby digital coins never did establish the financial backbone necessary to give the currency the stability it needed to sustain investor confidence. The reason I sold my inventory was due to the fact that I had no confidence that the American government would in the short term be able effectively regulate this form of currency. So, I made the decision to sell sooner than the rest of the investors."

"No collusion, no insider trading, and certainly no laws or ethics broken. Simply put, my hunch happened to be correct. Anyway, here's my prediction. Within my lifetime, when government regulation over digital coins are well established and that fact combines with the right economic cycle, the world will witness a guy who will be the first cryptocurrency trillionaire. And, Mr. Chairman, I can assure you, that I'm going to be one of those investors working pretty darn hard to end up being that guy.

"I have nothing further, Mr. Chairman. I'm prepared to answer any of your committee's questions."

The Chairman, who hasn't forgotten the contentious meeting he last had with Mark and Andrews in his office, says matter-of-factly, "Thank you, Mr. Sterling, for your brief statement. We will now enter the question and answer period of the hearing. I will use my prerogative as Chairman and will be the first member to ask the witness a series of questions. Each member will be allowed five minutes to ask the witness questions. We will recess for lunch, and if necessary, we will reconvene back here for the balance of the afternoon."

Chairman White, looking serious with a no-nonsense look in his eyes, begins with a hard-hitting below the belt question, "How would you compare your ethics and collusion standards during your cryptocurrency trading to the one hundred million contract where you seemed to have ripped off, oh, I'm sorry, defrauded the Nigerian government? And who gave you the insider trading information on that sham of a deal?"

Sterling glances at Andrews while thinking to himself that his suspicion of this hearing being more about revenge as opposed to public oversight is verified by the question, and calmly says, "Not so sure you have your information straight. In fact, it sounds like you very well may have paid someone for a dossier regarding my organization and myself who has provided you with inaccurate material. If I were you, I'd ask for my money back."

As soon as Elliot makes the "money back" comment, the entire gallery of visitors seated behind the witness table and the Senators erupts into laughter. The embarrassed Chairman, hearing the laughter and the smiles on some of the Senator's faces, pounds his gavel and shouts, "Order! There shall be order in these chambers! I warn the visitors that you must control yourselves. This is not a movie theatre. This is the United States Senate conducting a serious inquiry into the possibility of corruption and flaws with the regulation of our currency. There is nothing funny about this hearing. Any such outbreaks as I have just witnessed shall revert in me exercising my discretion to remove each one of you. I trust I've made myself clear!"

Senator White grabs a glass of water, takes a sip, and continues his aggressive line of questioning by stating, "Ever since you, Mr. Sterling, emerged onto the international scene, we got ourselves three dead US Congressmen. Your own brilliant attorney has been assassinated in front of your home. Your accomplice working for the Central Bank of Nigeria, the guy you allegedly paid off to wire you one hundred million dollars from the Central Bank, is being tried for treason and is about to be hung!

"Now how in Sam Hill is it that you invest just four hundred thousand dollars and by voodoo economics, you make one hundred million bucks? I'll answer that question for you. It's the same way you appear to have rigged the cryptocurrency market by investing a few measly millions and selling that off for billions! You are a master currency manipulator, aren't you, Mr. Sterling?"

Puzzled with what Nigeria has to do with digital coins, Sterling places his hand on his chin, thinks for a moment, then calmly responds to White, "Sorry Senator, but I'm not too sure what a 'currency manipulator' means, and since I sincerely don't know what the heck that is, my answer to you is no, I'm not. Now, just in case you weren't listening the first time, your information is false. Your allegations are slanderous. In fact, I'd be careful if I were you because the man sitting directly behind me is arguably the best attorney in all of Washington DC. I pay him quite a bit of money to advise me."

"I noticed that he was taking a bunch of notes as you were giving your reckless, unsubstantiated, and defamatory remarks. I assure you, Mr. Chairman, that if you continue down this path, I will be seeking legal counsel regarding your libelous accusations. This is not intended as a threat, please accept it as a fact."

White, who enjoys a good old-fashioned brawl, sarcastically answers, "Oh, I'm so concerned I offended you. We have so much evidence backing up my statements that you might be better off saving your money on legal defense and just stipulate to my comments! You may intimidate a lot of people Mr. Sterling, but I will assure you, you don't scare me. From this point forward, I'll ask that you please save the long-winded editorial comments for some other venue. Just answer the questions! Now here's my next inquiry. Why did the FBI place you under investigation for money laundering?"

Sterling grabs the mic and says, "There you go again, Senator, getting your facts wrong. The FBI opened an investigation into the death of Congressman Jared Baron and his two Congressional colleagues. I volunteered to be interviewed by the FBI to discuss whether I could shed any further light on the Congressman's dealings with Nigeria and his tragic death while visiting that nation. I answered the FBI agents to the best of my memory."

"Eventually, the FBI closed their file on the Baron matter, and unconditionally released me from any further questions. I reiterate. The FBI was investigating Baron, not me! And I still don't understand how Nigeria has anything to do with cryptocurrency!"

Senator White states, "It's your pattern of behavior that concerns us. This pattern is going to lead us to evidence that will assist us in investigating potential criminal conduct that this committee believes you may have participated in regarding cryptocurrency trading. Let's face it, Mr. Sterling, nobody invests ten million bucks and within a few months realizes a profit in excess of a billion dollars unless something fishy is going on. Believe me, we're going to find out what happened.

"We're just going to follow the money until we unravel the truth. My time has expired, and I yield to my colleague from California, Senator Richardson."

The Senator from California was a long-time acquaintance of Elliot and very comfortable with Elliot's long-established integrity for telling the truth. Senator Richardson simply asks, "To your knowledge, or that of your attorney, did you break the law regarding your Nigerian contract?"

Elliot responds, "No sir, I did not."

"And to the best of your knowledge or that of your attorney, did you break any laws regarding your trading of the cryptocurrency that made you over one billion dollars?"

Elliot answers, "No sir, I did not."

The Senator then abruptly says, "I have no further questions. I yield the remaining portion of my time. Thank you, Mr. Sterling."

The Chairman then says, "The Senator from Arizona is now recognized."

"Thank you, Mr. Chairman. Mr. Sterling, when did you first learn about the digital coins potential trade opportunity?"

Elliot stares at White seated next to the Arizona Senator and becomes suspicious that the two have collaborated on some perjury trap; he responds truthfully, "My Israeli attorney informed me that he had invested in the digital coins and told me that the developer of the coins, Yair Erdan, was attempting to find an investor for ten million dollars to take the cryptocurrency public. I met with Mr. Erdan who advised me that I could lose all of my money, and that he would provide no guarantees as to the potential success of the coins. I agreed to take that risk, and the rest is history."

The Senator does not follow-up the Erdan question, but instead randomly asks a question that only White would have known to ask, "Are you in the process of arranging a fifty-million dollar pay-off to the sitting Nigerian head-of-state?"

Without any emotion, Elliot responds looking back at the Senator and says, "No sir. I'm not."

The Senator then glances at White, insinuating that maybe he should stop from asking the next question, but nevertheless continues and states, "I'll remind you Mr. Sterling that you are under oath.

"Would you like to amend your answer?"

Elliot, now staring back at the Senator firmly says, "No sir. No need for that."

The Senator, who is clearly looking confused, nervously continues with his next question asking, "Who killed your attorney and why?"

Elliot, disgusted with the question, which had absolutely nothing to do with digital currency or the purpose of the hearings says, "The murder of my friend and attorney is the subject of an ongoing investigation, and under my counsel's advice, I have no further comment."

White, observing that his colleague was making no progress, steps in saying, "The committee will take a fifteen-minute recess."

After what felt as if an hour had passed, only Chairman White returned to the chambers. After everyone took their seats, Senator White addresses the room saying, "During the recess I had an opportunity to talk to the members of this committee and we have unanimously decided to postpone these hearings until next month. There are some Senators that would like to take a little more time to complete some further investigation based on some of the facts that were presented here today. So, we will resume this hearing in approximately thirty days. I'm going to excuse the witness at this time, but will expect the witness to return upon our request without further subpoena. Do you agree Mr. Sterling?"

Elliot looks back at Andrews, then says, "One moment Senator."

Andrews approaches Elliot at the witness table whispering back and forth for a couple of minutes. They conclude their conference and Elliot responds into the mic by saying, "That would be fine Mr. Chairman so long as Mr. Andrews' office is submitted a formal letter requesting my presence and providing a minimum of three weeks-notice to appear."

An agitated White says, "We're not asking you Mr. Sterling, we're demanding you to appear. You're not some privileged guy who gets special treatment. Since you are obviously unwilling to cooperate, let the record show that we will resume this hearing thirty days from today on the first Monday following said thirty days. We will issue you a subpoena with that date and deliver to your attorney. This hearing stands adjourned," as White bangs the gavel and abruptly stands and leaves the committee room.

With a smile on his face, Elliot stands to face Mark, Andrews and Yonatan as a swarm of reporters begin shouting questions at Elliot. Andrews comes to Elliot's rescue by saying to the reporters, "Please give Mr. Sterling a moment to collect his thoughts and we will meet you shortly outside these chambers in the hallway to answer your questions. Thank you."

As Elliot starts walking toward the hallway he says to Mark and Andrews, "I can't understand why this son-of-a-bitch White is acting like such a lunatic. I mean, this guy is dangerous. I don't know what happened when you guys met with him, but he's a madman with an axe to grind. We're going to need to get very tough with this guy because he's coming after me with everything he's got. We've got thirty days to figure out where he's coming from, and what we need to do to get him under control. I'm assuming, Mr. Andrews, you're going to figure that out for me. This man is out for blood."

Andrews responds, "We'll be ready for him. Now, are you ready for the press?"

Elliot says, "Piece of cake," as he steps into the hallway where the press is waiting for him like a pack of wolves.

The reporter from the main Washington DC newspaper shouts out, "Mr. Sterling, Mr. Sterling, everyone who invested in the same cryptocurrency as you did either broke even or lost money; how did you manage to make well over a billion dollars?"

Elliot answers the question, "Timing is everything! Of course, it doesn't hurt when you're not greedy and you sell into the strength of the market. I was firmly convinced that governments from around the world were aggressively preparing how to regulate digital coins. When the United States Congress decided to seriously look into regulatory action, I knew it was time to sell my position."

A heavy-set reporter with his greyish hair combed straight back asks, "Are you currently under investigation in Israel for insider trading?"

Elliot answers, "No, I'm not, unless you know something I don't know."

A well-recognized national correspondent for a major cable news network then asks the obvious question on everyone's mind, "Why is it that Senator White keeps implying that you're a crook?"

Elliot, who is annoyed at the question, simply answers, "You'll need to ask him."

The same reporter follows up, "The Senator has essentially determined that you have committed a crime. Do you think he's right?"

Looking straight at the reporter and deciding that he wanted to take the attention away from the recurring 'crime' questioning, Elliot decides to throw a curve ball at the mob of reporters.

"The other day Senator White was spotted with what appeared to be an attractive young female staff assistant checking into a ritzy hotel here in Washington. Now, just because he was at a hotel with allegedly his pretty assistant doesn't mean he's having an affair with her, right?"

The tactic worked to perfection as the reporters started barking out question after question regarding the incident ranging from the name of the assistant to wanting to know what she was wearing. Several of the reporters ask almost in unison, "Did you actually see the two of them together at the hotel, or were you simply told about the sighting?"

Seeing that he has accomplished his goal, it is now time to get away from discussing anything further about Senator White on record and Elliot says, "I have no further comment."

As if they had previously rehearsed, Andrews takes control and confidently addresses the news media, "Thank you all for your astute questions. Mr. Sterling is anticipated back here within thirty days. Please submit any written questions you might have to my law office and we'll be certain to get you a response as quickly as possible. We'll see you back here in thirty days."

As they make their way down the hall and out of the Congressional office building, Yonatan receives a call from the driver of their car, who advises them that the Capital Hill Police would not allow any parking in the reserved witness stalls due to overflow related to an event at the Capital being conducted by several Republican Senators. The officer directs them to the nearest parking garage located on Constitution Avenue. The driver suggests that they take the pleasant walk over to the garage because Constitution Avenue is in the midst of heavy construction work and the street is very congested.

Their plan is to meet on the third floor of the garage in the first parking stall adjacent to the elevator.

Yonatan thinks for a moment then addresses Elliot, "I just received a call from the driver of the car. He's telling us to walk over to the TQ+ Parking where he'll meet us on the third floor. I do not like this idea. We're wide open targets. I do not like the risk. We can take a taxi to the parking facility."

Andrews, who is very familiar with TQ+ Parking, says, "Don't be ridiculous! The parking facility is really nearby. I use it all the time. We certainly don't need a taxi! Besides, we could all use a good walk and some fresh air. Enjoy the scenery! Let's walk. Besides, the road construction will take the driver forever to get here. Tell the driver we'll see him in a few minutes."

The walk is actually very pleasant. The majestic Capital dome is magnificent to observe. The surrounding cherry trees are a beautiful sight. As they arrive at the parking facility, Yonatan seems relieved that there has been no incident, and vocally expresses his gratitude that his decision to allow the walk was the right one. Just as they are about to exit the elevator and turn toward the first parking stall, Yonatan senses danger. While simultaneously putting his arm out withholding anyone from exiting the elevator, he whispers to Elliot, "I don't see the driver!"

Within a moment of making that comment, a black man with an automatic weapon steps out of the car. Instinctively, Yonatan turns and tackles Elliot on to the floor of the elevator. He screams at Mark and Andrews, demanding that they drop to the floor. As bullets are flying every which way, Yonatan has the presence of mind to press the elevator button directing to the street level. While the elevator doors are closing, bullets are deflecting off the doors, with one ricocheting into Yonatan. Although Yonatan does not complain while the elevator is slowly making its way down, Elliot sees blood on his suit, prompting him to say, "I think I've been hit!"

Very alarmed, Mark says, "Hang in there. Don't move. We're going to get you out of here!"

With all the chaos going on, Andrews is calmly on his phone calling the Capitol Police and informing his office to arrange for an ambulance. As they reach ground level, Mark asks Yonatan to give them instructions, but notices that he isn't moving. He immediately realizes that Yonatan is bleeding from the left side of his body. It isn't Elliot who has been shot, it is Yonatan.

Instantly, Mark takes command saying, "Okay, everyone listen up, Yonatan is hit. It's not you, Elliot. Slowly, get Yonatan as comfortable as you can on the floor. Keep his head up and keep talking to him. Gabriel, stay on the line with the police. Nobody get off the floor. I'm going to keep the doors closed because I don't know where these assholes are. So, let's just stay put until the police get here. That's our best bet. Keep your hand on Yonatan's wound. Make it work like a tourniquet. You need to try to stop or control the flow of blood."

Mark grabs Yonatan's handgun and prepares himself by studying the firearm in the event he may need to use it. Elliot keeps talking to Yonatan, but Yonatan is not responding while the blood keeps flowing.

Although there is a pulse, Elliot fears the worst as they all sit on the floor of a cramped elevator, wondering whether any of them would get out alive.

Chapter 16

Three weeks passed since the tragic and senseless death of Yonatan. He was buried in the Mount of Olives adjacent to Jerusalem's Old City. The cemetery was the most ancient and most important Jewish cemetery reserved for very special people. Yonatan had served his country with military distinction and earned his right to be buried with the nation's celebrated citizens.

Elliot, Mark, Gabriel Andrews, and what seemed like hundreds of people attended Yonatan's final resting place. It was a moving moment when one of the top generals in the Israeli Defense Forces told of the brave and honorable life Yonatan had lived while eulogizing him. Little did Elliot understand the depth of the heroic history of his now deceased security consultant.

As he sat in his comfortable office at his home in Caesarea that afternoon, he kept replaying the events of that horrible moment immediately following his testimony before the Senate Committee on Banking.

Sitting in that elevator holding onto Yonatan, sensing that he would never make it to the hospital. That moment would forever be etched into his mind. Waiting to determine who would arrive first, the assassin or the Capital Police, had seemed like an eternity. Then came the shootout between the police and the killer where the bullets were striking the elevator door. And finally, the moment of truth as Mark, Elliot, and Andrews simply looked at each other without uttering a sound as they wondered what their fate would be that afternoon.

The sensation of hearing the words from the brave police officer who banged on the elevator door, saying, "It's over! It's over! You're safe!" These words, along with the image of the ambulance stretcher carrying the lifeless body of Yonatan, would live on in Elliot's soul for as long as he lived.

While sitting on a couch in his private office sipping Cognac, Elliot kept reading, over and over again, the Capitol police report confirming that his driver had been shot and killed, most likely in the garage, while the assassin waited for Elliot to arrive. The working theory pieced together by the police suggested that the

181

driver was caught by surprise at gunpoint somewhere near the Capitol as the driver casually waited for Elliot. The report suggested that the killer forced the driver to call Andrews and instruct them to come to the garage. Once the assassin had exploited all that he needed from the driver, he coerced him into the back of the SUV and shot him.

Since the assassin was killed and the driver was dead, all the police could do was speculate as to what might have happened. One thing for sure was that Elliot was very bitter about the whole ordeal.

Yonatan was dead, an innocent driver was murdered, and it appeared as if the Ambassador had stolen a ton of money from the Sterling Hedge Fund. No one had heard anything from Ambassador Mohammed, and to add insult to injury, General Yemi Muhammadu apparently was still alive.

Elliot could not figure out why the Nigerian government continued to place a price on his head, especially since everyone apparently had agreed to cooperate. The only explanation he could come up with was that the Nigerian right shoe had no idea what the left shoe was up to.

It felt like a coincidence that at the very moment Elliot was replaying in his head the Washington DC tragedy, Gabriel Andrews was calling from Washington DC. Elliot answers the phone, "How are you, Gabriel? Anything new?"

Andrews answers, "Yes Mr. Sterling, I have some information to share with you. I just got off the phone with Ambassador Mohammed. He informs me that the assassin was a mistake. The killer had been prearranged prior to Mark and I making the deal with the Ambassador. The assassin's orders were never rescinded because the General was dying and no one called it off!"

Andrews continues, "It became public knowledge that you were going to be testifying in Washington DC before the banking committee, and a low-level uninformed Nigerian government official mistakenly was responsible for the hit. The Ambassador expresses his heartfelt condolences for the outrageous and senseless killing of Yonatan."

Elliot responds with disgust in his voice, "Tell the Ambassador to shove his condolences up his ass. Yonatan is dead and his family grieves him dearly. They took the life of a great man and they should pay the consequences for his horrific death. Tell him to save his 'collateral damages' explanation for his son-of-a-bitch General. That bastard's government has cost me two of my very best men.

There are no words that will convince me that these people are anything less than terrorists!"

Andrews responds, "I feel the same way, Mr. Sterling, but nothing is going to bring your attorney or Yonatan back. Regrettably, this is the heavy price that was paid to conduct business with a ruthless military dictatorship. If there is any consolation, let me advise you that General Muhammadu died this morning. You have nothing further to fear. The government has declared fair and free democratic elections.

"Your previous dealings with the Republic of Nigeria are history. No one will ever bother you regarding your previous contract. The Ambassador has effectively had his contacts scrub the records effecting you and your company. This nightmare is over. Oh, and one last point, Mr. Sterling, the Ambassador has assured me that Stanley Roberts is alive and will be released from prison one week from today."

Emotionally having a difficult time processing this incredible news, Elliot asks, "Are you sure!"

Andrews says, "One hundred percent sure. In fact, I've got more sensational news for you. The Senate Banking Committee informed me that the hearing regarding you has been postponed indefinitely!"

Elliot looks at the receiver of his phone as if to imply that he couldn't believe all the newly received noteworthy information being communicated through the phone. "Let me get this straight. Roberts is about to become a free man. The General is dead. I'm no longer a Nigerian target. And White is calling off the Senate hearing! Any other disclosures?"

Uncharacteristically emotional or excited, Andrews answers, "No. I mean yes. Well, no to your question on any other disclosures. Yes, you accurately described the new facts."

Elliot digs further by asking, "Do you mean to tell me that I can get on the phone to Roberts' family and confirm in no uncertain terms that Stanley will be released? Do you have any idea how tumultuous this would be for Roberts' wife and children if it wasn't true? If you give me the green light to call Stanley's family right now, then I'll believe everything you're telling me. Do I make the call?"

Andrews says, "Be my guest. Call them."

Elated, Elliot composes himself, thinks for a moment, and asks, "Do you believe I should call the family now or wait until Roberts is airborne en route to the United States?"

Andrews answers quickly, "Wait until he's in the air. He'll be verifiably safe, and on his way to his new home."

With a broad smile on his face, Elliot says, "I agree, Gabriel. I was just cross-checking to see how smart you actually are. Alright. Tell the Ambassador that he's earned the balance of his fee, and that it will be paid pursuant to our agreement. I'm going to need a way for you to keep me very well informed on all of these latest moves. Don't think for a minute that I don't blame myself for the horrifying death of Paul Norman and Yonatan. You're right, Gabriel, I chose to get involved with the devil and I'll live with the consequences forever!"

Slightly over a week passed since Gabriel Andrews delivered his monumental good news on so many important fronts. Elliot wanted to believe that everything that Andrews had stated in that critical conversation was true. But the only confirmation so far was that several major cable news networks had reported the death of General Muhammadu. There had been no word on Stanley Roberts and there was very little formal confirmation indicating that the Republic of Nigeria was moving forward toward free democratic elections.

Elliot was becoming more and more skeptical with the lack of information regarding Roberts. Only the Ambassador knew the truth and it was about time Andrews confronted him in order to find out what the hell was going on. As Elliot is preparing to call Andrews, Mark—who recently arrived in Israel from Los Angeles—walks into Elliot's private office and says, "I think the Ambassador has set Roberts free! Andrews has been trying to get a hold of you, but your cell phone doesn't have any reception. I tried to call you and it goes to some dead spot. Anyway, it looks like Roberts walked out of his prison about four hours ago. As planned, he was secretly transported away from the prison and is, as we speak, aboard a British airplane en route to London. He will change planes in London then fly directly to San Francisco arriving there tomorrow at 6 PM.

"Andrews said to tell you to go ahead and let his family hear the good news! He also told me to tell you to inform his wife, and his daughter, Adeleye, that he has lost an enormous amount of weight. He is frail, in poor health, and has several broken bones that did not heal properly."

Elliot simply replies, "Give me your phone, Mark."

Mark hands over his phone, then Elliot dials Andrews' number. Within seconds, Andrews answers the phone, "Hello, Mark. Did you inform Mr. Sterling?"

Elliot interrupts, "This is Elliot Sterling. I need to hear it from your mouth before I call Adeleye!"

"How are you, Mr. Sterling. I trust everything is well with you. We have through some back channels confirmed that Mr. Roberts is on the airline's passenger list. As we speak, he's en route to London.

"Additionally, we have confirmed that Mr. Roberts is registered to be on the British Airlines flight from London to San Francisco due to arrive tomorrow at 6 PM. No one from our sources have actually seen or spoken to Mr. Roberts because the Ambassador changed the method by which Mr. Roberts was to be transferred from the prison to the airport. I can report that the Ambassador has personally assured me, in no uncertain terms, that he is free and on his way to the United States. Although he was not given any money or even a cell phone, for whatever it's worth, I believe Roberts is on that plane."

Concerned with the fact that no one had actually spoken to or seen Roberts, and that Mohammed changed the prison pick-up and airport routing plan, Elliot says, "Look, it sounds like Stanley is free, but I'm positive you won't bet your life on it. Until his family identifies this man in San Francisco, anything is possible. Yet, against my best instinct, I will inform the family that Stanley is on his way to America. I'm going to do it for three reasons. First, I don't think you'd be advising me that you trust the Ambassador unless you were very confident it is Stanley Roberts aboard that aircraft.

"Second, I'm confident you would never put me in a position with Stanley's family to raise their hopes that he was alive and coming home, unless you were sure of what you were telling me. Not only would you be placing me in a deeply humiliating position, but you would be torturing the family. I realize you're not guaranteeing Stanley's return, but you might as well have, because there's no turning back once I advise the family.

"Finally, as a practical matter, his family needs to be present at the airport to warmly welcome him home. For God's sake, Mr. Andrews, I hope he steps off that airplane in California!"

With no hesitancy, Andrews confidently says, "Tell Adeleye to go pick up her father tomorrow, but please warn her that he is frail and just released from a cold-blooded prison."

Elliot is silent for moment, then says, "Is Stanley going to live, or did Mohammed play me for a sucker by charging me a fortune knowing full well that the Nigerians were releasing him only because he's dying anyway? The Ambassador and his cronies could collect from me even though Stanley is so sick and battered that he's about to die."

Andrews answers, "We're about to find out that 5-million-dollar question. We have no clue until his family gets him to a medical facility for evaluation."

Elliot responds, "Alright, fair enough, but here's how I want to play this out. We will not pay the remaining fee we pledged to the Ambassador until Stanley is examined by a team of doctors. If he has reasonable life expectancy, we pay. If he's near death, we don't. So, as much as the Ambassador unilaterally amended our mutually agreed upon plan, we will reserve the right to make this medical amendment to our deal. Please pass this message on to the Ambassador. Do it gracefully, but do it with conviction. Understood?"

Andrews says, "Yes. I understand, but I don't agree. We made a deal, and we should honor it. Our arrangement is totally silent regarding the medical condition of Mr. Roberts. I recognize they have modified the agreement, but it still doesn't give us the right to act like thugs, even if they do. I will follow your instructions as you demand. Do your instructions stand?"

Elliot thinks for a minute, then says, "Yeah, the instructions stand. According to the Ambassador, Yonatan was assassinated by mistake although there should be peace per our agreement. So, if these guys can kill two of the finest people I've ever met right before my very eyes, then I can demand to make certain Stanley has a reasonable time to live. My decision is final!"

"I will implement your decision, but please take into consideration that the Ambassador may retaliate."

Elliot quickly responds, "That, Mr. Andrews, is a risk I'm willing to take. There will be no money to Mohammed until Stanley receives a reasonable clean bill of health. Listen, try to get an ID of Stanley when he departs the aircraft in London. If someone can shoot a photo, that would be great. For Christ's sake, it shouldn't be that difficult to get someone to talk to him and identify the man as the real Stanley Roberts. Keep me posted. Speak to you soon."

The moment Elliot hangs up the phone with Andrews, he begins to think about the words he would use to inform Adeleye of the terrific news regarding her father, along with the sobering reality concerning his fragile physical condition. He decides straight talk is the only way to go on the health issue.

As Elliot picks up the phone to call Roberts' daughter, he hastily puts the phone down. He thinks about how devasting it would be if the information Andrews had delivered to him is wrong. Elliot takes a moment to think and decides to wait until the aircraft has landed in London. Once on the ground at Heathrow Airport, someone could identify Roberts, making it much more comfortable to make that call. So, he simply waits at his desk, working on his routine Hedge Fund paperwork for the day.

Three hours pass. Elliot then picks up the phone and calls Andrews on his private cell phone. It doesn't take long before Andrews is on the line. "Yes, Mr. Sterling. How can I assist you?"

"You can confirm to me that the aircraft has landed and that you have a positive ID of Stanley. What can you tell me?"

Andrews responds, "The plane landed safely in London. The Ambassador assigned an escort to accompany Mr. Roberts to San Francisco. We have no picture, and the only confirmation we have at the moment is that from the Ambassador. I'm taking him at his word, but we won't know for sure until Roberts steps off the plane in California. Tell me, how did his daughter react to the good news?"

Elliot curtly answers, "I didn't tell her! Frankly, I didn't have the heart to tell her, then turn around and disappoint her if you were wrong. I was hoping you'd be able to provide me with a confirmation before I delivered to her such precious news."

Andrews responds, "I don't blame you, but if he's on that plane, there better be someone to welcome him home! Again, I don't guarantee it, but from the Ambassador's voice and confidence level, I'd say Mr. Roberts will be landing in San Francisco at 6 PM tomorrow. I advise you to be sure and have his family gathered at the airport to greet him. To tell you the truth, I'm way more worried about telling the Ambassador he's not getting the rest of his fee on time than I am Stanley showing up!"

"Alright. Okay. I'll call her. I'll call her."

Andrews states, "I'm relatively certain that the reason Mohammed sent the escort was to verify that Stanley was delivered as promised. In fact, I'm sure he'll be calling me the moment Mr. Roberts is in the hands of his family, demanding his remaining money. You really ought to reconsider paying this man off as opposed to waiting. He can cause you a ton of headaches. Think about it. Let me know your final decision."

"Not likely, Mr. Andrews, but I'll let you know. Call me when you hear from the Ambassador asking for the money. Tell the guy you've got to find me. Buy some time then tell him you'll get back to him shortly. Thanks for your good advice, counselor. We'll talk soon."

The risk of calling Adeleye was still plainly evident. There were two options available. Call or don't call. Elliot kept going back and forth in his mind, trying desperately to decide the honorable thing to do. After thirty minutes of internal deliberation, he grabs the phone and makes the call to his young friend in northern California.

Recognizing Mr. Sterling's name on the screen of her cell phone, Adeleye anxiously answers the phone, "Hello, Mr. Sterling? Is there something wrong? Did something happen to my father? Please don't tell me my father passed away in prison!"

"No Adeleye, he's very much alive. In fact, to the best of my sources, your dad is on his way to the United States."

The extremely astute Adeleye responds with fearful frustration, "What do you mean 'to the best of my sources'? Is he free or not? Please don't play games with your words! Where is my father?"

Elliot quickly realizes that he's trying too hard to be truthful, creating unnecessary anxiety for Adeleye. So, he pivots by saying, "My attorney has unconditional confirmation from the Nigerian Ambassador to the United States that your father was released from prison and is en route to San Francisco. He is scheduled to arrive at the San Francisco airport tomorrow evening at 6 PM."

Still feeling uneasy as to whether this is the truth because the source of the information was coming from the Nigerian government as opposed to Mr. Sterling, Adeleye asks, "Obviously, you have arranged for this miracle and I need to hear what you believe. Not what the Ambassador nor your attorney say, but what you believe in your heart and mind. Is my father free and coming home?"

Elliot silently thinks for a moment then confidently says, "Tell your mother that your father is on his way home, and I fully expect him to one day soon dance at your wedding!"

Adeleye bursts out crying for joy. Her reaction causes such emotion in Elliot that he too has tears in his eyes. It takes a little time before either one of them are sufficiently composed to talk until Adeleye finally says, her voice cracking, "Thank you, Mr. Sterling. You're an angel! You truly are an angel!"

Elliot responds, "Your father risked his life for your family and myself when he so courageously approved and wired my 100-million-dollar Nigerian contract funds. He honored his word to me and all I have done is honored my word to you. I assure you, I'm not the angel, he's the angel. Now, let's discuss something very important. Your father's health is very fragile.

"He needs immediate medical attention. I will make arrangements with Stanford University Medical Clinic to accept your father into their hospital. Please take him directly there from the airport. This could be a matter of life or death, so do not deviate from this course. Immediately get your father to the hospital. He will be examined from head to toe. The physical examination along with all the medical tests will provide you with a baseline regarding your dad's health. Please keep me informed as to his medical condition. Do you understand me, Adeleye?"

Adeleye sadly responds, "Yes, Mr. Sterling, I fully understand, but are you insinuating to me that my father could be dying? Are you withholding something I need to know?"

Elliot answer, "All I know for sure is that your father has survived a brutal prison. Anyone coming out of that place will suffer a major medical setback. Check him thoroughly and let's find out the real status of his health. I sincerely don't know anything more than that."

"I will do exactly as you say, Mr. Sterling. Please provide me with the name of his primary physician and the precise address of the medical clinic. My father hates going to the doctor, but he will love going back to his Stanford alma mater!"

Elliot ends the conversation by saying, "Take your mom to the airport, in fact, take your whole family. Your father will be overwhelmed with joy to see all of you present. Remember, the British Airlines flight is scheduled to arrive tomorrow at 6 PM from London. This will be an enduring memory!"

Adeleye closes the conversation by saying, "What you have done for my father and my family will forever be remembered. I can't express our gratitude in words simply because there are no words that can accurately describe the miracle of reuniting my father with our family. So, no matter what you say, you will always be considered an angel to us. I will call you soon with an update on my father's medical condition. Thank you again from the bottom of our hearts!"

As he hangs up, Elliot cannot help but reflect on the dangerous decision he has taken to raise the hopes of the entire Roberts' family. He has stuck his neck out as far as it could go regarding Stanley's return to his family. The ramifications of Stanley not being on that aircraft would be devasting not only to the credibility of Elliot, but to the raw emotions of Roberts' family. Elliot had made the decision to accept the advice and counsel of Andrews, and now all he can do is wait for the moment of truth.

That moment came at precisely 6 PM the next day when the British Airlines touched down at the San Francisco International Airport. As the aircraft taxied on the tarmac toward the gate, emotions were running at a feverish pitch. Adeleye and her mom kept hugging each other as the aircraft slowly made its way toward the terminal. Once the plane arrived at the gate, the members of Roberts' family stood at the very front of the passenger disembarking exit area trying to get a glimpse of Stanley.

As passengers began making their way pass this area, there was no sign of Roberts. In fact, it seemed as if every person on the plane had departed except the man they had come to greet. All of a sudden, Adeleye's mother began to cry out of concern that her husband had not made the journey home. Adeleye's sad stark-white face said it all. Mr. Sterling had been deceived as their joy turned to despair until Adeleye's sister flashed a radiant smile when she saw from a distance a person pushing a wheelchair.

The man in the wheelchair was her father! As Adeleye finally observed what her sister saw, she broke through a security barrier running to her father's outstretched frail arms as tears rolled down his cheeks.

The triumphant return of the patriarch of the family was a cherished moment, but it was evident that Stanley required immediate medical attention. To that end, Adeleye cut short his ceremonious return by transporting her father directly to the Stanford Medical Center where Elliot had previously texted her the address and the name of the attending physician.

Once Adeleye was certain that her father was comfortably resting in his private room, she called Elliot to again thank him and confirm that Stanley was in good medical hands. Elliot told her to keep in touch and to let him know the state of her father's condition. Adeleye told him she'd give him a progress report within a week.

Of course, it didn't take long after Roberts' return for Andrews to contact Elliot. As the cell phone was ringing, Elliot was contemplating whether to release the final fee payment to Mohammed or stick to his guns by waiting to determine the medical condition of Roberts. After the fifth ring, Elliot answers the call, "Hello Gabriel, I haven't made a decision regarding the Ambassador's money. Stanley made it back in one piece, but as far as we know, he could be riddled with cancer or fatal heart disease. Jesus, he could be dead in a week. I realize that Mohammed delivered the goods as promised, but my gut tells me to wait for the doctors to tell us he's got a good chance of living a decent life. What do you say?"

Andrews answers, "I agree with you, but these guys are rough characters. I don't need to remind you of that. If the Ambassador feels as if he was double-crossed, my gut says he'll retaliate. The guy that escorted Mr. Roberts to San Francisco has confirmed that Stanley has been delivered to his family. Mohammed just got off the phone with me asking whether his remaining fee has already been wired! I told him that first of all, we weren't even sure Roberts' was on the aircraft since no one had identified him from our team. I further told him that you have not been advised since you have been out of the country on holiday. Mohammed was told that I'd be in touch with him shortly."

Elliot responds, "Sounds like a bunch of bullshit to me. I don't think the Ambassador bought any of it. I'm confident he clearly understands that I have been acutely interested in Stanley's release and reunion with his family. I seriously doubt we can get away with much more than twenty-four hours before this guy goes rogue on us. And I'm pretty sure he's not going to accept our amendment where we don't pay until Stanley is told by his physicians that he has no life-threatening illness. That's not going to cut it, is it? By the way, how do you define 'shortly'?"

Andrews pauses, then answers, "By tomorrow at the very latest."

Elliot quickly responds, "I knew you were going to say that. Alright, here's my position. We don't pay another fucking dime until Stanley's doctor provides an opinion on the state of his health. If he's not dying of anything in the short term, we pay within one week from tomorrow. If he's diagnosed with an acute illness, we don't pay. That's my final position."

"I got it, Mr. Sterling."

Elliot goes on to say, "When you explain to this guy my position, don't show any weakness. Just tell Mohammed his fellow Nigerians have damn near killed Stanley, and that the family is concerned that he might not survive. Based on these observations, we don't pay until we hear the truth about his medical condition. If he has a reasonable prognosis to live, Mohammed will be paid forthwith as promised.

"I want you to inform the Ambassador that my position is final and unconditional. The worst thing you can do is make Mohammed think that I'm afraid of him. I'm pretty damn sure he needs us to pay him the money for his retirement more than I am afraid of a retaliatory move by a guy whose government is just about out of power. So long as you create the real perception that we are serious about our will and ability to pay, my bet is that he plays ball! Call him tomorrow morning."

Andrews answered, "I'll do my very level best, Mr. Sterling. Assuming Mr. Roberts' health is satisfactory to his family and you, please prepare your funds to be wired to the Ambassador within a week. I'll call you tomorrow with an update regarding my conversation with Mohammed. Thank you, and goodbye."

Andrews dedicated a substantial portion of the evening preparing on a yellow legal pad the different options available in order to effectively break the fee delay news to Mohammed. The more he reviews his notes, the more he is sure that the only way to approach delivering the bad news to Mohammed is to just come out with the truth. Worst case scenario, Mohammed could angrily blow up and revenge would be a real threat. Best case, he would understand where Elliot was coming from.

Either way, some form of definition is about to take place as he makes the call to the Ambassador.

Mohammed answers the phone with a serious tone of voice, quickly commenting, "When will I receive my funds?"

Recognizing that the Ambassador is an accomplished negotiator and diplomat, Andrews understood that the no-nonsense request for the money, tied to the lack of even a "hello", was intended to place him on the defensive. So, Andrews decides to immediately throw a punch, getting right to the point by saying, "You're not getting your fee at this time. The family is very concerned that Mr. Roberts is dying and that the only reason your government released him was the fact that he was dying. Therefore, you will only receive your money when the family is medically advised that Mr. Roberts has a reasonable life expectancy."

A belligerent Mohammed screams into the receiver, "That was not our deal! You got your man! I get my money! You have no idea what I'm capable of doing to Sterling! I demand my funds immediately!"

Again, recognizing that the Ambassador will tear him apart if he's not strong, Andrews responds, "You made some modifications to our agreed upon plan that you didn't have the courtesy to inform us of the change. Stop threatening us. We know who you are and we know what your government is capable of doing. Mr. Sterling has lost two of his best men due to your fucking brutality. It's the reverse. You don't know who we are and what we're capable of doing! Listen very carefully to me, Mr. Ambassador.

"You don't get paid until we confirm that the man you sent us is going to live. Period. End of discussion!"

Mohammed, now getting a clear picture of the situation, calms down, asking facetiously, "And when is that going to be, a year from now?"

Andrews, realizing he's gaining control of the conversation, says, "No Sir. Give us one week. We'll answer you within a week. If he's dying, no deal. You keep what we've paid you so far, but no more money. If the family gets a reasonable prognosis about his life expectancy, you get paid the two and a half million-dollar balance due. That's our modified deal. Take it or leave it."

Understanding that there is no opening to negotiate further, the wise and practical Ambassador asks, "How will I know whether Mr. Roberts is legitimately dying or not? As far as I'm concerned, Sterling could be deceiving me in order to save a lot of money. What proof will I ever see if you don't pay?"

Andrews thinks for a moment, then says, "That's a fair question. Either we wire you your money after the week is up, or I personally will show you medical proof that Mr. Roberts is dying."

The shrewd Ambassador understood that he had done the best he could under the circumstances and surrenders, saying, "Alright, Mr. Andrews, I'll wait a week, but if it turns out that Roberts mysteriously lives and I'm not paid, be assured that I will retaliate. Do we clearly understand each other?"

Doing everything he could to maintain his position of strength, Andrews answers Mohammed, "There you go again threatening us. You'll hear from me within one week. Have a good day, Mr. Ambassador."

Adamant to get the last word in, Mohammed says, "By the way, that's not a threat. It's a fact. Good day, Mr. Andrews."

Within moments of hanging up, Andrews promptly calls Elliot to report the results of the Mohammed conversation. As soon as Elliot answers, Andrews immediately starts him off by saying, "At best, you got one week to pay this guy his remaining two and a half million bucks or all hell is going to break loose. Here's some free advice. Don't mess with this man. Mohammed is serious, and he means business. It's not worth your life."

Elliot asks, "What do you mean my life?"

"You heard me, Mr. Sterling. Please, just follow my advice. Either Roberts is pronounced reasonably healthy, or he's not. If he is, pay this son-of-a-bitch. If he's not, you need to get me unconditional medical proof documenting Mr. Roberts' imminent death. You have one week. That's it. I'll wait for your instructions."

Clearly understanding that Andrews is dead serious, Elliot says, "I'm not too happy with the implied threat, but I'll get you the goddamn answer within a week. Just want you to know that I sincerely appreciate the hard work you did in buying me the extra week. I'm sure that wasn't so easy. You did a phenomenal job. Is that all, Mr. Andrews?"

"Yes sir. That's all. Thank you, Mr. Sterling. I'll wait to hear back from you."

Chapter 17

The week flew by quickly. It seemed as if life in Israel was beginning to develop a sense of normality. The Savor was selling like hotcakes all over the world. The profits were staggering. In fact, it had been reported in one of the leading newspapers that it had become "the rifle of choice" worldwide. The product was so popular that the Sterling Hedge Fund was having trouble keeping up with the phenomenal demand. Mark and Ben were doing a terrific job managing the business. They had not only become close business colleagues, but they had become amazing friends.

Elliot had been introduced to a real estate developer by the name of Noam Goldstein. He had a vision that there was a major demand in the City of Jerusalem for a new five-star hotel that Goldstein wanted Elliot to finance. The two agree to meet in Caesarea at Elliot's home in order to discuss the possibilities further. As he waits in his private office for Goldstein to arrive, Elliot decides that he will call Adeleye since the deadline is tomorrow—whether to release Mohammed's fee or not.

Just as he is about to place the call, he notices that he has a "missed call" from Adeleye, which meant that she most likely has the information he requires from her.

Adeleye answers Elliot's call on the first ring, saying enthusiastically, "Hello Mr. Sterling. I hope you are well. My father is going to live! He has developed some heart disease and chronic digestive complications. He also has broken bones from the torture he endured and that didn't heal correctly. But he will live!

"My mother wanted me to express how grateful she is for the miracle of you bringing him home to us. As for my father, well, he told me to tell you that you're a man of your word and that our family will from one generation to the next consider you a saint. God bless you, Mr. Sterling!"

Elliot pauses for a few seconds then says, "Please tell your father that keeping your word doesn't make you a saint, although I'll admit, it's getting tougher and tougher to find someone who actually means what they say and say what they mean. Tell your dad that keeping his word to me, while facing possible death consequences, was courageous and something I will never forget. Additionally, let him know that although I don't consider him a saint, he's arguably something more important to me. He's my trusted friend."

Adeleye, with her eyes tearing, says, "I will miss you, Mr. Sterling. My hope is that we will someday meet again. Please be certain to forward me your address so that I may write you from time to time."

Elliot responds, "That would be great! I'm sure we'll meet again sooner than you think. In the interim, please keep me informed as to your family's well-being along with your educational progress.

"When you graduate from UCLA, let me know what law school you will be attending. And of course, keep me apprised of your journey through law school. Hey, look, you never know when some billionaire living in Israel might be interested in hiring a young lawyer fresh out of law school.

"Make sure to send me pictures of the milestones yet to occur in your life, especially the one of you dancing with your father at your wedding! Let's for sure keep in touch!"

Adeleye completes the call by saying, "You're a good man, Mr. Sterling. I will always remember your courage and your kind heart."

Now armed with the medical facts regarding Roberts, it is time to give Andrews his instructions regarding Mohammed. Within moments of completing his call with Adeleye, Elliot is on the phone with Andrews. "I've got good news and bad news for you. What do you want first?"

Without hesitation, Andrews answers, "Let's hear the bad news."

Elliot says, "We've got to pay that son-of-a-bitch Ambassador two and a half million bucks!"

Andrews responds, "So, let me guess. The good news is that Roberts is going to live for a while."

Elliot says, "Correct. Tell Mohammed we appreciate his patience and we'll wire him his fee first thing tomorrow morning. I'm sorry to cut you short, but I've got someone waiting for me. Thanks for the spot-on advice. We'll speak soon."

Noam Goldstein was a very well-recognized real estate developer in Israel. He was famous for having the Israeli politicians in his back pocket. Goldstein was equally recognized for stiffing his subcontractors, often ending up paying them pennies on the dollar toward their contracts. As ruthless as his reputation was, he was equally known as a charming guy, a womanizer, and a winner. The moment he walks into Elliot's office, he flashes that charismatic smile and, in his Israeli accent, greets Elliot, "Do you mind, Mr. Sterling, if I call you Elliot? Please call me Noam."

Elliot responds, "I don't mind. That's what my friends call me. And, so far, I'll consider you my friend, although based on what I've heard about you, it might not be too long before we're in court battling each other."

Goldstein stares at his new "friend" and says, "I wouldn't believe everything you read. Besides, is that any way to speak to a friend?"

"Look Noam. I've heard every kind of bullshit that you could possibly think of. I've been in the real estate development business for over thirty years. I've seen it all. So, I figure if you've come all the way from your Jerusalem office to visit with me in my office, chances are you really need me. Now, since I probably have more experience and capital than you, how about you just cut to the chase."

Even though Goldstein understood he has just met his match, he still put on his charm by saying, "Aren't you at least going to shake my hand and ask me to take a seat?"

Having set the tone for his relationship with a shark like Goldstein, Elliot smiles, extends his hand toward him, and says, "I'll do better than that. How about some Cognac?"

The tall, rugged-looking, blue-eyed Israeli with a magnetic personality responds with amusement, "Now you're talking!"

As Elliot pours him a drink and they both settle into their chairs, Elliot says, "What do you want?"

Goldstein clears his throat and says, "I want you to make me a hard money loan for 300 million dollars so that I can build the best hotel in Jerusalem. I have an option on the property which is directly across the street from one of the most popular hotels in Israel. If I can show proof of my construction financing for the hotel, the property seller will allow me to exercise my option to buy the property. The seller insists that the buyer build out the land as opposed to holding on as a land speculator.

"At the moment, the Israeli banks are under strict government oversight and construction lending has become almost extinct. I need a Letter of Intent from The Sterling Hedge Fund showing your willingness to fund my project. Your Letter will allow me to exercise my rights to purchase arguably the best piece of commercial property in the entire country. This development is a no-brainer."

On the surface, Elliot likes what he hears and asks, "How many guest rooms?"

Goldstein replies, "We expect three hundred rooms."

Elliot, smelling some problems with the deal or perhaps serious potential governmental stonewalling to stop the hotel from ever being constructed, says "I'm not going to lend you the money, but I will buy you out. What's your price?"

Goldstein's demeanor goes from jovial to downright mean as he says, "There is no goddamn price, you greedy son-of-a-bitch! I didn't come here to sell my property, or my soul to you."

Elliot calmly responds, "First of all, I don't want to buy your soul, just your property. Second, I'm going to give you one opportunity to apologize for your stupid comment, and if you don't, I'm going to have you thrown out of my house. Your choice, Mr. Goldstein."

Goldstein looks down at the floor, expresses a grimace of pain in his face, and says, "I'm sorry for overreacting. It's taken me well over five years to assemble the real estate option I control for the hotel project. The last thing on earth I want to do is sell you, or anyone else, my option. I'm a real estate developer, and I've been waiting my entire career for an opportunity like this.

"I just can't allow for someone to come in at the last minute and steal it from me. Besides, you'll get eaten alive trying to work through the government's Rubik's Cube bureaucracy regarding a world-class hotel in the heart of Jerusalem. Believe me, you'll never make it out alive."

Thinking to himself that this poor bastard still doesn't get it, Elliot says, "Oh, I'll make it out alive. In fact, this development is going to be approved and built in record time. You want to know why?"

Goldstein, looking sick to his stomach, responds sarcastically, "Why?"

Now serious, Elliot says with confidence, "Because I'm going to pay you a bunch of money to be my development coordinator. You'll be paid based on performance, but it's going to be an obscene amount. You'll do all that charming schmoozing with the politicians you're famous for. You'll be the front man who gets all the press and glory you love. Just no ownership. That will be retained by the Sterling Hedge Fund. So, how much does it cost to purchase the property and what am I going to pay you for your services?"

Flabbergasted, Goldstein has a difficult time organizing his thoughts, but finally says, "I can't do this, Mr. Sterling."

Knowing Goldstein's notorious reputation for bluffing, and understanding that Goldstein had been shopping his request for construction financing all over the world including Los Angeles,

Elliot simply extends out his hand toward Goldstein and says, "I wish you well with your project. Let me walk you out to your car."

Quickly processing that not only has he met his match, but there might not ever be a better opportunity to get the hotel financed and built, Goldstein says in an uncharacteristically humble voice, "Let's roll up our sleeves and get this project built!"

Instinctively knowing that Goldstein has few, if any, options, Elliot says, "You made the right decision. I appreciate how painful this is for you, but sometimes it's better to get something rather than nothing. I also recognize that you bring value to the table. Together, we're going to get this done. You will run the day-to-day operations, similar to a baseball field manager.

"You will report to Mark Goldman. He has as much experience in land development as I do. He is my trusted associate. Let's just call him the General Manager. He'll oversee you. He will have the authority to correct you and even fire you, but he's too smart to do either if he thinks you're making the right moves. Don't challenge him because he won't hesitate to pull the trigger on you if he thinks he needs to. And, using all these baseball terms, I'll play the role of owner.

"I hold the veto power on all decisions. Let's just call it the final say. You will rarely hear from me unless things are going wrong or you need to speak to me. I will know everything that's going on through my people, but I will not interfere with your work until you are fucking up. At that point, I will not hesitate to throw you out. If you can live with what I've just said, then let's make a deal."

Mesmerized by how direct and straightforward Elliot is, Goldstein says, "I think I'm going to learn quite a bit from you, Mr. Sterling. Although I've always been my own man, I can live with the organizational chart and authority. As long as you don't take away my day-to-day decision-making authority where I'm able to use my experience and instincts, we're going to be fine. Sometimes, as you say in your American football, the quarterback needs to call an 'audible' at the line of scrimmage. I'm very good at that, so if you allow me to do what I think is right, we'll win together!"

Elliot understood and appreciates what Goldstein is insinuating. Yet, he is mindful that Goldstein would always need to be checked as he responds, "As long as we're winning, you won't hear a word from Mark or me. So, here's what we're going to do. You and I are going to get some food. By the time we finish eating, we'll make our deal. When we return, I'll have Mark Goldman; my attorney, Yitzhak Bennett; my accountant, Moshe Ariel; and Benjamin

Yaalon, my top Sterling Hedge Fund guy assembled here for a meeting. We'll get the attorney working on our contract, while the rest of us will concentrate on perfecting our business plan and strategies. Sound good?"

Amazed by the lightning speed by which Elliot had taken control, all Goldstein can say is, "Sounds good."

Goldstein and Elliot went on to have a productive meal and easily made a deal. Goldstein's compensation would be broken up based on performance. They agreed that the value of the services would equate to a fee of two and a half percent of the total cost of the projected 300-million-dollar project. If completed, the compensation would equal a fee of seven and a half million dollars. It was agreed that the payments would be made incrementally, starting with a 100-thousand-dollar bonus due upon the signing of the new agreement. This would follow by twenty-five percent paid at each of the following milestones:

1. Government entitlements and permits
2. All architectural and engineering plans approved by the Jerusalem government planning boards
3. Construction complete and a Certificate of Occupancy issued by the building department
4. Thirty days after the hotel opens and is operating for business.

Additionally, it was made abundantly clear between the two men that the Sterling Hedge Fund would be the sole owner of the hotel property, and Goldstein would be an independent contractor with absolutely no equity in the property. The two had shaken hands on their deal and it was time to meet up with the Sterling team.

All the men were patiently waiting in the formal dining room seated around the table waiting for Elliot to call the meeting into order. It didn't take long for everyone to shake hands and introduce each other.

Each Israeli associated with Sterling's Fund knew of Goldstein and his reckless reputation. None had ever actually conducted business with him directly or indirectly, yet they were very cautious going into business with a wheeler-dealer like Goldstein.

Elliot points at Mark, fresh from returning from Los Angeles, and says, "Proceed."

Mark, who had spent a moment talking with Elliot in the hallway outside the dining room, opens the meeting by saying, "I don't know you, Mr. Goldstein, but from what I hear about you from all these guys sitting around the table, well, let's just say, I already don't trust you. To tell you the truth, I can't understand how you'll ever be able to fit into a highly organized group like ours. So, why don't you do us all a big favor by just selling us the property, and you walk away a rich man."

The brash Goldstein, insulted by a foreigner and a man he had met for less than a minute, responds, "I think your name is Mark, if I'm not mistaken. Mark, why don't you go fuck-off!"

Not expecting that kind of reaction, Mark, the tough-guy Marine at heart, gets out of his chair, then dashes toward Goldstein intending to kick this guy's ass until Benjamin swiftly steps in between them.

Elliot, who can't believe the chaos in front of his eyes, yells at the top of his voice, "Both of you clowns, come with me," as he excuses himself from the rest of the group.

As they make their way into the private office, he sees a startled Felicia coming toward him asking, "Elliot, is everything alright? Mark, what's going on?"

Elliot, gaining his composure, responds, "Everything is fine. Just a misunderstanding that I will resolve in a moment. Mark and I will be over to see you after our meeting. I think he has some good news he wants to share with you. Don't worry, everything is good."

Felicia, trying to trust her husband, sarcastically says, "Doesn't sound so good to me. I'll see you two a little later." Since no one introduces her, the charming Felicia extends her hand toward Goldstein and says, "I'm Felicia Sterling."

Goldstein, not expecting the warm welcome, responds, "I'm Noam Goldstein. I'm very sorry for causing a disruption in your beautiful residence. Please forgive me."

Not buying any of Goldstein's tactics, the fiercely loyal and astute Felicia says, "Let me give you one warning. If you anger either one of these two men again in this home, I will personally see to it that you never step foot in my house again. Have a good day, Mr. Goldstein."

All tempers cooled down, especially after Felicia made her appearance. Elliot addresses Mark and Goldstein, "Look, Noam. If I got to choose between Mark and you, well, you're out. The question I have is whether I need to do that right here and now. I like the property and the development opportunity, but I don't need it. I'm a billionaire. I can pick and choose what I get involved with. Life's too short for this kind of bullshit. Mark can save you or cut you loose. So, Mark, what do you want to do?"

Grateful that his boss gave him the benefit of the doubt on the altercation with Goldstein, and equally appreciative that Elliot was allowing him to pass judgement on whether to procced with Goldstein, Mark does not immediately respond. He knows that if he decides to throw out Goldstein, the hotel project would be dead on arrival to the Sterling Hedge Fund.

Knowing that Elliot has made the decision to proceed, in spite of Goldstein's reputation, is weighing heavily on Mark. Obviously, his boss has decided that the potential profits and opportunity are too good to pass up. Mark is now figuring out what Elliot already knows. The only way to get the hotel development to become a reality was to hire this guy and keep him under tight control with an air-tight contract. This was precisely why Elliot had assembled all his top advisors to attend this meeting. Now, it boiled down to whether Mark could work with this son-of-a-bitch or not.

After thinking this through and knowing that Goldstein understood that Mark would not hesitate to throw a punch at him, Mark cleverly answers, "I really am getting better at this anger management thing. I'm sorry for having lost my temper. Just looking after our company. Noam, I kind of like your piss and vinegar bravado approach. It can get you in a whole bunch of trouble, but on the other hand, that swagger can convince a lot of people to do it your way. So, if you're willing to follow our Sterling Hedge Fund rules and you're willing to take some advice on occasion, I think I can work with you to get the damn hotel built. Just remember this, I may push you in order to get the best results, but you can't push me because you're going to lose."

Loving Mark's approach toward controlling Goldstein and recognizing he had him right where he wanted him, Elliot breaks the thick air by saying, "So, are you two going to kiss and make up? Come on, shake hands! Let's go get our deal done. We got a lot of very high-priced people sitting in the dining room just twiddling their thumbs."

The charismatic Goldstein suddenly makes his way toward Mark and gives him a bear hug. Not expecting that reaction, Mark takes it all in stride by hugging him back while smiling at Elliot. The drama is over and it is time to go back to work. As the men make their way back to the dining room, Goldstein asks Elliot, "How long have you known Mark?"

Elliot proudly says, "Since elementary school. Why do you ask?"

Goldstein stares at Elliot, then grins. "You're a lucky man to have a guy like Mark watching your back for all those years. No wonder you're so filthy rich! Okay, let's go add a hotel to your financial statement. I'm going to make this happen for you!"

As the meeting is reconvened, Elliot takes the floor explaining the deal in great detail. Each of his hand-picked associates took copious notes, including Goldstein. Elliot explains that there were three "big-picture" parts of the deal. The Sterling Hedge Fund was to be assigned all the rights to Goldstein's hotel property option. The option was $65,000,000 USD for the vacant property alone. Property values in Jerusalem had sky-rocketed in the last few years, making the price per square foot of land amongst the highest in the world.

The Sterling Fund would be required to exercise the option to buy the land within seven working days from the government's entitlement permit granting the right to build a hotel on the site. Every six months, the Fund was responsible to pay "option money" to the current owners in the amount of $250,000 USD in order to retain the option rights to the property. Elliot was clear to state that the option rights expired two years from now. All option payments were to be credited toward the eventual acquisition price of the property.

Elliot goes on to discuss Goldstein's compensation package, which would be paid in exchange for Goldstein releasing all equity rights to the hotel. Goldstein was entitled to 2.5% of all approved costs.

The anticipated development and construction costs for the hotel were agreed upon to be $300,000,000 USD. Therefore, the total compensation to Goldstein would total a staggering $7,500,000 assuming the hotel was successfully built. The payments would be split into 25% installments per each development milestone:

1. Government permits approved, known as the "entitlements"
2. Architect and engineering plans approved by the government, referred to as "A & E"
3. Construction of the hotel complete and a Certificate of Occupancy issued by the city of Jerusalem
4. The hotel was up and operating with guests occupying the rooms.

The final component of the contract was to include tightly drafted provisions granting the Sterling Hedge Fund the unequivocal right to terminate Goldstein for cause. The definition "for cause" was to be meticulously defined. In the event of a rightful termination, compensation due to Goldstein, if any, would need to be clearly delineated. This section of the agreement would additionally mandate that Goldstein would report to Mark, and that Mark would have the full authority to terminate Goldstein at any time subject to this section of the contract.

With the thorough explanation complete, Elliot goes around the table fielding questions from his associates. After about an hour of questions, answers, and general discussion, Elliot turns to Yitzhak Bennett and says, "Ball's in your court, Yitzhak. When you have the draft prepared, distribute it to everyone for comments. Let's try and get this signed by the end of the week. Anything else?"

Goldstein raises his hand and says, "All I ask each of you is that you give me a fair chance to do my job. Please bury any old perceptions you may have in your mind. I can do this job, but I'll need all of your help. I'm going to put the Sterling Hedge Fund into a position to win. Together, a world-class landmark hotel will be erected in Jerusalem, and you guys will be the illustrious owners. If you allow me to be me and if you judge me on my merits, we all will get along just fine. Thank you."

To the surprising delight of Elliot, his entire team of associates reacts to the upbeat message delivered by Goldstein by banging on the dining room table with the palm of their fists, then applauding in unison, demonstrating their support for Goldstein. The primary thought on Elliot's mind is how brilliantly Goldstein has taken a very negative perception of him and instantly converted it into a positive. There is no doubt that this guy possesses the skill set to win. That isn't the issue dominating Elliot's mind. It is whether this man could be trusted. Only time would reveal that truth.

Once everyone departed the meeting with their marching orders, Elliot invites Mark to join him and Felicia in the living room. As the two old friends walk side-by-side down the corridor from the dining room to the formal living area, Mark says to Elliot, "Man, that Goldstein character has a real gift of the gab. Jesus Christ, this guy is persuasive! But let me tell you something, Elliot. I wouldn't trust this guy as far as I could throw him. He's a con-man; I'm just glad he plays for our team!"

As they make their way into the living room, Elliot whispers back to Mark, "I was just thinking the same damn thing. We're going to need to keep a very close eye on him from start to finish. We need this guy for the hotel development project. He's effectively our seeing-eye dog. He'll walk us through the whole process, and he'll introduce us to the right people in government. With the proper controls in place, well, I think we can extract the best from this son-of-a-bitch."

When Mark spots Felicia sitting on her elegant apricot-colored loveseat, he can't help but say, "Felicia, I swear you're getting younger by the month. How the hell do you do it?"

Felicia answers with her quick wit, "Flattery will get you everywhere with me! But of course, you already knew that, didn't you?"

Chapter 18

Felicia and Mark greet each other warmly with a hug and kiss. As they sit down in a living room that resembles a picture right out of Europe's most fashionable architectural magazines, Felicia asks, "Which one of you two guys invited that creepy, loud-mouth man into this house?"

Elliot looks at Mark, and Mark stares back at Elliot. Neither one of them says a word until Felicia steps in, "I've seen those expressions on your faces before, especially when you're hiding something. Alright, enough already. Who is this guy?"

Understanding that Mark has to save his old buddy from a whole bunch of explaining to his wife, he jumps in, "We're going to build a world-class hotel in Jerusalem and Noam Goldstein is our third-party paid consultant. We're hiring him for two reasons. First, he knows all the government officials needed to obtain the required permits for the project. Second, he controls the hotel property option rights, which the Sterling Hedge Fund is about to buy for a ton of money. Other than that, he's total stranger."

Felicia stares at Mark and says, "Okay, that's very nice, but who invited a man like that into my home? Was that you, Elliot?"

Elliot looks at his wife and says, "Yeah. It was me. I want the hotel deal and he's our ace in the hole. I know he's loud and demanding and obnoxious, but I need him at the moment. Just trust me on this one. I've got this."

Felicia responds to her husband, "Oh, I trust you. It's the other guy I don't trust. Please, don't bring that man back to this house. If you think he's giving you some sort of a business advantages, well, whatever you and Mark decide, that's fine by me. Use him as you wish. Just keep him away from this home! So, Mark, how's your love life?"

Predictively shy when it comes to this subject, Mark humbly says, "Well, let me put it to you this way. I'm not married just yet, but according to Emma's doctor, she's going to deliver Paul Norman's baby very soon. That kid is going to be raised by Emma and me. I adore Emma and I've decided that I'm going to marry her about a month or two after the baby is born. So, I suppose my answer to your question is that my love life is pretty damn full. Thanks for asking."

Felicia gets up off the sofa and hugs Mark while saying, "Congratulations! You're going to make a wonderful husband and a terrific father. Where are you and Emma planning to get married?"

Mark responds, "Legally, we'll be married by a Justice of the Peace in a simple civil ceremony at City Hall in Beverly Hills. Emma will give birth in Los Angeles, then we'll be moving to Israel for as long as Elliot needs me here."

Felicia interrupts Mark, "This news is amazing! Elliot and I insist that your wedding reception be in our home, here in Caesarea. I'm not accepting any answer other than 'yes' to this proposal! Both of you need to invite your family and friends to come celebrate your marriage!"

The rugged, yet modest Mark says, "That's very gracious of you, Felicia. Of course, the answer is 'yes' with one contingency. Emma must be okay with it too. I'll call her later and give you the final answer by tomorrow. At least the 'best man' at my wedding reception won't need to travel. Oh, by the way, Elliot, if you weren't listening carefully, I want you to be my best man. You good with that?"

Elliot lovingly grabs hold of his life-long buddy and gives him a bear hug while saying, "I would have been deeply offended if you hadn't asked!"

Observing the emotional connection between these two best friends, Felicia sheds a tear of joy as she says, "Hey, Mark. Why don't you just call Emma right now while we're all sharing this moment. I'm pretty sure she's going to accept. If she agrees, I want to get started with the planning immediately.

"We've got lots to do, and very little time to pull off a sensational social event for the two of you. By the way, if she happens to say no, tell Emma I'm going to kill her when I see her!"

Smiling, Mark looks at his watch and responds, "Okay, alright. I'll try and reach her. Give me a few minutes," as he walks out of the living room to find some privacy.

In less than five minutes, Mark returns to the living room where Felicia and Elliot are awaiting Emma's response. Mark wastes no time and says, "Emma said to tell you 'yes'. She told me to be certain to thank you and Mr. Sterling from the bottom of her heart. Additionally, she wanted you to know that her wedding reception at your home will be one of the highlights of her life, and she is sincerely grateful."

Felicia cannot hold back her emotions as she blurts out, "I knew she was a keeper! Mark, you've picked yourself out a gem of a woman! A real winner! We're going to get along famously!"

Elliot, who is just sitting back listening and taking in all the beautiful dialogue, finally says, "Not only will this be a momentous day in both of your lives, but we'll have an opportunity to introduce ourselves to the Israeli business, political, and social circles. This event will mark a whole new life for all of us. I know I speak for Felicia when I tell you this reception will be breathtaking, warm, and a heck of a lot of fun. We love you, Mark!"

As the weeks went by, Felicia was meticulously planning for what promised to be an extraordinary wedding reception for Mark and Emma. Elliot seemed busier than ever running the Sterling Hedge Fund, which was becoming a labor of love. He had signed a tightly worded agreement with Goldstein regarding the hotel project and seemed to be getting along perfectly with him. While working in his home office on a routine Wednesday morning, Elliot receives an unexpected phone call from Goldstein. "Very interesting that you're calling. I was just thinking about you. How the hell are we doing? Getting any closer on the permits?"

Goldstein clears his throat and responds in his distinct Israeli accent, "We're doing well, Mr. Sterling. In fact, we're doing exceptionally well. This is precisely why I'm calling. I have arranged a meeting with the Minister of Finance. It appears he's going to recommend fast-tracking the hotel project approvals. The Minister loves what we propose to build. He thinks that everything you touch turns to gold! He specifically requested to meet you and insisted that you come to our meeting tomorrow in his official Jerusalem government office."

Elliot thinks for a moment, then asks, "What's the name of this guy? And how does he even know who I am?"

Goldstein answers, "His name is Gilad Regev. He's very familiar with you because everyone in the government who invested in digital coins either broke even or lost money. You're the only guy in Israel that made a profit. So, you're famous and they want to learn your secrets. Minister Regev is a very powerful man and has the ear of the Prime Minister. If he gives us the green light to proceed with our project, you can take his endorsement to the bank. We'll be home free."

Elliot responds, "Look, Noam, the politicians are your job, not mine. You handle it. Keep me out!"

Goldstein adamantly says, "I'm afraid I can't do that, Mr. Sterling. Minister Regev wants you in his office tomorrow morning at 10 AM. There's no choice here! Let me explain it to you this way. If you end up being a no-show tomorrow morning, you'll set back the hotel project for years. Men like Regev don't take no for an answer lightly. I insist that you attend for the sake of the project."

Elliot, starting to feel angrier by the second, says, "Listen, you fucking arrogant piece of garbage! You have no authority to be making appointments for me. You have no right to place me in this kind of position. You don't make commitments for me unless I pre-authorize them. Do you understand me?"

Goldstein, rapidly recognizing what a colossal error he has committed, goes into damage control by saying, "I'm so sorry, Mr. Sterling. I should not have accepted on your behalf without clearing it with you first. What a stupid mistake. I just used my instincts and seized the moment with the Minister because I saw it as a great opportunity to get the hotel development on a fast track. Please accept my sincerest apology for the terrible disrespect I showed you. Believe me when I say I meant no such disrespect."

Elliot is not buying any of Goldstein's explanations. What's crossing his mind is that he really has no choice but to attend the meeting due to the horrific downside to the hotel project schedule. Elliot was not about to set the hotel's construction schedule off by years. He clearly understood that he was going to need to reluctantly cave in to Goldstein and Regev for the sake of the project. The question is whether Goldstein or Regev have some nefarious motive for organizing the meeting. With no choice available, Elliot reluctantly says, "You win, Noam. I'll be at Regev's meeting. Don't ever compromise me again. Are you listening, Noam?"

Goldstein simply answers with, "Yes sir, Mr. Sterling! This will never happen again!"

The next morning, Elliot was picked up by his driver in his recently acquired black Mercedes Benz company sedan. They had left Caesarea at 7 AM in order to arrive in plenty of time for the 10 AM meeting with the Finance Minister. The trip had been calculated to run approximately two hours via Route 1 Highway into Jerusalem. They were to meet Goldstein at 9:45 AM outside the Minister's office complex. The trip went by quickly as the driver pulled up to the security detail in front of the building. It was abundantly clear to Elliot that he had arrived at the office of a very powerful man.

The night before, Elliot had conducted a little research to better understand who he would be meeting with. He learned that the

Minister of Finance was the main economic steward of the Government of Israel. The Minister was responsible for planning and implementing the government's overall economic policy, as well as setting targets for fiscal policy and the government's budgets. It was easy to conclude that Regev was indeed a very influential member of the government. He had graduated from Harvard with honors and enjoyed the full confidence of the Israeli Prime Minister. Regev was well recognized by his peers for an exceedingly high IQ, along with a weakness for young attractive Israeli women.

After jointly passing a rigorous security clearance, Elliot and Goldstein were escorted by a fully armed Israeli soldier to a reception area just outside the Minister's formal office. There they are greeted by naturally gorgeous young woman with a low-cut, white see-through blouse who smiles and starts speaking Hebrew to Goldstein. It was apparent the young receptionist knew Goldstein well and seemed to be speaking to a familiar visitor to the office. As their conversation drew to a conclusion, Goldstein faces Elliot and says, "The minister is running late. He was unexpectedly called into the Prime Minister's office early this morning on some complicated matter and will arrive shortly."

Elliot quickly says, "Every time someone in this country says "shortly", I'm in for a long wait!"

The wait would turn out to be well over an hour. On more than one occasion, Elliot desperately tried to convince Goldstein to talk to his pretty little girlfriend at the reception desk and reschedule the appointment. Goldstein wouldn't listen to any such request. All he kept telling Elliot was "that the wait will be well worth it".

At shortly after 11:15 AM, the Minister of Finance accompanied by an entourage of aides walks right past his receptionist, Goldstein, and Elliot without uttering a word. He enters his private office and an aide closes the door behind him. Elliot looks at Goldstein, and Goldstein stares back at Elliot with bewilderment. Just as Elliot is about to tell Goldstein he's had enough, the same aide who closed the door walks right over to Goldstein and says in Hebrew, "Our sincere apologies, the minister will now see you. Please come with me."

Goldstein and Elliot stand and follow the young assistant into the minister's office. As they enter the formal office, the minister greets them at an area in the office that resembles a small living room where there are two pastel yellow sofas facing each other. Regev is seated in one. Elliot and Goldstein are escorted to the other.

Goldstein extends his hand toward Regev as they exchange some pleasantries, then Goldstein quickly introduces Elliot.

The minister, a tall, very handsome, and distinguished grey-haired man in his late fifties, immediately opens the dialogue by saying in perfect English, "I just told the Prime Minister of Israel that I was about to meet with the only guy in the country to make a profit with those stupid cryptocurrency coins.

"That got his attention! The premier couldn't figure out whether to have you indicted for insider trading or to bring you into our government so we'd have the benefit of your brilliant advice. Which one do you think it should be, Mr. Sterling?"

Elliot is dead silent for a moment as he glances at a very nervous-looking Goldstein, then looks straight into the eyes of Regev as he addresses the question with one word, "Neither."

A surprised Regev responds, "That's your answer?"

Elliot quickly states, "Yeah. That's my answer."

The now annoyed narcissistic Finance Minister then says, "Does your answer imply the equivalent of what you Americans do when you're about to incriminate yourselves? You plead the Fifth Amendment."

Elliot calmly says, "For your working information, the Fifth Amendment of the United States Constitution is the section of the Bill of Rights that protects you from being held for committing a crime unless you have been indicted correctly by law enforcement authorities. It also prohibits self-incrimination and double jeopardy and mandates due process of law. The framers of the American Constitution were very wise."

"They demanded that no person shall be compelled in a criminal case to be a witness against himself. Effectively, a free man has the right to remain silent. So, since you now understand the foundation of the Fifth Amendment, you won't need to embarrass yourself using that amendment incorrectly while referring to me. Please take me at my word when I said 'neither'. I did no insider trading. I profited from cryptocurrency fairly and legally. I followed our company's analysis and I sold at precisely the right time without being greedy. As far as being an advisor to the government, I unconditionally have no interest. Are we clear, Minister Regev?"

Regev is blown away by the precision and poise exhibited by Elliot. He is not angry, he is uncharacteristically impressed. "Well done, Mr. Sterling. I just accept your answer at face value. And thanks for the civics lesson, but we're still going to insist that you advise our government!"

Feeling abused by this arrogant chump, Elliot says, "Is this why you dragged me down to your office? You want to strong-arm me into government service? You guys are really messed up. I've heard about these kind of moves in dictatorships, but not here. Not in Israel."

Reading Elliot's angry distrust and recognizing he better take control of the situation, Regev says, "I asked you come to my office in Jerusalem because we know that Noam does not have the money to develop a world-class hotel in the heart of Jerusalem. So, we figured out through our sources that you are the silent owner. By the way, we're very good at intelligence gathering here.

"Anyway, we decided that we wanted to speak to the real owner, not his representative. We're about to make a fast-track exception for your hotel project that is going to save you years of time and millions of dollars. If our government is going to grant this kind of accommodation, then the least you can do is allow us to grant it to the real principal. Wouldn't you agree, Mr. Sterling?"

Elliot's instinct was telling him that he was about to be shaken down for some kind of a bribe as he flippantly says, "Alright, here I am. What do you want to say to me?"

The minister sternly looks at Goldstein as if to say, "Why didn't you prepare your boss properly for this meeting", and goes on to respond to Elliot, "Since we're not going to indict you, and since we are prepared to approve the fast-tracking of your hotel project, we insist that you join the Prime Minister's Economic Advisory Board. It consists of only five individuals. These people are considered the best and the brightest when it comes to economics and finance. I'm the chairman and we currently have a vacancy on the Board due to an unfortunate death.

"We advise the Prime Minister on matters of great importance that shapes the fiscal policies facing the nation. We will clear you through our agencies, which will grant you the authority to receive the national security secrets of this country. This is an honor bestowed on very few people. The Prime Minister awaits your answer. Yes or no, Mr. Sterling?"

Quickly understanding that if he answers "no", the fast tracking for the hotel would very likely be withdrawn and a political target would be placed on his back. Elliot feels as if he has no choice but to accept. The question is whether the hotel project is really worth giving up his independence by having to subordinate to Regev. Although the position sounds rather interesting, it will be very complicated collaborating with an asshole like the minister.

Suddenly, Elliot says to Regev, "Give me a minute. I need to make a call."

Dumbfounded, the minister responds, "What did you say?"

Elliot repeats himself, "You heard me, I need to make a call."

"I'm offering you one of the most prestigious posts in the Israeli government, and you need a minute! Who in hell could you possibly need to speak to?"

Not paying attention to the minister, Elliot stands up and walks toward the door saying, "Excuse me, just give me a moment, I'll be right back," as he steps out of the room and finds his way to a private area in the reception room.

Goldstein, who is now terrified that his monumental hotel project along with his seven-figure fee are about to disintegrate, looks at the ceiling, takes a deep breath, and weakly says to Regev, "I'm sure that Mr. Sterling will return with good news."

Regev, who is infuriated by Goldstein's failure to prepare Elliot to cooperate prior to the meeting, lashes out at Goldstein, "The only thing I'm sure of is that you're an idiot!"

Elliot reaches Benjamin Yaalon on his cell and quickly briefs him on the situation. He then follows with the question, "Should I take the Board position or just walk out?"

Benjamin doesn't hesitate when he says, "Grab it, Elliot. Grab it!"

Elliot asks, "Because you're impressed with the Finance Minister?"

Benjamin laughs out loud as he says, "No, Elliot. Because it happens to be the most coveted Board seat in all of Israel. Any bank industry leader would die to have that seat. The best of the best fight to get appointed to that Board. The Sterling Hedge Fund will benefit beyond anything you can imagine. All future economic direction for the country is formulated through that Board. Our Hedge Fund depends on predicting future economic trends. There's nothing further to discuss. Accept as fast as you can say 'yes' before the minister changes his mind!"

Elliot responds, "But what about the fact that I can't stand this guy? He's impossible to work with. He'll stab me in the back just for fun."

Benjamin laughs again, saying, "Fake it. Get your ass on that Board. Stop talking to me and go tell him you accept. Do it now!"

Now doing the laughing, Elliot says, "I see you have no opinion on this matter. Oh, what you're willing to put me through for money, my good friend."

"No, Elliot. It's not just money. The powerful people you will meet will be very rewarding not only financially, but socially and in every manner you can think of. Trust me. Grab it!"

Elliot gets serious for a moment and says, "I hope this Regev guy doesn't end up getting me into some kind of big trouble. I don't trust this son-of-a-bitch, but you've never steered me wrong. I'll let you know when the deed is done. Thanks for your sage advice. I hope you're right."

As Elliot makes his way back into the minister's private office, he notices that Regev is nowhere to be found. In fact, no one is in the room. Not knowing what to expect, Elliot simply sits on the couch and makes himself at home, figuring that they'll return sooner or later.

Within ten minutes, both Regev and Goldstein appear through a side door that is camouflaged within the wall. Where that door led to was puzzling and clandestine. The look on Goldstein's face is blank. It reveals nothing other than Elliot's gut feeling telling him that these two guys are up to no good. Elliot doesn't say a word because he wants to hear what the minister has to say first. It reminded him of a good old-fashioned game of 'chicken'.

Finally, the minister breaks the ice and says, "If the decision was solely left to me, I would withdraw my invitation to have you join us on the Advisory Board. Any prospective Board member who hesitates, as you have hesitated, does not deserve to serve this nation in this capacity. The man who is saving you is the Prime Minister. He directed me to insist that you accept our offer. Personally, I hope you say no, but if you say yes, I will join with you to serve this nation with distinction. So, what's your answer?"

"My answer is yes with one condition."

Regev annoyingly responds, "And what is your fucking condition, Mr. Sterling?"

Thinking clearly about what Benjamin has just advised and understanding that the Prime Minister has his back, Elliot decides he needs to put this guy in his place while holding on to the invitation. Elliot clears his throat and says, "You probably get away with speaking down to most people because you consider yourself a very important man. Of course, you're the Finance Minister of Israel with a 350 billion US dollars Gross Domestic Product (GDP). Do you have any idea what the GDP is for China?

"Well, I'll answer that for you. It's 12 trillion US dollars. By the way, do you know what the GDP of the United States of America happens to be? The answer is 19.5 trillion US dollars! By comparison to world economic powers, Israel is just a small player. An important geopolitical nation, but a small fry on the world financial scene.

"So, let's get something straight here. You don't impress me as such a big powerful world financial figure. I'm an individual and my net worth is in the billions. You represent an entire nation and your GDP is only in the billions. I will accept the advisory position, but now I have two conditions. The first is that you will never talk down to me the way you just addressed me, or I will quit. The second is that you will provide the Sterling Hedge Fund with a letter confirming that the government of Israel will allow my hotel project to be fast-tracked. Do we have a deal, Mr. Minister?"

Knowing that the Prime Minister was demanding Regev to deliver Elliot on to the Board and highly impressed with Elliot's truthful comments, Regev simply bites his tongue and says, "Yes, we do."

Elliot extends his hand toward Regev, saying, "Good. I'll give you my best efforts and I'll work with you for the good of the country. Now, let's get this economy moving!"

A bewildered Goldstein, who can't believe what just went on, looks at the minister. Regev stares back at Goldstein and says, "If nothing else, this man has beitzim!" (Hebrew for balls)

As Elliot stands to leave the meeting, Regev says, "There are just two more things we need to do before you depart. The first is that I'd like you to divulge who you made the mystery call to."

Elliot answers, "I'd love to tell you, but then I'd have to kill you due to the high degree of confidentiality I maintain with that person. What's the second thing?"

"The Prime Minister has asked to meet you in person."

Elliot, stunned by the request, asks, "When?"

The minister says, "Right now. He's been here all day meeting with various Cabinet members about the national budget. The Prime Minister is a very hands-on sort of guy. Follow me. I will escort you to a ceremonial office the Prime Minister has here in the Finance Ministry. He's waiting for you. Come with me."

Elliot responds, "Why would he want to meet me? I'm sure he's got much better things to do with his valuable time."

Trying to convey a sense of humor, Regev answers, "I agree, why would he waste his time on you? All kidding aside, the Prime Minister believes your blend of practicality, experience, and thinking outside of the box is exactly what this country requires at this time in history."

Not quite convinced as to the motive of the face-to-face, Elliot asks, "How does he know so much about my practicality and thinking outside of the box?"

Regev quickly says, "As I told you earlier, we're pretty good at intelligence gathering here. Besides, he can't believe you outsmarted all of us with the digital coins. Frankly, he's very impressed with what you pulled off with those coins. Come, we're running late!"

As they're walking out the door, Elliot notices that Goldstein remained behind sitting on the couch. Out of curiosity, he asks Regev, "Two final questions. Why isn't Goldstein coming and how do I properly address the Prime Minister when I meet him?"

The short-fused Regev holds back from lashing out by saying, "Goldstein is not being summoned. Only you are invited. The Prime Minister's nickname is 'Shimi' although his real first name is Shimon. The public affectionately refers to him as Shimi, but you will refer to him as Prime Minister Weiztman. Just shake his hand, then refer to him as Prime Minister Weiztman, or simply Mr. Prime Minister. Please, let's move along, we'll talk as we walk. We're running very late."

The wide corridor floor is made from the internationally recognized Jerusalem stone. The black-framed photos dating back to the 1940s depicting Jerusalem are fascinating. They demonstrate the remarkable history of arguably the most famous city in the world. Elliot can't help but smile when he sees a photo of the then iron-willed Prime Minister Golda Meir personally serving tea to the then US Secretary of State Henry Kissinger. Elliot recalled that in one of their meetings, it was reported that Dr. Kissinger had stated to the Prime Minister, "Golda, you must remember that first I am an American, second I am Secretary of State, and third, I am a Jew."

Golda Meir famously responded, "Henry, you forgot that in Israel, we read from right to left."

As they arrive at the Prime Minister's working office, the security is visibly tighter with several armed military personnel guarding the entry from the reception area into the private office. Elliot is ecstatic to see that the security people all are armed with the Savor. Within minutes from checking in, Regev and Elliot are whisked into the office where the most important man in all of Israel is sitting behind a huge desk with what appears to be at least ten briefing notebooks.

The minister extends his hand and says in English with an Israeli accent, "Pleasure to meet you, Mr. Sterling. Anyone who can

216

sell that garbage cryptocurrency for a billion-dollar profit; is wise enough to negotiate the exclusive rights to sell our Savor rifle all over the world; and can throw the kind of multiple punches you unloaded on Regev, well, let's just say, you're my kind of man!"

Startled by how well Weiztman has been briefed, but puzzled as to how he knows what was said to Regev, Elliot responds with poise, "It's my honor, Mr. Prime Minister. Thanks very much for your kind compliments regarding the digital coins and the Savor, but I must say I'm quite curious as to how you know what I said to Minister Regev. Everything was stated privately to the minister."

The charismatic Prime Minister, with his confident firm posture, runs his hands through his long, wavy, grey and blond hair. He pauses for a brief second, stares at Elliot, and with his pronounced deep wrinkles on his forehead says without any apology, "As the Finance Minister told you, we're very good at intelligence gathering around here. Now, since you're soon going to be approved for our top security clearance, I'm going to let you in on my secret regarding Mr. Regev's and your confidential conversations. Here it is. I wanted to hear your conversation unfiltered so, I told Regev to leave the speaker on in his office. That's it!"

Elliot, who found the simplicity of the answer hilarious, just starts laughing out loud. Elliot didn't quite understand himself as to why he found the explanation so funny, but he couldn't stop laughing. Then, all of a sudden, the Prime Minister starts laughing in what becomes a special bonding moment between the two men who seem to really get each other.

Elliot looks at Weiztman and says, "We've got to teach this tactic to the American CIA." Just like two schoolboy buddies, they burst out laughing again. Obviously, these two guys, an Israeli Prime Minister and a self-made billionaire, have instantly become friends. This would be the beginning of what promises to become a fascinating relationship.

The laughter turns subdued as the wise Prime Minister decides to test his new best friend by seriously asking, "So, tell me, Elliot, are you really going to serve the nation or are you in it only for profit?"

Before Elliot gets a chance to answer the question, Weiztman, in his serious deep voice, asks, "Are you going to be one of these arrogant self-centered assholes that joins the Prime Minister's Economic Advisory Board solely to make money and profit from the information you come across? I've seen way too many of these bastards come and go. I need dynamic individuals who consider it their patriotic duty to help guide the nation to financial stability and strength. This country requires men of great vision.

"We need brain power, not our own citizens behaving like greedy financial terrorists. Israel is surrounded by fierce enemies from every direction who want to eliminate this country from the face of the earth. It's a miracle that we continue to survive. So, if you're in it solely for profit, I want you to withdraw your nomination right here and right now. I chose you, Elliot, because you're already filthy rich. I chose you because something tells me you're different. Am I right?"

Moved by Weiztman's words and the confidence he expressed in him, Elliot pauses, then says, "Well, Mr. Prime Minister, let me be perfectly honest with you, profit was my motive. Before I met you, I reluctantly visited with the Minister of Finance to get what I could get and then get the hell out of here.

"I had no intentions of being on any government board, not in America, and certainly not in Israel. I tend not to trust governments because I believe that power corrupts, and absolute power corrupts absolutely.

"So, when I was asked to join your Board, my natural inclination was to run as far away as possible. But then my business instinct, call it greed, kicked in and said, don't be stupid, there's a ton of money that can be made by joining, even though I knew I would be at odds with my good friend Minister Regev.

"Yeah, I'll admit, I started off just like the previous 'assholes' you described that have accepted this position to make money. But after processing your words, I'll assure you, that's not the way it's going to be for me. I'm going to serve this country with honor. Rest assured that I will not breach the trust you have bestowed upon me. In fact, I won't rest until we turn this country into a worldwide economic powerhouse. Together, we're going to vigorously move this nation forward like never before!"

The Prime Minister has a good feeling about his new-found friend. He realized this was precisely the guy he was looking for to serve in his administration. Using his sharp wit and keen sense of humor, Weiztman says, "Okay, Okay. I hear you, Elliot. How about I look the other way, and once in a while, you can make a little bit of profit here and there."

Again, the prime minister had hit Elliot's funny bone as they both burst out laughing. Upon sharing a good laugh, Elliot then composes himself and seriously says, "All joking aside, the only people who will profit from my service will be the citizens of Israel."

Accepting Elliot's sincerity, Weiztman closes the meeting by saying, "You and I are going to get along famously. By the way, I understand you have a home in Caesarea. I do too! So, as soon as I get down there next, I want you and your wife to come have dinner with Mrs. Weiztman and me. Yes, I'm aware that you have a wife, you know, all the Israeli intelligence stuff we talked about. Anyway, I want to get to know you better. Besides, we're neighbors!"

And just like that, Elliot had gone from being a highly successful, but relatively low-profile, Israeli businessman to a member of the Prime Minister's inner circle. He felt excited, yet concerned that with powerful friends came potentially powerful enemies. Elliot's instinctive genius kept warning him to be exceptionally cautious with Regev. He felt that this was a man that could not be trusted, especially the way the Finance Minister's facial expressions had telegraphed his obvious jealousy for the Prime Minister's respect in Elliot. It was apparent to Elliot that Regev would eventually engineer a way to throw him under the bus. No doubt, there could never be enough room on that advisory board for the two of them.

Chapter 19

Living in Israel had been a grand success for Elliot and Felicia. They had settled their major threat with the Nigerians, made a billion-dollar fortune beyond belief, and had risen to the highest levels of Israeli society due in part to the intimate relationship that naturally bonded with the Prime Minister and his wife, Shira. To put it mildly, life was very good for the Sterling family.

Felicia couldn't believe how quickly Mark and Emma's reception had crept up on her. She adored Emma's newborn baby and she loved observing the rugged Mark Goldman cuddle his daughter.

Although their wedding reception had started as a very controlled celebration, it had grown into a big-league social extravaganza. This event would surely catapult Elliot and Felicia Sterling onto every Israeli high society A-list and Felicia was determined to get it right.

Part of the pressure for Felicia was that Elliot had met so many high-level governmental acquaintances that he felt obligated to invite. He insisted that they be invited to assure that they wouldn't feel as if they had been intentionally slighted. The Prime Minister and his wife, along with five other ministers, had returned an RSVP indicating that they would all attend. Each member of Elliot's Economic Advisory Board had indicated that they were coming with their wives. Of course, all of the Sterling Hedge Fund associates, staff, and consultants were invited and had agreed to attend.

Felicia had on numerous occasions apologized to Emma and Mark about how uncomfortable she felt that the evening had grown into such a spectacle. So, she was especially grateful when Mark said, "We appreciate your kindness. We trust you both blindly. Whatever works for you guys, works for us."

On the morning of the grand reception, Felicia awoke at the crack of dawn. It was a magnificent morning looking out on her balcony as the sun began to rise over the Mediterranean coast. She was to meet the event planner in the already erected extravagant white tent where the celebration would be held. Felicia quickly threw her hair into a ponytail, put on an old white Stanford sweatshirt and some worn-out jeans. Without a shred of make-up, she briskly walked over to the kitchen to get some freshly brewed coffee. Within minutes, the natural beauty had made her way to the tented area on the grounds of her estate where the workers were well on their way towards laying down a gorgeous black-and-white checkered dance floor next to a small orchestra stage built the day before.

Felicia met the party planner, Abital, at the center of the room where the electrical technicians were busy at work installing special event lighting. Felicia and Abital greeted each other with a kiss, first on the right cheek, then on the left, as Abital enthusiastically says in her Israeli accent, "I'm passionate about beautiful, mood-provoking, and spectacular lighting! My team is dedicated to bringing out the elegance, ambiance, and theme of Mark and Emma's wedding reception through our lighting. I promise you, my dear Felicia, this party is going to be a world-class, awe-inspiring experience for everyone!"

Felicia calmly says, "The Prime Minister's wife assured me that there is no one in all of Europe or Israel that is better equipped to plan an event than you. I'm confident that Emma and Mark are going to have the time of their lives, and I'm equally sure our guests will experience a memorable evening.

"Okay, so explain to me the layout of the room and how the rhythm of the night is expected to go."

Abital, who is a serious, no-nonsense professional, responds, "Rather than stand here and talk, let's walk as I work. I'll point things out as we make our way through the room."

Felicia eagerly says, "Lead the way."

As they are walking, Abital explains that the party is organized as a self-serve food event versus waiter-served. An entire food pavilion was meticulously set up with stations ranging from carved roast beef to the most famous native fish in Israel called St. Peter's Fish, known in America as 'Tilapia'.

She points out that arrangements had been made to serve the "super-expensive" Karat caviar coveted by restaurateurs around the world. Abital winks at Felicia as she says, "Don't worry, I buy Karat at below wholesale. It never hurts to have a brother with the exclusive rights to this stuff."

They make their way over to the dessert section where Abital describes how Israel's most popular sweet recipes were at this very moment being prepared. She talks about the popular Rugelach, Halvah, and Israeli Chocolate Cookie Truffles. An animated Abital smiles with delight as she describes the Sweet Cheese Kanafeh and the warm Israeli Chocolate Cake. Abital says, "The Prime Minister goes crazy for Tahini Cookies, so of course, he will have an assortment from which to choose. Trust me when I say that Emma, Mark, and your lovely guests will be very well fed tonight. Oh, I forgot to mention, we'll have a separate ice cream parlor, along with a cappuccino, coffee, and tea station display!"

Felicia enthusiastically responds, "Tell me more."

Abital continues pointing out, "The hors d'oeuvre and appetizers will be arranged just outside the main tented area where guests will gather prior to entering the reception room. We will be tray-passing favorites ranging from sushi to chicken skewers. An open bar will be serving mixed drinks and wines featured from the Golan Heights and the Judean Hills. We will have a musical string quartet consisting of an ensemble of four players including two violins, a viola, and cellist. By the way, they are by far the best in Israel."

Feeling slightly embarrassed, yet curious to learn, Felicia self-assuredly asks, "What's a viola?"

With a warm smile, Abital answers, "Don't feel bad, it wasn't until recently that I learned what a viola actually was along with how it integrated into a string quartet. Anyway, a viola is a string instrument that is bowed or played with various techniques. It is slightly larger than a violin and has a lower and deeper sound magically complementing a string quartet."

Felicia, feeling appreciative of the explanation, seriously responds, "You know, I've seen that musical instrument more times than I can remember, and I have never bothered to ask what it was. I think I just thought it was a violin. I feel very enriched to have discovered a new instrument in my life. As they say, you learn something every day. Thank you for enlightening me. What about the main orchestra? Who did we hire for that?"

With great pride, Abital proclaims, "Tell Emma and Mark they better come prepared to dance. I mean it! These guys play all over Europe at the highest society events including royalty. This group is so good that they will have everyone in the room dancing all night long. Even the Prime Minister, who is notorious for being a terrible dancer, will be dancing his way toward exhaustion. They are truly that good! Believe me when I tell you that you will never use any other orchestra for your events other than these people. I can't wait until you hear them perform!"

Felicia says, "Sounds awesome! But will they play something soft and beautiful for Mark and Emma to have a traditional first dance before anyone else?"

Abital responds, "Absolutely. The beautiful couple gets the honor of the first dance. Then, this place is going to rock and roll! I guarantee you that your guests' feet will be hurting tomorrow morning."

Felicia asks, "What else can you tell me about this magnificent party?"

"We previously requested from Emma and Mark many photos of them and received quite a few. The cutest picture by far is the one of Emma, Mark, and the new baby. We even have a photo of Mark and Mr. Sterling as kids playing baseball together. I just love the one of Emma as a child. We have about ten pictures that we enlarged. They will be distributed throughout the venue. I have always felt that photographs like these bring much warmth to the party. These pictures really are fabulous!"

Felicia says, "We did a similar photo spread for my husband's fiftieth birthday party and the pictures were a big hit. To this date, people still talk to me about some of those photographs. Great touch. I'm looking forward to seeing them. I'd like Elliot to speak tonight about his life-long relationship with Mark and, of course, I want him to toast the new couple. At what point should he speak?"

In a formal professional voice, Abital responds, "The pace of tonight's event will be seamless. I will personally manage the party, and the flow will be perfect. Once your guests are seated in the tented area, Emma and Mark will be announced into the room by the orchestra lead singer, and they will proudly walk into the event as husband and wife with the spotlight on them.

"Thereafter, they'll graciously do the traditional first dance together, then, all hell will break loose as the orchestra will get this party rocking as they play the Horah (the Jewish wedding dance). We'll get Mark and Emma up on chairs as they have the time of their lives. After the Horah and your guests do some 'warm-up' dancing, everyone will take their seats. Mr. Sterling will then welcome everyone, make his remarks about his close friend, and finish with a beautiful champagne toast to the terrific new couple."

Very impressed, Felicia simply remarks, "Perfect!"

Abital adds, "You're right, the party will be perfect. Don't worry about a thing. Just enjoy the evening."

The balance of the day went by in a flash. All festivity preparation were done, and the party was about to commence as

Felicia and Elliot had made their way to the pre-reception area to greet their guests. Felicia looked drop-dead gorgeous in her Louis Vuitton evening gown. The spaghetti-strapped hand-embroidered dress with slits along each side was simply stunning. The metallic tones and silver bands with the unique Vuitton geometric pattern beautifully accentuated Felicia's sexy curves and waistline.

Elliot, who had lived a lifetime hating to dress in a tuxedo, actually looked very handsome wearing a Ralph Lauren classic black tuxedo. There was no doubt, Felicia and Elliot Sterling were about to become Israel's most glamourous and powerful couple. As scheduled, Prime Minister Weiztman and his lovely wife are the last to make their way through the reception line. They are graciously greeted by Elliot and Felicia. Thereafter, the Prime Minister and his wife are escorted by Elliot and Felicia to the table where they all would be seated together along with the Israeli Ambassador to the United States and his wife, Mark, Emma, and Felicia's best friends from Beverly Hills, Rachel and her husband.

Once they are properly seated, right on cue, a spotlight is directed to the main entry to the reception room where the lead singer of the orchestra says, "Ladies and gentlemen, please welcome for the very first time, Mr. and Mrs. Mark Goldman!"

Mark proudly holds his wife's hand as they slowly walk to the table of honor where his life-long best friend is waiting for him. The elegant and distinguished guests all stand and give them a respectful ovation as Elliot, Felicia, Mark, and Emma embrace. And, to the delight of the crowd, Elliot not only enthusiastically bear-hugs his friend, but gives him a big kiss on the forehead. Just as planned, the newly-weds are then announced to make their way to the middle of the dance floor.

Mark smiles at his new bride and embraces Emma as they start their romantic slow dance to the magnificent music of the orchestra. It is obvious to everyone in the room that these two people are very much in love. They appear to enjoy the dance even though the tall rugged Mark isn't much of a dancer. As they conclude their moment in the spotlight, Mark passionately kisses his wife on the lips while everyone in the room enthusiastically claps their hands in loud approval.

Instantly, the orchestra gets the party moving to the traditional Horah music as the tables empty and the dance floor becomes electrifying to the beat of the music. Before too long, the newlyweds are high above the dance floor sitting on chairs as Elliot and a gang of guests brace Emma and Mark as they are energetically swaying to the motion of the music. Everyone is laughing and smiling as the orchestra just keeps playing and playing. The euphoric look on Mark and Emma's faces says it all. This is going to be a night to remember.

Much to the obvious amusement of the guests, and as advertised by Abital, the orchestra had everyone, including the Prime Minister, dancing and smiling for well over thirty minutes after the Horah was over. Finally, the band leader says, "We'd like everyone to take their seats. A delicious dinner will be ready shortly for your enjoyment, and we're all going to be privileged to hear a few words from our gracious host, Mr. Elliot Sterling. So, please, ladies and gentlemen, take your seats at this time. Thank you."

Once every person is seated, Elliot briskly makes his way toward the stage and grabs a mic. He looks out over the debonair crowd and with tremendous charisma begins speaking, "Felicia and I warmly welcome you to a very special and emotional evening for us. We are especially honored to welcome Prime Minister Weiztman and his wife, along with the many dignitaries that have honored us with their presence here this evening."

Without any notes, Elliot begins his heartfelt story about two kids growing up in California without having too much other than each other. He tells the story about how they first met in kindergarten when Mark and Elliot claimed the same sleeping cot. Elliot remembers, "It wasn't such a big deal except it just happened to be the last cot available. The guy without the cot would need to rest on the floor." Elliot, now laughing out loud, goes on to say, "Before I knew it, out of nowhere, little innocent Mark punched me in the face! I reacted by kicking him in the groin. And that, my friends, was the beginning of a life-long friendship that has brought us here today. By the way, we were both sent to the Principal's office for a scolding, and that's before both of our mothers were called to come pick us up from our suspended day at school! That's a true story!"

As he looks out over a crowd of people laughing hysterically, Elliot makes eye contact with Mark and asks, "Hey, Mark. Did I get that right?"

Mark smiles and answers, "Almost. You're just missing the part about how I ended up with the cot, even after that 'cheap shot' kick of yours!"

Loving every moment of the narrative, the guests can't wait to hear more as Elliot continues, "Well, I left that part out because I wanted to spare you the embarrassment of having to explain to our guests how I felt so sorry for you after seeing you cry like a little baby. I just had to surrender the cot to you!"

By this time, it is sounding like two professional stand-up comedians naturally delivering their lines as the audience is roaring with laughter.

Elliot proceeds, "Seriously, meeting Mark Goldman on that day has forever changed my life for the better. Everyone in this room should be blessed to have a Mark Goldman in your life. A person who has your back no matter what. A man that you can rely on at the darkest of times.

"It is not a coincidence that Mark and I have spent our entire lives together since our comical beginning in that kindergarten room. This is a guy who will give you the shirt off his back. Actually, he once gave me the baseball jersey he was wearing during a little league game because I forgot to pack mine in my baseball tote bag. I'll never forget when Mark said, 'Here. You wear it. You're in the starting line-up and I'm only your backup on the bench. The team needs you more than they need me.'

"Imagine that. Here's a kid that could have been inserted into the starting line-up because I was stupid enough to forget my jersey and what does he do? He takes the jersey off his back and gives it to me so I can play, while he sits on the bench! I knew, right then and there, that this was a real friend. I also understood that Mark was a winner. A man willing to sacrifice for the good of the cause.

"We were inseparable throughout elementary school, middle and high school. We looked after each other as if we were brothers. We spoke every day until it was time for a new beginning. I was admitted to Stanford University on a tennis scholarship and Mark decided he would serve his country in the United States Marines. I will admit, this was a tough time for us. I was going the academic route and Mark was going to the School of Hard Knocks. I was worried I'd never see him again due to the dangers of being in the military, and he was worried that I would change for the worse by getting an education and forgetting about our friendship.

"Well, four years went by. I got an education, and Mark got a different type of education. We both grew up a lot during that time. When I graduated from Stanford, the first call I made was to Mark. I told him I wanted to start a real estate development company and I asked him to assist me. Neither one of us had very much money, but I knew that I wanted to associate myself with a fighter, a man I could trust to do the right thing when no one was looking. The same guy who took his jersey off his back so that I could play even though he had to sit.

"It took a hell of a lot of schmoozing by Mark and me, and a whole bunch of years before we finally got the Sterling Development Company off the ground. We built our company into one of California's premier real estate firms, and much of the credit for that success was due to Mark Goldman's honest hard work. Everyone who knows Mark understands that he's a no-nonsense clear-thinking problem solver. And, most important of all, he's a loyal friend and a man I trust and love with all my soul."

When the Prime Minister, then all the guests rose to their feet in a standing ovation, it was apparent that they were moved by the heartfelt remarks made by Elliot about his friend. But no one was more emotional than Mark as he stood up and walked over to Elliot and embraced him as a loving brother.

Felicia and Emma shed tears of joy witnessing these two life-long warriors share an iconic moment celebrating a beautiful life together as the guests spontaneously cheered out loud.

With his hand on Mark's shoulder, Elliot grabs the mic with a big smile and says, "I'm not done yet! This night also belongs to Emma. She's a highly intelligent young woman with the heart of a lion, and that of an angel. Her enthusiasm, her 'ruach' (spirit) for life, was obvious from the first day I met her in Beverly Hills. There is nobody on this earth that I would prefer for 'my brother' Mark to marry other than you, Emma. As the saying goes, you are a match made in heaven for Mark, and I know he loves you with all his heart. And so do we! Please hold your glasses up high with that expensive champagne my wife bought for all of you."

Elliot then proceeds to say, "May the marriage between Emma and Mark be full of good health, happiness, and grand success. May your lives together be spent in joy and Shalom (peace). And may you bring each other good for all the days of your lives. May God bless you, watch over you, and show you favor for the rest of your wonderful lives together."

Without prompting from anyone, the sound of silverware clicking against champagne crystal glasses could be heard reverberating throughout the room. Elliot knew exactly what was going on, but Mark didn't have a clue until Emma stood up and walked over to him as the chimes got louder.

Emma stands tall on her tippy-toes and whispers into Mark's ear, "They want us to kiss."

Much to the delight of the cheering crowd, Mark broadly smiles, grabs his wife, and lovingly kisses her on the lips for what feels like an eternity. The moment 'the kiss' is done, the orchestra leader half-jokingly remarks, "I've witnessed a lot of wedding reception kisses, but ladies and gentleman, that one belongs in the hall of fame! Okay, it's time for dinner and Mr. and Mrs. Sterling have asked me to please make yourselves at home. Enjoy the magnificent food. We'll back to perform for you shortly."

As the guests start moving toward the various food kiosks, Emma makes her way to Elliot and Felicia and spontaneously says, "Besides my husband, you are the most wonderful man I have ever met. Thank you for your inspiring words, Mr. Sterling. And you, Mrs. Sterling, well, I've never met anyone as gracious and charming as you! Thank you for planning this amazing party for Mark and I. This is a dream come true for me, and I will forever be grateful to the two you. I love you both!"

The night developed exactly as Abital and Felicia had planned. The food was delicious, the music was joyous, and the energy was unbelievable. No one had left because they were simply having way too much fun. One guest remarked to Elliot, "I've never seen the Prime Minister stay at a party for more than an hour. He's already been here for many hours and he's not going anywhere soon."

Mark, who had celebrated drinking with his friends and even with people he had never met, excused himself from Emma as he made his way up into the house to use the restroom. As he approached the powder room, he overheard a highly animated Minister of Finance Regev trash-talking Elliot.

Mark immediately recognizes that the man Regev is speaking to is Elliot's fellow member on the Economic Advisory Board. He decides to wait for a moment to continue eavesdropping on the conversation just to confirm what he thought is being said, is actually being said.

Mark listens for a minute as he hears a somewhat intoxicated Regev say, "Sterling is all show and no substance. He thinks he understands Israelis, but he doesn't understand the first thing about us. He's a fake, a phony, nothing but a scam. All Sterling does is kiss the Prime Minister's ass in order get favors from him for his business interests. I'm telling you, he's going to get us all fired! We need to get rid of him before he gets rid of us. This guy Sterling is in it for himself, not the well-being of Israel."

Mark has heard enough insults as he walks directly to Regev and confronts him, "Who the fuck do you think you are? What kind of a stupid, jealous jackass walks into a man's home and talks shit about him? You know nothing about Elliot Sterling. He works for Israel solely from his heart and soul. It costs him time and money to serve on the Prime Minister's Advisory Board, especially serving with an insecure idiot like you.

"The only reason you're going to get fired is because you are everything you accuse Mr. Sterling of being, and he is nothing like you. Elliot Sterling is a great man. A man of extraordinary vision, and if the Prime Minister is smart enough to listen to his advice, this country will start moving again.

"By the way, the street tells me you're corrupt as hell and an abusive misogynist. I really can't understand why your wife doesn't leave you. Everybody knows you're sleeping with your thirty-something receptionist. I'm surprised you haven't died from a heart attack. I even know you recently bought her a condo and a car. You are total garbage, Mr. Bullshit Finance Minister, so here's your options. One, you and your abused wife get the fuck out of here! Or two, I deck you right where you're standing. Oh, if your Ivy League education didn't teach you the word 'deck', it's slang for punching you in the face and knocking you on your butt! What's it going to be, asshole?"

Mark notices that the Advisory Board guy Regev had been gossiping with has long left the scene of the crime. Perhaps he didn't want to be associated with Regev's nasty lies or maybe he was just intimidated by Mark. The bottom line was that he was nowhere to be seen. As Mark stared at Regev to listen to his decision, the Finance Minister chooses to say nothing. Regev simply walks away without uttering a word, perhaps hoping that Mark would assault him so he could put him in jail. When he gets far enough away from Mark, Regev turns around and says, "You've just committed a very grave mistake! Thank you for verbally threatening me, I'll be filing a legal restraining order against you by a judge. I'm a very powerful man, Mr. Goldman. You're about to find out just how powerful I am. I feel sorry for you."

Mark responds, "The only guy you need to feel sorry for is you. Now, get the hell off this property! Listen carefully because this is not a threat, it's a fact. If you don't voluntarily leave this home within the next five minutes, I'm first going to deck you, then I'm going to drag you off the premises. Now you only have four minutes and forty-five seconds."

Without any further comment, Regev walks away clearly understanding that Mark meant every word he was saying. The question was would he call Mark's bluff? The answer came within the five-minute deadline. The Finance Minister and his wife had gathered their belongings and walked right past Mark without expressing a single word as they exited through the front door of the home on their way out. They were the very first to leave the reception, which was going very strong with no end in sight.

Now that the Finance Minister was gone from the party, Mark felt as if he had done the right thing even if Regev decided to retaliate. The issue for Mark was whether to disclose the incident tonight to Elliot or just let it slide until tomorrow. His instinct was to leave it alone through the rest of the party and figure out with Elliot what the appropriate consequences might be the next day.

Still slightly shaken by the unexpected altercation with Regev, Mark walks over to Elliot's private office and makes his way to the special liquor cabinet where Elliot keeps his favorite spirits. He grabs a bottle of Tequila and serves himself a double shot and chases that with another shot. Mark then takes a seat on the sofa and thinks for a minute about what transpired. For just a brief moment, Mark feels that perhaps he is in legal trouble because of the threat he made to a sitting Finance Minister.

Then he felt remorse for having reacted so aggressively defending Regev's insults of Elliot. But the more he thought about it, the more he decided everything was going to be alright. First, he had defended his friend from slanderous statements heard by Mark and the Board Member. He concluded that what he said, he would say it again. Second, he replayed the argument and concluded that the Board Member had walked away prior to his perceived "threat" having been made. Therefore, he concluded that any potential legal action by Regev against Mark would simply be a "he said, she said" allegation, since no one heard any words accept Regev and Mark. Yet, Regev would have to face the Board Member witness that Mark would produce as a "smoking gun", verifying the slanderous remarks made by Regev. Since there was no eyewitness as to what Mark had said, any potential judge would clearly understand that a close friend would have reacted with a vigorous defense.

The only issue really concerning Mark was what kind of retaliation the ego-driven Regev would seek. After all, he was a very high-level government official. One phone call by him could bring about a serious investigation which could cast a shadow on Elliot. For tonight, Mark concluded that he was personally in the clear. The only matter pending was how to control a loud-mouth Minister of Finance.

Mark figured that with cool heads the next day, Elliot and himself would turn circles around Regev. With his mind much clearer, Mark decides that the deep serious thinking moment is over and it is now time to continue partying with his lovely wife.

As Mark walks back into the reception, he sees Elliot, Felicia, the Prime Minister, and his wife collectively staring in one direction. The focal point of their concentration was the sight of Rose Sterling, Elliot's darling daughter, slow-dancing with the Prime Minister's tall and very handsome eldest son, Ethan Weiztman. Once Mark understood the picture, he started smiling at the intensity of the invasion of privacy of these two innocent kids. Mark is thinking, *Here's a young couple that probably just met for the first time tonight, and they have five adults observing every move they're making as if they're in a zoo.*

Mark walks directly to Elliot and whispers in his ear, "You really look ridiculous gazing at your daughter." Then Mark addresses all of them, "Give your kids some space! You got everyone in this place with their eyes fixed on them. Come on, let them enjoy a private moment!"

Not realizing how uncomfortable it was for Ethan and Rose, the Prime Minister asks, "Was it so obvious? Do you think they're actually aware we were looking?"

Mark answers, "Yes, and yes."

As the music stops, Ethan, a Harvard medical school student, and Rose walk over to their embarrassed parents. The charming Ethan addresses them with a charismatic smile, "I'm not the best of dancers, in fact, I'm not anywhere so good at it as Rose, but I trust we entertained you. In fact, it appears we may have entertained everyone in the room. Rose insisted we forgive you, and of course we will, but with your permission, Mr. and Mrs. Sterling, I'd like to take your daughter outside for a short private walk here in the neighborhood so that we might have a chance to get to know each other without two or three hundred sets of eyes focused in on us. Sound okay?"

Felicia answers, "Of course." Then adds with her adorable laugh, "Sorry, just too hard not to stare!"

Ethan looks at Rose, then Felicia, and says with an amused grin, "We forgive you, Mrs. Sterling. Now, if you will excuse us."

As Ethan and Rose are about to leave, the Prime Minister jumps in and seriously asks, "Are your mom and I excused too?"

As he continues to walk, Ethan looks over his shoulder and says smiling, "Yes Dad, the pardon extends to Mom and you too. Goodnight everybody."

It seemed as if no one had any interest in leaving the party. The music was going strong, and the desserts, liquor, coffee, and tea just kept flowing as the guests kept laughing and dancing. Finally, the Prime Minister looks at his watch and informs his wife that he's got to get up early the next morning for a Cabinet meeting. As they get up out of their seats, they walk over to Felicia and Elliot who are on the dance floor. The Prime Minister politely interrupts their intimate moment together.

"This has been a magnificent evening. You are both not only the best hosts in all of Israel, but Shira and I consider it an honor to call you our good friends. Who knows, perhaps soon we may even become mishpocha!" (Yiddish for a group of people related by blood or marriage.)

The Sterlings and the Weiztmans truly sealed their close bond this night as they hug and kiss each other goodnight. Showing a lot of class, the Prime Minister stops to congratulate Mark and Emma on their marriage as he and his wife, along with his security entourage, exit the reception.

The sensational party continued for nearly two more hours. It seemed as if it came to a close only because all the guests were simply exhausted as they warmly thanked and said goodbye to the Sterlings. What a grand success this night has been as Elliot, Felicia, Mark, and Emma sit in the residence's breakfast nook drinking hot chocolate and reminiscing about the party, life, and friendship.

Chapter 20

More than two months had gone by since the glorious party for Mark and Emma. Since Elliot had been clearly warned by Mark about the despicable words that Regev had said about him, Elliot had been very guarded in his relationship with the Finance Minister. The only interaction he had with him was at the Advisory Board meetings and they usually were on separate sides of the economic debate.

Mark had been advised by Elliot to do nothing further regarding Regev's comments. He was also told that Regev didn't have the courage to bring any charges against Mark, especially in light of the strong relationship Elliot enjoyed with the Prime Minister. That advice turned out to be correct. Regev did nothing legally against Mark and likewise did nothing ethically to apologize to Elliot for all of the slanderous statements he had made against Elliot.

During these months, Rose had fallen deeply for Ethan, and Ethan had fallen deeply in love with her.

Both families were delighted with the development of their relationship even though it was time for Ethan to get back to the Harvard Medical School in Massachusetts. Rose didn't quite know what to do with the realities of living in two different cities. She was ready to re-enter classes at Stanford University in California, which would be better than the distance from Israel. Nevertheless, it was still going to be two different cities.

Elliot had advised that they carry on with their education at their respective schools and that everything was going to turn out just fine. The Prime Minister had given similar advice to his son. Felicia had mixed emotions. She loved Ethan for Rose and thought that perhaps a short courtship and a fast marriage might be the best way to go. They could start their lives together, supporting each other through school, and perhaps with a little persuasion, Rose could transfer to Harvard to complete her undergraduate degree.

As Elliot was waiting for the monthly Advisory Board meeting to commence, he was in deep thought trying to determine whether Felicia was right suggesting that Rose should pull the trigger and proceed to marriage or whether it was smarter to wait. Felicia was normally very accurate on her thoughts regarding matters such as these, but it was clear in Elliot's mind that Ethan should pursue his education at his prestigious university and Rose should do the same.

They hardly even knew each other and it felt as if the best approach was to back off and let these two talented young adults develop naturally over more time. If there wasn't enough good character and love on both sides to get through this period, then it probably wasn't meant to be. Elliot decided that this would be his final position just as the Prime Minister made an unexpectable appearance in the room.

Out of respect for the Prime Minister, everyone in the suite stands, then immediately sits back down at his prompting. He starts by addressing the Board, "Shalom. I understand that you did not expect me here today. I felt as if I should address you concerning a serious matter that I will share with each of you with confidence. Finance Minister Regev will be indicted on corruption charges tomorrow by Israel's attorney general. The charges are being brought after a two-year investigation.

"The Finance Minister will face multiple counts of bribery and three counts of breach of trust. This is the first time in Israeli history that a sitting Finance Minister faces criminal charges of this nature.

"Mr. Regev has called the prosecution's indictment 'outrageous' and an 'unprecedented witch hunt' carried out by his opponents. I have spoken at length with the attorney general and I have concluded without a doubt that the evidence is overwhelming against Regev. I have asked for, and received, the resignation of Mr. Regev, effective immediately. Further, I have made the decision that I will ask Elliot Sterling to become the Chairman of this Economic Advisory Board."

The Prime Minister refrains from speaking for a moment, looks at each member of the Board, then addresses Elliot, "I apologize for the short notice, but as everyone in this room knows, your country needs you. So, do you accept your appointment, Elliot?"

Not allowing Elliot to utter a word, the Prime Minister smiles and instantly says, "Thank you, Mr. Sterling, I never had any doubt you'd accept. Of course, I've taken the liberty of having brought with me Judge Abramowitz to administer the oath of office right this very moment so that you can proceed with leading our Board without missing a beat."

Having no intentions of accepting the chairmanship, Elliot responds with a calm grin on his face, "I'm honored, Mr. Prime Minister, at your confidence, but there are far more qualified and much more deserving people on this Board to hold the chairmanship.

Respectfully, I refer you to one of them. I humbly withdraw from your nomination. Thank you."

The Prime Minister, who has already made up his mind and knows that every member of the Board is staunchly loyal to him, says, "Does anyone here volunteer to replace my nomination of Mr. Sterling?"

Not one person says a word. Then the Prime Minister continues, "Does anyone here have an objection to my nomination of Mr. Sterling?"

Again, not one comment is made except by Elliot, who says, "Yeah, me! I object!"

The Prime Minister walks over to Elliot, puts his hand on his shoulder, then looks him squarely in his eyes. "Sorry. Too late. My Cabinet has already voted to approve you as the next Chairman of the Economic Advisory Board. So, I ask you to raise your right hand and allow Judge Abramowitz to swear you in. Since I have the President of the United States visiting me tomorrow, I really need to go!"

Elliot clearly sees the handwriting on the wall. "I believe you call this Israeli democracy. I call this a benevolent dictatorship. Alright, you win, Mr. Prime Minister, with one minor condition."

The Prime Minister curiously asks, "And what's your condition?"

Elliot answers, "Mark Goldman is sanctioned by you and this Board to be my official assistant. He is to be granted clearance to participate in the meetings and will be regarded as an official staff member of this Board. We have a deal, Mr. Prime Minister?"

Laughing out loud, the Prime Minister says, "You are way too easy, Elliot. Of course, we have a deal. Mark will be provided with his proper credentials and can start conducting official business next week.

"Very well, Judge Abramowitz, please administer the oath. I really mean it, I must go."

Reluctantly, Elliot raises his right hand as Abramowitz administers the oath in less than one minute.

The Judge shakes Elliot's hand as he congratulates him on becoming the Chairman of arguably the most influential and powerful Board in Israel. The Prime Minister follows, shaking Elliot's hand and saying, "Finally, this Board is going to have the leadership and vision to accomplish big things. Very good decision, Elliot" as the Prime Minister winks at Elliot.

Elliot winks back at the Prime Minister, saying, "I'll do my best."

As the Prime Minister starts walking toward the door, he says, "Thanks to all of you for your understanding. Please give Mr. Sterling your cooperation, undivided attention, and your straightforward talk. We have much to accomplish and I would appreciate all of you to cooperate. Let's get this country moving again! I'm relying on each one of you to come through for me. Please don't let me down. Oh, by the way, I'll name a new Minister of Finance within a week. Who knows, it might even be one of you."

After a series of formalities are read for the record by the Clerk, Elliot stands at his chair, takes off his coat, rolls up his sleeves, and says, "I call this meeting to order. As you all know, this is not a job I asked for. In fact, I do not like having the enormous responsibility of being the chairman of this Board.

"But since it appears that I have become a victim of our Prime Minister's forced persuasion, I do pledge to each of you that I will do my best to guide this Board and this nation toward unprecedented prosperity. And finally, if any one of you finds an objection to have my business associate, Mark Goldman, be a member of the staff of this Board, I will remove him from consideration. The reason I have insisted in his participation is that I believe he's going to help make us better. For sure, he makes me better. So, by a show of hands, who here is in favor of Mr. Goldman becoming a staff member of this Board."

Every hand went up almost in unison. To the delight of Elliot, he says, "Let the record show that it is by unanimous consent that the Board agrees to the appointment of Mark Goldman to serve in the capacity of staff member to the Economic Advisory Board. Thank you, gentlemen, for your vote of confidence.

"Over time, I am quite certain that you may even end up thanking me for this recommendation!"

With that bit of housecleaning taken care of, Elliot decides that he will set his vision for the economy and his agenda for the Board members by taking the floor. "We have much to accomplish here for the country, but if we are always participating in wars or military conflicts, we will never be free from the financial influence the United States has over us. We will never truly be able to be a wealthy country if our defense budget keeps draining the economy. We must learn as a nation to control our defense spending by staying out of military conflicts, especially including tensions along Israel's southern and northern borders. Don't get me wrong, our military forces should be second to none, but our leaders must keep us out of war. We do this, our economy will blossom beyond recognition."

The Board members had never associated the strength of the economy of Israel with defense spending. Military expenses were just a way of life. Every member (except Elliot) had served in the Israeli Defense Forces (IDF) and had never seriously thought about the colossal price the nation paid toward military expenditures.

As simple as the concept Elliot had brought to light, no one had really given it much analysis. Military spending was just seen as a necessary national stupendous budget item. It really never seemed to faze anyone in the government, until this moment. All of a sudden, one member from his seat spontaneously began to pound the table in approval of the idea. Then, a second, and a third, then all the members clapped their hands in appreciation of Elliot's military comments.

Elliot looks around the room, chuckling and saying, "I guess you liked that recommendation. Well, if you liked that one, you're going to love this one. The state of Israel is going to develop into an energy power! We are going to become an independent country that will not depend on anyone for its energy needs. The eastern Mediterranean, better known for conflict and strife, will become a mecca for oil exploration. Israel, who is at the mercy of volatile, largely unfriendly neighbors for fuel supplies will one day soon have enough natural gas for itself and to sell to others. With this Board's leadership, Israel is about to become the 'poster child' of a natural gas rush that will transform us from energy paupers into princes!"

The Board members are so excited with this idea that they each stand to give Elliot an electrifying standing ovation. One member shouts out, "From your lips to God's ears! Tell us more. Please tell us more!"

Elliot passionately continues, "Mark Goldman has researched and reported to me that there is a natural gas field about 50 miles west of Haifa known as Tamar. We now know that a Texas energy company has located massive offshore fields 80 miles from Haifa. This a monster natural gas field!"

"This new offshore oil development will not only make Israel self-sufficient, but will eventually allow us to export oil! Did you hear me? Export oil! Mark my words, we will soon be able to build partnerships that will create a gas pipeline that will run from here and link us to the gas economy of Europe. It will reach our Arab neighbors. This idea is destined to become a remarkable revolution and I guarantee you, as sure as I'm standing here, the State of Israel will emerge into an energy powerhouse."

"An independent Israel will not ever need to depend on anyone for its energy needs."

The members are mesmerized with the vision that Elliot is outlining for them. One by one they keep reciting out loud, "Mazel Tov. Mazel Tov!" (Good luck. The constellation of good stars and destiny.)

They didn't want him to stop. The members wanted to hear more from their leader. So, Elliot continues, "This nation is blessed with brain power. The future is tied to technology. I say let's become known for our research and development for high technology companies. We will become the Silicon Valley of the Middle East and Europe. This will not only contribute to our economy, but will be a brilliant way to assist in developing our domestic military industry by focusing a portion of our R&D on military technology giving us an edge over our neighbors."

"I see us becoming a state-of-the-art country to work with when it comes to electronic warfare systems and innovative medical imaging. My Hedge Fund research tells me that the international computing industry has shifted the emphasis from hardware to software products, which human capital plays a much greater role. We will become one of the first nations to compete in global software markets."

"I predict that one day, not too far out in the future, more than fifty Israeli companies will have initial public offerings on NASDAQ and other international stock markets. Before you know it, the international investment community will be referring to Israel as the greatest 'Start-Up' nation' in the world! Sound feasible to all of you?"

A gentleman well into his seventies and traditionally the quietest Board member stands to his feet and says to the laughter of the entire Board, "I'll bet my old sweet ass it's feasible. Let's get started!"

The Board meeting lasted for hours with Elliot enthusiastically outlining one economic idea after the other. He talked about the importance of the diamond industry both from the trade and manufacturing side of diamonds. Elliot's vision included Israeli diamond companies supplying the stones that would eventually garnish a vast amount of the diamond jewelry sold worldwide. He emphasized that Israel's diamond polishing factories would soon become the most advanced in the world.

He told the members that Israel was already well recognized for experienced diamond polishers and that a marketing campaign would be launched by the government reminding the world markets that Israel has a rich tradition of know-how and expert craftsmanship second to none in this field. Elliot confidently predicted that Israel is so good at this that it will eventually expand its manufacturing capabilities to various offshore locations such as India, China, Africa, and elsewhere.

The new Board Chairman concludes the marathon meeting by reminding the members that the tourist and the agriculture industries have just scratched the surface of their potential. And he tells them with pride that the Ashkelon Desalination Plant converting seawater to fresh water will eventually be able to convert 15,000 to 16,000 cubic meters of seawater to fresh water EVERY HOUR with the goal of supplying 15 percent of Israel's annual water supply. Technology that the world will eventually need.

"You see, gentlemen. We have enormous potential, and yes, we can reach these goals if we collectively have the will to achieve them. No more fighting amongst each other. No more hidden agendas. Let's get this nation leading the planet in innovation. I know we have the brain power. Together, we will to get there! Our tiny country is about to become an economic powerhouse with your help and ideas. Let's pledge to work together to assist the Prime Minister to get this nation moving again. We can do this!"

"This meeting stands adjourned."

Again, a standing ovation for their new leader, along with a sincere tear of joy from its oldest member.

Nearly six months had gone by from the date Elliot had been appointed Chairman. Since that initial Board meeting, the name Elliot Sterling had become synonymous with "patriotic financial genius". He had captured the attention of the finest economic minds throughout Israel. In fact, his reputation had become so famous and well respected that even the taxi-cab drivers on the streets of Tel Aviv knew exactly who he was. It seemed as if the country had discovered a new national hero. He was the guy with the ideas and vision to begin an Israeli economic modernization of a nation desperately in need of a financial renaissance.

Even Mark Goldman's national profile had begun to rise as a direct result of his involvement with Elliot and the Committee. He had built a reputation and the nickname "Mr. Fixer". The Board members consistently went to Mark with their questions, and Mark consistently got them their answers.

Mark loved every moment of his interaction because he understood that he was on the cutting edge of information, which was organically assisting the Sterling Hedge Fund to grow at a staggering rate.

Although Elliot and Mark never openly discussed this fact, they both knew intrinsically the net effect of serving on the Economic Board.

As time passed, the investigation into the former Minister Regev got nastier and nastier. Not only was he facing decades in prison for bribery and corruption, but new allegations of sexual harassment were looming. And to make matters worse, the government attorneys were forcing Noam Goldstein to provide inside information to the government in order to build the case against Regev. Goldstein had been named as an unindicted co-conspirator in the legal case against Regev. Almost immediately thereafter, Elliot terminated his services regarding the Jerusalem hotel project.

The Prime Minister decided that he would hold off naming a new Finance Minister in order to allow Elliot an opportunity to get a grip on the Economic Board and start implementing his ideas.

Instead, the Prime Minister delegated the duties of Finance Minister to the Economic Board, allowing that group to de facto serve as a committee handling what would normally be under the administration of the Finance Minister. Since Elliot was the Chairman and their leader, he effectively served as the ceremonial Finance Minister, appearing at official government meetings when required.

In fact, most dignitaries that Elliot met referred to him as "Mr. Finance Minister". This was a role Elliot was beginning to become very comfortable playing until one day the Israeli press questioned his true loyalty in a newspaper headline reading: THE SILENT AMERICAN—ELLIOT STERLING.

The article questioned whether an American who maintained dual citizenship with the United States of America and with Israel should actually be entrusted with the country's top secrets. It openly suggested that Elliot was only in it to enrich his Hedge Fund business and that the Prime Minister was a "sucker" for thinking Elliot could maintain dual loyalties to his "true homeland as opposed to Israel". The piece went on to suggest that the Prime Minister was either naïve or making "a ton of money with this foreigner".

It didn't take long before the phone rang in his private office in Caesarea with the Prime Minister initiating the call. As Elliot answers the call, an assistant with a clear Israeli accent says, "One moment, Mr. Sterling, the Prime Minister will be with you shortly."

Elliot responds, "Certainly."

It takes about a minute before the Prime Minister's familiar voice comes on the line. "Well Elliot, that newspaper article makes me out to be a crook and stupid. It makes you come across as a manipulative monster. What do you think?"

Elliot quickly responds, "I think I should immediately resign and take away their ammunition!"

The Prime Minister instantly responds, "No, Elliot! That's precisely what these bastards want you to do! We're going to do the exact opposite. I'm going to offer you the post. There is no one more qualified for the job than you. I want you to be my Minister of Finance. The country loves you and I need you. I want to announce this to the media and the nation today."

Taken by complete surprise, Elliot reacts, "Have you totally lost your mind, Mr. Prime Minister?"

Prime Minister Weiztman says, "Wrong again, Elliot. Financially speaking, you are by far the best thing that has happened to this country in a long time. Your ideas are cutting edge. You know what to do in order to modernize our economy. You're my first choice, Elliot, so give me your answer! Let's get this announcement scheduled for later today. Do you accept my offer?"

Elliot thinks for a moment then says, "The press is going to eat us alive with your offer! Do us both a favor. Pick one of the very capable members on the Economic Board. I insist you make this easy on yourself. Pick someone else!"

Weiztman pauses, then says, "And lose you and Mark Goldman. That's not going to happen! You're the 'chosen one', Elliot. You're it! You, my good friend, are going to be the next Israeli Minister of Finance. I need you to make your way up to Jerusalem by the end of day. Meet me at Beit Aghion (the official residence of the Prime Minister) for a joint press conference. I will make the official announcement, then you will say a few words. Agreed?"

Elliot, somewhat dazed at the fact that he has been asked to become the Finance Minister of a nation, smiles while responding, "I hope I don't live to regret this decision. Alright, I accept."

Now smiling from one ear to the next, the Prime Minister says enthusiastically into the receiver of the phone, "Good man! You're a good man, Elliot! I'll see you at 4:45 PM sharp at Beit Aghion. I'll schedule the press conference for 5 PM, which will give us plenty of time to make the evening news. By the way, the nation thanks you for agreeing to serve our country and I thank you personally for your sincere commitment to the well-being of our beloved Israel. See you later this afternoon."

At precisely 4:45 PM, Elliot was awaiting the commencement of the press conference while being briefed by the Prime Minister's chief of staff as to the sequence of events that were scheduled to occur.

At 5 PM, Prime Minister Weiztman enters the room saying, "I've spoken to the rest of my Cabinet and they unanimously endorse this move of naming you Minister of Finance. So, let's get this show on the road. I'll speak first, then you'll say a few words. Then we'll hold a brief press conference"

As the two men enter the room, all rise out of respect, then take their seats as the Prime Minister steps up to the lectern while Elliot remains standing to his right. The Prime Minister greets the press, "Good evening. Thank you all for coming on such short notice. Today, we're going to introduce to you the man who I will nominate to be the next Finance Minister of Israel. I expect the Knesset to approve the nomination in short order. Mr. Elliot Sterling is a highly experienced international businessman and the current Chairman of the prestigious Israel's Economic Advisory Board. I introduce to you my choice to serve this nation as the next Minister of Finance."

To a polite, yet partisan crowd, there is a soft applause with all eyes on the nominee. Elliot slowly walks toward the podium as the sparse group stands out of their seats and gives Elliot a standing ovation.

Elliot puts both hands on the lectern, stares at the crowd, and humbly says, "Oh, by all means, please be seated."

Making eye contact with Felicia who has accompanied Elliot to the press conference, he begins without any written notes, "Thank you, Prime Minister Weiztman, for the confidence you have bestowed upon me. If confirmed by the Knesset, I will work tirelessly toward earning your trust, and the nation's trust as Israel's Minister of Finance. Additionally, I'd like to thank the members of the Economic Advisory Board, which I consider a great honor to have so closely worked with over the previous months. The nation owes each of them a debt of gratitude for their dedication and patriotism."

Elliot looks straight at the members of the press and opens his formal comments, "I was born in America and I come from very humble beginnings. Although we didn't have much money, my mother always made sure we had a roof over our head, plenty to eat, and decent clothing to wear. We never felt poor or disadvantaged. In fact, we always felt secure because we had each other. That security is all I ever needed growing up. I learned from a very early age that there is no substitution for hard work. If you earn what you have, not only will you appreciate it, but you'll fight hard to keep it."

As Elliot glances at Felicia, she winks, signifying he is right on track with his remarks. With the confidence of his wife, Elliot continues, "While attending Stanford University, I quickly realized that the world was made up of a diverse population with many cultures and philosophies. Just because I thought something was true, it didn't necessarily mean that everyone shared my opinion. This was a very valuable lesson that helped shape my life through my business career to this very moment."

Pausing, Elliot continues, "I have been very fortunate throughout my lifetime to share a life with my remarkable wife, Felicia, and our two loving children. I have also been very fortunate to live a life alongside my close friend and business associate, Mark Goldman. To a certain degree, they all complete me. They have kept me grounded and focused.

"As for the nation of Israel, I see a terrific future. My economic vision for this country has no boundaries. We will become a global financial force in modern technology. I predict that we will one day surpass Silicon Valley with our innovations, and we are well on our way toward becoming an energy independent nation. Our tourism, agriculture, textile and our diamond industry will thrive. Israel, at peace, will economically develop like no other country in the world.

"Just like in my early days, we don't need anyone else but ourselves to find security and success. The unity of the people of this country will be vital. Together, we will become the envy of the world not only from an economic point of view, but as a model nation for the world to emulate. I thank the Prime Minister for this honor and will be pleased to take a few questions."

The press was so impressed with the spontaneous remarks of the future Finance Minister that they did what was never done before by this group of journalists covering the Prime Minister—they applauded out of respect for what they had just heard. It wasn't just a few of the media, it was unanimous and thunderously loud. Even the Prime Minister could not believe what he was experiencing as he remarks with a big smile and a laugh, "Perhaps I should have been introducing Mr. Sterling as my successor. Very well, let's take the first question. Yes, you in front, go ahead."

A young reporter introduces himself and asks, "Mr. Sterling, as an American, isn't hard for you to differentiate your loyalty for America while serving Israel? How can the Israeli people be assured that your policies won't be swayed by your United States interests?"

Elliot stares right into the eyes of the reporter and answers, "You may be too young to know the background of the fourth Prime Minister of Israel, Golda Meir. Anyway, she was born in Kiev, then immigrated to the United States as a child with her family and was educated in America as a teacher before going on to become one of Israel's greatest Prime Ministers. I'll say no more."

For the next thirty minutes, Elliot had the press corps eating out of his hands. He had them laughing and agreeing with him. He answered all of their questions with confidence and with ease until finally, the Prime Minister closed the press conference with a simple "thank you" to the members of the press.

Elliot had won the moment. He had gained the Israeli media's respect that would lead to the public opinion of the nation being favorable for an American-born citizen holding the prominent position of Finance Minister. It could not have gone any better, which would assure Elliot's approval by the Knesset.

Chapter 21

Nearly a year had passed with lightning speed since that memorable press conference. Elliot had been confirmed unanimously by the Knesset. Gilad Regev had been convicted of corruption charges and was waiting for his appeal. He also continued to face an upcoming trial on serious sexual harassment charges. Although Noam Goldstein was never formally indicted due to insufficient evidence, it was publicly known that he was just as guilty as Regev and had vanished from the Israeli business scene.

Elliot had gone about his business with great seriousness and placed the country on a trajectory toward economic respect around the world. The Israeli public had credited him with raising the standard of living. There was no doubt, Elliot Sterling had become the most popular politician in Israel. In fact, the word on the street was that he might one day become the next Prime Minister.

On what seemed like a routine Monday morning, Elliot was in his office at his home in Caesarea organizing some final matters before being picked up by his government chauffeur for transport to his Jerusalem office. He had an important meeting scheduled with the US Treasury Secretary to discuss a new trade treaty. Mark had been working on the details of the new treaty for months, and today would be the first face-to-face between Elliot and the American Treasury Secretary.

As Elliot is about to close his briefcase, a special ring on his cell phone signifies it is the Prime Minister. He immediately answers the call and is asked to wait for the Prime Minister. Within seconds, the Prime Minister says in a distressed voice, "Elliot, it's my son, Ethan! These bastards have my son! He's been abducted! Oh, my God, he's been kidnapped!"

Alarmed at the seriousness of the news, and simultaneously worried at the devastating effect this would have on his daughter, Elliot maintains his composure, calmly saying, "I'm on my way to Jerusalem right now to help you. I guarantee you we're going to get Ethan out of this. Did this happen in America?"

The Prime Minister says, "Yes. In the parking lot basement of his apartment near the Harvard Medical School. His bodyguard was shot and instantly killed. Our Mossad intelligence agency advise that Ethan was most likely injected with a drug to knock him out then concealed in a bag and clandestinely driven out of the parking lot in some vehicle, probably a van. We're working on obtaining the surveillance videos. Please tell Rose immediately."

"The cable news networks are about to go live with the story. She needs to hear it from you first. Tell her what you told me. Give her hope that Ethan is getting out of this alive. Listen Elliot, cancel your driver. I'll have a helicopter pick you up in about twenty minutes and fly you to Jerusalem. Let's engage the American Treasury Secretary to work on this right away. Please pray to God that your daughter's fiancé lives to see their Chuppah! (A canopy under which a Jewish couple stands during their wedding ceremony). I got to go, Elliot. I'll see you here."

Elliot immediately advised Felicia who took the news very badly. She was crying and frightened for Ethan. She was horrified picturing Ethan in the hands of these monsters and thinking about the pain Ethan's parents were feeling. Additionally, she was very worried about the negative effects this nightmare would have on Rose. In fact, she told Elliot that she should probably get to Stanford to be with her during this ordeal. Elliot did his best to calm her down, but he was under enormous pressure to call his daughter before she heard about it on the news or from a friend.

Elliot reaches Rose on her cell phone and says, "Listen sweetie. Ethan has been kidnapped at Harvard. He's alive, but we don't know much more. The Israeli and American governments are using all their collective power to free him. I need you to stay calm and have faith. What can I do for you?"

Rose, who is shocked, stays composed and responds, "Daddy. This is what you can do for me. Get him out alive! Get Ethan out alive!" And with that said, she bursts out crying uncontrollably.

Elliot, who cannot stop her from crying, says, "I promise you, Ethan is coming out. Now, I must go. I'm going to pass you to your mom. We'll keep you informed. If you need Mom to get to Palo Alto or you want to come home to Caesarea, just tell us what you need. Be very careful. I love you."

As he hands Felicia the phone, he can hear the noise from the helicopter, which has landed in his spacious backyard. Elliot grabs his briefcase, gives his wife a kiss and hug, and says, "I'll call you as soon as I can with an update. I love you and tell Rose I got this."

The flight to Jerusalem is very efficient and quick. Before he knows it, Elliot is escorted into a private room several levels underground from the offices of the Prime Minister. He's escorted into the room where a high-level command post has been established for the sole purpose of rescuing Ethan Weiztman. The Prime Minister is seated in between the director of the Mossad, (Israel's equivalent to the American CIA) and the director of Shin Bet (Israel's equivalent of the FBI).

Elliot is told to take a seat at the table. He glances at the Prime Minister whose face looks pale and distraught. Then he starts listening intently to the General in charge of the Mossad. "We believe it's Hezbollah as the probable proxy for Iran. The intelligence we've gathered so far indicates that the kidnapping was planned by two Americans. We've been able to identify the Americans who we believe were recruited by Hezbollah, the Shia Islamist political party and militant group based in Lebanon.

"The Hezbollah paramilitary wing is the Jihad Council, and its political wing is Loyalty to the Resistance Bloc party in the Lebanese parliament. Our working theory is that they ordered it. We are confident nothing will happen to Ethan until they make their demands."

The General continues, "The moment we have the garage video camera images, we'll get the license plate of the vehicle the kidnapper's used and hopefully we'll identify the assailants. We'll figure out where they have Ethan hostage very shortly thereafter. The American FBI and the CIA are on the case as well as the Boston Police Department. I'm sure that within the next hour we'll have a very good idea where these assailants are and what they want."

An aide to the Prime Minister enters the room and advises that the President of the United States is on the phone. The Prime Minister picks up the line as the President says, "Shimon, I got everyone in my government that's worth a damn desperately trying to figure out how to free your boy. I wouldn't bet against us. Now, I know you guys over there like to do your own thing when it comes to this kind of stuff. It's better to let us handle this, Shimon. We'll keep you up to date with each step we take. Our Treasury Secretary is over there to meet with Finance Minister Sterling. We'll keep all lines of communication wide open. What else can I do for you?"

The Prime Minister responds, "Thank you, Mr. President. I think you're doing everything you can.

"Here's what I know from my vast military experience and from everything I have learned as Prime Minister. If we don't act fast, they're going to kill my son, Mr. President. These bastards are going to kill my precious boy! So, I'm not going to promise you we're going to just sit back and let you handle this. We will do what we must do to save Ethan, but of course, we'll keep you informed. Please provide us with any information you have. Every second is vital. Thanks very much for your cooperation."

The President responds, "I'm going to pretend I didn't hear the part about you doing what you must do. Remember, this is our jurisdiction and you don't want the left foot and the right foot tripping all over each other! Did you hear me, Mr. Prime Minister?"

Prime Minister Weiztman can barely maintain his composure as he solemnly responds, "I hear you, Mr. President. Now, I need you to clearly hear me. This is my son we're talking about and I will do whatever I need to do to save his life. We thank you and your government for your assistance. Shalom, Mr. President."

The President seriously answers, "Listen, Shimon. I'd probably do the same thing, but remember this, don't put American citizens at risk! I'll be praying for Ethan. Let's keep in touch."

The moment the Prime Minister hangs up his call with the President, he addresses all assembled in the room, "The President means well, but my instincts tell me that the Americans are going to get Ethan killed. So, I direct the Mossad to immediately create a plan to rescue Ethan. As we have done exceedingly well over the years, get our people in and out as quickly as is humanly possible. Work closely with the Americans for as much information as possible, but I want our people in charge of the entire operation to free Ethan. We know how to do this better than anyone else on the planet. In this instance, it will be better for us to ask for forgiveness from the Americans than permission to act. I want my options presented within two hours."

Just as the Prime Minister completes his instructions, the Director of Shin Bet announces, "We've got the video of the parking lot showing that there were two assassins who murdered our bodyguard while simultaneously kidnapping Ethan and stabbing him with an injection to put him to sleep. We have confirmed the license plate on a white van. And, yes, indeed the American kidnapper was recruited by Hezbollah to carry out precisely this type of assault! We agree with the Prime Minister, time does not favor us. My guess is that we'll be hearing from Hezbollah directly, or the kidnappers within hours. By the way, Mr. Prime Minister, their initial demands will be outrageous, so you really need to consider what your bottom-line is going to be."

The Director of Shin Bet looks at the Prime Minister and says, "With your permission, I will go ahead and show you the video we've received from the Americans regarding the parking lot camera documenting the entire kidnapping. I draw your attention to the middle of the room's center screen."

The surveillance video showed in great detail the entire gruesome kidnapping. All eyes were riveted on the screen as the bodyguard is splattered with bullets, killing him instantly. The kidnappers used an AR-15 style lightweight semi-automatic rifle to murder the guard. Then it can be seen that as Ethan is shocked by the commotion, one of the kidnappers runs up from behind and injects him in the neck with a drug, which almost instantly paralyzes Ethan. The kidnappers quickly grab Ethan's body and throw it into what appears to look like an oversized burlap potato sack. Within minutes, the very well-prepared kidnappers had Ethan inside their van and out of the building parking lot without any resistance.

A shaken Prime Minister addresses the group, "I've seen enough. Turn it off. Please have my options ready for me as I requested. I'll see you back here in a couple of hours. Thank you all for your efforts."

The Prime Minister retires to his private office to console his panic-stricken wife and think about his own options. Elliot leaves the room to meet with the United States Treasury Secretary. He previously had Mark shift the meeting place to the Prime Minister's office as opposed to the Finance Ministry's office due to Ethan's crisis. As he walks into an elaborate conference room, Elliot greets the Secretary with a hardy handshake and says, "Welcome to Israel. We thank you for coming."

The Secretary responds, "The President of the United States directed me to come as we pledge our full support to Israel. We're here to assist you with military, economic, and diplomatic support."

Elliot responds, "Prime Minister Weiztman extends a warm welcome to you and asked me to tell you that we are prepared to cooperate with the United States in any manner we can. This nation looks at America as our greatest ally, and your country should always count on Israel as a strategic cornerstone in the Middle East. We are prepared to sign the first of many Economic Treaties that will mutually advance the economic vitality of both of our nations. Please count on us to be your partner in any 'Peace Initiatives' that will bring stability to the region. We are prepared to have the United States play the role of honest broker to maintain the peace in this area of the world. We want peace, not war.

"As a practical matter, our economy will grow during times of peace as opposed to draining the country's resources in times of war.

We stand ready to vigorously pursue peace with our neighbors, but we will not hesitate to go to war at any time to defend our nation."

The impressed Secretary says with a smile, "For an American living in Israel, you seem to know what you're talking about. All kidding aside, we know we can work with the Prime Minister. Having you in the government with your American business and political background, well, that just makes things that much easier. By the way, your Mark Goldman is efficient, courteous, and downright knowledgeable. You sure you don't want to trade him back to us?"

Elliot responds, laughing, "Even if I wanted to trade him, I'm afraid he couldn't live on your government's salary! Alright, so we'll go through some of the big-picture points on the new trade treaty, and then we'll organize an East Room signing event at the White House as soon as the President and the Prime Minister can match up their schedules. Sound good?"

The Secretary quickly responds, "Perfect."

Elliot then proceeds to get to the urgency of the moment. "We'll need your help to save Ethan."

The Secretary does not hesitate in his response. "Just tell me what I can do and I'll try my best."

Elliot stares directly into his eyes and says, "Have one of your people open up a back channel with Mark Goldman and tell us what you find out about Ethan's case. I know that the Secret Service runs under your direct authority. Assign your best man to follow Ethan's kidnapping, then have him inform Mark with up to the minute information. Mark will in turn keep our people informed."

Very uncomfortable with the request, the Secretary says, "Now, you know I can't do that. Besides, what's in it for the United States of America?"

"Well, for starters, we promise that you will be the first to know if we launch a full-scale military assault on Lebanon. Or we decide to send our Israeli Mossad Special Forces to America in the dead of the night and under the radar to rescue Ethan. Look, the Prime Minister is going to do whatever he has to do to save his son. All I'm asking is that we rely on you for accurate information so we can intelligently make the right decisions. You have my word we won't put American citizens at risk. Can we count on you?"

The Secretary looks at Elliot and says, "You owe me big time, Mr. Minister. Alright, I'll get you the information. Just remember one thing. If anyone should ever ask me on the record whether I knew of this practice, I will categorically deny any involvement. You read me?"

Elliot answers, "Yes sir, I read you. Since time is so critical, could you please immediately get in touch with your people and get this started? I'll set you up with an office here and I'll have Mark join you to organize the logistics of the back channel, and of course, finish up the details of the treaty. Every second counts. I'll inform the Prime Minister of your generous cooperation. He'll be very grateful. We'll see you at the White House soon. Thank you, Mr. Secretary."

After leaving his meeting with the Secretary, Elliot walks directly to the Prime Minister's office to inform him of the "back channel" and to see if there is anything new regarding Ethan. He desperately wanted to know if there were any new developments so that he could inform Rose and Felicia. As he briskly walks toward the Prime Minister, he couldn't help but remember in horror that infamous day when he too was assaulted at gunpoint in a similar parking structure predicament. His mind flashed a vivid image of a lifeless Yonatan, his brilliant bodyguard, killed that day. It was alarming to think that his innocent future son-in-law was facing a horrible death by terrorists committed to evil.

The receptionist recognizes Elliot and tells him that the Prime Minister has been expecting him and to go right in. He finds the room filled with political and military aides discussing how to manage their way out of the crisis. Mrs. Weiztman is composed and sitting virtually by herself as she contemplates the harsh reality of the moment. The Prime Minister is on the phone to the Director of the Mossad.

Once he finishes the conversation, Elliot is signaled to come sit with him.

Elliot takes a seat and immediately informs the Prime Minister of the back channel arranged by the Treasury Secretary and Elliot. Weiztman is, of course, very grateful for the American cooperation, but he re-emphasizes, "Elliot. Listen to me. The Americans are going to get my son killed. We'll take the information, but we must handle this ourselves. Period. No further discussion!"

Elliot, feeling at a disadvantage because he has no military or Mossad experience, as well as not wanting to upset the Prime Minister, simply says, "I guarantee you that when Ethan is free, it will be due to the fact that we had the American intelligence. Don't underestimate the American FBI and CIA. They know what they're doing."

Weiztman says, "No doubt they know what they're doing. They just don't know enough about this enemy like we do."

A young political aide interrupts the conversation, "Everyone has returned and they're prepared to present options for Ethan's release. It's time, Mr. Prime Minister, to proceed to the central meeting."

Before the Prime Minister returns to his top-level meeting, he speaks briefly with his military Chief-of-Staff who oversees all the military branches in Israel. The Chief-of-Staff hands him a sealed envelope and advises, "These are the options my military experts have organized. You will probably hear much repetition from the group waiting for you next door. The grave truth is that there are very few good alternatives. The plan labeled 'Option 1' is what we recommend you adopt. Obviously, Mr. Prime Minister, once we've heard out the group, we can discuss all options and decide on the best plan."

A weary Prime Minister thanks his Chief-of-Staff and slowly gets up out of his seat to make his way to the meeting. As he enters the room, everyone rises out of respect, then sits back down as the head of Mossad starts off the briefing, "Your son was expertly moved from Massachusetts to Mexico then onto Syria. It is unclear at the moment whether he is currently in Syria, Iran, or Lebanon. With assistance from the CIA, we believe that Ethan is alive and will be used as a negotiating bargaining chip by Hezbollah.

"From a security standpoint, we can't understand how these terrorists were able to get Ethan out of the United States undetected. Although we do not have any evidence, our working theory is that a high-level American official was paid a lot of money to turn his back while Ethan was ushered out of the country. We will investigate that later, but for now we'll stay focused on Ethan's whereabouts and safe return."

Shocked that the Americans were, first, unable to locate his son, and second, unable to keep him in the United States, the Prime Minister asks, "Did the Americans at least apologize for the blunder?"

The Mossad Director quickly answers, "No Sir. They didn't."

As the Prime Minister gestures with his hand, signifying to the Mossad Director to continue with the briefing, the head of Shin Bet interrupts, "Excuse me, Mr. Prime Minister, I've just been informed that we have the kidnapper's demands. The demands are openly from Hezbollah. So, here they are. One. All economic sanctions currently in place by Israel and the United States will cease immediately."

"Two. The United States and Israel will remove Hezbollah off their official designated 'Terrorist State List'. Three. The divided areas A, B, and C of the occupied West Bank, which was part of the Oslo Accords, will be immediately implemented. Hezbollah demands that an interim Palestinian government, the Palestinian Authority, be granted powers of governance in Areas A and B."

"They also demand talks brokered by the United States to create a two-state solution as the original intent of the Oslo Accords. Military control by Israel over the entire divided areas A, B, and C must cease immediately. And, Four. The United States release five hundred million dollars frozen in American financial institutions back to Hezbollah or Lebanon. Upon a written document agreeing to these terms signed by Israel and the United States, along with the simultaneous release of five hundred million dollars, then, and only then, will Ethan be released alive. If there is no response to their demands by midnight tonight, the Prime Minister's son will be buried at sea."

After the Shin Bet director completed the reading of the harsh demands, the room was so silent that you could hear a pin drop. Not one word was said for well over a minute. The Prime Minister was emotionally disturbed as he placed his hands over his face in obvious pain to hear such unrealistic demands that effected the fate of his beloved son who would not even be granted the dignity of a sacred Jewish burial.

Everyone in the room understood that none of the demands would be met and that Israel nor the United States would ever agree to negotiate with terrorists. And everyone clearly understood that the Prime Minister and his wife would be obligated to place the nation of Israel over the life of their precious son, Ethan.

The first man to break the silence is Elliot Sterling. He stands onto his feet, looks over the room with an air of confidence, and says, "I say we fight back! We have nothing to lose. They already have Ethan and are threatening to kill him. Everyone in this room knows we're not going to give into their demands.

"So, let's play hardball right back at them. Here's what I propose we do. First, tell them that we demand Ethan be released by midnight tonight. In exchange for his release, Israel and the United States will agree to have all of their demands heard before the United Nations. The United States will agree not to exercise their veto power in the Security Council in order to have these demands

253

fairly debated and voted upon without American veto influence. Israel and the United States will abide by the wisdom of the United Nations Security Council delegates to deliberate and vote on whether the demands are a legitimate request. The UN will serve as the arbitrator."

The Prime Minister, who is listening intently, asks, "Or what are the consequences if they say no?"

Elliot seriously answers, "Or we blow Lebanon, Hezbollah, and its people off the face of the earth!"

The Prime Minister then looks directly at Elliot and asks, "How in hell do you think you'd ever get the Americans to agree to give up their security council veto. That isn't going to happen!"

Elliot looks back at the Prime Minister and says, "That's not the problem. I've got this. Just leave this part to me! My biggest challenge is not whether the Americans will agree to cooperate with us, it's to get the President of the United States to make his final decision within the next few hours. So, as you can see, we don't have a second more to waste on this decision. Let's do this! We'll call the kidnapper's bluff, then raise the ante! It is my opinion that the US will play ball with us and Hezbollah is going to fold. This is our best chance to get Ethan out alive and give up nothing except future talks."

A wide-eyed Prime Minister looks out over the room and asks, "Who opposes this plan?"

As he waits for the answer, the Prime Minister opens the sealed envelope his military Chief-of-Staff had handed him prior to entering the room and silently reads 'Option 1' to himself.

The opposition voice comes from the director of the Mossad. "With all due respect, Minister Sterling, you are going to start World War Three if we do what you suggest. It is a reckless and irresponsible solution which will guarantee Ethan's death! You don't know the first thing about Middle Eastern military and geopolitical negotiations. This idea is nonsense and suicide!"

Waiting to see what other comments would come forward, Elliot doesn't say a thing. The Prime Minister asks, "Who else has an opinion?"

The head of Shin Bet is next to speak. "We know that Hezbollah and Lebanon are on the brink of financial collapse. The economic sanctions are strangling them. If they believe they have a real chance at getting their five hundred million back through the United Nations, they might just blink.

"The balance of the Arab world will look very favorably upon the Oslo Accord being relitigated before the United Nations without an American veto. If the leaders of Hezbollah and Lebanon believe that we mean business, they might just cave-in. They give us back Ethan and they get the world to hear their case. Ethan doesn't mean anything to them except just one more Jewish body, but the possibility of getting back their money and a real UN deliberation might sound pretty good as opposed to being blown off the earth.

"The plan could work, but I don't see the Americans giving up their veto power. In fact, I don't believe the current American President is comfortable with the Oslo Accords. And, for sure, we wouldn't tolerate a 'two-state' solution as it is described in the Oslo deal. But I don't mind getting tough with these bastards as long as Mr. Sterling can deliver on what he says he can do."

Shaking his head, the Mossad director says, "Now I hear two naïve people in the room."

The Prime Minister stares at the Mossad director asking, "What's your solution?"

The director answers, "We figure out where Ethan is and then we pull him out. We are the best in the world at counter-terrorist hostage-rescue missions. The Israeli Defense Force commandos will get Ethan out, just like we did at the Entebbe Airport in Uganda. We'll have his location spotted within the few hours. We'll inform Hezbollah that the only way we will pay them and cooperate is that we pick up Ethan ourselves.

"Additionally, we'll tell them that we're going to pay them in cash, not a wire that can be reversed. Between the Americans and our people, I guarantee you we'll identify exactly where these terrorists are holding Ethan. He will be freed, and Hezbollah will never receive one penny from any of us. Mossad can coordinate this operation, but we must start planning right now."

Elliot takes the floor, responding, "You're right, I don't have your kind of expertise at Middle Eastern military operations. But let me tell you what I am an expert in. Finance. I'm an expert in finance.

"Hezbollah and Lebanon desperately require capital. Their people are demanding food and water. They don't have money to arm themselves or to even pay for their military personnel. Their infrastructure is going to hell. They can't take it anymore. I'm telling you, they're going to accept our deal, and the Americans are going to fully cooperate with us."

Elliot pauses for a moment, deciding whether he should close his argument or push harder at the risk of deeply insulting the director. He decides for the sake of Ethan he must continue. "I don't need to be a General in this region to tell you that you don't have enough time to plan a flawless rescue. It would be reckless and irresponsible to play with Ethan's life. Your 'Rambo' tactics will undoubtedly get him killed. If these guys end up murdering the son of a sitting Israeli Prime Minister, believe me, it would be an act of war and totally naïve to think that Israel isn't going to retaliate with a vengeance, including blowing their asses off the face of earth. Give me your support, and we will win!"

Without any prompting, the room erupts with applause. The right option had crystalized into overwhelming support by the high-level officials listening to the case Elliot had presented. The only step pending was the Prime Minister's blessing. To that end, the Prime Minister addresses the group, "I don't believe any of us really know exactly what the right option might be. Everything I hear has risks for the nation and for my son. All I know for sure is that negotiating with terrorists will only result in the worst possible consequences. So, as I weigh out my decision between the seasoned recommendation of our distinguished Mossad leader and the wisdom of our Finance Minister, I am conflicted between which will bring the best results for our country, and then for my wife and I personally."

A tired and pained Prime Minister takes a deep breath as he looks in the direction of the director of Mossad saying, "You have served this nation with great honor and I have never questioned your judgement, but I will today. We will pursue Mr. Sterling's option and I will ask that you give him your full support. That is my final decision. As for you, Mr. Sterling, I pray that you will deliver on what you have so eloquently predicted. The nation is with you. Godspeed."

Elliot stands and says, "Thank you, Mr. Prime Minister, for your confidence." Then he starts walking toward the Mossad director and addresses him, "I ask for your support. I can't succeed without your experience and cooperation. I need you. The nation needs you and Ethan's life will depend on your sound advice."

Not knowing how the director is going to react, the eerie silence is torture for the Prime Minister and everyone present. The director seems to be processing the words he is about to use to tell Elliot to go to hell. But instead of saying a word, the director simply extends his hand in order to shake Elliot's hand, signifying his support. The room immediately explodes into a deafening cheer of joy.

Chapter 22

After everyone had left the critical strategic meeting, only the Prime Minister and Elliot remained in the room. The Prime Minister addresses Elliot, "The reason that I chose your option is not entirely because you suggested it. Prior to this meeting, I had asked my military Chief-of-Staff to brief me with my options. He is this nation's greatest expert when it comes to military affairs. His number one option was to call Hezbollah's bluff and refer this matter to the United Nations. He didn't quite advocate blowing Lebanon off the face of the earth, but pretty close.

"Anyway, I compliment you on your thinking. I'm very impressed that you were able to instinctually approach the solution to this problem damn near the same way as an accomplished life-long military man."

The Prime Minister grabs a bottle of Sullivan's Cove Scotch sitting on a table his staff had arranged. To relieve his stress, he lights up a cigar and pours himself and Elliot a drink, saying "L'Chaim." (To life) He asks, "What's it going to take to get the Americans to fully cooperate?"

Elliot responds, "It's not whether the United States will cooperate, it's more like how quickly can we present our option to the President of the United States. It just takes time for an American President to complete his deliberations and make a final decision to proceed. This is why I must say 'Shalom' to you right now and concentrate on meeting with the American Treasury Secretary who is standing by, waiting for me. We'll get our back channels up and running right away. The Treasury Secretary will be able to get through immediately to the President and get the ball rolling."

As a very emotional Prime Minister gets up to leave the room, he turns to Elliot, shedding a slight tear while saying, "Our nation, and my son's life, depends on your steady hand. Please bring Ethan home to his mother and to your daughter!"

The look on the Prime Minister's face said it all as Elliot began to feel the grave responsibility placed upon him to bring a successful result. This was the challenge of his lifetime. The nation and the world would be watching. The Prime Minister and his wife had placed their son's life in Elliot's hands. The thought of explaining to Rose or Felicia a possible tragic ending to Ethan's life while Elliot was in command seemed overwhelming. Obviously, the role of hostage negotiator was not the skill set he ever thought would be required to successfully serve as Minister of Finance, but this is where he found himself.

To be frightened or feel a lack of confidence was the last emotions he should be thinking about. Elliot needed to lead with mental toughness. So, he did. First, he called Mark and told him to meet him immediately. Second, he called the American Treasury Secretary and informed him he was on his way to meet him within the next five minutes. He called the director of the Mossad and requested he join them in the meeting with the American Secretary.

The last person to arrive at the meeting with the Treasury Secretary was Mark. He excuses himself for being late, but with his charismatic charm and an air of total confidence, Mark says, "Let's kick some butt on these assholes!"

The Treasury Secretary starts laughing out loud as he says, "Now that's the spirit I like to hear! Alright, Elliot, tell me what you need in order to get the Prime Minister's boy out alive."

Elliot stands and addresses the Mossad director, Mark, and the Secretary by pacing in the room as he explains the time sensitivity and the details of his game plan. He starts by clearly expressing in plain intelligible words that he needs the Secretary to get on the phone and tell the President of the United States to stand down when it comes to exercising the American veto at the United Nations.

Elliot explains that under his plan, the demands made on Israel by Lebanon via their proxy Hezbollah would be bypassed to the United Nations Security Council where the merits of the Oslo Accord would be deliberated. He advises the Secretary that in order to assure the appearance of a fair decision, the United States would be required to temporarily set aside their veto power. Elliot goes on in great detail to inform the Secretary that further demands included the proposed elimination of financial sanctions imposed by the US on Lebanon, along with a formal request to officially remove Hezbollah from the State Department's 'Terrorist List'.

Then, Elliot concludes by informing the Secretary that the kidnapper's demanded the return by the United States of their "frozen" five hundred million dollars.

The Treasury Secretary appears numb. No facial expression and not a word of response until he finally snaps out of it with a stupid joke in bad taste. "I'd advise the Prime Minister to start making funeral arrangements. There is no way the President is going to sign off on these demands. I don't even think the UN has jurisdiction on half the stuff you're asking us to do. If I were you, I'd go back to the drawing board. No one is going to get the President to agree to this kind of bullshit."

Elliot does not get rattled. He takes the opportunity to put the Secretary on the defensive, saying, "Your attempt to make a joke at Ethan's expense was in very poor taste. If you can't present this to the President, then please step aside and allow me to present the proposition. Just hurry and get me an audience with him. We have no time to waste!"

The Secretary responds, "Sorry for the dumb joke. It's not funny! I sincerely apologize. Yeah, okay, I'll agree to have you make the presentation to the President. I wouldn't even be able to get the words 'Oslo Accord' out of my mouth before he would vociferously stop me!"

Elliot glances at the Secretary, then Mark while thinking to himself, *This may not turn out well!*

Mark decides to enter the discussion. "Look, we don't expect the President to implement any of these bastard's demands. The goal is to save the life of Ethan without appearing to be negotiating with terrorists. After Ethan is released, we will spin it to the world as if some rogue Hezbollah assholes kidnapped the Israeli Prime Minister's kid and placed some whacky demands on the United States and Israel. So, in order to save the life of Ethan, we'll say we heard out their demands at the UN.

"If the United Nations elects not to hear the demands, or no conclusion is decided, the matter will die for lack of a final decision. In the meantime, Ethan will be free and the world will go on to its next crisis."

The Secretary responds, "If I heard you right, you just want the President to play the game with no intention of allowing any of the demands to be taken seriously by anyone in the United Nations. You want Hezbollah to believe America is on board solely for the purposes of getting the Prime Minister's son out alive without firing even a single bullet. Is that what you're telling me?"

Mark answers, "Yeah. That's what we're telling you."

The Secretary gathers his thoughts, then says, "I think we can do that. You Israelis are experts on delaying and confusing diplomatic agreements. Every time America comes up with some peace plan, it seems as if Israel finds a way to make it disappear in thin air. Personally, I don't think there will ever be peace in the

Middle East, but we sure as hell don't want to see the Prime Minister's son butchered by thug terrorists.

"The way I understand it, Ethan is not political. He's a medical student trying his best to become a doctor. He's an innocent bystander who is a victim of terrorism. I think the President will be empathetic to the truth here. I'm pretty sure that if the shoe was on the other foot, Israel would step up and assist the President if heaven forbid it was one of his kids or some other serious security challenge.

"Give me a few hours to track down the President, his national security advisor, and the Secretary of State. We should be able to help you with this. By the way, just one more question."

Mark responds, "Go ahead."

The Secretary asks, "What's your Plan B if the kidnappers say no to your proposal?"

Mark answers, "The Prime Minister has given the order to blow Lebanon off the face of the earth."

The Secretary looks at the silent Mossad director and comments, "I was afraid you were going to say that. All righty then, let me go to work. See you back here in a few hours. Let me know if you hear anything new. All the backchannels are hard at work, so, pretty soon we should collectively figure out exactly where Ethan is being held. Let me remind you, please don't commit the United States of America to any deal with the kidnappers until we give you the green light. Thank you, gentlemen."

The Secretary was correct. It didn't take long before the CIA and the Mossad had determined precisely where Ethan was being held. He was located in Bekaa Valley, Lebanon. This was an important strategic place for Hezbollah due to their precision missile project and the manufacturing of explosives. The area was heavily guarded, making it very difficult to pull off any kind of a 'Entebbe' style rescue mission.

Although it was unclear which specific prison barracks Ethan was assigned to, it was with one hundred percent certainty that he was there. Their intelligence gathering also confirmed that Ethan was being moved around in the middle of the night throughout the facility to assure that the Israelis did not try and pull off some type of dramatic rescue or air strike.

The Hezbollah hostage negotiator had sent a cold message to the Israelis reminding them that they had until midnight to agree to their demands, or Ethan would be hung. They warned that the Israelis should not wait until the last hour to agree to their demands. They concluded their message by saying, "Don't test our will. We will not hesitate to kill the Prime Minister's son and we are prepared to fight until we destroy the evil American empire along with every last Israeli."

The Treasury Secretary had requested that the American Israeli Embassy's military attaché assist him with the kidnapping ordeal. The attaché had been sharing information with Mark and vice versa. The whereabouts of Ethan and the most recent threats received in the terrorist's communique were being transmitted to the Secretary in real time. The rescue coordination with all agencies in the American and Israeli governments were being handled flawlessly, but so far there was absolutely no clue as to the American President's decision. It was now well over three hours without the Secretary indicating one way or the other what their position was going to be.

At exactly 9 PM, three hours before the deadline, the Prime Minister enters the command center.

Elliot is discussing with Mark how to create more urgency with the Secretary in order to insist on a decision. Both Elliot and Mark rise to shake the hand of the Prime Minister who has dark rings under his eyes and looks as if he has aged significantly. Before Elliot can say a word, the Prime Minister angrily says, "We have no more time to wait for the President's approval. I want you to personally inform the Secretary that if we don't have the President's green light within fifteen minutes, we will do what we must do. My son will not die without a fight for his life. I am the Prime Minister of this nation and we will not allow for any of our citizens to be executed in cold blood by terrorist without us putting up a fight. We know where Ethan is and we're going to go in there and get him. You have fifteen minutes, Elliot."

The Prime Minister says nothing further. He simply turns around and makes his way out the door, realizing that not only was he about to lose his own son, but he was very likely going to lose the sons of other Israeli parents in a high-risk rescue attempt he was fifteen minutes away from ordering.

The desperate decision to pursue a rescue had been made, even though Mossad nor the IDF had nowhere near enough time to prepare. The Prime Minister had lost confidence in the President and Elliot understood that this was a "Hail Mary" attempt to save the Prime Minister's only son.

Elliot and Mark feel defeated and discouraged as they walk toward the office where the Treasury Secretary is working. Suddenly, Mark spots the Secretary briskly moving toward them. The moment they are within talking distance, the Treasury Secretary says with a sigh of relief, "The President says to tell Prime Minister Weiztman to go get his son out of harm's way. You have our blessing on every aspect of the plan. Now go kick these bastard's asses!"

Even though they are standing in the Israeli Prime Minister's administrative offices, Mark is so excited with the decision that he can't help himself but to express the United States Marine Corps battle cry out loud, "Oorah!" which organically makes the Secretary laugh out loud.

Elliot then grabs the Secretary's hand to shake it, and with overwhelming joy, he leans over and gives the United States Secretary of the Treasury an unconventional bear hug, saying, "On behalf of the Prime Minister and a grateful nation, please extend our deepest gratitude to the President. And on a personal level, thank you, Mr. Secretary. You have done God's work! You're a brilliant man with a wonderful soul and we owe you big time! Please excuse us as we must immediately inform the Prime Minister."

With this vital information in hand, Elliot and Mark briskly make their way to the Prime Minister's office to break the news. As he enters the Prime Minister's office, he sees Mrs. Weiztman in tears and the Prime Minister in heavy discussions with the director of Mossad. The seated Prime Minister slowly looks up to make eye contact with Elliot and with great skepticism asks, "What is the answer?"

With everyone in the room listening intently, a proud Elliot answers, "The President of the United States said, 'go get your son out of harm's way'!" The room ecstatically explodes into cheers, as Mrs. Weiztman's tears of sorrow instantly convert into tears of joy, and the Prime Minister is overpowered with emotion.

With a burst of renewed energy, the Prime Minister hugs Elliot and vigorously shakes Mark's hand saying, "I haven't quite figured out what it is about you two guys, but you always seem to win. I'm just glad you play for our team. Thank you for your thoughtful work and the results you have produced so far, but now comes the hard part! It's going to take a master negotiator to get Hezbollah to defer their demands to the United Nations. I'm not certain how you're going to pull this off, but you got things under control so far, so please, carry on, just get me my son back alive!"

With the full mandate of the American and Israeli governments behind him, Elliot says with conviction in his voice, "I'll get him back."

The Prime Minister whispers, "From your lips to God's ears. Please let me know where I can assist. You have the vast resources of the government behind you, so don't hesitate to call on me."

As Elliot is about to speak with the director of Mossad, Mrs. Weiztman approaches him.

"Thank you, Mr. Sterling. You bring great hope to us. Please do all that you can to bring my son back home to us alive. I'm confident that you will. May God be with you."

Elliot responds, "I'm not only going to bring Ethan back to you and the Prime Minister, but I also promised to bring Ethan home to my daughter! So, to that end, please excuse me."

Elliot takes the Mossad director and Mark out of the room and into a secure private office. He opens by saying, "What's the best location to make the hostage exchange?"

Without any hesitation, the director says, "There are two border towns where the exchange works. The first is the Israeli town of Zarit where we will propose to pick-up Ethan. The second is the Lebanese town of Ramiyah where Hezbollah will bring Ethan."

Elliot stops to think for a moment. He looks over at Mark, he stares at the ceiling then addresses the director, "Alright. It's time to lay out our counterproposal to the terrorists. Who's going to speak for the Israeli government?"

The Mossad director smiles when he responds saying, "We have been preparing for this moment and have the hostage negotiator on standby for my order to deliver the message to the kidnappers.

"He is the head of a team of highly trained and equipped elite counter-terrorists/hostage-rescue operations unit. The YAMAM is the name of this special forces unit and they are a part of the Border-Guard Force which collaborates with the Israeli National Police. Due to its task-oriented training, which is primarily dedicated to the art of rescuing hostages, this unit is now our leading outfit in this field. The commander of YAMAM will be our chief negotiator."

Elliot peers at Mark again and Mark winks back at Elliot, signifying his sign of approval. Before Elliot can say anything further, the director adds, "You should also understand that the Sayeret Matkal is the elite special operations unit of the Israeli Defense Forces. Under normal protocol, and for decades, Israeli policy regarding hostages has required counterforce as the only acceptable option. Sayeret will be on standby if heaven forbid they are needed. We're breaking protocol to pursue your United Nations plan due to the unprecedented circumstances surrounding the Prime Minister's son."

Elliot asks, "Anything else I should know?"

The director adds one more detail, "At the direction of the Prime Minister, both YAMAM and Sayeret Matkal have been for the past few years converting all of our soldiers to learn the Judean combat system. It is the most sophisticated advanced close quarter combat system the world has ever seen. The Prime Minister has instructed me to use only Judean combat-trained soldiers regarding any part of this operation."

The director continues, "The Judean combat component will add an additional layer of expertise for the YAMAM team who will be assigned to peacefully collect Ethan at Zarit or, if by force, at the Bekaa Valley in Lebanon commanded by Sayeret Matkal. As you can see, Mr. Finance Minister, we are militarily ready for whatever circumstances come our way."

Although Elliot senses a bit of resentment by the director for having to pursue the diplomatic course as opposed to the military counterforce option, he disguises his true feelings and says, "Very good. I like what I hear. So, go ahead. Give the order to the YAMAM commander to make our counteroffer."

The director responds, "I can only execute this order if it comes directly from the Prime Minister."

Sensing some tension in the air between his boss and the Mossad guy, Mark attempts to lighten up the mood by asking the director, "Where can I get Judean combat lessons?"

The director maintains his serious tone and responds, "California."

Annoyed, Mark considers the answer sarcastic and more forcibly responds, "Where I come from, it's downright disrespectful to speak to a colleague with such contempt. I asked you a pretty simple question, now give me a fucking courteous answer."

The director makes eye contact with Mark, pauses for a second, and repeats himself, "California. If you're not a member of our military, or high-level border patrol, or police, then no one here in Israel is prepared to teach it to you. The creator of Judean combat was a distinguished former member of a special forces unit in the IDF. He now lives in California. He floats in and out of Israel for consultations, but I'm sure, for a fair fee, he could be persuaded to teach you. He goes by the name 'G'.

"Trust me, this guy's brilliant. If you find him, tell him I recommended you. Now, can we get back to launching our mission?"

A humbled Mark replies, "His name is G? You're serious, aren't you?"

The director, who has had enough of the small talk, says, "I need to get my instructions from the Prime Minister. So, let's not waste any more time!"

Elliot, who has also had about enough from the director, says, "I have direct authority from the Prime Minister to act on his behalf. Just in case you have amnesia, you happened to be sitting right next to me when he granted the authority. In fact, it was witnessed by more than twenty people who gave us their thunderous approval. You may have memory loss, but you're not deaf! I'm not asking you, I'm directing you to act. Inform the YAMAM commander to deliver our position to Hezbollah now or I will do it myself!"

Understanding the chain of command and the fact that the Prime Minister has delegated his authority to the Minister of Finance, the proud, but fiercely patriotic Mossad director faces Elliot with upright military posture and formally responds, "I will respect the Prime Minister's wishes placing you in charge of this mission and I am prepared to follow your instructions. For the sake of Ethan, I hope you know what you're doing."

The director walks away from Elliot to go meet with the YAMAM commander, but Elliot says in a forceful voice, "Just a moment, Mr. Director. I'm not quite finished." As the director abruptly stops, Elliot continues, "Just two more things. First, I know exactly what I'm doing. And second, don't fuck up my message with the YAMAM commander! Now you may go."

Although Elliot realized he may have antagonized the one man he needed to assist him with the complicated rescue, he knew he must take control by putting the director in his place, especially in the event of an unexpected emergency requiring his split-second instructions be carried out by the director.

Elliot received confirmation from a high-ranking assistant to the Mossad director that at precisely 10 PM, the joint Israeli and American counterproposal had been delivered by the YAMAM commander to his Hezbollah counterpart. The assistant indicated that the message was delivered orally by special phone securely dedicated for the sensitive hostage discussions. Additionally, the proposal reduced to a written communique outlining the counter deal points and delivered via a simple email attachment. When Elliot asks the assistant whether the Prime Minister has been briefed with any of this information, the answer is "No".

The first thought that crosses Elliot's mind is that it appears that the Mossad director has done his job and not interfered with the chain of command. He then contemplates what a terrifying next two hours are going to feel like waiting for an answer from committed terrorists.

As Mark and Elliot are discussing the various possible scenarios that might arise, the Mossad director enters the room at approximately 10:30 PM. He greets Elliot and formally says, "The YAMAM commander would like to have a word with you. Since he can't leave the command center nor his special phone, he would appreciate if you would join him."

Elliot responds, "Sure, I'll come by in about fifteen minutes or so."

Prior to making his way to the command center, Elliot takes Mark with him to update the Prime Minister. He finds him seated reading the main Jerusalem newspaper. Elliot gets right to the point indicating that the offer has been made, but more than a half hour has gone by "with stone-cold silence". Elliot goes on to inform him that he is experiencing some difficulties keeping the Mossad director respecting the fact that a non-military man like him is leading the mission.

The Prime Minister responds, "You're in charge, Elliot. You act on my authority and with my blessing."

With the vote of confidence from the Prime Minister, Elliot and Mark briskly walk to the command center where they are escorted to the YAMAM commander and the Mossad director. Once they arrive, they are asked to be seated as the commander says, "Thank you for meeting with me. Let me give you my candid assessment of the situation. I believe we are on a failed mission. The enemy has not responded, and it is my experience with Hezbollah that they will unconditionally reject our proposal.

"They will see it for what it is, a ploy to get the Prime Minister's son back alive. We offered no guarantees that we will follow through with our word. I think this plan is going to get Ethan killed without us even putting up a fight. Do we have your permission to immediately go to Plan B?"

Elliot glances at Mark, then at the commander and director, then looks back at Mark and says to Mark, "Do you want me to tell them, or do you want to tell them?"

Since Mark knew exactly where his childhood friend and boss is going with this, he winks at Elliot and says, "I'll tell them." He then faces the two gentlemen and calmly says, "You do not have permission to go to Plan B. The only permission that is granted is for you to stay the course! Any questions?"

The commander jumps out of his seat and proclaims, "You just gave Ethan his death sentence!"

Elliot responds, "No sir. I've given Ethan the only chance he has to live. Your so-called Plan B is not only going to kill Ethan, but very likely will result in other courageous IDF soldiers to be slaughtered. You are ordered to follow my instructions. There will be no Plan B. Am I clear, Commander?"

With a sarcastic tone, the commander answers, "Perfectly clear, Mr. Finance Minister, but I do have a request of you."

"And what's that, Commander?"

The commander sits back down and says, "Since you have so much confidence in your strategic plan, I will insist that you stay here in the command center with the director and myself to help guide in real time any fast-moving developments that come our way. Now, that is my political answer to you. But the real reason I want you in here with me is because I want you to experience first-hand how you will single-handedly allow the only son of the Prime Minister to be killed by his kidnappers while we sat back and negotiated with fucking terrorists!"

Elliot decisively responds, "I will definitely stay right here for as long as it takes, but you are relieved of your duties. You are no longer in charge of the negotiations. Who is your top assistant?"

Shocked, but no longer feeling distressed with the course of action, the patriotic commander answers, "My top assistant is Lieutenant Commander Gantz."

Elliot calmly says, "Okay. Where is he?"

The director points to what appears to be a thirty-something handsome young man standing next to him and says, "That's him."

Elliot takes control of the situation. "Very well. Thank you for your services, Commander. You may now leave. Alright, Lieutenant Commander Gantz, you're my chief hostage negotiator. Do you understand the plan of action?"

Gantz instantly responds, "Yes sir. I was responsible for writing your plan which we ultimately submitted to the enemy. I have studied it from all conceivable angles. I know it inside and out."

Elliot says, "I, along with the director of the Mossad and this entire assembled staff are ready to assist you. You got a big job in front of you so, go prepare some more while we wait for their response."

Elliot then addresses the Mossad director and asks, "You on board?"

The director, who is impressed by Elliot's convictions and decisive thinking, answers, "Yes, Sir."

All the waiting seemed to make the entire command center on edge. There was very little interaction between the members of the team. It appeared as if the only thing anyone was doing was staring at computer screens waiting for some reaction from rogue terrorists. Elliot had expressed concern to Mark that perhaps the morale was very low due to the open exchange and firing of the commander. It was as if the majority of the rescue team agreed with the previous commander that the plan was doomed and the only thing everyone was waiting for was to receive official notification that Ethan was dead. The pessimism was growing exponentially by the second due to the kidnapper's silence.

At 11 PM, the sleepy room begins to buzz. The military personnel are chatting and the young Lieutenant Commander begins barking out instructions to his people. Before Elliot has any idea as to what is going on, the young Lieutenant Commander brings what appeared to be the official Hezbollah response over to where Elliot and Mark are seated.

A grim-faced Lieutenant Commander gets right to the point. "Mr. Minister, our proposal has been denied. I will read you the communique: 'Your proposal is rejected in its entirety. There will be no deals here, only our deal. If we do not receive your Prime Minister's acceptance to our demands by midnight, the hostage will be executed. Do not test our will any further.' End of statement. I am requesting further orders, Sir."

Elliot had always taught Mark not to outwardly reveal on his face how he was feeling under pressure. One of his favorite expressions was, "Your face is your sword". So, even though Elliot feels worried, he maintains a self-assured and poised composure. "You'll need to give me a few minutes."

The Lieutenant Commander and the director excuse themselves in order to give Elliot a moment to think through his next move. Elliot glances at Mark but does not say a word, and Mark remains silent because he understands that his boss is contemplating the best next step. The silence continues for nearly five minutes until Elliot says to Mark, "I keep asking myself, if this was my kid, what would I do? Would I send in a special forces unit to try and rescue my own child? Would I just cave in and give these bastards what they're asking for? Or would I have the courage to call their bluff even at the expense of my own kid's life? How do we save Ethan's life without compromising the country's integrity?

"I know two things for sure. First, you're never going to win making a deal with the devil. And second, negotiating with terrorists is a bad precedent. What can you tell me, Mark?"

Mark looks his friend in the eyes and says, "I'm no expert in this Middle Eastern shit, but I do know that every time we gave into our business enemies, we lived to regret our weak decision. I say these sons-of-bitches are going to cave in if they really believe we're okay with losing Ethan, but if we do lose Ethan, we're going to blow these fuckers off the face of the earth. If they realize that we have prepared for the death of Ethan, which is their only bargaining chip, then I believe they'll have no choice but to take our deal. Think about it; if they kill Ethan, they've just killed their country, themselves, and their families in exchange for Ethan, who means nothing to them. That's my two cents."

Elliot remains silent, then asks Mark to call over the Lieutenant Commander and the director so that he can give them their instructions. As he is waiting for the them to arrive, Elliot thinks about whether he should consult with the Prime Minister before his final directives are given. He makes a split decision that he will not inform the Prime Minister due to the fact that he would not be in an objective position to think clearly in a matter that affected his son.

The two men stand in front of Elliot in military attention as they wait to hear his critical instructions.

Although inwardly terrified out of concern for Ethan's life, Elliot addresses the two military men with stone-cold precision and conviction, "Inform Hezbollah that our previous position is final. Advise them that we insist that the Prime Minister's son be released unharmed to Israel immediately. If not, we will consider this an act of war. The consequence of not retuning our citizen forthwith will result in an all-out attack on Lebanon, Hezbollah, and any of their affiliates.

"Tell them in no uncertain words that Lebanon will be literally blown off the face of the planet. For those Hezbollah leaders and members located outside of Lebanon, we will hunt them down and kill them one by one. Finally, make it clear that they have until midnight to communicate their unambiguous answer or we will immediately mobilize into action. Do you understand my instructions, Lieutenant Commander?"

The ashen-faced young commander and the very pale-looking director glance at each other as the Lieutenant Commander dutifully answers, "Yes Sir. One question, Sir?"

Annoyed, and with a short fuse, Elliot responds, "What the hell is your question?"

"Has the Prime Minister approved this plan of action?"

Elliot instantly says, "The Prime Minister has granted me unconditional authority. Now, go do exactly as I have instructed and do it quickly!"

Without any further comment, the reluctant Lieutenant Commander and the Mossad director take the message back to the command center to systematically roll out the message to Hezbollah. Within fifteen minutes from receipt of the instructions, the Lieutenant Commander returns by himself to update Elliot advising him that the official communique had been sent precisely as dictated. The only thing left is the treacherous wait for the response by midnight. Elliot thanks the Commander, then with a tired and humble smile says, "God is with us, so get your men ready to pick up Ethan in Zarit."

Chapter 23

It was 11:45 PM and Hezbollah was dead silent. Elliot was naturally very concerned that he may have taken the wrong decision. The thought of having to inform the Prime Minister and his wife of a failed mission that cost them their son's life was haunting him. Then there was the terrifying thought of breaking this same news to his daughter Rose and to Felicia. The pain and humiliation of announcing to a nation in mourning that he alone had made the decision to pursue diplomacy, as opposed to brute force, with terrorists would leave a life-long devastating scar on Elliot.

Facing the agony of defeat, Elliot asks one of his aides to summon both the director and the Lieutenant Commander. He is mentally preparing himself to accept that he has made a grave error.

It was time to discuss the real possibility of Elliot resigning from the Cabinet and turning over the next military steps to the "experts". Additionally, he asked Mark to request that the Prime Minister be available to meet shortly for an update on the operation. The vision of Ethan and Rose dancing at Mark's wedding reception kept swirling in his head. Elliot was desperately trying to come to grips with what seemed to be lining up as an unmitigated disaster.

As the director and the young Commander are walking toward Elliot, he notices that they both reverse their course and begin briskly walking back toward the command center with a military intelligence officer. Elliot looks at his watch indicating 11:59 PM. Something dramatic is going on and Elliot isn't going to wait to find out what. He springs up and jogs toward the command center with Mark. What he sees is the Lieutenant Commander intently reading a lengthy communique from Hezbollah, but still leaving an anxious Elliot with no clue regarding Ethan's status or a final answer.

Without any emotion, the Lieutenant Commander looks up from his seat right into Elliot's eyes and calmly says, "The enemy has blinked. Please take a seat while I explain their response."

Elliot, Mark, and the Mossad director circle their chairs facing the commander as Elliot says, "Alright, let's hear it."

The very impressed commander begins, "Mr. Minister, Hezbollah will agree to our demands with one major exception.

They request that the Secretary General of the United Nations put in writing his acknowledgement that the UN will in fact debate the following issues: 1. Elimination of financial sanctions imposed on Lebanon. 2. The elimination of Hezbollah off the 'Terrorist List'. 3.The return of the $500,000,000 'frozen' by the United States government. 4. Revisiting of the 'Oslo Accord' main diplomatic matters regarding a 'two-state solution' and Palestinian authority over the West Bank Areas 'A' and 'B'.

"If we provide Hezbollah with a written letter to this effect signed by the Secretary General, they will agree to release 'the hostage' at the designated location of Zarit. If we are in agreement, we are to inform them immediately. They have given us until 8 AM to produce the letter from the Secretary General. Upon receipt of an 'acceptable' letter, the hostage will be taken to Zarit and released at precisely 10 AM at the official border main crossing gate."

Although ecstatic with the news, Elliot reacts cautiously, "I'm encouraged, but worried that these bastards have something hidden up their sleeve. Getting the United Nations to cooperate with Israel on such a letter is virtually impossible given the diplomatic realities of the world. And even if we get the goddamn letter, the way they've phrased their communique with the word "acceptable" letter gives these assholes a way out. So, what do you think, Mark?"

Mark sits back in his chair and says, "Write them back immediately and advise them they'll have the letter by 8 AM. Tell them to prepare to have Ethan delivered to Zarit at 10 AM. End of story!"

Accustomed to Mark's clear thinking, Elliot responds with a soft chuckle, "Jesus, you drew that opinion quickly! Seriously, I think you're probably right. At minimum, we're keeping Ethan alive at least for the next eight hours while we figure this thing out. The trick is going to be in getting the Americans to convince the Secretary General to write the goddamn letter. But I think you're right, we need to buy time for Ethan. There's no choice here.

"We must get in touch with the President of the United States to engage the UN Secretary to play ball. Jerusalem is seven hours ahead of both Washington DC and New York City. So, it's about 5 PM at the White House and the United Nations. Gentlemen, we got a lot of work to do and not much time to do it in. Any further comments, Lieutenant Commander, or Mr. Director? By the way, any chance we're getting played by these guys?"

The astute young Commander responds, "Mr. Minister, it's my opinion that their counter-offer is real. I believe that if we get them the letter, Ethan will be delivered alive to us. One brief observation, though.

"Hezbollah's communique is silent on the part about the United States releasing its veto power during the Security Council deliberation. I recommend we also stay silent when we respond. This will help us later with Hezbollah at the UN. So, Mr. Minister, can you get the letter from the Secretary General?"

Elliot responds truthfully, "Don't know the answer at this minute, but I'm going to try like hell! Alright, keep the veto issue to ourselves. Mr. Director, anything further to add?"

The director says, "I don't smell an ambush. I think they mean business, Mr. Minister." Then with a smile on his rugged face and with deep respect, the director says, "Besides, we stay the course!"

A proud Elliot glances at Mark and says, "Okay, Commander, send off the message accepting the counterproposal. Tell them to have Ethan at Zarit at 10 AM. Mark, find me the Treasury Secretary. I need him to call the President, so he can get me over the hump with UN Secretary General."

While Mark is tracking down the American Treasury Secretary, Elliot makes his way to the Prime Minister's office in order to brief him on the situation and the anticipated following steps. As he enters the Prime Minister's office, he observes that Mrs. Weiztman is seated next to her husband looking gravely concerned. Elliot greets them both warmly while he sits down and says, "We have an important breakthrough concerning Ethan. Hezbollah will release Ethan if we can get the United Nations Secretary to write a letter agreeing to debate the merits of their demands and our related counterproposals."

Mrs. Weiztman begins crying for joy that the news is not that of her son's demise. The Prime Minister is overwhelmed with hope that Ethan might soon be returned to them alive and says, "You're a miracle worker, Mr. Elliot Sterling, you're a miracle worker! I knew you could do this. I just knew it!

"You're going to need to engage the President of the United States to pull this off. The UN will never assist Israel in such a request. But they won't deny an American request. Tell me how I can help you."

Concerned that he may have raised the hopes of the Weiztmans, Elliot remarks, "We are, as we speak, lining up the American Treasury Secretary to assist us in presenting this to the President. We strongly believe that the President will help us, although it is very important to understand that there still remains a possibility that he'll say no. Should that become the case, please stand by, Mr. Prime Minister, because we will need you to get on the phone and twist the President's arm to say yes. He won't deny your request, but I'm going to try to do this without making the rescue come off as a personal request."

Weiztman responds, "You've brought us this far, so keep using your instincts. If Ethan is released, where and when will you pick him up?"

Elliot says, "Zarit, tomorrow morning at 10 AM."

The Prime Minister shakes Elliot's hand and simply says, "Godspeed!"

Mrs. Weiztman, mentally battered and wiping back tears from her eyes, looks directly at Elliot and says, "We thank you for your valiant efforts. Please, bring home my son and bring back your daughter's beshert." (Yiddish for divinely foreordained spouse or soulmate.)

Feeling the tremendous weight of her comments, he kisses Mrs. Weiztman goodbye and says, "God will be with us!"

The moment Elliot steps out of the Prime Minister's private office, he is instantly greeted by Mark who informs him that the Treasury Secretary was unexpectedly recalled back to Washington D.C. for an "emergency" Cabinet meeting. Mark explains to Elliot that apparently American banks had panicked because of a massive amount of US home mortgages that had been mysteriously underwritten and packaged as worthless loans.

The banks were becoming increasingly nervous when they realized they would be forced to absorb the losses, thus causing the banks to stop lending to each other. They obviously didn't want other banks giving them worthless mortgages as collateral, and none of these entities wanted to get stuck holding the bag. As a result, interbank borrowing costs, typically referred to as "Libor", rose. This mistrust within the banking community was causing a brewing financial crisis requiring the United States government's intervention to head off what promised to be a catastrophic shortfall in the American banking cash reserves.

After listening carefully, and with a grim face, Elliot says, "Now what?"

Mark responds, "I've lined up the Treasury Secretary aboard his plane to call us in fifteen minutes. You'll have an opportunity to explain the urgency we have regarding the Secretary General's cooperation. Clearly, the President and the Treasury Secretary are preoccupied, so make your words count!"

Elliot and Mark make their way to a secure office to prepare for the very important call from the Treasury Secretary. Mark's cell phone rings almost exactly fifteen minutes from the time he had indicated the Secretary would call. He answers the mobile call and launches directly into the business at hand, "We understand that you and the President are facing a critical financial challenge and we appreciate the importance of your time at this moment. So, thank you for the call. We'll be short and to the point. By the way, Mr. Secretary, you're on speaker phone. Okay Elliot, the floor is yours."

With that introduction, Elliot says, "Hezbollah will release the Prime Minister's son if we provide a letter from the United Nations General Secretary agreeing to take up a debate and deliberations regarding the issues you and I have previously discussed including the Oslo Accords, financial sanctions, the $500,000,000 USD 'frozen' funds, and the 'terrorist state' designation. So, get us a credible letter from the UN Secretary by 6 AM Israeli time and we get the Prime Minister back his son. No letter. No return of hostage. That's it."

The American Treasury Secretary is silent for a moment then says, "Are you asking for anything the President hasn't already approved?"

Elliot and Mark quickly respond in unison, "No!"

The Secretary reacts, "Alright gentlemen, I've got my marching orders. Give me a couple of hours to locate the President or the Secretary of State. Since the President has approved the general game plan, I may have the State Department personnel concentrate on getting you the letter. The President's hair is on fire regarding our financial crisis, so his attention span is not going to be on the Middle East. He likes your Prime Minister and if the State Department can't get this done in the name of the President, I'll do my best to have him make the call directly to the Secretary General. I'll get back to you as soon as I can. Okay, I've got to run. Talk soon."

Elliot and Mark respond, "Thank you, Mr. Secretary."

They look at each other as the phone clicks dead with Mark saying, "You did a terrific job of getting to the heart of the matter, but I don't think this guy is even going to talk to the President! Shit, he scares me! This thing could go either way. Sounds like the United States government is involved in a huge mess, and it looks as if this son-of-a-bitch is going to lay off the letter we need to some low-level State Department bureaucrat. I'm not liking our chances right now."

Elliot immediately says, "I think you got it read right, but we have absolutely no choice other than to get Prime Minister Weiztman involved to call the President. And, even with that move, I'm not so sure the President is going to take the Prime Minister's call for at least another twenty-four hours. If I get Weiztman to make that call, we run the risk of alienating the Treasury Secretary for going around him."

"Perhaps even worse, the Treasury Secretary will wipe his hands clean and be relieved that we took him off the hook to get this done for us. I don't know. I'm thinking we leave it alone. Let the Secretary do what he's got to do. What do you think? Should I try and get Weiztman on the phone with the President?"

Mark takes a little time before answering then clearly says, "No. Let the Treasury Secretary run with this. There's no doubt that he understands that Ethan's life depends on whether we get this letter or not. It's on him to do his level best to honor our request. Will he? Well, we're about to find out in a couple of hours. Let's stay with the Secretary."

Without hesitation, Elliot says, "I agree. The hard part is going to be sitting around waiting for this all to develop. In the meantime, let's go over and brief the Mossad Director and the Lieutenant Commander as to what's going on. They both must be ready to either pick up Ethan or go to war."

Elliot and Mark spent the next 45 minutes briefing the command center along with the Prime Minister as to what was transpiring between the Americans and the United Nations. No one really believed that Elliot was actually going to get an acceptable letter from the Secretary General, but nobody expressed anything other than optimism that the letter would be produced. As the time passed, any optimism by Elliot was rapidly being replaced with pessimism. It was already 5 AM Israeli time and not a word from the Treasury Secretary.

Elliot is exhausted and barely able to keep his eyes open. He is second-guessing himself as he expresses to Mark, "I should have allowed the Prime Minister to call the President himself. We're running out of time. I'm going to get on the phone and call the Treasury Secretary!"

Equally as tired, Mark slowly says, "Look, Elliot. The way I see it, the Secretary is working on it. He just doesn't have anything to tell us except that he's working on it. My hunch is he's waiting on the Secretary General. Give him another 30 minutes."

A worried Elliot answers, "I hope Ethan will still be alive in another 30 minutes," as he closes his eyes in frustration, trying to get a catnap in while continuing to painfully wait.

Both Mark and Elliot had dozed off when suddenly at 6 AM, the Lieutenant Commander flanked by the director says, "Excuse me, Mr. Minister, we have received a copy of the letter from the United Nations General Secretary."

Precisely at that moment, Mark's cell phone rings as a drowsy Elliot says to the commander, "Hold on for a second, let me see if that's the Americans calling Mark."

Mark flashes a smile and a thumbs-up to Elliot as he passes the call to him. "The Treasury Secretary wants to speak to you."

Elliot grabs the phone as the Treasury Secretary quickly starts explaining, "No one here in Washington wanted to touch this type of letter with a ten-foot pole. I couldn't get the President's Chief-of-Staff, let alone the President, to even listen to me about the letter. There wasn't a soul at the State Department including the Secretary of State that would stick their neck out for this kind of a letter. So, I did it myself! I was able to reach the UN General Secretary and told him that I speak for the President of the United States. I asked that the Secretary General accommodate the President as a personal favor and write the letter."

The Treasury Secretary asks Elliot to hold while he covers the phone to privately speak to his aide, then the aide returns to the phone to say he'll be just another minute as he must take another call from a United States Senator. Finally, the Secretary returns. "Sorry Elliot, it's a madhouse around here. Okay, where was I? Alright, so the Secretary General says to me he'll do it for the President."

The Treasury Secretary then starts laughing out loud as he continues the story, "Then this guy tells me off the record that he has no problem with this because by the time this matter is placed on the official United Nations Docket, Hezbollah is bound to do something so stupid someplace in the world that the Secretary General will have no choice but to pull it off the Docket indefinitely anyway!"

As Elliot chuckles and starts profusely thanking him for his amazing work, the Treasury Secretary interrupts Elliot, "Don't thank me yet. The letter is not as strong as I would have liked. In fact, it's pretty darn weak. I did the best I could under the circumstances. You're going to have to make a lemonade out of a lemon. This is all you're going to get. There will be no amendments.

If the Prime Minister loses his son because of this piece of shit letter, my sincerest apologies and condolences.

"There's nothing further I can do. Please let me know if you get him out. The United States of America stands ready with our ally if you declare war against Lebanon. Good luck, Mr. Finance Minister."

An inwardly demoralized Elliot professionally responds with dignity and strength, "The government of Israel thanks you for your efforts, Mr. Secretary. On a personal level, I'm grateful for your act of courage in stepping up in attempting to help an innocent young man when no one else seemed to care. Be assured that I will inform the Prime Minister of what you have done by sticking your neck out for his son in the name of humanity and in the face of evil. I know you did your best and that's all anyone could ever ask of you. We'll keep you briefed. Good-bye, Mr. Secretary."

Mark immediately sees the pain in Elliot's face and says, "That didn't go so well, did it?"

Elliot, now angry and annoyed, responds only with, "Give me the goddamn letter so I can read it!"

Mark hands him a copy, saying, "It's worse than you think. I have mixed emotions as to whether we should even forward it to the kidnappers. The letter is weak. Very, very weak."

Elliot grabs the letter and carefully reads each word. He then looks up at Mark, the Lieutenant Commander, and the Mossad director and says with serious concern, "Doesn't sound so good, does it?"

The Mossad director is the first to respond, "The letter is very fragile. Hezbollah will see words such as 'we intend' or 'may convene in the future' or the word 'might' as very ambiguous. This communique establishes no concrete guarantee of anything. Basically, it's total bullshit."

The commander then says, "I have read the letter thoroughly and I whole-heartedly agree with the Director. If it was solely up to me, I wouldn't forward such a letter to a terrorist. In all likelihood, this letter will be the nail that seals the coffin shut for Ethan. My recommendation would be to request more time from Hezbollah, then ask the United Nations for a clean new letter amended by us."

Elliot turns to Mark saying, "Alright, I got two who say not to send the letter. What do you say?"

Since Mark had time to think while the other two had been expressing their opinions, he comes right out saying, "If we don't send the letter, Ethan is for sure going to be a dead man. If we do send the letter, he 'might' be a dead man. So, I say send the letter.

What do we have to lose? If they accept, we get our man back in one piece; if they deny, he's a dead man anyway. Send it. Who knows, they may feel this is their best way out of this sticky situation. After all, we did threaten to blow these bastards off the face of the earth."

The commander jumps into the conversation, "Why are you opposed to sending a letter to them requesting more time while we figure out how to either get a better UN letter or mount a surprise rescue mission?"

Mark says, "First of all, we don't know whether we can even get anything else out of the UN. Second, there's no way you can put together an effective rescue mission. It just too late in the game to be changing our plan. As we told you earlier, we need to stay the course. Period."

Elliot steps back in, "Let me assure you, we're not getting anything else out of the United Nations or the United States. We can only rely on the current letter we have obtained. I don't profess to be a strategic military thinker, but my gut tells me that if we proceed with a military rescue mission, not only do we lose Ethan through a failed attempt, but we lose some of our very best Israeli soldiers. I'm not going to take that risk. So, here are your orders, Commander. Send the letter exactly as it is written.

"Make certain that you inform Hezbollah that we will meet them in Zarit at precisely 10 AM to pick up Ethan. Go ahead. Send it! Send it right away!"

A skeptical commander and a weary director are very concerned with their instructions, but are duty bound to follow the chain of command as they jointly acknowledge the order, "Yes Sir, Mr. Minister."

At exactly 7:30 AM, the commander returns to formally advise Elliot and Mark that the United Nations letter has been sent to Hezbollah as written. The Commander informs them that the "enemy acknowledged receipt of the letter with no additional comments."

Elliot asks, "Are you prepared to pick up Ethan?"

Very reluctant, and unconvinced that there would be any such rescue, the commander responds, "Not at this moment."

A furious Elliot says, "What the fuck are you doing? Get your best people to Zarit immediately! You still don't get it, do you? Listen carefully to every word I'm saying. Ethan Weiztman will be released at 10 AM at the border town of Zarit! Now, go get your ass over to the command center and organize the team to get him out of there. Did you hear me, Lieutenant Commander?"

"Yes, Mr. Minister."

A disgusted Elliot responds, "Good. Now go get it done and tell me the moment you have any official response from these assholes!"

"Yes, Sir."

The atmosphere in the whole command center area was unbearably tense. It seemed that as each minute ticked by the intensity got greater. Mark understood just by looking at how pale Elliot's face was that the ordeal was taking a toll on him. There were no smiles; in fact, it was quite the opposite. Mark glances at his watch, which now reads 9:30 AM. He looks at Elliot and reluctantly says, "It's 9:30 AM and no word from Hezbollah. Should we wait them out or send them some sort of a reminder?"

Elliot, barely audible, says, "No. We wait."

The sand at the top of the hourglass was just about empty. Ethan's release by 10 AM was becoming increasingly unreal, until dramatically, it happened. At 9:50 AM, just ten minutes before the crucial time limit, the commander and the director rapidly approach Elliot with the commander excitedly saying, "He will be released! Ethan will be released at 10 AM at Zarit! As you have commanded, our special forces are on standby waiting to collect him. Minister Sterling, I want you to know that you have the finest mind I have ever had the privilege of serving with. On a further private note, I would go to battle for you anywhere and at any time you were in charge. Sir, thank you for your leadership and bravery."

In an impromptu moment, and out of shear respect, the Lieutenant Commander and the Mossad director stand at full military attention and salute Elliot with a great admiration. In a sense, they appear to be acknowledging the birth of a new dynamic Israeli leader. Elliot reacts by saluting them back. "Thank you for your kind words, but the mission is not over. We need to see Ethan back in these offices with his parents. Go get him and bring him here safely, then we'll celebrate."

The commander responds, "As we speak, we have the best Judean combat-trained soldiers waiting at the designated Israeli/Lebanon border crossing location. Zarit is less than 150 miles away from Jerusalem. If Ethan is released at 10 AM, he'll be flown here and will arrive by noon. Here is a copy of Hezbollah's final communique surrendering to our demands. Please keep it as a memento to your outstanding leadership on this historic day. We'll inform you the moment we confirm Ethan is safe."

Elliot then turns to Mark and shakes his hand, but holds back from celebrating until they receive a confirmation that Ethan is free. After a brief discussion, they conclude that Elliot should hold off from informing the Prime Minister and his wife until they know for sure that Ethan is released.

They also conclude that Rose and Felicia would only be informed once they have Ethan in their hands.

An assistant to the Lieutenant Commander makes his way toward Elliot to inform him that the command center has picked up a visual live feed via satellite positioned on the precise Zarit border crossing location where the prisoner transfer is about to take place. The assistant invites Elliot and Mark to join them in order to view in real time the release of the Prime Minister's son. Elliot instantly stands and eagerly follows the assistant toward the command center.

As Mark and Elliot take their seats in the command center, they notice on a big screen a figment of what resembles Ethan's face. The visual definition is grainy and not clear. Five armed Hezbollah terrorists dressed in military garb are escorting what appears to be Ethan, who looks frail and limping. The Israeli military contingent consists of five IDF special forces soldiers. They all meet at the gate on the precise border line separating Lebanon and Israel. Everyone in the command center have their eyes glued to the screen and you could hear a pin drop.

The moment of truth had arrived as a Hezbollah terrorist grabs what is now clearly identified as Ethan by the arm and walks him to the edge of the Lebanon border where he is met by one IDF soldier standing virtually on the edge of the Israeli border. Without one word being said, the terrorist releases Ethan's arm as Ethan limps onto his homeland without incident. The Israeli special forces officer grabs him and then all five IDF soldiers circle around Ethan, keeping him in protective custody as they whisk him away to an awaiting military vehicle.

At that moment, there is thunderous cheer and applause in the command center. Everyone is overjoyed with emotion. Grown men who had experienced ferocious combat and military battles are literally tearing up. The Lieutenant Commander and the Mossad director could be seen hugging each other. Elliot and Mark stand to embrace as the commander approaches Elliot and says, "You alone, Mr. Minister, own this victory. Normally, I would thank my team for their hard work, but today I bestow that honor on you."

An exhilarated Elliot says, "Thank you for the gesture, but these are your people and you led them to this victory. I just gave you a little guidance. We were all in this fight together, and we won this fight together. Let them know that we are proud of them. Tell them to go home to their wives and families or significant others and feel a sense of honor for what they all accomplished here today. We recaptured the Prime Minister's son without a drop of blood and we executed our plan to perfection. You did good, Commander. Now, go tell the director and all these people how grateful we are for their extraordinary and dedicated hard work." Then, with a wink and a very tired smile, Elliot says, "By the way, Commander, I'd go into battle with you any day too!"

Elliot turns and walks out with Mark to a spontaneous enthusiastic applause by each person in the command center. Everyone there recognized that it was Elliot, with the assistance of Mark, who had developed the winning strategy and had the presence of mind to stay the course with the game plan. As Elliot is walking out the door, he turns around, points at the director, then does a fist pump toward the command center team, provoking a cheer that could only be equated to the reaction of a walk-off home run in the bottom of the ninth inning to win the seventh game of a world series baseball game.

As Elliot leaves the room, he rushes to break the good news to the Prime Minister who is anxiously waiting to hear the fate of his son. Elliot is escorted into the Prime Minister's office where he sees both the Prime Minister and his wife being consoled by the Chief Rabbi of the State of Israel. Elliot doesn't even wait to reach them, blurting out loud, "Ethan is safe and coming home!"

Mrs. Weiztman bursts into tears of joy and the Prime Minister shouts out with tears in his eyes, "Thank God! Thank God! Thank God!"

First the Prime Minster hugs his wife, then the two of them step over to bear-hug Elliot. Suddenly, the Rabbi joins in on the celebration, jointly hugging the Prime Minister and Elliot, saying, "Our prayers have been answered! Mazel Tov, Mazel Tov!" (A Jewish phrase expressing congratulations.)

Chapter 24

The Prime Minister's office had instantly converted from a subdued and extremely depressed environment to full of life. As word spread throughout the government that Ethan was free, the Prime Minister's office had become a highway of well-wishers expressing their heartfelt congratulations for Ethan's release. The entire country of Israel was rejoicing as television and radio news reports were airing nationwide.

Each of the American cable news networks and the international media from Moscow to London and beyond were reporting on the spectacular release of Ethan. The fact that there was no military conflict related to the incident was making major headlines. The Prime Minister and the Israeli Defense Forces Commander were being hailed as brilliant for successfully settling the conflict without bloodshed, yet not a word was mentioned about Elliot or Mark.

In the meantime, Elliot joyfully informed Felicia and Rose. Both were on their way to Jerusalem from Caesarea to reunite with Ethan. The Prime Minister had earlier been briefed by Elliot regarding the fact that Ethan appeared to be walking with a bad limp and looked frail. He was informed that Ethan had been taken to a hospital in Haifa for a medical evaluation along with the practicality of getting a warm shower, clean clothing, and some fresh food. Ethan was expected to arrive at the Prime Minister's Jerusalem residence, Beit Aghion, at approximately 2 PM.

While waiting for Ethan, Rose, and Felicia to arrive, Elliot and Mark had checked into the elegant King David Hotel to get a couple of hours of rest and clean up for Ethan's big arrival. As they were walking through the lobby of the hotel, Elliot puts his arm on Mark's shoulder and says, "We did it again! But this one might just go down as the hall of fame move for team Sterling and Goldman! No doubt, we're awesome together!"

Mark turns and looks at Elliot and says, "All I do is assist a masterful and skilled leader that has accomplished astonishing milestones without me. I'm not your equal, I'm just the guy who's got your back."

Elliot stops walking and says to Mark, "Don't underestimate yourself. You're my partner in every sense of the word. You're my brother, and we made it to this remarkable stage together. I'm here because we're here together."

As they start walking toward the elevator, a very upbeat Elliot loosens up with his childhood friend and says with his patented charismatic smile, "By the way, I concede that you're my equal and all that stuff, but you need to concede that I'm much better-looking than you! You don't need to answer that, just go get some rest. Let's plan to make it over to the Prime Minister's residence by 1:45 PM. No doubt, that rendezvous is going to be exceptionally exciting!"

After resting, Elliot and Mark make their way back through the lobby and out the front entrance of the first-class hotel. As they step outside, they are met by a swarm of photographers and the news media.

There are more than two dozen reporters who keep shouting out questions while photographers keep flashing photos. This literally looks like a circus.

Overwhelmed with the volume of news coverage, Elliot keeps walking trying to locate his government black sedan. A young male reporter shouts out a question that captures Elliot's attention.

The reporter asks, "Did the government of Israel pay a ransom to Hezbollah for the release of the Prime Minister's son? Did Israel negotiate with terrorists?"

Entering the back door of his waiting car, Elliot simply answers, "No, and no," as the car drives off.

The Prime Minister's Jerusalem residence was near the King David Hotel. The estate had an elaborate security fence along the entire peripheral boundary. It looked like a fortress. IDF soldiers carrying the Savor rifle were visible everywhere. Mark had never seen such heavy security at a private home. Once inside the residence, they are immediately greeted by the Prime Minister who escorts Elliot and Mark into a private study.

The Prime Minister informed Elliot that he had spoken with his son from the hospital and he was happy to report that under the circumstances, Ethan was in relatively good health with the exception of an apparent broken foot, which had occurred during the earlier stages of the kidnapping. He was scheduled for surgery the next day in Jerusalem to correct the problem. Other than being exceedingly thin and totally worn out, he appeared to be in good spirits and in relatively good shape.

The Prime Minister informed Elliot that Ethan was running about one hour late and that he specifically requested that he and Rose be allowed to share some private time before any press appearances. He wanted to be sure that Elliot was present so that he could personally thank him for the remarkable decisions he had made in order to ensure that he come home alive.

After all the pleasantries are dispensed with, the Prime Minister says to Elliot, "I have an announcement. No one knows about it. In fact, I didn't even know about it until late this morning when I made the final decision. Mark, you're welcome to stay if you wish. So, here goes."

Elliot looks over to Mark and then to the Prime Minister, who says, "After a long consultation with my wife and some key loyal ministers, I have decided to step down from being Prime Minister of Israel. The kidnapping of Ethan has had a profound effect on Mrs. Weiztman and me. So, I will call for a new election and step down within three months, and I ask that you replace me as Prime Minister!"

Elliot starts laughing out loud as he looks at Mark, who is not laughing. Based on the tone of the Prime Minister's voice and the look in his eyes, Mark instantly understood that this was not a joke.

Now realizing that the Prime Minister is dead serious, Elliot says, "Are you out of your mind?"

The Prime Minister responds, "No. I'm not. First of all, the Lieutenant Commander and the Mossad director have just a few minutes ago held a press conference on national television. They informed the nation that it was you, and you alone, that set the remarkable strategy, then led the effort to secure Ethan. They called your military strategy brilliant. They both stated with conviction that you are a hero and a great new Israeli leader. The Mossad director asked the Knesset (the unicameral national legislature branch of the Israeli government) to issue a rare Proclamation memorializing your extraordinary service to the nation. You, my friend, are about to become the most popular man in Israel!"

Elliot humbly responds, "I just had a hunch as to what might be the correct course to get back Ethan alive and without any bloodshed. I was driven by the fact that he is your son, and frankly, by the fact that my daughter is in love and prepared to marry Ethan." Then with a broad smile on his face, he adds, "Oh yeah, and also by the fact that my wife would have killed me if I didn't bring him back alive. So, does that qualify me to be an Israeli Prime Minister? Hell no!"

The serious Prime Minister says, "Not necessarily all by itself. But when you add the incredible leadership and booming economy you accomplished as Minister of Finance, along with the trust you have created amongst the vast members of the government, I'd say you're ready. Of course, it doesn't hurt that you're a billionaire or having me quietly guide you behind the scenes. Let's do this!"

Elliot responds, "I'll give it some thought, Mr. Prime Minister, but in the meantime, why don't you pour Mark and I some of that famous Macallan Scotch you only break out on special occasions."

The Prime Minister pours all three of them a drink and raises his glass saying, "To the brilliant leadership of Elliot Sterling. To the man who saved my son's life! And to the man whose daughter will become my son's wife. Your life's work has brought you to this crossroad. You're a hero to this nation and your destiny will be to lead it toward staggering greatness. To the next Prime Minister of our beloved State of Israel!"

Mark chimes in with a verbal applause, "Hear, hear!"

Elliot reacts with, "Thank you. But let me add Mark Goldman to all this recognition. Mark has been at my side since I was a kid. You should know, Mr. Prime Minister, that without Mark, I would not be standing here today. So, let's raise our glasses to a devoted friend, a great partner, Mr. Mark Goldman!"

As they finish their drinks, an aide to the Prime Minister enters the room and informs them that Ethan would be arriving to the residence within the next five minutes. They are told to make their way to the entry porte-cochere in order to greet Ethan upon his triumphant arrival.

On his way toward the entry, Elliot stops to share a private moment with Rose and Felicia as they hug and cry for joy that Ethan is returning safely to his parents and his bride-to-be. Rose stares into her father's eyes and emotionally says, "Thank you, Daddy. I knew you would bring Ethan back to me!"

Feeling very proud of her husband and with tears dripping off her cheeks, Felicia says, "You just gave our daughter her life back. She loves Ethan and she's now going to have a beautiful wedding! All because of her amazing father. I love you, Elliot!"

It was an exciting moment to see the motorcade slowly make its way to the entrance to the Prime Minister's home. The car carrying Ethan was now directly under the porte-cochere where a military officer was about to open the door. A receiving line had formed with the Prime Minister and his wife at the front, followed by Rose, Felicia, Elliot, and about ten other government and political figures.

The magic moment of Ethan's return was about to be witnessed by the entire country as it was being carried live on national TV. As the door to the backseat was opened, Ethan Weiztman slowly made his way out of the automobile to thunderous applause and a roar of jubilation!

The fragile Ethan is assisted by his father and mother who instantly hug and kiss their son in what seems to last for an eternity. Then, Ethan spots Rose and moves to embrace her to a second deafening cheer of approval by all those present, including a smiling Prime Minister. It was a memorable moment that was certain to make an impression on the nation. Not one word was said by either Ethan or Rose. They just clung to each other, grateful to God that they were reunited against all odds.

Finally, as that shared moment was over, Ethan breaks his silence spontaneously, saying to Rose in her ear, "I will never leave you again. You are the love of my life."

Rose, who has inherited the wit and charm of her Mother, responds by joking, "I told you'd regret the day when you went back to Harvard without me."

Ethan breaks out laughing at Rose's comment and kisses her on the lips to yet another boisterous cheer as he and Rose make their way to Rose's parents. Ethan, a former member of the Israeli Defense Forces, decides even in pain, to stand at formal military attention as he greets Elliot with a salute, showing his highest form of respect for the man who saved his life, and his future father-in-law.

Elliot returns his salute as they both then collapse into a hardy hug joined by Felicia and Rose. The magnitude of raw emotions at that moment in time is simply breathtaking.

Everyone gathered inside to sit for a formal late lunch with Ethan, a now former hostage and the guest of honor at the Prime Minister's residence. The only issue was that neither Ethan nor Rose were anywhere to be found. They had been last seen walking away into the residence, but not since.

Obviously, they had much to get caught up on, but they also needed to be respectful to their parents and the over 50 invited guests. Just as the Prime Minister was about to summon his aide to find them, Ethan and Rose, holding hands, walk into the grand dining area in the residence to the warm applause of the hastily assembled group.

As the two take their seats at the table with the Prime Minister and his wife along with Elliot, Felicia, and Mark, the Prime Minister stands to make an emotional toast to his son without any notes. The moment he starts to speak, his voice cracks as he says, "The fact that Ethan is here with us today stands as a testament that there is a God, the Master of the universe, who has spared my son's life. It also demonstrates the remarkable resilience Ethan has shown us throughout this terrifying ordeal. He's a courageous young man and I am so humbled to be able to call him my son. I am extremely grateful that Ethan has been returned to his beloved mother and to Rose, the extraordinary young woman he will soon marry. So, please raise your glasses. To Ethan, my son, a man of great valor!"

Everyone in the room stands and breaks out in applause as they take a sip of their champagne. Once the guests are seated back down, the Prime Minister continues, "There is one more person I wish to acknowledge here this afternoon. He is our Minister of Finance. But today he's much, much more than that. Elliot is my personal hero! He is the brilliant architect of the successful military and diplomatic strategy that returned Ethan back home to Israel without going to war and without one drop of blood spilled. Let me put it to you this way, this man is a natural-born leader, his will is made of steel, and he has a vision like a prophet. Elliot Sterling, please stand and be recognized!"

Elliot, not expecting to be acknowledged on an afternoon that he believed solely belonged to Ethan, embarrassingly and slowly gets out of his seat to stand. As he looks out over the assembled guests, he spots the Lieutenant Commander and the Director of Mossad standing and cheering in loud applause. This prompts the entire Israeli Cabinet to stand, and then everyone, to give the American businessman turned Israeli political leader a standing ovation. It doesn't take long after that for the small crowd to organically start demanding, "Speech, speech, speech!"

The Prime Minister grabs the microphone and says, "Come on, Elliot, say a few words!"

Hesitantly, Elliot walks over to the mic and humbly says, "Thank you. Thank you very much. I'm having a lot of trouble finding the words to help you all understand the exuberance and pure joy I feel to see Ethan reunited with his parents and my daughter. Everyone on our team did their part to assure that Ethan would return to the land of Israel a free man. I do not stand here alone. I represent the enormous efforts of people like my associate, Mark Goldman, along with the leadership of the Mossad and YAMAM.

"I especially want to acknowledge the courageous direction of the Prime Minister who gave me the confidence and encouragement to pursue our mission from a position of strength even though it effected the life of his loving son. Our collective decisions resulted in a strong message to the terrorists that dare threaten this nation. We will defeat you no matter what your threat might be. The return of Ethan Weiztman to his homeland will forever stand as a testament to our resolve. Thank you."

What was becoming a norm for Elliot whenever he spoke publicly, the place simply went wild with cheers and heartfelt applause. Ethan made his way to his future father-in-law and gave him a hearty hug. Thereafter, it seemed as if everyone in the room had converged to shake Elliot's hand. It was a picture-perfect moment witnessed by the Israeli press as the clever Prime Minister accomplished his mission that afternoon. Elliot had become the most charismatic politician and leader in the nation.

Chapter 25

The day after the luncheon for Ethan was the day that Elliot Sterling became a household name throughout Israel. His name was splattered throughout the nation including print media and social media. Every television news network and radio affiliate were talking about Elliot. It seemed as if Elliot's picture could be seen everywhere one looked. In fact, his fame was growing rapidly in Europe and in the United States. He was the man responsible for rescuing the Prime Minister's son right from the hands of terrorists without a drop of blood having been spilled.

The Israeli newspapers led with bold headlines stating: ELLIOT FREES ETHAN!

Elliot was quickly gaining fame as a national hero and military genius. Even the highest-ranking generals in the Israeli defense forces were giving Elliot serious praise for his tough-minded military strategy. At the end of the day, Elliot was able to lead the effort to rescue the Prime Minister's son from the hands of no-nonsense terrorists without going to war. Most citizens in Israel had believed that Ethan's abduction would surely lead to a protracted military conflict, leaving many Israeli young soldiers to die.

Elliot was being credited with the brilliant strategy that left no dead and no war. In turn, public opinion regarding Elliot's favorability rating in the country shot through the roof overnight.

Elliot does not realize how instantaneously famous he has become, but Mark grasps immediately what is going on when he says to Elliot, "You have every news outlet in the country wanting to get a face-to-face interview with you. Let me break some news to you, you are a celebrity phenomenon in this country. You're a rock star. Everyone wants to talk to you! Personally, I think you're way overrated."

Laughing out loud hysterically, Mark and Elliot look at each other, then continue laughing like a couple of school kids giggling in a play yard. When the two old friends finally compose themselves, Mark seriously says, "You realize that Prime Minister Weiztman is pulling all the media strings. He's choreographing a symphony for you with the Israeli national press. The goal he has in mind is to make you the next Prime Minister of Israel. This guy is not screwing around, Elliot. He's dead serious, and if you aren't on the same page with him, I suggest you tell him right away."

Elliot quickly responds, "At first I thought he was just making me feel like perhaps he was grateful for the effort to save Ethan's life, but now I think you're right, he's serious. And no, I don't want the job. Not only am I under-qualified for the position, it's not what I want for Felicia or my kids.

"I got to break the news to the Prime Minister before he does something stupid, like commit me to his national political party without my consent. Hey, Mark. Do me a favor. Let the Prime Minister's assistant know that I need to meet with the boss."

Within thirty minutes of the request, the meeting was confirmed at the Prime Minister's office. As Elliot and Mark made their way to his office, they discussed virtually every angle needed in order to be prepared to inform the Prime Minister that Elliot had no interest in taking his job. In fact, they strategized as to why the Prime Minister should continue leading the nation.

When they enter the prestigious office of the Prime Minister of Israel, they instantly feel the power and prestige of the occupant. The Prime Minister is comfortably seated on an exquisite pastel-colored apricot loveseat, texting a message to an undisclosed person. He looks up at Elliot and asks him to please take a seat because he has something important to tell him.

The Prime Minister gets right into it, "Elliot, and Mark, other than my wife, nobody knows what I'm about to tell you. So, listen carefully."

Once he determines that Elliot is listening, the Prime Minister looks straight into his eyes and says, "I have been diagnosed with pancreatic cancer. It's unclear how long I will live. I want you; I am asking you to take my place as Prime Minister. The country needs you. I need you."

An ashen-faced Elliot glances at Mark, then addresses the Prime Minister, "I am so sorry to hear this. I had no idea except for your weight loss, which I attributed to the stress associated with Ethan's abduction. How do you feel? What can I do for you? Let me arrange for the Mayo Clinic in Rochester, Minnesota, to organize their specialists to get you treatment. They're the best in the world."

The Prime Minister stares into Elliot's eyes and says, "My dear Elliot, you're not listening to me! I just told you what you can do for me! Take over the office of Prime Minister. I will help you. I'll show you everything you need to know. Just trust me. As far as the illness, well, I got a lot of faith in God and the Israeli doctors. I am positive they're both going to take good care of me. Now, let's get back to politics!

"I'm going to resign from my office within two months. I will simultaneously resign my seat in the Knesset. I want you to take over both by running in the special election for my seat in the Knesset. You will be elected by a landslide after I endorse you. Once you win the special election, you will announce your run to become Prime Minister."

Elliot, shocked by Weiztman's illness and overwhelmed by all this talk of becoming a Prime Minister, says, "It's such an honor that you would even consider me. I am at a loss for words, except that you picked the wrong guy. I don't understand the first thing about Israeli national politics. It's way above my paygrade. How about I stay as Minister of Finance and you pick some other competent guy, or woman, and we all remain friends?"

The Prime Minister clearly responds, "We're already friends. What I need is my new Prime Minister!"

Starting to see the handwriting on the wall, Elliot tries once again to get out of the plan by saying, "Frankly, I don't even know what I have to do to qualify to run for the office of Prime Minister. I mean really, this is laughable. It's not going to work. The Israeli opposition party is going to eat me alive.

"I'm not your guy, Mr. Prime Minister. Really, I sincerely mean it, I'm not the right choice."

Prime Minister Weiztman slowly responds, "You're exactly the right choice. You are what's needed in this country to unite a terribly divided nation. The people need a leader that can bring them together as opposed to living in a country that is ready to burst into civil war. As we sit here today, you've become Israel's most popular politician. Use this political capital wisely. Lead this nation out of this crisis and you will forever be remembered for what you have accomplished.

"I no longer have the strength nor the time to do this. But you do. Use your magnificent leadership skills. Modernize this nation and make it a worldwide financial powerhouse. You can do this. You will do this!"

Elliot keeps looking at Mark, desperately trying to evoke some help to get him out of this rapidly emerging critical decision, but Mark stays silent, leaving the decision to Elliot. Mark understands that the Prime Minister wouldn't be asking if he has any doubt as to whether Elliot can lead the nation.

Mark realized that Elliot wanted no part of national politics, but he also knew that the Prime Minister was offering Elliot the greatest honor of a lifetime. An opportunity to become the head of state of a nation. So, he just stayed silent, allowing for Elliot to take the decision without any influence from his close friend and advisor.

Elliot takes a deep breath and says to the Prime Minister, "I'm not saying yes, but please explain to me the logistics of what I need do to get on the ballot."

The Prime Minister instantly begins explaining the process, "I am the head of the Centrist Party. I control thirty-five seats in the Knesset (the Israeli Parliament). My party, recognized as the Centrist Party, did not win an outright majority of the seats required to control the Knesset. By the way, that's typical in Israeli national elections.

"So, party leaders generally become Prime Ministers by cobbling together a Parliamentary majority with the help of a group of smaller parties. These smaller, middle of the road parties have chosen to form a coalition supporting my leadership in order for me to capture my current 65-seat majority. Those 65 seats, out of a total of 120, is what keeps me in power. Although technically we only need to control 61-seats, I'm going to deliver those same 65 seats to you so that you will maintain a ruling majority, and that, my friend, will make you Israel's next Prime Minister."

Elliot understood the explanation and thanks the Prime Minister for making it easy to comprehend. He then addresses Mark, "Sounds doable. We just need to govern toward the center. Currently, Israel is a 'Center-Left' country, so, the Prime Minister's political job is to rally enough left-leaning voters to defect toward the center. As a party, we must rely on the labor movement and bring them into a big open tent known as the Centrist Party. I think I got it!"

The Prime Minister begins clapping, saying, "Look at you! Mazel Tov! I couldn't have said it any better myself. You see, you're a natural!"

Elliot stares at the Prime Minister and says, "To be honest with you, I can't stand politicians. Their level of hypocrisy turns my stomach. When you combine the intense personal media scrutiny that my family and I would be required to tolerate, and you tie it to the scoundrels in the politics, along with the real family security risks, well, I just can't do this. I'm not going to put Felicia and my two girls into that fishbowl. In fact, if you're not going to be the Prime Minister, I don't even want to continue as Finance Minister!

No sir. I respectfully decline. It's a bad fit. You got to trust me on this."

A serious Weiztman responds, "God is testing you, and there is only one correct answer."

First glancing at Mark, and then looking straight into the eyes of a very ill Prime Minister whose life expectancy appeared frighteningly low, Elliot decides not to answer the question. Instead, he decides that this is not the correct moment to make a decision and pivots, saying, "Okay, okay. Let me at least have a chance to consult with my wife and my daughters. I've got a big business running here, lots of important associates, and a bunch of employees. Oh yeah, and I shouldn't neglect the major hotel development I have under construction in Jerusalem. Give me a couple of days to think this proposition through a bit. I mean, you're talking about becoming a head of state, for Christ's sake!"

The Prime Minister, looking frail, jokes, "Wrong religious reference, but you're certainly on the right track concerning my suggestion that God is testing you. All kidding aside, of course, talk with your family. Take a peek at your business interests, then make a well-informed decision. But take my political advice, the momentum for you to win the election for Prime Minister is there for you to grab."

"These things don't line up that often. The country needs you and, in my opinion, nothing else is more important. Don't wait too long in making your decision. Thank you for your consideration."

The men shake hands as Elliot and Mark briskly make their way to the waiting car arranged to drive them back Caesarea. As they are about halfway home, Elliot breaks a relatively silent trip by saying to Mark, "So, tell me. What do I do?"

Half asleep, Mark awakens knowing how humor and fun are capable of quickly making a bleak situation seem a lot more positive. "Hunter S. Thompson is credited as having said, 'Life should not be a journey to the grave with the intention of arriving safely in a pretty and well-preserved body, but rather to skid in broadside in a cloud of smoke, thoroughly used up, totally worn out, and loudly proclaiming "Wow! What a ride!"' I say we take the ride. You were born for this moment, Elliot. You will lead Israel to its rightful place amongst world powers, and I'll be right next to you all the way!"

Unable to hold back his laughter, Elliot responds, "Yeah, sure. Tell that to my wife. She's never going to accept this. She's under the belief that one day, in the not too distant future, we'll be heading back to the States to live in Beverly Hills. When I tell Felicia to prepare herself to become the First Lady of Israel, well, she's simply going to strangle me.

"I'm telling you right now, this Prime Minister gig is not going to fly with her. Believe me, when I envision running the country with you at my side, I'm all in, but I just can't put Felicia and the kids through this. And what about the Sterling Hedge Fund?"

"I mean, the sky is the limit with what we can accomplish. We have a real possibility of eventually becoming one of the biggest hedge funds in the world! Listen, I think we're going to need to gracefully back down from the Prime Minister's request. This is just not going to work."

Mark quickly assesses that the main obstacle in Elliot's mind is Felicia's probable objection. He thinks for a moment then says, "Look. Felicia is a real humanitarian in her heart. For as long as I've known her, she has continuously promoted the wellbeing of underprivileged children. Felicia has been at the forefront of advocacy for abused women. She cares deeply about correcting poverty and she has never stepped away from a fight to stop bullies. What about decent mental health care for everyone."

"Felicia will enjoy a serious platform by which she can advocate for her convictions here and all over the world. She's going to be spectacular at this once she settles into the role. I can't even image the splash she's going to make socially. Just thinking about Felicia entertaining heads of state or traveling to the White House or other European nations as the First Lady of Israel, she's going to be a natural.

"No, Felicia isn't going to kill you, she's going to thank you!"

Elliot does not say anything for the next 30 miles of the car ride and then suddenly says, "Yeah, I think you may be right. Felicia will be a great First Lady. And the more I think about it, our Hedge Fund will probably have more opportunities than ever before with me as Prime Minister. I'll just need to place the Fund into a blind trust and let Benjamin, Moshe Ariel, and Yitzhak Bennett run it."

Now understanding that the tide is turning, Mark responds, "You and your family will make contacts all over the world. The Sterling Hedge Fund will be left in good hands and is all but guaranteed to grow. Elliot, take this opportunity, you won't regret it!"

As their car drives through the main security gate and up toward the residence, Elliot spots Felicia, Rose, and Ethan walking. He asks the driver to stop and pull the vehicle to the side of the road. He informs Mark that he's going to finish the walk with his wife and daughter as he gets out of the car saying, "Thanks for the advice. I'll see you a little later. Say hello to Emma for me."

Excited to see her husband, Felicia greets Elliot with a passionate kiss and a hug and says, "You're just in time to hear the wonderful news. Ethan is going to ask Rose to get married! He was waiting for you to return from Jerusalem to ask for your permission. So, here we are, Ethan, go ahead and ask!"

Ethan, who was not expecting Felicia to blurt the news out quite that fast, collects his thoughts, faces Elliot, and formally says, "Mr. Sterling, it is with great humility and with the highest level of sincerity that I ask you for your consent allowing me to marry your daughter, Rose, the true love of my life."

Shocked at what is happening before his very eyes, Elliot looks at Felicia and Rose. Both are crying from pure joy. Then with a heartfelt smile and shedding a tear, Elliot replies, "There is no one else I would rather have marry my daughter than you, Ethan. Of course, you have my permission!"

Hugging in an impromptu group hug, Elliot asks Ethan, "Does your father know of this decision?"

Ethan responds, "No sir. I wanted your concurrence first. My mom and my father love Rose and they are going to be over the top when I call them. As you are probably aware, my dad is not so well and I'd like to get married as soon as possible. Rose and Mrs. Sterling are good with that as long as you agree."

Thrilled for his daughter and for Felicia, Elliot responds, "As far as we're concerned, you guys can get married whenever you both agree on a date. I haven't asked Felicia, but I'd love for you to be married at our home. It would be our great honor. You okay with that, Felicia?"

With her very quick wit intact and with her beautiful smile, Felicia answers, "Which home are we talking about, Beverly Hills or Caesarea?"

Rose instantly starts laughing, then Ethan can't stop laughing before Felicia says, "Of course, it's okay. There's no better place on earth than to marry our daughter right in the garden of our home so long as Ethan agrees."

With a straight face, Ethan answers, "Now, Mrs. Sterling, which home are we talking about, Beverly Hills or Caesarea?"

Everyone bursts into out loud laughter as Felicia enthusiastically answers, "Right here in Israel! This is going to be the wedding of a lifetime. I can't wait for you to inform your parents.

Let's go back to the house. They deserve to hear the good news and pick a date. Then, let's gets this wedding started!"

As they all start their short walk back to the residence, Elliot says, "Ethan, go ahead and give your parents the exciting news, but let's hold off on the date, at least until this evening. How about all of us have dinner together in the dining room at 6 PM? Felicia, could you please have Erica join us? Erica is in Jerusalem at the University, but if she leaves within the next couple of hours, she can get here in plenty of time for dinner."

"Perfect, see you all this evening."

Felicia, sensing that there is more to the dinner than just marriage talk, gets right to the point, "What's going on, Elliot? What's wrong? You're scaring me a bit. What do you need to say? How about you just simply tell us right this second?"

With a big grin, and sincerity written all over his face, Elliot explains to his wife, "It's a surprise. Nothing to be worried about. Nothing to be alarmed about. Just an announcement I want to make in front of the family. Something I want to share with all of you about the future, which will require a little feedback. Trust me, nothing bad and certainly nothing that can't wait until dinner. If you insist, well, I guess I'll need to tell right now, but I think it will ruin the family moment. I'd prefer to enjoy the marriage announcement for a few hours. My stuff can wait until dinner."

Knowing her husband well, Felicia understood Elliot didn't want to talk about whatever was on his mind until dinner. She recognized that if there was anything even remotely urgent requiring conversation, Elliot would already have spoken to her. So, she elects to let it go until dinner, saying in her charming way, "This better be good!"

Elliot winks at Felicia saying, "Oh. It will be. Trust me. It will be."

The conversation walking back to the residence was pleasant and full of enthusiasm for the upcoming wedding. The young couple had gone through a lot and they were both very emotional about the fact that God had spared Ethan's life. They were both determined to make the most out of their lives together including the planning of a beautiful wedding celebrating life and their future.

By the time dinner was ready to be served, Ethan had informed his parents of the good news and both the Prime Minister and Elliot had shared their well wishes by phone. As the entire family gathers for dinner, including Ethan, they all sit down at the magnificent table setting Felicia has organized, which includes porcelain bread, salad, and dinner plates, sterling silverware, and Baccarat fine crystal wineglasses. The handmade white tablecloth with floral designs is stunning. The candelabra lighting finished off the ambience of the formal dining with a touch of class tailormade for a special evening.

Although Mark and Emma were not technically 'family' members, they were nevertheless invited to the dinner. Felicia considered them family and wanted them present to celebrate the marriage announcement, and whatever Elliot was about to disclose. Mark was the closest person in the world to Elliot aside from his wife and kids, and Felicia knew that he would not have wanted this evening to proceed without his lifelong friend and his wife present.

As the dinner is about to get started, a highly emotional Erica stands unannounced at her seat and raises her glass. "Let me be the first here this evening to toast my sister, Rose, and my future brother-in-law, Ethan. I've never met a more perfect couple, and to tell you the truth, I doubt I ever will. Both of you bring out the best of each other. I am so excited for your future and I can't wait for your wedding day! I love you, Rosie, and I love you, Ethan. L'Chaim!" (To life.)

Elliot glances at Felicia and then addresses Erica, "That was beautiful, unexpected, but beautiful. Thank you, Erica. So, since we are a bit out of sequence, I'd like Ethan to say a few words. Go ahead, Ethan, share some thoughts."

Ethan collects his thoughts, then speaks from the heart, looking at Rose, "From the moment I met you, I knew you were the woman I was going to marry. A kind, intelligent, beautiful woman with a charming sense of humor. I also understood that I would be marrying into the magnificent Sterling family. I really mean when I say, I love you, Mr. and Mrs. Sterling, and I love you, Erica. I hope I will always make you proud. And I promise you all that I will always do my very best to take good care of Rose for the rest of our lives."

Rose, Felicia, and Erica are simultaneously crying as they feel the warmth and sincerity of Ethan's words. Elliot immediately says, "Your words mean a great deal to us, and we feel the same for you."

Elliot continues addressing Ethan and Rose, "So, when's the big date?"

Ethan glances at Rose and answers, "Sunday, July 27 at 3 PM right here in your magnificent backyard garden. It going to be spectacular! Can we fit 400 guests in the garden?"

Elliot thinks for a moment and says, "I think so. We'll just make it fit."

Felicia chimes in, "I am so excited! This is going to be the most beautiful wedding ever. We've got slightly over three months to pull this off. I'll get started with all the planning as of tomorrow! Wow, we've got a lot to do, and not a whole lot of time to do it in. Every moment counts!"

Elliot looks over at Mark and smiles as he says, "I don't think my subject matter here tonight is all that important compared to the marriage of my daughter. I think we cover my theme perhaps tomorrow night. Or some other day."

Felicia interrupts him, "No. No. Go ahead, Elliot. Tell us what's on your mind. Let's hear it. I'm sure this is really important to you and our family. Go ahead. We're all ears."

Elliot clears his throat, looks at Ethan, and calmly says, "Your father, Ethan, has asked me to become the next Prime Minister of Israel. Of course, I must run and be elected, but he has pledged his entire political machine behind my candidacy. As you know, your dad is very ill and he will be resigning the office soon. He wants the country to continue with his political philosophy and method of governing, and he chose me as his successor.

"I told him that the only way I would even consider the job is if my family fully endorsed the idea. He knows that if any of you are opposed to this, I will withdraw my name from consideration. I realize this is a lot to ask of all of you to make the sacrifice regarding public life at a head of state level. But I am confident that our family will step up and make a difference for the good of the many lives we will touch along the way if we choose to embark on this journey."

Elliot pauses for a moment to look into the rather shocked faces of his family and continues, "I also believe that Felicia will blossom into a magnificent First Lady that will have a worldwide platform to make a difference for the well-being of many people's lives. This is a once in a lifetime opportunity.

"There are less than 200 heads of state in the world. If elected, I will be one of them representing amongst the most famous and important nations on earth. I'm prepared for the challenge, and Mark has agreed to be right there by my side as he has been since I was a kid. If you all give me your blessing, we'll start the campaign by advising Ethan's father that I accept the challenge. If you say no, then I say no, and life will just go on, except that I will resign as Finance Minister when Ethan's dad resigns."

Ethan stands and says out loud, "You got my support! The country loves you! You're going to make an incredible Prime Minister and I will help you in any way I can!"

Everyone in the room is supportive except Felicia, who has not said a word until now. "What about your safety? What about our safety? We've been through a lot, Elliot. No political position is worth your life or that of any member of our family. Come on, we just saw what happened to Ethan. I mean, this kind of stuff happens to high-profile Middle Eastern politicians.

"Elliot, we have everything we could ever have dreamt for. We don't need fame or money or political power. We need you to be alive and with us. I don't want to go to sleep every night thanking God that you made it through another day. Or whether our family is safe! Don't you remember why we originally decided to come live in Israel?

"Well, let me remind you. We were afraid for our lives regarding the Nigerian threat at that time. I can't go through this again. I'm petrified every day that something terrible will happen to you as the Finance Minister. Now multiply that by ten as a sitting Prime Minister. I was worried sick when Ethan was abducted. I don't want any of us to worry everyday about this. I love you very much, Elliot, but I just can't support this! Not this time. I'm sorry, I just can't do it. Please forgive me!"

Upset, Felicia excuses herself and abruptly leaves the dining room to everyone's heartfelt pain for her.

Embarrassed, Elliot addresses his family, "I'm so sorry I ruined this beautiful moment for you, Rose and Ethan. It was stupid of me to even have brought the subject up in light of the marriage announcement. I should have disclosed in advance my plans to Felicia privately.

"Had I known that she would have reacted so strongly, opposed to the idea, I would have dropped the subject with her and we wouldn't even be talking any further about it. What a boneheaded mistake! Anyway, that's water under the bridge. Please forgive me for exercising such bad judgement. I'm going to excuse myself and go apologize to my wife. Let's all get back here tomorrow evening and finish off what we started the right way. See you all tomorrow. And, congratulations, Rose and Ethan."

Both Rose and Erica stand and approach their dad as Rose says, "You didn't do anything wrong, Dad. On the contrary, we're very proud of you for rising to such a prominent position of respect in this country. Go talk to Mom. Tell her we're with you on this. She just loves you and our family so much that she can't even consider the thought of losing you. You need to explain to her that you will have the very best security guards in the world and so will we."

"You're going to be the finest Prime Minister that this nation has ever seen, except for Ethan's dad, of course. Seriously, we all endorse you, now go get mom turned around. We'll all be back here tomorrow night. You can try the Prime Minister announcement thing all over again, except this time you're going to have unanimous consent."

Elliot is so touched by Rose's comments and his two daughter's support that he embraces them both and says, "Thank you for the vote of confidence. I'll do my best to speak to your mom. If she still says no, then that will be the end of discussion, period. I'm not willing to upset your mom any further if she wants to kill the subject. Either way, we will return here tomorrow evening and carry on with celebrating the marriage good news. And I'll let you all know whether we're going to pursue the Prime Minister position. Wish me luck. See you all tomorrow night. I love you all deeply."

Elliot finds Felicia sitting on a loveseat in the bedroom reading a book. She seems composed and no longer angry. As he approaches her, Elliot whispers, "I'm sorry for upsetting you. I should never have put you in that position in front of the family. Please forgive me."

Felicia responds softly, "I'm sorry for walking out of the room like a two-year-old in a childish rage. The thought of reliving the insecurity and fright of the Nigerian nightmare just got to me. We got through it, but at what expense. Paul was murdered like a dog and Yonatan is dead. I don't think I had a peaceful night's sleep until we finally settled into our life here in Caesarea.

"And to tell you the truth, I still worry every day that something might happen to you or Rose or Erica. Let's face it, we've been looking over our shoulders for far longer than I choose to remember. The high-profile position of Prime Minister takes us right back to square one as it relates to safety and security."

"Jesus, Elliot, we all just experienced the horrifying kidnapping of Ethan. One of our daughters could be next! An Israeli Prime Minister wears a target on his back. If you are assassinated, the country will mourn you for a month, then replace you with a new Prime Minister, but I will be a widow for life. Your children will become fatherless. Come on, Elliot, do you really want that for us? Let's get out of here, let's go back to the States. We can make a phenomenal life for ourselves, our kids, and our kids' kids in Beverly Hills.

"Let's go home."

Elliot sits down next to his extraordinary wife that he loves with all of his heart and says, "I'll do whatever you ask, but first listen me out. If, after I finish my explanation, you say go back to Los Angeles, then we pack our bags and we go. Fair deal?"

Felicia, who has always viewed her husband as bigger than life, just nods her head, signifying her approval to proceed with the explanation.

Elliot gets right to the point, "Ethan's dad has pancreatic cancer and his prognosis is not good. He's not going to live long. The Prime Minister spent a lifetime building a political coalition that took him to the highest levels of Israeli international leadership. The political party he built, one man at a time, is what keeps Israel at peace with their hostile neighbors.

"He is concerned that if his successor is not of his political persuasion, the entire Middle East will be at war within six months from him stepping down from office. His worry is that many young Israeli soldiers will die, and that the economy will fall into a crippling recession. Effectively, everything that he worked his entire lifetime to accomplish will result in a disaster if he doesn't hand-select his successor.

"He wants that successor to be me and no one else. I said unconditionally 'no' to his passionate request for the very same reasons you expressed. He just won't take no for an answer. He told me that he would place his entire political machine and campaign finances toward assuring that I would win. Ethan's dad has with great confidence advised me that I and everyone else in the family will be afforded the best security in the world.

"I didn't say yes or no, I informed him that I needed to consult with you and our kids before I could even consider his offer. That's why you and the kids and I find ourselves at this juncture."

Felicia, who is distressed at the news concerning the Prime Minister's medical condition, yet intently listening to her husband's explanation, asks, "Anything else?"

Elliot answers, "Yes, there is. I believe I can make a serious difference in the lives of Israeli citizens. In fact, I believe I can make a difference in the lives of millions of people from around the world as the head of state of Israel. I never thought in a million years that I would find myself in a position like this, but now that the opportunity is right before me, I want to seize it and run hard with it. The only person I would give this up for is you.

"Just say the word, and I'm done. Oh, and one last thing. I sincerely believe that you will make the greatest First Lady this nation has ever seen. Your voice and your work will be recognized across the planet. Okay, that's it. Your wish is my command. What's your wish?"

Felicia was dead silent. She appeared to be in deep thought literally saying nothing while staring across the room with no facial expression. Her mind was cluttered with bad thoughts genuinely fearful that something terrible was going to happen. Yet, she was keenly aware of what a unique opportunity it would be for her family if her husband was to become the head of state of a country like Israel.

She realized that Elliot was born for a challenge like this and was ready to lead. On the other hand, Felicia understood that her family would never be same. Their privacy would be trampled. The travel and stress of the job would most certainly take a toll on her husband's health. She worried not only about his health, but his safety and, perhaps most importantly, the security of her family.

Elliot also stayed silent. He knew his wife was weighing the options and when ready, she would declare her position. Felicia clearly understood Elliot's explanation as to how he had gotten to this point, but she was conflicted and reluctant to sacrifice her husband just because Prime Minister Weiztman had worked all of his life for a country he was born in and loved. She suddenly breaks her silence, "What did Rose and Erica say?"

Elliot responds softly, "They offered their support and have encouraged me to proceed."

"I know that Mark is in favor of this. Since you were kids, you've both been looking for the next adventure. Now, look at the two of you. Ready to lead a nation. Not bad for a couple of kids growing up in poverty, and about to make it on to the world scene. It's hard for me to be selfish by stopping you from pursuing this awesome opportunity. I guess I just don't want to live in fear that one day you won't come home to me. I'm sure that you and our family will be carefully looked after.

"But let's face it, there's no guarantee. Raising our profile to this level makes us a prime target for some lunatic or a rouge nation to cause us devasting harm. Having said that, I'm not going to stop you. So, let's do this. Just don't get yourself killed or make me remind you that I told you so."

Fraught with emotion, Felicia's eyes were welling with tears. Not because she had a change of heart regarding her decision, but she felt as if she had just lost her husband to politics and a nation. She deeply loved her husband and the thought that she couldn't have him the way they had lived their entire life was giving her tremendous anxiety.

Understanding Felicia's pain, Elliot comforts her by holding her hand and saying, "You're the finest woman I have ever met. I love you for setting your personal feelings aside and allowing me to pursue this course. I promise you I will do my very best to keep our personal life as normal as I can. We'll just need to create a routine that works. We can do this. I want you to join me as often as you can when it is necessary for me to travel.

"Just think about all the good we're going to accomplish together. We're going to make an enormous positive impact on people. We're going work together to make this the greatest chapter in our lives. I promise you I will not take unnecessary security risks. Don't look at this as a setback, view it as a terrific opportunity to leave a legacy of decency and great accomplishment.

"The world will forever associate the Sterling family name with a proud record of unprecedented achievement."

Now embracing her husband tightly and feeling the security of his confidence, Felicia whispers in his ear, "Okay, Mr. Future Prime Minister, show us the way! We'll break the news to the family at dinner tomorrow night, but I'm pretty sure your daughters knew I was going to trust you and follow your lead anyway. I always have."

These are the magic words Elliot needs to hear from Felicia. Nothing would stop him now from charging ahead with the hard-fought campaign to become Israel's next Prime Minister.

Chapter 26

A considerable amount of time passed since the family had reconvened for their final dinner where Felicia had given her unconditional endorsement in front of the family, authorizing Elliot to pursue his ambitious goal of becoming Israel's Prime Minister. Since that time, Prime Minister Weiztman had announced to the public that he would be stepping down and retiring from government due to his serious illness. He had enthusiastically named Elliot as his successor and asked the public to embrace Elliot as the next Prime Minister.

The press and the people of Israel had taken an immediate liking to Elliot and began referring to him affectionately as "Eli". He had easily won a seat in the Knesset, previously held by the Prime Minister, and breezed through the primary to become his party's nominee for Prime Minister of Israel. Clearly, Prime Minister Weiztman's well-oiled political machine had tilted the advantage toward Elliot.

Their established grass-roots organization understood exactly what they were doing. They almost made it look easy, until it was announced that they were going to go head on with a worthy primary opponent, Menachem Kahlon, the right-wing soldier politician who had served as the 15th Chief of General Staff of the Israel Defense Forces (IDF).

Kahlon didn't know much about Israeli politics, but he was a popular military war hero with a no-nonsense approach to dealing with Israel's antagonistic Arab neighbors. He was a fiscal conservative and had developed a working coalition with the country's Orthodox religious party. His right-wing affiliation had no tolerance for a two-state solution, which would allow for the Palestinians and Israelis each to maintain sovereign land for their people. These two candidates were destined for a dogfight.

The first poll was released on the question of who the public would like to see as Prime Minister. Elliot was holding a narrow margin advantage with 53% favoring him against the 47% who thought Kahlon would do a better job. The poll contained a margin of error of 5% and the conclusion was that the election was simply too close to even make an educated guess. Elliot's campaign officials immediately claimed "front-runner" status, but Kahlon's people countered saying, "The only poll that counts are the results on election day."

Several news articles were questioning whether a billionaire could actually separate his business interests from the public's interest. The news media seemed to be implying that Elliot had a direct conflict of interest when it came to the Savor Rifle or the brand-new Jerusalem Hotel that was about to be completed by the Sterling Hedge Fund.

Kahlon picked up on this right away claiming that Elliot was running for Prime Minister in order to enrich himself and his family. Kahlon kept hammering at his talking point saying that Elliot was from Beverly Hills and knew nothing about the Israeli military nor the real Israeli culture. At one campaign rally he said out loud to the large assembled crowd in Haifa, "Go home Mr. Sterling, the United States needs your tax dollars one hell of a lot more than Israel needs your corrupt business intentions."

Elliot had read these words in the main Jerusalem newspaper and was furious. He summoned Mark and two of his top political advisors to discuss "the best way to address an Israeli creep like Kahlon."

Naively, Mark says, "I would ignore this asshole!"

The top political advisor in the country, Naftali Litzman, says, "We can't afford to ignore Kahlon. He is very well known for repeating a lie over and over again until he gets the results he's looking for.

"We're going to draft a statement under Mr. Sterling's signature, which is going to address the conflict of interest issue head on. You, Mr. Sterling, you're going to place all of your financial assets into a blind living trust!"

Elliot glances at Mark for a short moment then remarks, "That's easy for you to say, but much more difficult for us to enact. These things take months and months, if not years, before they can be organized properly. I've worked my entire life to gain what I have, and I'm sure as hell not going to throw together some bullshit blind trust. Before I'd do anything like that, I'd need to consult a lot of my most trusted advisors. We just don't have enough time to do this the right way. So, I'm sorry, Mr. Litzman, there will be no blind trust at this time. Perhaps after the election."

Litzman sternly addresses Elliot, "Then I'm afraid, Mr. Sterling, you will lose the election."

Elliot stares at Mark, then Litzman, and says, "If I lose, I guess the nation will never find out how good a Prime Minister I might have been. Sorry, Mr. Litzman, we're just going to ignore this asshole. We'll present our ideas and our vision for the future. If we lose, we lose!"

Proud of his boss for standing up for the integrity of the Sterling Hedge Fund and for backing his sincere advice, Mark says, "I'll call for a board meeting to organize how best to segregate our business interests from those of our political interests."

Litzman instantly steps in by arrogantly saying, "You can organize all you want, but Kahlon, the press, and the Israeli voters are going to eat you alive. I reiterate, no blind trust, no victory. Please don't embarrass Prime Minister Weiztman. Save yourself a lot of time and aggravation. Get out now!"

As Elliot and Mark had done so many times together throughout their long-standing career when it came to people like Litzman, Elliot simply looks at Mark with that familiar special look and asks, "Should I tell him or do you want to tell him?"

Mark says, "I'll tell him. We're letting you go, Mr. Litzman. Thank you very much for your services. We'd appreciate you abiding strictly by the Confidentiality Agreement you signed. We wish you well."

A very agitated Litzman gathers his papers and throws them into his briefcase. As he walks out of the room, the terminated political consultant responds in his thick Israeli accent, "You, my friend, have just committed political suicide!"

Mark, who just can't hold himself back, responds, "And you, you arrogant prick, have just blown a chance to work for the next Prime Minister of Israel. Make sure the door doesn't hit you on the butt on your way out!"

Once the commotion dies down and Litzman is gone, Mark says to Elliot, "I'm really glad you got rid of this guy. He's nothing but trouble. I think you need to call the Prime Minister and let him know that you just fired the best-known political advisor in the entire country of Israel. I think he needs to hear it from us as opposed to Litzman's spin on it."

Elliot agrees, "You're one hundred percent right. I'll call him right now," as he takes out his cell phone and dials the Prime Minister's personal line.

Minister Weiztman answers on the first ring, saying in a frail voice, "Elliot, how are you? Anything new on our kids' wedding? How's the campaign going?"

Elliot responds, "Everything is fine, Mr. Prime Minister. Felicia is in charge of the wedding, and the only thing I know for sure is that this shindig is going to be the finest wedding in Israel's proud history! Can't wait to see you on the dance floor! How are you feeling, Shimon?"

The Prime Minister soberly responds, "To tell you the truth, Elliot, I'm worn out. The treatment for advanced metastatic pancreatic cancer is hard on the body and soul, but I'm hanging in there. Anyway, I'm certain you didn't call me for advice on wedding plans or cancer. So, what can I do for you?"

Elliot goes straight to the point, "I just fired Naftali Litzman. He's arrogant and insubordinate. To tell you the truth, I'm not so sure he's up to date on the modern Israel. Anyway, I'm sorry I threw your referral out. I hope I didn't embarrass you. I just couldn't work with this son-of-a-bitch."

The Prime Minister quickly asks, "Was there something in particular that was the breaking point?"

Elliot responds, "Well, besides being a guy who thinks he knows it all, he was demanding that I place all my assets into a blind trust immediately. I told him I didn't mind doing this, but it would take time for me to accomplish it the right way. He didn't want to wait. He wasn't asking me, he was telling me what to do. So, I fired him."

The Prime Minister asks, "And then what happened?"

"Litzman told me that I was going to lose the election because of the lack of a blind trust, and he also told me that I had committed political suicide. Was he right?"

Minister Weiztman pauses for a few seconds, then says, "Hell no, he wasn't right. Litzman was educated in the United States and majored in political science. American presidents are always forced to place their assets into blind trusts, but that's not necessarily true here in Israel. Many of our Prime Ministers never had that much money, making blind trusts rarely, if ever, a part of our political discourse.

"Now, in your case, well, you're rich and the press is going to pressure you to disclose your assets. I guarantee you, this bastard Kahlon is going to raise the issue every time he opens his mouth. So, you better come up with a game plan regarding your billionaire status. The people of Israel are going to demand that you show us where the conflicts of interest might be found. The citizens will want to know that you are not just running for the highest government office in Israel in order to improve your financial security. What's your plan, Elliot?"

Without much further thought and with no hesitation, Elliot responds, "My accountant, Moshe Ariel, and my attorney, Yitzhak Bennett, will prepare a comprehensive financial statement that will clearly demonstrate my assets and liabilities for the Israeli people to review. I'll be prepared to defend the statement. Should I win the Prime Minister's office, I will additionally pledge that within twelve months of taking my oath of office, I will transfer my assets into a blind trust, which will be administered by Benjamin Yaalon, a top executive in the Sterling Hedge Fund. This is my plan. If I lose the election on this issue, I'll be okay with that. I consider my position fair and transparent, and this is my final decision."

The Prime Minister silently thinks for a brief moment then says, "That sounds perfectly reasonable to me. I can live with that plan. You got my blessings. By the way, I never liked that guy Litzman either. In fact, half the time I thought he was full of bullshit," as both men begin laughing out loud to the delight of Mark who is listening to the conversation.

The Prime Minister continues, "I've got the perfect replacement for Litzman. A man I fully trust. His name is Ariel Lashman. He was Litzman's assistant for many years until he quit to start his own media relations company. This young man can run your national campaign. He's a Columbia University undergraduate in communications and a Yale law school attorney."

"And trust me when I tell you, this man gets our national politics! Ariel is made to order for you. You're going to like this guy and more importantly, you're going to win with him. As soon as I hang up with you, I'll call Ariel and make the arrangements to have him meet with you in your home in Caesarea at 1 PM tomorrow afternoon. This man is brilliant and he'll be an absolute perfect fit for you. Agreed?"

Elliot jokes, "He can't be any worse than the last guy you recommended. Just kidding. Of course, I agree! Send him over tomorrow at 1 PM."

The next day at precisely 1 PM, Ariel Lashman arrived in Caesarea for his interview with Elliot. Just as the Prime Minister had predicted, these two men got along famously. They spoke for hours on end about a range of subjects spanning from political philosophy to campaign strategy. Remarkably, they seemed to agree on virtually everything including Elliot's solution for how to handle disclosure of his vast wealth. By the end of the evening, they had made their financial arrangement and Ariel was hired as the national campaign manager for Elliot's run to become the next Israeli Prime Minister.

Ariel had a deep intellectual curiosity and his enthusiasm was remarkably contagious. The glint in his eyes wasn't just pride, it was a fire burning inside him to succeed. To Ariel, anything less than the best was failure. To that end, Ariel was determined to make Elliot the next Prime Minister of Israel, and no one like Kahlon nor the press, or anyone else were going get in the way of that mission.

As Ariel is about to leave their long meeting and go back to Tel Aviv where he resides, he says to Elliot with a sparkle in his eyes, "I know the country and I have my pulse on the mood of the nation. I guarantee that you will be the next Prime Minister of Israel. All you need to do is be you. Elliot Sterling, no one else. You've got what it takes. Only a handful of people are born with the gift to lead, and you got it! I'll navigate you through this, and you follow your instincts. We're going to win, and we're going to win big!"

Elliot calmly looks at Ariel with a charismatic smile and asks, "So, now what?"

A serious Ariel answers, "Later tonight, I'll email you our schedule for the campaign rally events which I will be arranging along with the talking points you will use during our stops around the country. Your first rally will be in Tel Aviv at the Kings of Israel Square in two days. Make sure your words sound as if they're coming from the heart as opposed to reading from prepared remarks."

Elliot assures Ariel that he'll always speak from the heart and then asks, "By the way, how many people do you expect to attend the Kings Square event?"

Ariel stares into Elliot's eyes and says, "Thousands of adoring Israeli citizens will come to listen to the next Prime Minister of Israel. You're not going to get a second chance to make a great first impression. I suggest you try your best to get it right."

Elliot responds quickly, "Thousands! Are you joking?"

Ariel says, "No sir. I'm not joking. The venue is an open-air square, and it's going to be jam-packed. Bring your 'A' game. Your comments are going to be covered by the national media and will be broadcast live on television during prime time. This is going to be your time to shine. The nation is going to love you, and I can't wait for the whole country to get to know you not as a billionaire, but as genuine, charismatic man who gives a damn about Israel! Any other questions?"

Elliot thinks for a moment and asks, "When are you going to issue a press release regarding my financial statement?"

Ariel answers, "The financial press release will be in the hands of the media by noon tomorrow. So, if you are confronted by the media on any of this financial stuff, all you need to say is, 'Please read the financial statement in its entirety, then I'll be happy to answer questions.' Keep your answers short, sweet, and to the point. Best not to engage in any follow-up questions.

"After we release your financial statement, we'll hold a press conference where you will answer any question they have for you. We'll do this once, and that will put the financial issue in the rear-view mirror. Okay, I'll call you tomorrow, Mr. Future Prime Minister."

Realizing that if he won the election, Elliot would be required to turn over operational control of the Sterling Hedge Fund. To that end, Elliot had Mark arrange for the Board to meet at his home in Caesarea the next day at 10:30 AM. At this gathering, Elliot would be prepared to discuss various topics ranging from his stepping down as the chairman of the board, to the formation of a blind trust, and the release of his financial statement to the public.

The following day at 10:30 AM, every member of the Board is seated in the dining room prepared to hear what their leader had to say. Elliot had spent a great portion of the night preparing to address his loyal Board members. He begins, "I don't consider this a farewell meeting. I am comfortable calling it an information session. So, by chance, if you haven't heard yet, I am running to become the next Prime Minister of Israel." As he gets to the end of that sentence, each member of the Board stands up as they give Elliot a standing ovation and loudly clap and cheer.

Elliot is humbled by the amount of sincere respect he feels at that moment. In fact, he gets a little choked up as he starts his opening remarks. "Thank you, thank you very much. Please take your seats. Together, we formed one of the most successful hedge funds on the planet. Our presence is everywhere and, our product is in demand. We not only sell rifles, but we build hotels, and our real estate holdings are world-class. Our brand is so well respected that Wall Street firms insist on hiring us as their financial services consultants. To put it mildly, we are exceedingly good at what we do!"

Pausing for a moment to sip some water, Elliot transitions by going straight to why he called the meeting, "I expect to win my election, therefore I'll need to be stepping down from our beautiful company, this masterpiece we started together. When I do finally depart from our hedge fund, my successor will be Benjamin Yaalon, and I will expect that you give him the same courtesies as you have extended to me."

Elliot points to Benjamin and says, "Stand up, Ben!"

Benjamin stands and salutes Elliot, then acknowledges the Board members by waving as they enthusiastically clap, signifying their approval of Elliot's choice to succeed him.

As Benjamin sits down, Elliot continues, "My opponent, Menachem Kahlon, is going to try to smear me as a con artist interested in using the office of Prime Minister to line my own pockets in order to benefit the Sterling Hedge Fund. So, all of us must do what we can to demonstrate that this Board and I will be independent of each other should I be elected Prime Minister.

"I'm going to take two important steps to show some daylight between my potential government position and my personal business dealings. The first move will be to produce a comprehensive personal financial statement indicating precisely what my assets and liabilities show. Moshe Ariel will be in charge of completing that task. I will release my financial statement to the media as a good faith effort to demonstrate full financial disclosure. Any questions, Moshe?"

Moshe stands, and with his typical dry wit, asks laughingly, "Last time I checked, you were a billionaire. Has anything changed in the last couple of days?"

Elliot rapidly answers, "Yes. 8,605,119 Israeli citizens have only recently begun to figure out I'm a billionaire. And I got news for you, Israelis will not tolerate some guy from the United States coming here and hustling their government out of money in order to self-benefit. So, Moshe, it's your job to show the citizens and the press what I own and what I owe. Thereafter, we'll just let the voters decide how they want to deal with my political fate."

Elliot carries on, "The second step will be to transfer all of my assets into a 'blind trust' within one year after the election. Benjamin Yaalon and Yitzhak Bennett will jointly administer this trust."

The Board meeting went on for several hours, deliberating about various decisions. It was concluded that the Savor rifle would be introduced to the American market with a focus on law enforcement accounts. The Savor was selling so well, and the stock value had risen so high, that each of the Sterling Hedge Fund Board members had increased their wealth considerably. Elliot's financial assets had gained well over half a billion dollars by virtue of the Savor rifle alone.

The Board allocated much attention toward the new hotel in Jerusalem, which was scheduled to open within a month. The hotel management had reported that the main wedding and special events rooms were already booked for the balance of the year. Additionally, the room reservations for the opening twelve weeks were set at ninety percent occupancy. Given this information, the Board unanimously authorized raising the fees in both categories, concluding that the initial rates were too low.

As the Board meeting drew to a close, it was evident that the Hedge Fund was doing phenomenal business. Although everyone was exceptionally pleased with the performance of what was shaping up to be one of the world's most lucrative money funds, Elliot realized that his business was about to become a huge target for Kahlon and the Israeli media.

Walking away from the Board meeting, Elliot tells Mark, "The good news is we have created an extraordinary Fund. But the bad news is my run for the Prime Minister position will take us from being a fiercely private entity to a very publicly scrutinized business. Our enemies will try and take advantage of us anytime they see an opening. It's going to be your job, Mark, to be the silent liaison between Benjamin and me. If I win the election, let's make damn sure the Sterling Hedge Fund honestly continues to grow. We must never allow this company to become the victim of evil forces."

Mark responds with, "Will do, boss."

As Elliot is bidding goodbye to Mark, he says, "The new campaign guy has me speaking in some major outdoor Square in Tel Aviv tomorrow evening before thousands of people on primetime TV. I'd like you to join me. We'll drive together. Meet me here at the house. A car will pick us up at 1 PM."

Mark asks, "Is there anything you'd like me to do to help you prepare for the event?"

Elliot responds, "I'll receive some talking points from the campaign guy later tonight, but I just plan on speaking from the heart. Once I get into it, I should be alright. There is one thing though I'd appreciate you checking out for me, and that's security. I promised Felicia I'd take security seriously for the sake of the family. The venue is totally open to the public and is an unsecure Square. Sort of like a park.

"Frankly, it wouldn't be that difficult for some lunatic that feels like killing a billionaire or the next Prime Minister to show up and shoot me. The campaign manager—by the way, his name is Ariel Lashman—has spoken to me extensively about politics and what it will take to win, but I didn't hear a word about security. Can you dig a little deeper for me on this? You good with that, Mark?"

Mark looks at Elliot with a serious impression on his face. "Are you kidding me? There is nothing more important than your security. I'll start with Lashman and work my way down to the actual guys responsible for your well-being. I'll get right on it. Let me have Lashman's private cell number. I'll brief you tomorrow in the car regarding what I've discovered. Okay, I'll see you tomorrow at 1 PM."

Elliot spent the rest of the evening and well into the late night preparing for his speech the next day.

Although he was nervous, he understood that the majority of the people had a very favorable impression of him. He read the comments provided by Lashman, but drew the conclusion that he could better connect with the voters by simply talking to them. So, in typical Elliot Sterling style, he throws the talking points on his desk and concentrates on memorizing his own comfortable talking points.

At exactly 1 PM the next day, Elliot and Mark entered a black sedan which they would ride together to Tel Aviv. The sedan was accompanied by two identical black sedan cars. There was a total of six security guards traveling with the entourage all heavily armed with the Savor rifle and other semi-automatic weapons. Their interim destination was the Hilton Tel Aviv Hotel located on the Mediterranean Sea where Elliot had originally stayed when he and Felicia initially arrived in the country. The short trip was scheduled to take less than an hour.

Elliot immediately turns to Mark and half-jokingly asks, "What can you tell me about my security? Do you think I'll make it out alive tonight?"

Mark, who is not laughing, responds, "The Shin Bet is Israel's secret service and FBI rolled into one. These are some of the same guys we dealt with during Ethan's kidnapping. They're very good at what they do. Shin Bet are responsible for protecting the Prime Minister and those running for that position, such as you. Our biggest worry is allowing ourselves or them to be lulled into a false sense of security."

"Complacency is one of the greatest enemies of a personal security detail. It is particularly threatening when a very long time has elapsed from the time when a Prime Minister has actually been seriously threatened. We will operate on the assumption that a candidate for Prime Minister will be protected to the fullest extent conceivably possible. From this point forward these people will be guarding you 24/7, and it doesn't matter whether there is actual intelligence about a threat or not, the key is never to lower your guard."

Listening carefully, Elliot bluntly asks, "Alright, I heard all the comments. Now answer my question. Do you think I make it out alive tonight?"

Mark is dead silent for a moment, then answers, "Yeah, you do, but for a lot of reasons, I'm worried about your security."

With a concerned look on his face, Elliot remarks, "What the hell does that mean?"

Mark spends a moment to organize his thoughts then says, "What that means is that the word on the street is that although the Shin Bet leaders respect you, they don't consider you one of them. They resent that you didn't serve in the Israeli military. They don't like that your native language happens to be English as opposed to Hebrew. And, from what I hear, they think you're trying to buy the election versus win it on the merits. Kahlon is one of them, and he's spreading as much shit as he can about you with the establishment guys in Shin Bet. This makes me nervous."

With a worried look on his face, Elliot says, "I can't have these guys guarding my family! Forget about me. We're talking about my family! No way can I allow this! I need to hire my own people. What kind of crap is this? I'm running to be Prime Minister of Israel. Who cares whether I speak English or Hebrew? Everyone speaks English here."

"The only thing that matters is whether I can effectively do the job, not some Rorschach test for Israeli nationalism. You know, this kind of conversation makes me think that Felicia was right. The risk to my wife and kids is way too high. This doesn't feel right anymore. It sure as hell isn't worth risking the security of my family, or my life. From what you're explaining to me, it's obvious, I'm just not one of them. Everything I do will be reviewed from every possible angle with cynics bending over backwards to prove how I'm deceiving the public. This type of hatred can lead to assassination. I better get out of this thing before it's too late!"

Mark carefully measures his thoughts and says, "Look, I'm no expert on Israeli society or politics. I know what I've heard, and I sincerely believe we face a risk. Can we beat it with our own bodyguards?"

"Possibly. Can we turn around some of these assholes in Shin Bet? Time will tell. At least now we're aware of what we're up against. We've got a fighting chance to weed out some of the Kahlon hard-liners and replace them with our people. In the meantime, I think Shin Bet will do their jobs, but if you become Prime Minister, well, we'll need to stack the security deck in our favor."

Elliot thinks, then says, "Alright, we'll move forward with the campaign for now. I want you to immediately bring in some of our own people to assist with security, especially regarding Felicia, Rose, and Erica. Inform the Shin Bet people that you're hiring some of my private security guys out of an abundance of concern for my family. Tell them that I want to be overly cautious because of my family.

"Make sure that Shi Bet thinks they're in control. The truth is I want our guys to keep an eye on what Shin Bet is up too. Even though Shin Bet will be doing the reconnaissance work prior to me arriving at our campaign stops, I want our people cross checking Shin Bet, and I want them reporting to you off the record. I'm granting you my authority to take whatever action you deem appropriate.

"You're the only guy I'm going to trust my family with, or my life on. Understood?"

As their black sedan makes its way toward the entry of the exclusive Hilton Hotel in Tel Aviv a few hours ahead of the primetime TV campaign event that evening, the former Marine and lifelong friend of Elliot accepts the grave consequences of his assignment with a simple, "Yes sir!"

Chapter 27

Ariel Lashman was sitting in front of his personal computer in the elaborate Presidential Suite he had arranged for Elliot. The plush and very impressive suite was located on the top floor of the hotel with expansive views of the gorgeous Mediterranean Sea. Campaign aides were tediously busy working on the finishing touches of the all-important campaign rally for Elliot scheduled to take place in three hours.

As Lashman is pounding away on the keyboard of his computer he sees Elliot out of the corner of his eye and immediately stops what he's doing, stands up, and shakes Elliot's hand. "We have perfectly choreographed this evening's event. The networks will carry us live, our billboards featuring your face are up all over the area where you will speak, and our grassroots people have effectively gotten the word out to the voters who work and live in the area. We expect thousands upon thousands of people to pack the Square tonight. You, Mr. Future Prime Minister, are going to kill it and we are going to ride this momentum all the way to election night. The polls now favor you. Let's face it, this election is yours to lose. And I don't like to lose. Have you organized your thoughts?"

Speaking with the confidence of a champion, Elliot responds, "Perfectly."

Loving the response, Lashman laughs out loud to Elliot's self-assuring comment. "Is there anything you need from me? If not, I need to excuse myself and get back to business."

Elliot stops Lashman in his tracks and says, "Yeah, there is. I want you to meet my business associate, and my friend for as long as I can remember, Mark Goldman."

Lashman extends his hand toward Mark as he says, "So, you're the famous Mark Goldman. The man behind the man! It's a real pleasure to meet you. I'm sure we will be working closely on this campaign together, and please let me know if you need anything. Very good. I'll go back to working on getting our man elected Prime Minister."

As Lashman starts to walk away, Mark says, "Hey Ariel, there is something I need."

Lashman stops walking. Turns, then faces Mark. "And, what is that, Mark?"

Mark responds, "What is this campaign doing about security tonight for Elliot?"

Lashman answers, "Shin Bet is totally in control of security for Elliot and his family. They work with the campaign regarding scheduling, events, so on and so forth. But when it comes to security, they call the shots. Period."

Mark looks at Elliot, then Lashman and says, "From now on, everything you turn over to Shin Bet, I want you to give me a copy. Every meeting you or your staff conducts with Shin Bet, I want to be in on it. Sound good, Ariel?"

Lashman answers, "If Mr. Sterling tells me it's okay, then consider it done."

Elliot understands exactly what Mark is doing and camouflages it by making a joke, "It's a self-interest thing. He just wants to make sure I don't get killed so he has someone to hang around with all the time. He wouldn't know what to do with himself if something happened to me. This guy worries way more than my wife!"

Lashman starts laughing and says to Mark, "The Shin Bet agents will be here in the suite within the hour to go over the final details and itinerary for this evening's event. I'll see you then."

As Lashman returns to his laptop, a young campaign staffer steps up to Elliot and says, "We've prepared a briefing for you regarding Kahlon. Mr. Lashman believes our information may assist you with your final finishing touches for tonight's campaign rally."

Elliot responds, "Sure. Follow me," as he moves to a beautifully decorated living room parlor in the suite. Elliot and Mark take a seat on a gorgeous pastel green sofa with apricot designer cushions. Mark instructs the campaign aide to sit on a chair next to the sofa.

The staff member starts by pulling out a news article from the main Jerusalem newspaper, which had a headline stating, KAHLON CLAIMS STERLING HAS PRICE ON HIS HEAD. The young man goes on to explain that Kahlon claims to have evidence suggesting that Elliot had stolen money from the Nigerian government and they had ordered him killed. The article alleges that Elliot participated in an illegal contract that produced an illegal wire transfer to Israel in the amount of one hundred million dollars. The story names Benjamin Yaalon, Elliot's friend and banker, as his accomplice.

It goes on to detail that Benjamin is currently serving as a top executive in the Sterling Hedge Fund, which was illegally funded by the "dirty money" from Nigeria. Kahlon is calling for a criminal investigation and is quoted as saying, "I believe that Sterling is a fraud and should immediately terminate his candidacy for Prime Minister."

Elliot glares at Mark then asks the young man for the article. "This guy sounds desperate. I'll read the full story and respond to the accusation in this evening's talk. Okay, what else you got?"

The staffer pulls out a magazine article where Kahlon is quoted as saying, "How can you trust a man to be Prime Minister with zero military experience? Elliot Sterling shouldn't even be in the same room as me when it comes to the Israeli Defense Forces. He's nothing but a foreigner, a stranger, and he has no business governing Israel."

Elliot, now realizing his opponent was a down and dirty street fighter, calmly responds, "I guess Kahlon has never heard of the former Prime Minister Golda Meir, a naturalized Israeli citizen by way of the United States. In fact, for the longest of time, it is reported that she didn't even know what an army division was, yet her role in the famous Six Day war is legendary. Well, thank you for your briefing. It has been very helpful. Please do me a favor. Tell Ariel I'd like to speak to him."

The staff member asks, "Now?"

Elliot says, "Yes. Right now."

The excruciatingly busy Lashman breaks away from his computer and asks, "You wanted to see me?"

Elliot says, "Yes. Please take a seat. Kahlon is a liar. He's just throwing shit up against the wall to see what sticks. So, here's what I plan to do. First, I will address this matter tonight during my speech. Second, I'm going to make available a full disclosure to the media of my United States lawsuit against the Republic of Nigeria. This way, they can read my complaint filed against the Nigerian government. It's all public record anyway since the suit was filed in the Los Angeles Federal Court.

"The media is going to dig for this stuff anyway, so we might as well just turn it over to them. Just wanted to get any thoughts you have on the matter."

Lashman reacts quickly, "Brilliant. We expose everything because we have nothing to hide. We then simply move on with the campaign. Sounds like the advice I would have given you. Spin this Nigerian story your way tonight. Push Kahlon back on his heels regarding military experience. He attacked you, now it's your turn to swing back."

319

"We got a national audience this evening. Put him on the defensive and make him look foolish. Go after this guy! I just know you're going to have the crowd on your side and the nation eating out of your hands. I can't wait!"

This was exactly the kind of response Elliot was hoping to hear from his campaign manager. Elliot knew instinctually what he thought he should do, but he drew confidence from an experienced Israeli political expert advising him to do precisely what his instincts said. With that in mind, Elliot excuses himself telling Mark and Lashman he was going to retire into the bedroom for the next forty-five minutes to collect his thoughts and get in a nap before the big event.

As Elliot moved to the bedroom, Mark made his way to the Shin Bet meeting already in progress. He sits in on the security deliberations for approximately forty-five minutes and concludes, to his surprise, that they are unconditionally dedicated toward the safety and security of Elliot. With that peace of mind, Mark excuses himself.

Recognizing that he is running late, he walks at a very fast pace toward the bedroom where Elliot is resting. He knocks on the door, but no one answers. After several attempts, Mark no longer knocks, he just pushes the door open and approaches the bed where he finds Elliot soundly sleeping.

After several attempts to awaken Elliot by politely shaking him, Mark gets aggressive and shouts Elliot's name while simultaneously pulling on his arm. That did the trick as Elliot with half a smile says to Mark, "Down, boy. Relax. I'm up. I'm up."

Getting more nervous by the second, Mark says, "Elliot. It's starting to get very late. You've got to move it. Get in the shower, and let's get the hell out of here."

Elliot begins to sense the urgency of the event and quickly begins to change his demeanor. He understands the importance of the moment, and that he's running late for the critical prime time event.

He rushes toward the bathroom and closes the door without saying anything. Mark uses the downtime waiting for Elliot by selecting a black pin-striped suit and red tie from the closet. It doesn't take long before Elliot is ready. The Shin Bet entourage is standing at the door ready to escort him to a waiting car.

The security detail use the back-loading elevator to discreetly escort Elliot, Mark, and Lashman through the lobby to a waiting black sedan with the engine running. They swiftly enter the car as the Shin Bet guards carrying semi-automatic weapons close the door behind them. In front of their car is an identical black sedan, and immediately behind them is a similar automobile. The three cars instantly depart the hotel entry en route for the campaign rally and the most important night of Elliot's political career.

The Kings of Israel Square in Tel Aviv was just minutes away from the hotel. Lashman had arranged for a small trailer to be set up nearby the main stage and speaker's podium. As the three cars approach the designated entry point to the Square, armed guards from the Israeli Defense Forces (IDF) stop the lead car for questioning.

In an instant, the IDF guard waves them through and the cars make their way to a secure parking area steps away from the trailer. The moment they park, four Shin Bet agents stand alongside the door Elliot is about to exit. The lead Shin Bet guard taps on the glass where Elliot is seated then abruptly opens the door and hustles Elliot, Mark, and Lashman directly into the trailer without a hitch.

The trailer was outfitted with two comfortable sofas, a wet bar, a large screen TV, and a full-length mirror. Elliot and Mark take a seat on one of the sofas as Lashman stands making calls to his field representatives scattered throughout the open-air Square in the middle of the city. Mark addresses Elliot enthusiastically, "Did you see the amount of people out there? I mean, that place is wall to wall human beings. It feels like a crowd you'd see at a major concert event. Wow!"

As Elliot is about to comment, Lashman comes over and says, "There are so many people in the Square that the Fire Marshal was threatening to stop the rally, but one of our staff took care of the Marshal. There are well over five thousand supporters who've come to hear you speak. This is an amazing turnout. It's going to look spectacular on national TV. Get ready. You're up in five minutes."

Those five minutes seem like an eternity to Elliot as he listens to the Mayor of Tel Aviv address the huge audience. He quips to Mark, "The Mayor is telling everyone what a terrific guy I am, but the truth is I've never met or spoken to him. I hope when I go on stage, I don't thank and shake the hand of the wrong guy."

Marks laughs out loud, "Just walk straight to the podium. The Mayor will want to be on national TV, so I guarantee you he'll be extending his hand out to you. In fact, I'll bet you ten bucks he gives you a big bear hug."

As he hears the Mayor announce, "And let me introduce to you the next Prime Minister of Israel!", Elliot takes a deep breath.

Looks at himself in the mirror and says to Mark, "Wish me luck."

Mark affectionally hugs his life-long friend and says, "You got this. Go get 'em, boss!"

Elliot stands up straight and walks onto the stage waving to the adoring crowd and hearing a deafening roar. He goes directly to the podium where the Mayor gives him a bear hug, much to the amusement of Mark who is standing with Lashman on the side rails awaiting the critical address to the nation.

When the Mayor leaves the stage, Elliot keeps smiling and waving at the mass of humanity in front of him as the TV cameras roll. He keeps repeating, "Thank you! Thank you very much!" But the crowd vigorously continues clapping and cheering, and then suddenly starts chanting, "Eli, Eli, Eli!"

Elliot can't believe his eyes or ears. The moment is simply electric. Like nothing he had ever experienced in his lifetime as he finally leans into the microphone and says, "Shalom, Tel Aviv!"

With those simple words, his supporters go wild. "Eli, Eli, Eli!"

After a few minutes of further applause and chanting, Elliot finally gets the opportunity to speak. He starts off his remarks by thanking Prime Minister Weiztman for his support. He then graciously acknowledges the Mayor of Tel Aviv for his kind words and enthusiastic introduction. Throughout his hour-long talk, Elliot is able to lay out for the Israeli citizens his vision of the future. He speaks from the heart when he declares that the Israeli Defense Forces would have the full financial support of the government headed by him, making IDF the best equipped and organized military Israel has ever seen. To a rousing ovation, he promises that no country on the planet would ever threaten Israel again because the world would be on notice that Israel will be prepared to vigorously defend its nation and aggressively strike back with a vengeance.

Elliot went on to articulate what he saw as a cornerstone to his economic policy. He laid out his plan for offshore oil drilling. Elliot described these oil reserves as incredible, and he declared he would immediately authorize access to this untapped natural resource. He told the public "that the days of oil dependency would be over during a Sterling administration." He spoke with clarity as he outlined a comprehensive infrastructure plan to build highways and bridges and new water pipelines. Elliot spoke about bringing bigger and more tourism to Israel through international marketing campaigns.

He passionately spoke about making Israel "an economic powerhouse" through his vision of establishing Israel as the "Start-Up Nation" where high technology companies, similar to Silicon Valley in the United States, would concentrate their development in Israel. Elliot declared that during his tenure as Prime Minister, Israel would become "the world's foremost tech hub". He predicted an exodus by titans in the tech industry, which would leave areas like California and relocate in Israel.

Once Elliot had articulated his commonsense vision of how he would lead the nation, he turned his comments toward Kahlon's attacks by calmly tearing apart his opponent's accusations one by one.

The speech to this point had connected perfectly with the mood of the nation. Israel was looking for a strong leader who was not afraid of its terrorist and antagonistic neighbors. The people were looking for peace through strength. They demanded a military force second to none, and they wanted their leader to fund the IDF with the best fighter jets and military equipment money could buy. The crowd loved Elliot's passion for building a nation around a military and economic power.

Elliot had skillfully articulated to the people that the real image of a powerful IDF would prevent war and that by staying out of war, the Israeli economy would be allowed to significantly grow. The Israelis were deeply nationalistic and they had connected with a man that they could trust to lead from a position of strength. The country was starving for a charismatic leader with vision, and they found their man in that Square that night.

Now that the nation understood what his policies were, Elliot was determined to clear his name of the bad impression Kahlon was spreading through the media, especially the Nigerian smear. So, he starts with a story while he smiles and says, "My opponent would like you to believe that I stole one hundred million dollars from the Nigerian government. Now imagine this, I sign a contract in Nigeria in the offices of their highest government central bank. I meet with the chairman of this government's bank and the Minister of Finance while in Nigeria. All of my contract documentation is signed before a notary, my attorney and the bank's attorney. This is all witnessed by more than half a dozen Nigerian top government officials. The Nigerian government promises to pay my earned proceeds immediately.

"The Nigerian government does not pay their obligation to me because they demand that I pay all income taxes in advance before they will release my funds. I say to them, in what country do you pay taxes in advance on income you haven't even received? Their answer was, if you want to be paid your contracted money, you must first pay your taxes. Reluctantly, I prepaid the Nigerian government hundreds of thousands of dollars in taxes. Do you think they released my contract proceeds?"

Elliot continues, "The answer is no, they did not. So, I sue the Republic of Nigeria in the United States Federal Court to collect on my contract. And, guess what, before we actually get to a final judgement, but after a long court battle, the Nigerian government wires me my full earned proceeds from that legitimate contract. So, what do I do with those funds? I turn around and wire every penny of that earned contract and invest it right here in Israel."

The reaction of the crowd is thunderous applause as they start shouting once again, "Eli! Eli! Eli!"

Elliot closes his masterful defense by saying, "In the coming days, I will release my entire Nigerian lawsuit to the media in the interest of transparency and answer any questions that might be asked of me regarding this matter. So, I ask you, Mr. Kahlon, am I the fraud, or are you the fraud? My Nigerian contract was legitimate. I made my arrangements with the highest levels of government. I paid my taxes in full.

"I sued the Nigerians in an open United States Federal Court. The Nigerian government paid the contract in full through their government's Central Bank. And I invested all my contract funds in this country. Therefore, Mr. Kahlon, I call on you to retract your slanderous accusations, or it is you who must step down from this campaign!"

The five thousand supporters simply go into a frenzy. They slip into a state of uncontrolled excitement knowing that Elliot has tactically eliminated any doubt about his character that Kahlon had attempted to damage.

With his mission accomplished on the Nigerian matter, Elliot turns his attention to the elephant in the room. His lack of Israeli military experience. Instead of trying to defend it by weak acknowledgements that he had no meaningful military leadership, he just goes straight into explaining how a person with judgement, tied to seasoned military advisors, can easily get the job done. Elliot jumps straight into the example of the great Israeli Prime Minister who came from the United States with absolutely no military experience to make his point.

Elliot now seamlessly shifts the conversation to rebuttal Kahlon's scathing remarks about how Elliot "was a foreigner and nothing more than a stranger" in Israel. Kahlon had painted a picture of Elliot as having zero military experience, effectively a subordinate to Kahlon's expertise "who didn't even belong in the same room" as Kahlon regarding the Israeli military.

Elliot looks straight out at his audience and into the TV cameras and says, "Mr. Kahlon. Have you ever heard of Golda Meir? Well, just in case you haven't, let me give you a little history lesson. Golda Meir was born in the Ukraine and became a United States citizen by virtue of her father. Eventually, Golda became a naturalized Israeli citizen. This 'foreigner' went on to become one of the most well recognized Prime Minister in the history of Israel. And, by the way, she didn't have any military experience. In fact, it is well reported that Golda didn't even know what an army division was. But she had extraordinary judgement!"

Approving where Elliot is going with the story, his five thousand admirers jump right back into their now famous chant shouting, "Eli, Eli, Eli!"

Once they stop their demonstration of support, Elliot continues, "Now, I hope you're listening, Mr. Kahlon, because I'll let you in on a well-recognized secret. This 75-year-old 'foreigner with no military experience presided over a stunning victory for Israel in the famous 1967 Six Day War also known to many of you as the 'Yom Kippur War'.

"Golda Meir played a significant strategic role during this war which resulted in Israel controlling land that made the country four times its previous size. Egypt lost 23,500 square miles of the Sinai Peninsula and the Gaza Strip. Jordon lost the West Bank, East Jerusalem, and the Golan Heights. Not bad for the 'stranger' from America, a seventy-five-year-old grandmother with no military experience! So, do you now believe me when I tell you that a foreigner without military experience can be effective? Judgement counts, and I have that judgement!"

To use the idiom originally coined in the United States, the place went bananas! The Square with over five thousand people present simply went crazy with enthusiasm and admiration for by far and away Israel's most charismatic politician. Elliot went on to complete the speech by pointing to the military leadership he had demonstrated during Ethan Weiztman's kidnapping. He proudly spoke about how he had successfully directed the commanders of the prestigious YAMAM counter-terrorism unit in order to return Ethan home safely.

Elliot finishes his remarks, "I wish to conclude my comments here this evening by promising to all Israeli citizens that if you elect me your next Prime Minister, I will move this great nation forward in spite of all the obstacles that we face. Together, as a united country, we will prosper like no other nation has ever seen before. So, let me leave you with my favorite quote originally authored by George Bernard Shaw and made famous in a speech delivered by the late American Senator Robert F. Kennedy, the brother of President John F. Kennedy."

He says, "Some men see things as they are, and ask why. I dream of things that never were, and ask why not?"

Elliot pauses, then looks out into the crowd and says, "Now, let's go out and win the office of Prime Minister! God bless you! And may God continue to bless this great nation of Israel!"

The assembled crowd reacts with a stirring applause signifying their overwhelming approval, shouting in unison, "Eli, Eli, Eli!" As Elliot slowly makes his way off the stage waving, shaking hands, and smiling at the assembled crowd, he points a finger at Mark, and with a big smile Mark points right back.

The country had witnessed the beginning of a shift from the old power elite to the new independent-thinking Elliot Sterling. The major TV networks instantly began commenting "that this guy has what it takes to win the national election." Israel was abuzz with the prospect of electing Elliot their next Prime Minister.

Chapter 28

Six weeks had gone by since the booming success of Elliot's speech at the Kings of Israel Square in Tel Aviv. Ariel Lashman's decision to nationally televise that campaign rally had proven to be brilliant. The audience watching that evening had become overwhelmingly impressed and convinced that Elliot was the right man at the right time to lead the nation toward a new beginning. He had captured the spirit of the country, and the polls had him ahead by double digits. Kahlon was so far behind that there were rumors his campaign was virtually out of money and on the verge of suspension.

Nevertheless, Elliot kept running hard by crisscrossing the country. He had visited literally every major city and area throughout Israel. Each campaign rally attracted overflowing crowds, the likes that had never been seen before. Elliot had become an overnight sensation with daily newspapers and television stations covering every move he made.

The election was two weeks away and although the polls seemed to be indicating a landside, Elliot ran as if he was behind. Lashman's strategy was to push the campaign to continue raising money while outworking the opposition candidate. For those reasons, it was decided to go where very few candidates running for Prime Minister had ever gone.

Lashman had studied the Israeli electorate and decided that the nation needed much better representation in the southern region of the country. So, Lashman focused in on the City of Eilat, a southern Israeli port and resort town on the Red Sea, near Jordon. Elliot had earlier been flown by his private jet to Eilat and had been resting in the posh Queen of Sheba Hotel suite where he was scheduled to speak in the main ballroom later that evening before one thousand campaign contributors and supporters.

Lashman had arranged for many business leaders scattered from around Israel to come listen first-hand to the likely new Prime Minister. His spin to the corporate elite leaders focused on the simple concept, "support a winner, it will pay off big dividends later." Each one of these hundred chief executive officers were considered Israel's cream of the crop business aristocracy. They secretly formed a small power structure. The individual ante paid by these men to be present was ten thousand dollars apiece collectively representing one million dollars.

They all attended for one reason, and one reason only. Buy influence with Elliot Sterling. Prime Minister Weiztman had worked hard to establish the relationships and each of these men were prepared to continue their support of Elliot. Although he had met a few of them during his term as Finance Minister, Elliot had no real personal relationship with any of them. So, this would be an exceptional opportunity to get to know them since Lashman had a prepared private cocktail hour immediately following Elliot's public address.

The business leaders were seated in the front rows of an enormous banquet room in the hotel that had accommodated and overflow crowd which would listen to the next Prime Minister of Israel. The electricity for the upcoming speech could be felt in the air. The country was preparing itself for the greatest economic expansion and international respect the nation had ever experienced. Everyone present, intrinsically understood that Elliot would be the man to lead them to this unprecedented place.

The President of the Technion, also known as the Israel Institute of Technology, was given the honor of introducing Elliot. Lashman had selected him because The Technion was the oldest university in the country. It was ranked as the best university in Israel and the Middle East. Their highly advanced engineering programs symbolized exactly what Elliot was envisioning when he alluded to making Israel the new Silicon Valley of the world.

So, with the words uttered by the Technion President, "Allow me the honor to introduce to you the next Prime Minister of Israel," Elliot waves to the crowd and slowly walks toward the podium to a standing ovation and the now familiar cadence of "Eli! Eli! Eli!"

It took a while before everyone took their seats and Elliot finally got a chance to say, "Shalom, Eilat! Many thanks to Dr. Izzy Gould for that gracious introduction. I think being the President of the Technion may just rival the importance of being the Prime Minister of Israel. Trust me when I tell you that if I become Israel's Prime Minister, I will constantly be seeking the advice and the good counsel of Dr. Gould and the Technion faculty."

He continues his opening light remarks, "As I look into the prestigious group assembled here today, I see the chairman of the board of Israel's largest cable TV, internet, and phone company."

Smiling and now unable to hold back his own laughter, the charismatic Elliot looks straight at the internet giant's CEO and jokingly says, "Hey, listen, I've been trying to call your company's customer service, but they put me on hold so long that I always end up hanging up. So, while I have your undivided attention, do you mind lowering my bill slightly?" The audience and the CEO burst into a roar of laughter.

As the smiling cable executive is about to respond to the future Prime Minister of Israel, two men wearing dark grey suits with the hotel's plastic name tag identification on their lapels start calmly walking from opposite sides of the room toward the podium. They have the appearance of being official hotel personnel. Perhaps even security personnel. But it is unclear to the Shin Bet agents as the two suspicious men stop in the middle of the room between the first row and the elevated platform where Elliot is about to speak.

One of the two men looks directly at Elliot, and the other faces the assembled one hundred business titans gathered in the first two rows.

The Shin Bet agents had seen enough and instantly charged toward the two men with their semi-automatic weapons drawn, but it was too late. The Islamist terrorists yell in Arabic, "Allahu Akbar! Allahu Akbar!" (God is the greatest!) as they jointly detonate their highly explosive suicide bomb vests packed with ball bearings, nails, screws, bolts, and other objects that serve as shrapnel to maximize the number of casualties.

The explosion resembled an omnidirectional shotgun blast. And although the two bombers were instantly obliterated by the explosion, their last evil thought was how grateful they were that God had bestowed something upon them that they would have been incapable of attaining were it not for divine benevolence. God was greater than them.

For the rest of the room, it was utter chaos. The two simultaneous explosions had caused death and destruction. Everyone was in shock and despair. The blasts had gone outward toward those that stood directly in front of the killers. Mark's first instinct was to run toward Elliot who he could not see.

A Shin Bet agent grabs him while telling him to stop. Mark shoves the agent aside and keeps running frightened and with urgency toward his beloved life-long friend, his brother.

Mark wasn't the only one frantically trying to get to Elliot. A swarm of Shin Bet agents were doing everything possible to maneuver through the wreckage to get to the future Prime Minister of Israel. The scene was an unmitigated disaster. An unimaginable nightmare. The torn apart bodies of many of the important businessmen were scattered on the floor in front of the podium where Elliot was speaking.

Mark cannot stop thinking about the tragic real possibility that Elliot has been killed. His emotions are too much to handle as he muscles his way through the wreckage and the security personnel trying desperately to control an uncontrollable set of circumstances.

As Mark finally gets to the podium, he sees Elliot lying on the floor bleeding and unconscious. He screams at the Shin Bet officer not to move Elliot until a doctor arrives. He crucially pleads to the agent to concentrate only on finding a medic. Mark then takes full control of the fight for his friend's life.

It didn't take long for a young doctor to arrive with a Shin Bet agent. He instantly clears everyone away from Elliot, then makes a call to his paramedic associate, urgently ordering him to come to the scene. The doctor takes Elliot's pulse and singles a thumbs-up to the agent that the patient is still alive. He then carefully examines his body to determine if any limbs have been severed. The doctor states out loud that the entire body is intact, much to the relief of everyone surrounding Elliot.

Mark immediately introduces himself and indicates that he is Elliot's chief of staff and a close personal friend as he asks, "Is Mr. Sterling going to survive?"

The doctor answers, "Mr. Sterling is in shock, bleeding with serious wounds from the blast, and is in grave risk of losing his life. We need to get him to the hospital and to the operating room immediately! My paramedics will be here within minutes and we will do our best to save his life. We recognize that the country needs him to live, but frankly, this doesn't look good."

Just as the doctor predicted, the paramedics arrived and were carefully working to move Elliot to the hospital. The Shin Bet agents had cleared a path to the awaiting ambulance and the agent's cars.

As the doctor's team was gently moving Elliot on to the gurney, a cell phone on the floor near Elliot starts vibrating. Then it stops and rings again. Mark recognizes the phone as Elliot's and determines that it must have fallen out of his suit pocket upon Elliot's impact to the floor. As he waits for the paramedics, Mark leans over, picks up the phone, and sees on the screen that it is Felicia who is frantically calling for the third time.

This time, Mark answers and hears Felicia hysterically say, "Thank God you're alive! Are you alright? It's all over the news!"

Deeply saddened he must deliver the harsh news, Mark closes his eyes and says, "This is Mark. Elliot is badly hurt. He is unconscious and we're moving him to the hospital. I'm right here next to him."

In deep despair and very scared for her husband's life, Felicia asks, crying hysterically, "Is Elliot dying?"

Seeing that the medical team is now on the move with Elliot, Mark responds, "We're on our way to the hospital right now. I'm sending a helicopter for you and the girls. You'll be with Elliot shortly. Our guy is going to pull out of this."

Felicia, who can't control her emotions any further, angrily asks once again, "Is my husband dying?"

For a moment, Mark thinks and asks himself, how would Elliot want me to answer this question, then he confidently responds, "Your husband will be dancing at Rose's wedding. Look for the helicopter, I'll keep you updated."

It was a mad dash to the waiting ambulance. Mark insisted on riding with Elliot as they position him in the emergency vehicle and whisked him away to the medical triage team ready to immediately go to work on saving his life. It took about ten minutes before they arrived as the ambulance and four Shin Bet cars tore through the streets of Eilat arriving at the emergency doors where a sea of paparazzi photographers and news reporters had already gathered to record the breaking news.

The medical surgeons along with a small army of nurses and technicians efficiently took control of Elliot as they rolled him away into the corridors of the hospital. Before he even understood what had transpired, Mark lost sight and control of Elliot. He was now in the hands of God and the medical team.

Now joined by Lashman and several Shin Bet agents, Mark is escorted by the hospital's Chief Executive Officer to a private waiting area as they settle into what promises to be an excruciating painful period of time before anyone would learn Elliot's true fate.

The man in charge of the Shin Bet agents comes up to Mark and asks, "May I speak with you?"

Mark, who is very upset with Shin Bet and the horrible circumstances in general, answers, "What the fuck went wrong with you guys! How could you allow something like this to happen? Somebody is going to need to answer for this! Now, what the hell do you want?"

The Shin Bet agent responds, "I am in charge and I will need to answer for this. But in the interim, it is my responsibility to keep Mr.

Sterling and his family safe. I have been instructed by Prime Minister Weiztman to report to you as Mr. Sterling's chief of staff and I'd like to brief you if you will permit."

Mark cools down and says, "Sorry about that. Alright, go ahead. What do you need to tell me?"

The agent responds, "First of all, we have the hospital secure. It is possible that the terrorists could attempt a second strike to try and complete what they started. Because of the news media, they realize that Mr. Sterling survived. We are seriously concerned for Mrs. Sterling and her daughters. I know they are in flight here as we speak. This is not the best place to be at the moment even though we understand that they will want to be with Mr. Sterling at this time. The helicopter will land on a pad on the roof of the hospital. The family will be brought right here to this room. Please advise them that they are not to leave this area without our escort. This also applies to you, Mr. Goldman."

Mark answers, "Got it. Do you have any idea who did this?"

The agent says, "Yes. It was Hezbollah in retaliation for Mr. Sterling's involvement in Ethan Weiztman's kidnapping. They claim they were deceived by Mr. Sterling. They have publicly taken responsibility for this terrorist act. We've got fifteen people dead, including the top executive of the internet company along with some other prominent businessmen. Despicable monsters who I assure you will pay heavily for the evil they've done!"

Mark looks at the agent and says, "These animals think that they were deceived? Let me get this straight. They go out and kidnap an innocent young man. My boss outsmarts them by getting Ethan Weiztman out alive, and they feel deceived! What kind of creatures are these bastards?"

The Shin Bet agent answers, "They are ruthless killers with no regard for the decency of human life. Regrettably, we have lived with this type of enemy our entire lives. This is nothing new to us. We will retaliate stronger than ever, but trust when I say, we will face terrorism again in the not so distant future. This is our norm living in the Middle East."

"We pray that Mr. Sterling has a speedy recovery. Our nation needs him to survive and lead us to the time where this is no longer the norm. Excuse me Mr. Goldman, we've just been informed that the helicopter carrying Mrs. Sterling and her daughters has arrived. I'll greet them and we'll all return to this room within ten minutes."

Escorted by four Shin Bet agents, Felicia, Rose, and Erica somberly walk into the guest surgery waiting area. Each of these women display a seriousness on their faces. Their hair is tied back in a simple ponytail, and none of them are wearing a shred of makeup.

Felicia makes eye contact as Mark delicately approaches her. They embrace as Felicia bursts out crying. Mark does his best to comfort her, yet realizes that it would be better to let her release all the stress and deep emotions she felt. It takes a while before she composes herself then instantly asks, "Where is Elliot?"

Before Mark answers the question, he requests that Rose and Erica gather in closer so that they too could hear his explanation. He starts by solemnly saying, "Elliot is in surgery to remove shrapnel located in his body due to the bomb explosion. The biggest medical challenge is related to his lungs which were adversely penetrated by the blast. I'm not going to sugarcoat this. Elliot is in critical condition. The surgery will take several more hours. We're going to leave it in God's hands."

Not a word is said by Felicia or either of the girls. Felicia appears shocked as all three of them have tears running down their cheeks. The thought of losing Elliot feels real and devastating to this close-knit family. It's as if time has just stopped. What would life become for Felicia without her beloved husband? How would Rose and Erica cope with the premature death of their father?

Several hours passed until finally the chief surgeon, still wearing his blue medical sanitary scrubs, appears in the waiting room to address the family. In a serious voice, the doctor gets right to the point, "We removed a good deal of shrapnel that was lodged throughout the left side of Mr. Sterling's torso. This posed no remarkable threat to his internal organs, except one. We were forced to remove Mr. Sterling's lung due to severe damage from the debris. This part of the surgery took approximately six hours. The other lung is functioning well. I can assure you that one lung can provide enough oxygen and remove enough carbon dioxide. A healthy person with two lungs has a lot of reserve function, so if one lung is removed, that person can still function normally, without shortness of breath."

Then came the all-important punchline. "Your husband will fully recover. He will be confined to the hospital for about ten days. Please remember that it is totally common to feel tired for 6-8 weeks after surgery like this. His chest will hurt and be swollen for about 6 weeks. It may ache or feel stiff for up to three months. You should also know that for the first 2-6 weeks after arriving home, Mr.

Sterling may have trouble sleeping for more than three to four hours at a time. This will get better as he heals and becomes more active."

The calm and serious surgeon finishes by addressing Felicia and the two girls, "Mr. Sterling is truly a very lucky man to be alive. By the way, I'd be willing to bet that he was an incredible athlete because it appears that a split-second instinct to dive toward the floor upon impact of the bomb is what saved his life. We are all fortunate that your husband will live to lead Israel during these times."

Now shedding tears of joy, Felicia extends her hand and says, "Thank you, doctor, for saving my husband's life. There are no words that can express how grateful my daughters and I are for what you and your wonderful staff have accomplished for my husband. As far as I'm concerned, all of you have been put on this earth to do God's work. We trust we will be able to return the favor to you one day. By the way, he was one of the most competitive athletes you will ever meet. My husband attended his university on an athletic scholarship. Thank you again, doctor."

As the doctor leaves the room, Felicia impulsively grabs her two daughters and forms a tight group embrace, signifying how grateful they all are with the message the doctor just delivered. Neither one of them say anything. It is a moment to celebrate the fact that Elliot would live and be blessed with a "normal" life. A moment that each of them would cherish for the remainder of their lifetimes.

Felicia then approaches Mark and asks him to follow her to the back of the room where no one can hear what she is about to tell him. Once they reach that destination, Felicia firmly whispers, "Please listen carefully to me, Mark. Elliot will never go back into politics! He will not become the next Prime Minister of Israel. After he recovers from his stay in the hospital, I will be taking him to Caesarea for his rehab over the next three months. After he fully recovers at our home in Caesarea, I'm taking Elliot and my family out of Israel and back to our new home and simple lifestyle in Beverly Hills. Did you hear me, Mark?"

Mark answers, "Perfectly."

Careful not to upset Felicia and unwilling to speak for Elliot under the circumstances, Mark further says, "I'm ready to set up shop anywhere in the world. You and Elliot just tell me when and where."

After revealing to Mark what her plans were, Felicia visually appeared relieved, showing some color in her face as opposed to that scared ashen look when she had first arrived. With the assurances by the doctor and the kind response by Mark, she was ready to get some well-deserved rest. Felicia informs her daughters and Mark that she was going to lie down on one of the lounge seats, close her eyes, and hope to get a few minutes of sleep. Felicia emphatically instructs everyone that she is very anxious to see Elliot, and to wake her in the event the doctors authorize a visitation.

With Felicia now comfortable, Mark decides to walk over to the man in charge of the Shin Bet agents and asks, "Any further threats we should be aware of?"

The agent quickly responds, "No, but we are preparing ourselves because the Prime Minister and the Minister of Defense are likely planning a strategic military air strike on the Hezbollah terrorists camp where it is believed the Eilat bombing incident was planned, trained, and ordered. This military operation will be executed with pinpoint precision. Regrettably, that move will result in this hospital and the Sterling family placed on a heightened state of alert. Of course, I will advise you the instant I hear anything, Mr. Goldman."

The final person Mark wanted to speak with was Ariel Lashman who was pounding away on his laptop keypad. Lashman stops typing and looks up at Mark asking, "How you holding up?"

Mark, worn out from the dramatic day, says, "My best friend on the planet is lying in bed with one lung removed and clinging to life on a ventilator after a terrorist bombing attack. Under normal circumstances, I'd say that's pretty fucked up! But for now, my answer is, I'm a very happy guy because my friend is going to live, and for this moment, that's all that counts!"

Lashman responds, "That's a beautiful perspective as it relates to Mr. Sterling, but my problem is that I personally invited each one of those 15 businessmen who lost their lives today. Innocent people!"

Mark, who had been so focused on the survival of his life-long friend, had completely forgotten about this side of the tragedy. Silently, he played back in his mind the horrible scene of those accomplished men scattered all over the room's floor. These images made him visibly upset as he holds his hands to his face and says, "May God rest these fine men's souls and bring comfort to their families. Please determine when they will be buried so that either I or someone representing Elliot will be present. We will not forget these patriots!"

Lashman, impressed with Mark's compassion, says, "We'll find out and let you know. It's a shame. These guys were just doing their jobs of promoting their businesses and participating in the political process. I'd hate to be the one responsible for informing their wives and children. All I can tell you is that we need Elliot Sterling back on the saddle running the country within the next three months. I'm setting up a game plan to finish the campaign. He'll be elected by potentially the largest landslide in the history of Israel even with his medical condition."

"We'll then form the government and swear him in as Prime Minister as soon as the doctor permits. The Knesset and the Israeli people will accommodate Mr. Sterling with whatever time he needs to rehabilitate before officially taking over the government. I figure this will take three months. Since you'll be his chief of staff, implementing his decisions will be seamless. This will work out just fine."

Mark did not interrupt Lashman because he wanted to hear what was going through his mind. As soon as he finishes, Mark emphatically says, "Slow down, partner! First of all, when it comes to the campaign and the government, the only thing that matters is Elliot's health and recovery. Everything else is secondary. Are you hearing me, Ariel? This man has survived a terrorist bombing. The doctors just tore a goddamn lung out of him! Let me assure you. No one in the family, including me, is even remotely considering politics at this time. Period!"

Lashman courteously listens to Mark's passionate statement, remains silent, then says with conviction, "Of course, Mr. Sterling's health and recovery is of paramount importance and priority. But don't forget, I get paid to elect him the next Prime Minister of Israel. So, unless you want to fire me, I need to be mindful about the election and politics. Perhaps that's what Mr. Sterling would like me to be thinking about, or perhaps not, but until he tells me differently, I'm going to continue to do my job!"

With a sarcastic smile, Mark gets tough. "Man, your reputation precedes you. Ariel, you really are a ruthless political junkie. Okay, let's talk politics. Maybe Elliot chooses to continue with the campaign, maybe he doesn't. I guarantee you that his family are all going to insist that he get out. I am going to advise him to get out. The risk no longer justifies the reward. This is my friend. He's my brother, and trust me, no political office, not even being Israel's Prime Minister, is worth his life. Enough is enough!"

Lashman stares back into Mark's eyes and says, "Elliot Sterling, whether you like it or not, is going to win the national election in a landslide. I wouldn't be surprised if he carries better than 70% of the vote.

"Whether he accepts to become Prime Minister is a whole different story. I agree, this will be up to his family and Mr. Sterling. All I know is, the people of Israel want him. This is not some ordinary political office for Mr. Sterling to occupy; this office will be the making of a once in a lifetime world leader, and in my humble opinion, sometimes a risk like this does justify the reward."

Mark listens carefully to Lashman and says, "Hey look, the election is in less than three weeks. Obviously, Elliot is not going to be doing any more campaigning. It's possible he won't even be out of the hospital. Should he happen to win the election under these circumstances, then Elliot, Felicia, and his kids are going to make a final decision. Now, if I were a betting man, I'd place all my money on resignation. I guess we all just need to wait and see what the hell happens. So, for now, you're not fired; not yet, anyway."

Lashman responds with a smile, "Fair enough. In the interim, I will continue to do my job. With your permission, I'd like to release to the Israeli press, and for that matter, the entire world, a written press release indicating Mr. Sterling's medical condition and prognosis. Additionally, I want to organize a press conference right here at the hospital. We'll have the surgeon, me, and perhaps you. We should set the narrative straight before the media speculates and reports it without facts. Do I have your permission? Would you and Mrs. Sterling like to attend?"

Mark instantly responds, "Go ahead, set that stuff up. Mrs. Sterling will not be attending, and I will not be participating. I suggest you throw in a Shin Bet official at the press conference. I agree, get this done as soon as possible. I just looked out the window and it's a media circus out there. I guess the world wants to know how Elliot is doing so go tell them how he's doing."

Chapter 29

Three months had gone by since the horrific terrorist bombing incident. Elliot had been confined to the hospital for well over a month before he was finally released to his home in Caesarea. During his convalescence, he had won the Prime Minister election in a landslide, just as Lashman had predicted.

To the delight of Felicia and the girls, Elliot made a full recovery with no apparent symptoms other than the fact that he was breathing on one less lung.

As a courtesy to the new Prime Minister-elect, the Israeli Knesset had granted an unprecedented 100-day extension before Elliot was to formally take office. This meant that he had less than ten days to finalize his cabinet and take the oath of office. But that was the furthest thing occupying his mind on this day. Today, his oldest daughter, Rose, was going to be married to Ethan in the sprawling backyard of Elliot and Felicia's home in Caesarea. This promised to be a well-deserved magical moment for the Sterling and Weiztman families.

As Elliot sat in his home office working to catch up on a few pending matters, Felicia and the maid-of-honor, Erica, attended to a multitude of last-minute details regarding the wedding and Rose's needs.

The backyard looked exquisite with perfectly lit white tents and a gorgeous white wedding Chuppah (wedding arch where the bride and groom stand during their wedding ceremony). The beautiful pastel flower arrangements on the Chuppah and throughout the tented area were extraordinary. The white walkway scattered with rose petals leading to the Chuppah appeared as if it were arranged for a princess.

The perfectly manicured lawns and landscaping looked like a photograph taken from a fairytale. This place felt like the wedding of the century was about to take place.

The security surrounding the residence and the entire neighborhood was beyond belief. There were surveillance helicopters in the sky and hundreds of armed soldiers from the IDF. Bomb-sniffing dogs could be seen throughout the backyard, the front entrance to the home and at the entry to the residential compound. There were surveillance cameras everywhere. Shin Bet had strategically set up SWAT sharp shooters ready to fire at any given moment. No stone had been left uncovered when it came to the safety and security of this wedding.

The tradition in Jewish weddings is to provide a marriage contract, known as a Ketubah. It was about to be signed in Elliot's office with both the former Prime Minister and the newly elected Prime Minister ready to witness the proceedings. Effectively, the Ketubah outlines the rights and responsibilities of the groom, in relation to the bride. It is written in Aramaic with specific language outlining the groom's financial obligations to the bride and is then signed in the groom's presence by two male witnesses.

The Ketubah is considered important because it is a legal and moral commitment that clearly defines that the principal obligations of the groom is to provide his wife with food, clothing, and affection along with other practical obligations. Later, during the wedding ceremony when the groom places the ring on the bride's finger, the Ketubah is then read aloud.

The first to arrive for the Ketubah signing in Elliot's office was Prime Minister Weiztman. An assistant rolled him in by wheelchair. He looked frail and weak, yet happy to have lived to witness this day.

Once all the warm greetings are exchanged, Weiztman dismisses the assistant and gets right to the issue on his mind, the mandate the people of Israel had given Elliot to lead and lead vigorously.

Now in private, Weiztman angrily shouts, "Okay, Elliot. Tell me there's no truth to the rumor that you are about to resign from the constitutional obligation and the unconditional trust the people of Israel have bestowed upon you. Forget about what I did to assure your victory! You have been awarded the great privilege of having been elected Prime Minister. Now, act like it!"

Since both Weiztman and Elliot were living through difficult health challenges, and especially given the fact their children were about to get married, Elliot was bewildered at Weiztman's aggressive comments.

But out of respect for his political mentor, he calmly responds, "Today our kids will be married and we will become family. Since the day Rose was born, I have been waiting for this moment. Now that this beautiful time has arrived, I would appreciate if I could concentrate on her wedding. If you want to talk politics tomorrow, I'll be ready."

With a sad look in his eyes, Weiztman says, "Elliot, I'm very ill. I don't have much longer to live. I'm blessed that God has given me life to enjoy this day, but who knows what tomorrow will bring for me. I'll regret if I don't get a chance to tell you what's on my mind while I can. So, I'm going to express it."

"You owe it to the families of all those gifted businessmen who lost their lives just to come out and support your efforts to become Prime Minister. You owe it to the doctors that saved your life, and you owe it to a nation who elected you in a landslide. Don't be the guy who sends the message to Hezbollah that their terrorist tactics have won! I guarantee you that if you walk away from this obligation, you will regret it for the rest of your life. There you go, I said what I needed to say."

Moved by the words of a great man who is dying, Elliot decides to respond, "If the decision was mine alone, I would be sworn-in and consider it the greatest honor of my life. I came very close to losing my life, so to be perfectly honest with you, it is Felicia and my daughters who will have the final say. They are terrified to lose me. They just don't want me to take the risk anymore, and frankly, I'm going to respect their wishes. But I'll tell you what, I got about ten days before I need to officially inform the Knesset and take office. I promise you, after the wedding, I will seriously take those days to revisit this decision with them. If they agree, then I can serve this nation with peace of mind. We got a deal?"

With a bit of a smile, Weiztman softly responds, "Deal."

With that score settled, Elliot turns to Weitzman with a twinkle in his eyes and says, "How about you and I celebrate Ethan and Rose's marriage with a L'Chaim?"

Weitzman soberly says, "I'd love to, but my doctors prohibit me from drinking any alcohol."

Not willing to take no for an answer, Elliot responds with his quick wit, "What's it going to do, kill you?"

Finding humor in the comment, Weitzman and Elliot burst out laughing as Elliot pours them both a glass of his best Scotch. Just as he is pouring the drinks, an entourage of people led by Ethan, Mark, and the Rabbi enter the office to witness the long-standing tradition of the marriage Ketubah signing. Elliot had invited the chief surgeon who saved his life along with the young doctor who acted decisively at the scene of the bomb blast to be present. He greets them both with a hug and starts pouring drinks for them along with everyone in the room.

The signing event could not have gone any better. It marked the very definition of celebration and good will. Elliot was so pleased to see the joy in Prime Minister Weitzman's face. He knew deep down in his soul that his daughter was about to marry the right man for her. Everything about this moment just felt right, and all of the pain Elliot had endured throughout the terrorist bombing seemed like it had occurred a long time in the past.

With the signing complete, and following tradition, the group of men that had entered the room with Ethan now exited the room circling him while singing and clapping as they escorted Ethan toward the Chuppah and his soon-to-be wife.

As everyone cleared the room, Elliot chose to briefly remain in his office by himself in order to gather his thoughts a few minutes before the wedding ceremony.

Elliot catches his breath, then takes a seat at his chair while propping his feet up on the desk. He closes his eyes and reflects upon the image of the day Rose was born. He remembers Felicia's beautiful smile as the new proud parents just stared in awe at the miracle of their new baby girl. Elliot remembers thinking to himself about the awesome responsibility of raising a child with principles and ethics.

He and Felicia wanted their child to grow and become an adult with a noble character. His mind wandered, picturing Rose in her first elementary school play where she landed the lead female part. He experienced firsthand how she grew to nurture and love her sister Erica.

As Elliot continued reminiscing about Rose's life development, he remembers how proud he was of her as a captain of her high school tennis team who won their division championship. He recognized her intellect and leadership skills from a very young age, but it was her kindness and empathy that he respected the most about her. And Elliot would never forget that day that she received a letter from Stanford University, which turned out to be a turning point in her life. She did not open that letter until she gathered her mom, sister, and dad together to share in what was either going to be the ecstasy of victory or the bitterness of defeat. He famously remembered her reading the first line of that letter:

"Congratulations…" as the entire family cried for joy as they heard her spontaneously give credit to her parents and Erica for always encouraging her to study hard and do better. Rose had grown up to be a very loyal daughter who easily surpassed her father's dream of raising a principled child with a noble character.

Elliot understood what exceptional judgement she possessed by virtue of the man she was about to marry.

It was time to make his way over to the Chuppah to enjoy one of the sweetest moments of his life. As he gets ready to leave his office, he thanks God for bringing him from a life of poverty as a kid to a life of great wealth. He was so grateful for his beloved wife Felicia and for his two remarkable children. He felt blessed to have survived the bombing attack, and yes, he was very proud to have been elected Israel's Prime Minister. At that moment, he thought to himself, *My life has been lived well beyond a billionaire*.

Elliot stands up from his desk, straightens his bowtie, and puts on his elegant black tuxedo coat. As he is about to leave his office, he notices a large manila envelope partially hidden amongst some other mail. Although he is in a rush to get to the wedding ceremony, he is curious who was sending that envelope with a handwritten address to his attention. So, he decides to take a peek at who it is from.

As he grabs the envelope, he instantly sees that the return address indicated it is from Adeleye Roberts, Stanley Roberts' daughter. Without hesitation, Elliot opens the envelope, which includes a large photo, with a handwritten note that reads:

"Dear Mr. Prime Minister,

On that dark day when my father was abducted by the Nigerian government, I will always remember when you confidently told me to advise my mother that she would see the day that my father was in America dancing at my wedding. This is a recent photo of my father and I dancing at my wedding in San Francisco! Your prophetic words came true, and my family and I will eternally be grateful. By the way, the nation of Israel has shown great judgement in electing a brilliant leader like you. Good luck with that fascinating journey.

Warm regards,
Adeleye."

As he drops the photo on his desk and makes his way toward his daughter's wedding, Elliot clearly understands that the direction of his destiny is Israel.